A
CROWN
OF
BLOOD
AND
BONE

BY

SLOANE MURPHY

A Crown of Blood and Bone
The Shadow Walkers Saga #1
Part of The Seven Realms Saga
Copyright © 2020 Sloane Murphy

Published by Hudson Indie Ink
www.hudsonindieink.com

A Crown of Blood and Bone/Sloane Murphy – 1st ed.
ISBN-13 - 978-1-913769-10-9

There is no light without shadow, just as there is no happiness without pain.

- ISABEL ALLENDE

ONE

THEN

Looking into his piercing, bright blue eyes, I question how we managed to get to this point. After everything we've been through, I refuse to accept that ending up here, with him in my arms and me praying to a god I don't believe in, is the end of our story.

There have been so many moments throughout history that could've killed either of us. Where we could've killed each other. But we survived it all. The rise and fall of empires. Wars of the world. The breakdown of the world we once knew.

There was never a moment at any point in our past that I ever thought I'd be the one hoping beyond all hope that he'd survive. That he wouldn't leave me. Especially not like this. When he has given so much for me, which is something I would have never thought possible.

I scream as I lift him onto my shoulders, and his groans of pain are matched by mine. I will save him even if it's the last thing I ever do.

Because a Dracul—my immortal enemy—saved me. In more ways than I ever knew I needed saving.

A CROWN OF BLOOD AND BONE

TWO

NOW

"Colt, I am not having this conversation again," I sigh, blowing my hair out of my face as I struggle with my bags up the stairs to my apartment. The summer heat is stifling, making my hair stick to my face.

"Remy, come on. You can't be serious about marrying that douchebag. He couldn't be more wrong for you if you'd picked up a total stranger off the street, blindfolded!" he shouts through the phone. Colt might be my favorite brother—the one I'm closest to—but he's also been gone since his disappearing act twenty-one months ago, just after his birthday. A disappearing act that kind of broke me because I didn't hear from him for six months. Then I broke all over again when Creek, my bestie, ghosted me in favor of joining Colt's world-fucking-tour thirteen months ago.

"You get to have an opinion when you've spent a decent amount of time with him and are actually present in my life, Colt. Even then, your opinion doesn't necessarily weigh in on the decisions I make about my life. Because it's exactly that, my life," I tell him as I fumble with my keys to open my front door.

"Fuck!" I screech as I trip forward over my cat, Sushi, and try not to drop my bags. My phone flies, and I huff again.

"Fucking cat," I moan at him, dropping the bags on the counter before lying on the floor to dig my arm under the couch to pull my phone from its hiding place under my sofa.

"Fall over the cat again, Remy?" Colt asks with a laugh when I finally pick my phone back up and huff. I roll my eyes even though he can't see me. I clamber back to my feet, trudging to the counter to put my groceries away as Sushi wraps himself around my feet, meowing at me to feed him like the little dictator he is.

"Fuck you, Colt. Just because I'm clumsy doesn't mean you get to make fun of me from a million miles away." I tear open a packet of cat food from the grocery bags and put it down for Sushi before refilling his water.

"Aw, come on, sis, you know I love you just the way you are. You're my favorite sister."

"I'm your only sister, dickhead." I laugh nonetheless. "Are you coming home anytime soon?"

"That's actually why I'm calling… Creek and I land in two days, would you mind grabbing us from the airport?" I can hear the cheesy grin in his voice, and even if he did disappear on me and steal my best friend away in the process, I can't deny him.

"You're home for my birthday?"

"Of course, we wouldn't miss your twenty-first for anything."

"Well, considering I haven't heard from Creek for a little over a year, I didn't really know if he'd be around. You left before my last birthday too, so sorry if I didn't expect you to be around for this one." I hate how whiny I sound, but Colt and Creek were the two people I was closest to in the entire world, and then they just both up and left with barely any explanation.

"He's been going through some stuff, and I'm sure he'll tell you all about it when we're home," I can hear his sigh through the phone, but I don't soften. "He's missed you a lot you should cut him a little slack."

"Maybe, or maybe he can learn what it's like to be ghosted without any reason or explanation. Your bromance is strong, I'm sure you'll dry his tears."

"You and I both know that's not how it's going down, Remy," Colt mutters, and I roll my eyes as I put away the last of my groceries. I'm headed for the refrigerator and last night's leftover mac and cheese when he asks, "So, you'll get us from the airport?"

I sigh, snagging the mac and cheese and popping into the microwave. He's lucky he's my favorite. "I will, as long as you both promise not to talk shit about Jack on the drive home. It's three hours to the airport, I can't deal with the bullshit for that long."

"Fine… but you really need to dump the douchebag." I head back to the fridge to grab a can of Pepsi Max—it's my ultimate weakness, and I know I'll need comfort foods if Colt's going to keep spewing bullshit the entire time we talk. "I know Creek made his opinion clear before he left, and from what Dad and Bauer said, the guy's a real tool."

"Seriously, Colt? Give me a break. You met him once, for about ten seconds before you disappeared halfway across the world." The impact of the statement might hit a little less with the bite of mac and cheese I shove in my mouth on the way to the couch. I drop down, balancing the soda and pasta before continuing, "Maybe when you spend some time with him, you'll see what I see. You'll see how much he loves me."

"That man loves numbers and facts. He's a fucking robot."

"There is nothing wrong with wanting to be sure about things, Colt! We can't all be as spontaneous as you. Some of us want to make calculated decisions. Like mine to move to pre-med next year instead of dance. It's a better life choice. I'm still going to dance, but just for fun." I wince at the word-vomit, knowing he's not going to like what I just told him. But it's better to break the news when he's on the phone, so I can't see the disappointment I know would be on his face if he was standing in front of me. A sudden, loud thud makes me pull the phone from my ear with a laugh. I guess I'm not the only one with butterfingers today.

It's faint, but I can just make out Colt muttering to himself, "Stupid fucking phone, stupid fucking slippery bastard case. I hope the screen isn't smashed." There's a spatter of cursing before I hear the fumbling noise of him picking it back up.

"Baby sister, you have danced your entire life. One year engaged to the biggest douchebag on Earth—because who the fuck proposes on the anniversary of your mom's death, by the way—one year, and your entire fucking plan has changed. This is bullshit and you know it!" His voice rises with each statement until he's eventually shouting, and then Creek calls out in the background. My heart stutters at the sound of his voice, and I shake my head. Stupid, traitorous heart. That door closed a long time ago, and it's never going to open again. I love Jack, and he loves me. He'd never leave me the way my family has.

"A lot can change in almost two years, Colt. You've been gone a long time. Maybe you don't know me as well as you used to." Some of the fight goes out of me for a moment. I've faced a lot of abandonment over the years, and nothing hurt quite as badly as Colt running off and Creek following right after him. I shake the dark thoughts away before they can press to close and heave a sigh. "I'm going to go; I have a big night planned, and I need to sort shit out."

"Don't lie to me, Remy. You have a night with the new episodes of *Chicago*. I'm still addicted, and it's all your fault, so I know exactly what your night consists of."

I stick my tongue out at him even though he can't see it. "Fine, yes, I have a date with the boys in blue, but I am done having this argument. Text me the details of your flight, and I'll get you both from the airport. Okay?"

"Okay, but this isn't over, Remy."

"If you say so, Colt."

"I love you, baby sis. Always have, always will. I know you don't believe me yet, but I have your best interests at heart, and that guy isn't right for you. I'll text you later."

"Love you too," I say, hanging up the phone even though that argument definitely isn't finished. Not by a long shot.

"Babe, look at this place," Jack thrusts his iPad screen in front of my face as I'm trying to put on my mascara. "Imagine waking up on your twenty-first birthday with this view. We should celebrate every chance we get. Life is all about the memories, right?" I swallow the sigh that threatens before smiling at him. He's been so excited about making sure I have the best birthday, and I love him for it, but birthdays are not my favorite thing.

"It looks amazing, like paradise," I admit as I look at the sea cottage. I've never even been on a plane, but this place really does look like paradise, even if it is a day's flight away.

"What better way to celebrate, than just you and me and our own piece of paradise, away from everyone and everything?" he asks as he wraps his arms around my waist and kisses my neck. I sigh contentedly and sink into his embrace, shaking off the stress of starting a new year at college.

"It will be the perfect break before the chaos begins. My residency. The wedding planning. It's exactly what we need."

He kisses me again and squeezes me.

"My treat for your birthday," he tags on the end, and I try not to roll my eyes. Jack is a trust fund baby, and growing up the way I did, it makes me a little uncomfortable when he throws his money around, but this is my birthday. And he's right, time is precious, and we should make all the memories we can.

"Plus, the anniversary of when we got together is the day after your birthday. We could try to make a proper vacation out of it. Think of all the things we could knock off your bucket list. Skydiving, swimming with turtles, cave diving, zip lining through the jungle. We could have so much fun before adulting and life becomes a heavy reality for us both."

"It sounds like heaven, but remember, we'll need to have dinner with my family too. Colt and Creek are coming back."

"How could I forget?" His arms slacken around my waist, and he turns me to face him. The frown on his face, deep with his dislike for my family, hurts my heart. "Your dad and brothers hate me. I can't wait for us to move away from your oddball family after the wedding. And don't even get me started on your so-called best friend."

"Hey, they're not that bad," I counter, but we've had this conversation more times than I can count. My family aren't exactly The Brady Bunch, but they're good people. "And they don't hate you, they're just very protective of me. I'm the baby. It's just the way they are."

"If you say so, babe, but I don't want our kids growing

up the way you did, with the weird survivalist bullshit. It's bat shit crazy."

I smile at him—he's not a fan of my family, which is the root of most of our arguments. They might be crazy and more than a little different, but they're mine. Still, I swallow my objections. I don't want to argue with him. Not today.

"I know you don't, which is one of the reasons we're why we're moving, you'll remember. Now, let's look at this trip some more before I have to get to work. You should get to the hospital too; you don't want to be late for rounds."

"I've got time, how about we celebrate today being a great day again?" Jack says suggestively and I laugh as he picks me up. My legs wrap around his waist instinctually as he lowers his lips to mine. He kisses me until I'm breathless and forget about anything but him as he walks us into the bedroom. I scramble back onto the bed and he crawls over me before kissing me with so much heat my toes curl.

"I don't think I'll ever have enough of you," he whispers into my ear, as before he rolls us so that I'm straddling him. I kiss him again, groaning as I feel him harden beneath me. My phone rings, interrupting the heat of the moment. "I swear if that is your fucking brother... cock block," he mutters as he pushes me off of him.

I dig my cell out of my pocket, ignoring his grumbles, and see my favorite person's name on the screen. "Fallon, you okay?" I answer the call with a smile, and Jack rolls his eyes. It's not just my family he's not a fan of. He's not a fan of my "kooky" friends either. His words, not mine.

"Bitch, that is not how you answer the phone. Is that asshat fiancé of yours staring you down while you're on the phone again? That shit is so freaking toxic." I sigh at her words, the chasm between Jack and the rest of the people I love is great. I really wish they could see the side of him that I get to see. The loving guy who wants to look after me, to take me away for my birthday, to make me smile. All they seem to see is a controlling, rich dickhead. I just don't get it.

"I'm great. Thanks, Fallon. Wonderful of you to ask."

"Oh, don't even. You know I love you; he just rubs me the wrong way. There's something about him that just screams bad juju," her southern accent comes out a little thicker with the emotion in her voice, and I fight off a smile. I always thought she'd sound a little like a southern belle if it wasn't for all of the cussing "Anyway, I was actually calling because I heard that fine-ass brother of yours is heading back to town for your birthday. You want me to come with you to get him?"

"How did you…" I pause, realizing that some mysteries are left as just that, mysteries. "In fact, I don't want to know the answer to that. Your obsession with Colt still gives me the heebie jeebies."

"Girl, it ain't no obsession, it's straight up lust. Have you seen that boy lately?"

"No, he hasn't been around for nearly two years, remember?"

"You got to get over that fire," she says, and I roll my eyes. Jack signals to me that he's going to go, and I blow him a kiss with a wave. He looks angry, but that's a problem for future Remy. I tune back into Fallon, rolling my eyes at her defense of my brother and Creek. "He left because it was what he needed to do. You'll understand eventually. Same with your boy, Creek."

"Is there a reason you called? You know, other than to talk about dickbag one and two?"

"Nope, you know I'm firmly Team Creek. That boy lost his damn mind when he found out you were getting engaged." Here's another argument that I don't feel like getting into today, rearing its ugly head again. "You didn't even notice he was acting weird. You know Jack told him like two weeks before he even asked you just to piss Creek off. And then Creek, who is so obviously in love with you, had to watch you with Jack knowing you'd likely say yes. *Which you did!*"

"Fallon," I try to interrupt her, but she just barrels on.

"I'm not surprised at all that he left. I'm just surprised

that you are."

Yup, she's hitting me with all of her bullshit. "Don't start, Fallon. Creek and I were never like that, and you know it. You were right there with us—we were The Three Musketeers. You were as worried as I was when he didn't even bother to say goodbye."

"No, I wasn't." She scoffs, and I roll my eyes. *Yet again.* "I knew he was gonna go. It's not my fault you couldn't see past your worry and anger. If he's coming back, though, maybe you two can work through all your issues and finally fall madly in love."

"My life is not some romcom, Fallon. I love Jack. Creek coming home doesn't change anything. We're friends. Or at least we were."

"Yeah, you keep telling yourself that, girl. I'm telling you, I'll voodoo Jack's ass if he don't sort his shit out and clear the path for my boy Creek."

I huff a sigh at her. This is one thing we've never seen eye to eye on, especially since she knows I crushed on Creek for a while when we were teenagers. But it was just a stupid crush.

"We both know your voodoo is all in your head." We're both aware that I don't believe in the bullshit voodoo thing, but despite that she constantly brings it up. "Anyway, to answer your first question, no, I don't need you to come with me. I can handle those two idiots on my own. I've got to run, though, I'm supposed to be at the bar in thirty because Shelly called in sick again."

There's a hint of disappointment in her voice as she says, "I *guess* you can wrangle them on your own. And you can't always be in denial, by the way, it's as real as you and I. I guess I'll let you stay in denial about Creek for now, but one day, you're going to see just how right I am."

"Uh-huh, if you say so. I'll talk to you later—love you!"

"Love you too, in-denial girl."

The airport arrivals area is so freaking busy that, for once, I'm thankful for my height. I'm not exactly supermodel tall, but being five-foot seven means I don't have to jump up and down to look for these two bozos. I wait for what feels like forever, watching as the arrivals area slowly empties, and I start to think that maybe Colt gave me the wrong flight details. I check the time on my cell again and search back through my messages from Colt to make sure I have the right information. He better not be punking me.

But I pull up the text, and… nope.

This is the flight number he gave me. What the actual fuck.

I turn to go sit down and settle in for the long haul when a voice shouts from behind me.

"You leaving already, little bit?" I turn in the seconds before I'm lifted off the ground and spun around. I can't help the squeal that escapes my lips. "I missed you so much, little sister!"

"Put me down you big idiot, you'll drop me!" I tell him, and thankfully he puts me back down. I take a step back, wondering who the fuck this is and what the hell this stranger did with my brother. Behind him, I spot Creek, and my jaw nearly hits the goddamn floor.

"What the fuck did you two do while you were traveling? Fall into a tattoo gun and mainline steroids?" The words fall out of my mouth, my filter's never been great but what the hell? The two men in front of me are not the ones who left. They both look like they've grown about six inches and packed on about two hundred pounds of muscle, which they decided to then cover in ink. "Who even are you?"

"Don't do me like that, little bit. I'm hot!" Colt waggles his eyebrows at me, making me realize his fucking eyebrow is pierced too, and I can't help but laugh at his stupid ass. Apparently while his looks changed completely, the rest of him stayed exactly the same. He wraps me up in a hug and I groan, but despite my anger at him fully ditching me, I'm so happy he's back. I'm just not going to let him know that, that would be too easy.

"Come on, Hulk. A girl needs to breathe." I laugh, and

he releases me with a sheepish look before slinging his arm over my shoulder.

"Hey, Remy," Creek says quietly when I push Colt's arm off, turning and coming face-to-face with my former best friend.

It takes every ounce of willpower I possess not to fucking drool over the man-god in front of me. Holy. Fucking. Hell. His long, dark hair is up in a man-bun, his beard is long but hot as fuck, and every inch of his beautifully muscled skin is covered in ink of some form. *Think about Jack, you love Jack. This guy is a huge dick bag. Remember he's a dick bag.*

"Creek, I see you decided to join my brother's steroid and ink marathon. I guess that's why it's been radio silence, huh? Let's go, I've got things to do."

He runs his hand down his face, his eyes pleading with me not to give him shit, but he was my best friend. He's the guy who didn't leave my side for two weeks when my mom died so I didn't feel alone, and then he dropped me thirteen months ago like I was nothing but trash, and I haven't heard from him since. I shove my cell back in my jacket and head toward the exit without looking back.

I hate being a bitch to them, but also, fuck them. I'm here, and I definitely didn't have to be. They're the ones who left. Ugh, I hate being so conflicted. These guys are my family, but like, who just ups and leaves without so much as a goddamn goodbye and then ghosts you for over a year? Yeah, I'm petty about it, but then, neither of them has given me an explanation as to why they both left. Colt at least reached out since Creek disappeared and let me know the man was with him, so I wasn't just worrying he was dead somewhere. Which I legit was for the first week he went MIA since he left without any fucking word and never bothered to reach out. Like I said, dick bag.

I climb in the front seat of my '87 Mustang, my baby that Bauer has been helping me modernize a little. He might be a pain in the ass, and like eight years older than me, but the guy is a genius under the hood of a car. Colt lets out a whistle when he sees her. "Damn, Bauer really has been helping you make this beauty shine. He always did love machines more than humans."

"Will you guys get your asses in here already?" I sigh. I have a dance class this afternoon, and if they don't get a move on, I'm going to miss it. I take them both in, and eye my back seat, trying not to laugh too much. Creek sighs as Colt laughs, before folding himself almost in two and climbing into the back of the car, his knees by his ears because there is no space for someone his size back there.

"If I'd known you two had like, tripled in size, I'd have asked Bauer for his truck."

"You and I both know our big brother would never let you drive his truck." Colt rolls his eyes as he gets into the passenger side and slams the door shut.

"If you hurt Betty with your ridiculous meathead muscles, I'm going to break you," I growl at him and pat the dashboard. Betty was my mom's car, and I always loved it. Dad gave it to me when I got my license, and she's been a pet project of mine since then... Well, with Bauer's help.

"I'm not going to hurt the damn car, and the ladies love these meathead muscles." He wags his eyebrows again, and I can't help but laugh at his ridiculousness. I spot Creek in the rearview mirror watching me but decide to not pay attention to it.

"I'm sure they do, buddy. Let's get this show on the road. I need to drop you guys off and head out."

"You're not hanging out?" Creek asks quietly, and it's almost like I can feel his relief. It stings, and I bite my lip.

"No," I tell him sharply and put the car into gear, ending the conversation.

THREE

"Babe, are you almost ready?" Jack shouts from downstairs just as I'm finishing setting my long hair into curls.

My birthday isn't until tomorrow, but I'm full to the brim with anxiety. Dinner tonight is meant to be a way for me to celebrate finally turning twenty-one, but it's really just going to be one big macho, bullshit-fest between my family and Jack. I hope Maddie and Fallon help me keep the testosterone in check because it's sure to be off the charts. I shudder even thinking about my eventual engagement party, but I don't want to go there. One disaster at a time and all that.

"I'll be down in a minute." I shout back from his bathroom while straightening the dress I'm wearing. I touch up my eyeliner and give myself a once over before grabbing my shoes and heading downstairs to where Jack's impatiently waiting.

"You look hot, babe! You sure we have to go?" he says with a playful laugh, but the tension around his eyes confirms it's not really a joke.

"Come on, it won't be that bad, and I promise we won't stay too late, okay?" I tell him, hoping to placate him even though guilt eats at my stomach for dragging him with me when he obviously doesn't want to go. I bite my lip and contemplate telling him he doesn't have to come with me, but I know if I show up alone, I won't ever hear the end of it.

He rolls his eyes at me, handing me my purse as I slip my heels on. "Let's just get this over with, yeah?"

I swallow the lump in my throat. If it wasn't my birthday, we wouldn't be doing this. I love Jack, and I love my family, but having everyone in one room is just a nightmare. I swear I feel more stress over this than I did with my exams to get into med school. Jack opens the door for me and gestures me ahead, so I smile at him and place a chaste kiss on his cheek before heading toward the car.

The drive to the restaurant is tense, and despite trying to make conversation, it ends up being a pretty quiet ride. We pull into the parking lot behind the restaurant, and I look over at Jack, noticing the tightness in his shoulders, the set to his jaw, and the white-knuckle grip he has on the steering wheel. My stomach flips. Maybe I should've come alone.

He climbs out and slams the door as I unbuckle, making me flinch. What a night this is going to be. I slip out, rounding the car to join him and reach out to take his hand in mine. He rewards me with a small smile. We walk into the restaurant, and I can't help the big smile on my face. My family and friends have come here for my birthday for the last eight years, and I have so many happy memories here.

The hostess waves us to the private room in the back we always book, and Jack wraps his arm around my shoulder as I lead us through the restaurant. I feel him take a deep breath as I push the door open to the room and noise explodes around us.

"Happy birthday!" voices shout, and I can't help but laugh. Bauer is closest to me and picks me up in a bear hug, which is such a signature Bauer move.

"Happy birthday, baby sister. Welcome to the grown-up table," he says in my ear before dropping me back on the ground. Not even a second later, Maddie, Creek's mom, wraps me up in her arms with tears in her eyes.

"I can't believe how quickly you grew up!" I sink into her embrace, soaking up the love from her, the woman who became everything I ever needed after my own mom passed. I squeeze her tightly before she releases me and takes my face in her hands, shaking her head. "Too quick."

I laugh at her and turn to find the rest of our small group, my dad, Colt, Creek, Fallon—my other bestie—and her little sister, Rebel. Jack stands off to the side, excluded from the group, as if trying to keep himself from catching their crazy as he so delightfully calls it. I roll my eyes and finish saying hello to the group before taking my seat at the table, with Dad to my right, and Jack to my left. The noise dies down as our server comes in and takes everyone's drink orders.

Jack squeezes my hand under the table, and I offer him a small smile. I heave a deep sigh of relief because so far, so good.

"So, Colt, how long are y'all back for?" Fallon asks, a wicked smile on her face as I groan internally.

"Well, since you asked so nicely, I think me and the man bun are finished with our adventures for now. It's time to come back home," he says to her as he winks at me. My gaze drifts to where Creek sits next to him at the table. He's stiff as a board, and his jaw is clenched. He looks at Jack sitting by my side, who is equally as tense, I can feel the stiffness of his posture from where he's pressed closely against my side.

Awesome.

"Are you guys really sticking around?" I ask, my gaze

bouncing between Creek and Colt as the table goes quiet.

"We are," Creek says, turning his gaze from Jack and hitting me with those bright green eyes of his instead. There's so much emotion in his eyes. He's always been so expressive, I've always been able to tell exactly how he's feeling in just a look.

"I guess you guys should take the next few weeks spending as much time together as you can then. We'll be moving after the wedding in a few months," Jack says, and the table explodes. My dad looks like he's going to slit Jack's throat with the butter knife clenched in his fist, while Fallon couldn't look more disgusted if she tried.

"Over my dead body," Colt says while Bauer pins Jack with a look that could be classified as deadly.

I drop my head into my hands because this is not how tonight was meant to go. Happy Birthday to me.

Jack smiles and that's enough to have my dad and brothers all start yelling over one another about how they'll kill Jack before they see me leave the state and all I want to do is crawl into a fucking hole.

"Come now, boys, I'm sure they're not going far, right?" Maddie, ever the diplomat, speaks up, trying to calm my thunderous father and brothers.

"Well, erm…" I sigh.

"We're heading over to the East Coast. I have a once-in-a-lifetime opportunity with a fellowship in Boston,"

Jack tells the table, and I can almost feel the rage rolling off my dad in waves.

"I forbid it," he says, his voice booming across the room. Fallon sends me an apologetic look while Rebel sits next to her, wide-eyed.

"Dad, come on… You can't do that." I take his hand, but he snatches it away.

"The hell I can't!" he booms, eyes flashing in my direction before turning the ire of his gaze toward Jack. "And you, Boy Wonder... You and that giant stick up your ass have a lot to learn if you think any differently."

"This. This right here is part of the reason why we're moving. Your family has no idea about real life or boundaries," Jack says to me before turning to speak to my family "Remy and I are engaged. We're going to be married. There isn't anything you can do to stop it." Jack levels my dad with his stare, a battle of two titans fighting a war of wills in a look alone.

"Watch me," Bauer says, his voice lethal as he pulls a gun and lays it on the table.

"You see! You're all fucking crazy. Who the hell brings a gun to dinner?" Jack shouts, standing and yanking me up with him. "Come on, babe. We're leaving. This is ridiculous."

"You let go of her right the fuck now," Creek growls as Jack's fingers press into my upper arm. I try not to wince at his grip, but I'm pretty sure it's going to leave a mark.

"You don't get to speak to me like that," Jack says, pulling me toward the door, which Colt and Creek block jump up to block.

"You guys, it's fine. We should just go," I say, tearing my arm from Jack's grip. Jack looks at me like I've lost my mind, because obviously we should never show that we're not a team in front of people—I hate the fakeness of it all, and I'm tired of it—so I lift my chin and look him in the eye. "You started this. You couldn't just let me have one nice night with everyone I love.

"As for you two, I appreciate the sentiment, but standing up for me now after ditching and ghosting me for over a year is too little too late. Maddie, Fallon, I'm sorry. I'll be over for dinner in a few days, but we're just going to go."

"Okay, sweetheart, you take care, and happy birthday," Maddie says from her chair, her hand on my dad's shoulder. I'm pretty sure if it weren't for the light touch, he wouldn't still be in his chair.

"Love you, girl." I can't miss the concern in Fallon's eyes as she blows me a kiss and Rebel gives me a little wave. I turn back to the door, but Colt and Creek haven't moved.

"Please, you guys," I say quietly, and their faces drop. I can't quite read them, but the disappointment coming at me from every corner of the room is overwhelming. They separate, framing the door, and Jack storms out as soon as there's space.

"I love you, little bit," Colt whispers, dipping to kiss my cheek as I start to leave. I dart from the room trying not to let the tears in my eyes stream down my face.

I drag the covers up over my head and sink into my pillows, ignoring the shitty week I've had. It's my twentieth birthday, which means it's also a week to the day before the seventh anniversary of my mom's death. A senseless, stupid moment of time, which spun my entire life out of control.

I remember that day, a week after my thirteenth birthday, like it was yesterday. We were meant to go shopping… to go get our hair done. A rite of passage, she'd said. She just had to pop out for some grocery shopping first. She and Maddie had a weekly shopping date, though I knew it was actually because my stupid brothers ruined my cake for my belated birthday party. I heard her yell at them the night before when she thought I was asleep. So she said she'd go shopping and then she'd be back. That's what she told me, at least...

I remember baking in the kitchen, Bauer and Colt were outside playing football with Creek, while Fallon and I were eating more of the cookie dough than we were baking. My dad was out in the shed, doing whatever the hell it was he did out there.

Then the kitchen phone rang.

I answered the phone laughing. Maddie's voice sounded strained, but I didn't think anything of it when she asked for my dad.

I yelled for him to come to the phone, and he ran in from the shed, his face pale. It was like he knew. He picked the phone up off the counter, and I went to the oven to pull the cookies out. His cry rang out around us as he fell to his knees, and the guys all came running in. My father doesn't cry. Ever. But it was the noise he made, like a wounded animal close to death, that I remember most vividly. His hands shook as Bauer took the phone from him and raised it to his ear. He listened before mumbling his acknowledgement and hung the phone back on the hook.

Bauer grabbed the keys to his truck, his twenty-first birthday present from Mom and Dad earlier that year, and lifted my dad off the floor. Colt took Dad's other side without any word.

"There's been an accident. We need to get to the hospital," Bauer said calmly, with my dad just standing there like he was numb. I remember putting the cookie tray down, burning my hand but not thinking much of it because it was obvious something really fucking bad was happening.

The ride to the hospital took what felt like forever, with me cramped in the back with Fallon, Creek, and Colt. I don't remember seeing anything of significance until we got to the hospital. Bauer led the charge since Dad was completely spaced. Creek and Colt walked with him until we saw Maddie, and it was like Dad suddenly came back to life. She strode right up to him, pulling him in and letting him hug her tightly.

"She's in surgery; but Denny, it's not good," she said, her voice breaking over the words. A nurse led us all to a waiting area just after that, and I sat there, one hand in Creek's, the other in Fallon's, just waiting. No one said it, but it was obvious.

I felt a tug at my heart, and tears fell from my eyes. I knew right then, without anyone even telling me. A few minutes later a doctor arrived and took my dad and Maddie aside. That was the second time I've ever seen my dad cry, but I already knew.

My mom was gone. I'd felt it.

Maddie came back into the room and crouched down in front of me, calling Colt over while Bauer went to my dad.

"I am so sorry," her voice cracked, and the tears ran faster down my face.

So today, on my twentieth birthday, I sit in bed wrapped up in my blankets, like I do most birthdays until my family dinner tonight. I do the same thing every year, and tradition is tradition even if Colt and Creek disappeared off the face of the Earth this year. This year can go eat shit. The only good thing about it so far has been Jack. He's been my rock, especially since those two disappeared. Colt's been gone nine months, and Creek, well he up and disappeared just after his birthday a month ago. I haven't heard shit from either of them, but I know they're together from Fallon, Maddie, and Dad.

Asshats.

"Babe? You up?" Jack's voice rings out through my apartment. I grumble incoherently back, but I hear his laugh as his footsteps get louder. "Come on, it's your birthday, and I made breakfast."

The comforter is ripped away from me, and I groan at the sudden onslaught of light. I guess he opened the damn blinds too.

"Happy birthday, beautiful." He leans down and kisses me, and despite me hating my morning breath, he doesn't seem to care. He pulls away and grabs a mug from my dresser and hands it to me, full of the bitter black nectar that he knows is the way to my heart.

"Thank you," I sigh and smile.

"You're welcome. Now come eat breakfast. I hate that

I have to work today, but tomorrow, we celebrate. I know it's not a good time of year for you, but we should try to make some good memories. Your mom wouldn't want you to be sad forever."

I shrug noncommittally. This entire week is my most hated time every year.

The next day, he packs my suitcase into his car along with his and drives us for hours out to his parents' cabin on the lake, surrounded by mountains. The place's beauty is almost indescribable, and yet I feel nothing but hollow. Jack's smiles and laughter ring out around me as we pull up to the cabin, and I paint a smile on my face, but I can't really feel it.

"Come on, babe, this is going to be amazing. Just you, me, and the lake. There's even a hot tub out back." He winks before climbing out of the car.

I take a deep breath and will myself to feel something. Anything. For Jack's sake more than mine. I know he's trying to do something nice for me, but this just isn't me. I'm not a luxury cabin in the woods kinda girl. Especially not this week. I pull myself together the best I can and climb out of the car to join him—he's already at the door, unlocking it and opening the cabin. Though, I'm not sure cabin is the right word for this place. Lake house, maybe? It's all wood and glass, open spaces, and so freaking modern.

My cell pings in my pocket, and Jack steps in front of me in a heartbeat, his hand out. "No cell phones while we're here, babe. This is us time."

I hand over my phone, trying not to roll my eyes. Phone or not, I'm probably not going to be great company this week.

We spend the week hiking, going out on the lake, having picnics, and trying to enjoy the time together. I'm not exactly party central, but I do lose myself to it all a little. But today's the day, and we're headed home. I have dinner with my dad tonight, the same as every year.

"Come on, babe. Let's just go for one more quick walk, and then we'll head off," Jack says with a playful smile. I'm reluctant because I don't want to be late to see Dad and Bauer, but I smile and nod because I can see how hard he's trying. I grab my jacket and follow his lead out to the trails.

We walk for about half an hour before Jack veers off the track and pulls me with him out onto a vista, looking down over the lake.

It's so peaceful.

"This is beautiful," I tell him softly. Mom would have loved this place.

"You are beautiful, Remy, even in your darkest moments. You are all that is light and right in this world. I knew it the moment I saw you, even in that dingy little dive

bar with the worst live music I've heard in my entire life. I knew then, what I know now, and nothing has changed since that moment. I love you, Remington Bennett, and I will love you always." He takes a deep breath and goes down on one knee. Horror and happiness clash inside me. What is he doing? Why now? Why today?

"So today, on your darkest day, I want to be that light for you. For now, and for always. Will you, Remington, do me the honor of being my wife?" He looks up at me, so hopeful and full of love. I feel myself nodding, saying yes, but it's like I'm not myself. Not today. Why today? If it was any other day, I know I'd be so happy. So I find myself agreeing and kissing him. Because I do love him.

I do.

A CROWN OF BLOOD AND BONE

FOUR

"You all packed and ready to go, babe?" Jack pops his head around the corner and into the bedroom where I'm just throwing the last few things into my bag.

I smile up at him as he steps into the room, wrapping his arms around me as soon as he's close enough. "Yeah, I'll just be two minutes. You good to go?"

"I'm ready for anything as long as it's just the two of us."

"I'm sorry it's not the break you wanted." I sigh as he kisses my neck but smile nonetheless.

Last night might have been a disaster, but today we're going away for the weekend. Just the two of us. It's not an escape to paradise, but he's been working so hard; and between studying and dancing, I've been all over the place too. Plus, after last night, I just want to shake it off. Knowing how much tension there is between the most important people in my life sucks. I just hope that they all love me enough to accept my decisions. Accept that I know what will make me happy.

"Babe, as long as it's you and me, we could be in a goddamn igloo and I'd be happy." He kisses me again before taking a step back so I can spin in his arms. I place my hands on his chest and smile up at him. I've always loved that he's a bit taller than me. It's shallow maybe, but I'm not a short girl, and it's nice to feel small sometimes.

"You and me forever." I smile before I lift up onto my tiptoes to kiss him again.

"Now then, no more distractions, otherwise we'll never leave." He laughs but holds me tighter.

"I don't see any problem with that, everyone thinks we're gone anyway. We could just hole up in here for the whole weekend. No phones, no outside world."

"That sounds like heaven, but I might just have a surprise waiting for you."

I laugh at him because of course he does.

"You shouldn't have."

"It's your twenty-first birthday, babe. It only happens once. We're doing it in style."

"What does that mean exactly?" I ask, skeptically.

"It means get your ass in gear so we're not late!" He

laughs and smacks my ass before hightailing it out of the room.

I can't help but laugh back. This week is usually the worst week of the year for me, but Jack is really trying, so this year, I'm going to try too. Mom wouldn't have wanted me to be miserable. She'd have probably kicked my ass for being so sad for so long. My heart pulls a little, but I know the smile on my face is meant to be there, so I grab my bag and head down to find Jack.

He's already outside, so I grab my keys and lock up before I jump in his car.

"Ready?" he asks with a huge smile.

"Always."

We pull up to the airfield, and my jaw drops. "What the…"

"Surprise!" Jack exclaims as we pull up to a private jet.

"Surprise?" My eyes dart between him and the plane, half-excited, half-wincing at how much money he's spent on me yet again.

"I know how much you've been wanting to go to New York, and I know you always had plans to go with your mom on your twenty-first, so I wanted to do something special for you. We're taking my dad's jet, and we'll do a city flyby since it'll be dark when we arrive. I've booked a hotel for the weekend, and I have so many other things planned. I know you hate it when I spend my money on you, but it's mine to spend, and I can't think of anything better to spend it on than making you happy."

My mouth opens and closes uselessly, and for the first time in a while, I'm speechless.

"Jack, you shouldn't... I mean... holy fucking shitballs. New York?" The words fall from my mouth, my eyes widening as it sinks in. "This is amazing, thank you so much!"

I wrap my arms around his neck and kiss him, trying to pour every single emotion into the movement. He pulls back, his eyes dark with heat. "More of that in a bit, babe. Let's board so we can get into the air!"

A private car brings us from the airport to our hotel hours later, and I'm at a loss of words over the entire day. It's been one of the best days of my life. I've never even flown, let alone like that on a private jet. It was just... magical. And to be here now, in the one place I've always wanted to see with the lights eating the darkness around us. It looks like everything I ever imagined it would, and I fully understand why it was my mom's favorite city on Earth to visit.

"Mr. Crawford, so lovely to have you staying with us." A man with white hair opens the door to the front of the hotel and ushers us inside with him. "It's lovely to see you again. Everything has been organized as you requested.

Your room is the penthouse as always, your room keys are here. If you need anything at all, please do not hesitate to call down to the concierge." He swipes the plastic in his hand and another door opens, leading to stairs. We follow him down and come into a small room with coat hooks. Jack takes my jacket with a smile as the man opens another door, leading us into what looks like a freaking apartment, not a hotel room.

"We hope you enjoy your stay," he says with a smile before turning on his heel and retreating. His footsteps echo down the hall until the swish of a door closing lets us know he's gone.

"Jack this is… I have no words."

"You like it?" he asks, taking off his shoes and coming to stand beside me as I take everything in.

"Like it? How could I do anything but love it? This is more than I ever dreamed. Look at this view!" I look out of the windows to the sparkling sea of lights below us, the view highlighting the beauty that is Central Park. "Thank you so much, Jack, this is everything."

"I just want you to be happy, Remy. If I can be a part of that, I'll do everything in my power to make it so."

I laugh as I run up the stairs, the bright light pouring into a bedroom that's full of windows. The white curtains move with a breeze filtering in through open doors that lead to the balcony. The sound of gulls outside lures me toward the open doors, and the smell of the ocean offers me a sense of tranquility.

"I know you don't think that running is something that will save you from me." His deep but happy voice fills me with joy, and I feel instantly at peace.

"Then don't give me a reason to need saving." I laugh as he wraps his arms around me from behind, his hot breath on my ear. I'm not one to feel like I need to be protected, but that's exactly how I feel right now, and it's so freeing rather than stifling like I imagined.

He kisses my neck, and I can't help the groan that slips from my lips as his hand reaches around to cup my breast, squeezing gently. His teeth scrape down my neck, and I shiver in his arms.

"You are wearing far too many clothes," he breathes as he spins me in his arms. The skin of his bare chest pebbles under my touch.

"I guess you should do something about that then." I smile, standing on my tiptoes to capture his lips with my own. It doesn't matter how many times I kiss him, I lose myself in him as if each time were the first. He reaches behind me and pulls at the bindings on my corset, which falls to my feet.

He kisses down my neck. He works his way down

my naked chest, capturing one nipple in his mouth while pulling at the other with his hand before swapping his attention. My hands plunge into his hair and pleasure shoots through me. Who knew someone so forbidden could be exactly who I needed?

"Please." The moan falls from my lips, and I feel him smile against my skin before his lips move south. His fingers make quick work of the leather bindings, and he peels the pants down, taking my panties with them.

I gasp as his tongue laps against my wetness, and his growl makes my knees weak. He wraps his arms under my thighs and lifts me, his head still between my legs, and drops me on the bed.

"Fucking divine." His voice against my pussy makes me shiver before he licks my clit again. The sensation makes me shudder and moan incoherently.

"Oh shit." I bite down on my lip as he slides two fingers inside me, hooking them just right to reach the part of me he knows drives me insane. His attention doesn't let up as he drives me over the edge, making me cry out.

He leans over me and kisses me, still covered in my juices, and I can taste myself on his tongue. I stroke a hand down his body, undo the button on his jeans, and reach inside, feeling how hard he is under my touch. He groans, kissing my neck again before biting down leaving his mark on me. He pulls back and looks down at me, his eyes wild.

"I need to feel you, baby." He pushes down his jeans and boxers before lowering himself down to me, kissing me again as he takes both of my hands and raises them above my head, pinning me with one hand. He slides into me in one thrust as his head rests on my forehead, giving me only a second to adjust to just how big he is. The pain quickly subsides, and I raise my hips to let him know I'm good. His free hand finds my clit as he fucks me, holding me prisoner beneath him. The noises he pulls from me don't sound human, but at this point, I have no control of my body, I am his plaything. My orgasm rips through me completely as he releases my wrists and grabs my hips. He slows until I start to come down and then pulls out before flipping me on to my stomach.

"Ass in the air, Remy," he rasps, sounding as if he's barely maintaining control of himself. I get onto my knees, and his big hands grasp my waist and pull me back toward him before gripping my hips. If I was anyone else, that shit would leave a bruise, but I love that he isn't gentle with me. He plunges back into me and steals my breath, fucking me like he's scared he's going to lose me. He reaches around me and pulls me up so I'm kneeling, his chest against my back, and he wraps his hand around my throat.

"Mine," he growls and bites my shoulder as I come again. He keeps his pace and then quickly follows, letting go of my hair so I fall forward. He falls with me, shifting us on the bed so I'm lying on his chest.

"Always, Angel. In this life or the next. There's no one else out there for me. It's you and me," he says, kissing the top of my hair, and I breathe contentedly.

"Always."

I wake up happy to be back in my own bed. Stretching out with a smile on my face, when my dream comes back to me. I feel like I should fan myself after that dream. I clench my thighs together tightly, unsure whether or not I should be happy that Jack isn't here right now. I've never had a sex dream before, but hell yes to my imagination for the one it conjured last night. I know for sure I've never been around that guy before, but something about him felt familiar.

I sigh as his face eludes me. All I really remember is his voice and how he made me feel. I guess that's why they're dreams and not reality. I sigh, throwing the covers off and climbing out of bed despite the clock telling me it's four in the morning. I throw on some running gear and head out to the kitchen, braiding my hair as I go. Sushi wraps himself around my legs, demanding his breakfast. I feed the little dictator and scratch behind his ears before I grab a bottle of water and put in my ear buds. I tuck my key into my leggings along with my phone and head out.

After that dream, I feel restless. Surely I shouldn't be dreaming about someone who isn't Jack, especially after we had such a nice weekend away for my birthday. I felt closer to him than I have in a while, which was nice.

I head for the stairs, waking up enough to feel glad that I'm getting an early jumpstart on my workout. I run down the stairs, and the music blares through my headphones as I make my way out of my apartment building. The park is only six blocks from here, so I start at a steady pace, trying to clear my head; but all I can think about is the guy in my dream.

He felt so real. More like a memory than a dream.

But I know I've never met him before. His eyes flash in my mind as I reach the entrance of the park, and I pause, stretching before I continue my run. I search my mind for more. Have I met the man in my dreams? Surely I'd remember someone like that.

I shake my head. I'm being ridiculous. It was just a dream. I take off again and start a lap around the park. As I eat up the miles, my mind finally clears. I feel at peace again and less like I've betrayed Jack in my sleep. Ridiculous I know, but it is what it is. Especially since this is the second guy I've dreamt about in two weeks that isn't my fiancé.

The sun starts to rise as I finish my lap, and I decide to stretch out on the grass before heading back to my apartment. My phone rings in my pocket, and I answer it without looking, trying to calm my breathing as I do.

"Hello?"

"Remy?"

"Morning, Dad, up with the sun still I see?" I tease, and he gently grumbles over the line. My dad's not the softest of men, but I've always been a bit of a daddy's girl.

"You sound like you've been up longer than me. You okay?" His concern filters through his gruffness and makes me smile.

"I'm fine, Daddy. What's up?"

"I just wanted to make sure everything's okay for today?" he asks, and his voice changes. It's strange, almost as if he's nervous.

"Of course, when have I ever missed this?" I rub my chest at the pang of sadness from thinking about my mother. Every year, with the exception of last year when Colt disappeared, we've all gotten together at the house for dinner. We eat my mom's favorite meal and remember her in our own special way. The anniversary is hard for all of us, more so because it's so close to my birthday. It's also my engagement anniversary with Jack, but this is something I've done forever, and I know he understands that it isn't going to change.

"Of course not, I just wanted to check since Wonder Boy was spouting off at dinner the other night." I sigh, yes, dinner was an excruciating clusterfuck, but I guess I shouldn't have hoped for anything more.

"Dad, come on. Please don't."

"I do not like that boy, Remy. He isn't right for you."

"You and every male in our family keep telling me so; but like I keep telling you, it isn't your decision, and he makes me happy." I hate how much it hurts that my family despises Jack, but I know how much I love him. My family is much too overprotective after my mom, I doubt they would like anyone I was with.

"Hmmm, we'll see," he mutters. "You'll be over at the usual time?"

"Yes, Dad, six sharp. When am I ever late?" He laughs, my penchant for being on time is something he says I get from my mom. Since he's usually running behind, I can completely believe it.

"Never. I'll let you go. Be safe, Remy."

"Always, Dad. Love you."

"Love you too," he says before the line disconnects, and I sigh. He never calls to make sure I'll be at Mom's dinner, it's just a given. He sounded on edge, but this time of year always messes with us all, so I don't read too much into it. I pick myself up off of the ground and stretch again. I'm going to be sore from sitting down so long, but there's not much I can do about it now. I jog home as the sun finishes rising, trying not to let thoughts of my mom crash down over me.

FIVE

I pull up to my dad's house, relishing in the fact that it still feels more like home than anywhere else. I get why most people think it looks creepy as fuck, but that's part of its charm. The looming darkness, the gothic feel. I used to pretend when I was little that it belonged to an evil queen, and I was a trapped princess.

The wind whistles through the trees that line the property as I climb the steps to the porch, letting myself in. The house still smells the same as it always has, except now the scent of Mom's favorite meal wafts down the hall from the kitchen. I still, listening to my dad and brothers laughing, probably talking about Mom and her epic clumsiness—the same clumsiness I seem to have inherited. Even if I have seemed more agile as of late.

"You going to come and say hello or keep lurking at the door?" My dad's voice booms through the hall, and I laugh softly, shutting the front door behind me. I have no idea how he always knows I'm home, but he always has and probably always will. Trying to sneak out when I was younger was a total bust, every single time.

The click of my heels echo as I make my way to the kitchen, and I find more faces than usual. My entire family is there, but so is most of Creek's. Maddie sits at the table with Nirvana, his little sister, sitting next to her. "Oh, hey guys. I didn't expect to see everyone here. Nirvana, you finally home from school for the summer?"

"Yeah, Mom decided I could grace you all with my awesomeness this evening rather than staying at school for another night." Her voice twinkles, light, as if no darkness has ever touched her. "Dad couldn't make it, though. He's away on business again, but I'm way better company anyway."

I smile at her as she comes at me with open arms. She's younger than the rest of us. She's in her junior year at a boarding school for geniuses because her brain amazes everyone.

"Smells good, Dad." I smile at him, and he steps in to hug me once Nirvana releases me. He squeezes me tighter than normal, and I sigh. I can't even imagine how much it must still hurt for him. Mom was the love of his life.

They were childhood friends who became high school sweethearts before getting married and staying happily so until the day she was taken from us. It breaks my heart every time I think about it.

"Hey, sweetheart."

"Hi, Daddy," I whisper and hug him tightly back before letting him get back to preparing the feast I know is coming.

"How are you doing, Remy?" Maddie asks me softly as the chatter starts up again, pulling me just out of earshot of everyone else.

"I'm okay; it's just hard. It's always hard." I sigh.

"I know. It doesn't get easier like everyone always says, but this isn't the end of her journey. She'll be at peace." She pauses, her face staying soft despite the twitch of her eye as she asks her next question. "How are things with Jack after the other night?" She isn't team Jack either.

"It's fine. We went away for a few nights to celebrate my birthday and stuff. It's just hard when the people you love don't get along, y'know?" I smile at her before turning to grab a drink from the refrigerator.

"I can understand that. It's not that we don't like him necessarily. It's just that we don't feel like he's right for you. He's so uptight and straight-laced. He's a white picket fence and two kids kinda guy, and you were always much more of a free spirit. It's like he suffocates that part of you,

59

and we don't like to see the girl we love disappearing in front of us."

"I'm the same person I've always been, but my priorities have changed. And if you guys loved me as much as you say, you'd be happy that I'm happy. But enough, tonight isn't about me. Let's just help Dad set the table. You know how flustered he gets."

"Okay," she says softly, pausing for a moment as she takes me in. "You know I love you like a daughter, right? I just want you to be truly happy on your own path."

"I know. I love you too, Mads."

She smiles, and we head to the table, joining in the laughter over Colt's stupid story about supposedly fighting some ninja while he was in Japan for a while. I roll my eyes and help Dad set out the food. It always seemed strange that this was Mom's favorite, but it just always was. An English roast, with chicken and all the trimmings. So weird, but also so freaking yummy. Everyone takes their seats, slightly closer together tonight with the Winchesters here, but it still feels like family, even if I am still mad at Creek.

"My Emily would have loved seeing all of you here, around this table, celebrating love and family. It's been too long since she was taken from us, but I know she's still out there, looking down on us, waiting for our next adventure together. She wouldn't have wanted our sadness or tears, so tonight we remember her how she would have wanted us to. With love and laughter." My dad's voice cracks a little. It's always so strange to see such a big man break, but no one pays attention to it, and we all dig in as he carves up the bird.

Dinner was an event, full of laughter and stories about stupid stuff Mom did. There were new stories this year from Maddie, who grew up with Mom and Dad. Her and Nate, Creek's dad, grew up on the same street as them. It's so weird to me that such a small place could create so much love and links. Even my dad's best friend, Wing, grew up right next door to him, in between his and Nate's houses. I can't even imagine growing up like that. This house is out in the middle of nowhere, with a driveway a mile long and acres of land behind it, though it never felt lonely out here either.

I finish washing the last dish and hand it to Nirvana to dry before drying off my hands. She finishes the last dish, taking her time wiping the moisture away before softly saying, "I'm heading out, I've got Mom's car keys, and I'm heading to Kayla's. Creek's going to drive her home in his car later... I miss you, you should come see me more, especially if you're moving away like Mom said."

"I'm sorry, I've been a crappy friend lately. Is everything

okay with you?" I ask her, realizing just how wrapped up in my own bubble I've been since Creek disappeared.

"Yeah, I'm okay. I mean it sucked having Creek ghost me, and then you fell off the face of the Earth too, but I get it. You guys have always been like two sides of the same coin. I was so shocked when he went and left you behind. I will never understand boys."

"Ditto. They don't make any more sense, no matter how old you are." I smile at her.

"I guess it's a good thing I like girls too then." She says it so quietly I almost think I don't hear her, but I smile widely at her.

"Nirvana, really? That's so cool! I'm so proud of you and honored you'd tell me. Do your mom and brother know?" I hug her tightly. I can't imagine knowing myself so well at that age. Hell, I hardly know who I am now!

"Not yet," she shakes her head gently. "I'm going to tell Mom first since I'm not sure how Creek will take it. He's always been so overbearing but also so freaking cool. I still worry, though. He's been gone a while, and he seems different since he came back." Worry clouds her eyes, and my heart breaks for her.

"Sweetheart, you have absolutely nothing to worry about. As far as your brother is concerned, you hang the moon, and you always have. But if he's a dick about it, you tell me, and I'll kick his ass. Meathead or not." I wink at her and she laughs, the worry gone from her face. It warms me from the inside out. "I'm always here for you, okay? Even if you just need to vent or cry. You have my number."

"Thanks, Remy. I have to go, I can feel my phone buzzing in my pocket, and I just know it's Kayla losing her shit. I love you."

"Love you too, Nirvana. Always."

"Always," she says with a wave before grabbing her bag, hugging her mom and Creek before running to the door. I get myself a drink and head back to the table. Now that Nirvana has left, everyone seems so much more serious.

"Remy, you should sit. We need to… discuss some things with you," my dad says. I laugh at how serious he sounds, but everyone else at the table looks bleak, so I stop. I turn to my brothers, Bauer's jaw is clenched as the rage rolls from him in waves, and Colt can't stop fidgeting uncomfortably. Creek won't even look me in the eyes, and Maddie only offers me a sad smile.

"What's going on? You guys are weirding me out," I say, taking a seat opposite my dad.

"Before I start, I want you to know that we never wanted to lie to you, but I need you to listen to everything I have to say before you ask any questions or lose your shit, okay?"

"Way to keep me calm, Dad." I roll my eyes and take a

sip of the whiskey I poured, glad now that I have it.

"I'm serious, Remington. I need you to listen," my dad says, and I nod tightly. "Okay, right. You think after doing this a few times, I'd be more prepared to tell you, but you're my little girl, and this shit is hard." He swigs back the amber in his own glass, and I look to the others around the table, who all seem just as uncomfortable.

"Remy," Maddie starts. "Our families are different. I know this is all going to sound more than a little unbelievable, and I really wish your mom was here to help tell you because she always had such a way with words."

She takes a breath and looks at me before continuing. "Remy, you, we, all of us. We are what is known in our world as Hunters. Hunters are an elite being, descended from angels. We are Nephilim. We are faster, stronger, smarter than you could possibly imagine." I sit, staring at her like she's lost her mind, but that doesn't make her stop speaking. "We were created to help keep the balance in the five factions of the world. The Nephilim, the Dracul, the Lycans, the Witches, and the humans. The humans have no idea about any of this, and that is how it must always stay."

I burst out laughing because I just can't help it. What the actual fuck?

"This is no laughing matter!" My father's voice booms, so loud I flinch. My laughter dies away as I realize he's deadly serious.

"Hunters are the peacekeepers of the world. We hunt the Dracul and the Lycans, who feed on humans and kill indiscriminately. They are a drain on this earth and need to be wiped out for the good of everyone," he says, before standing and pouring himself another drink.

"Remy," Maddie sighs before continuing, "I know this all sounds unbelievable, but what your father tells you is true. We couldn't tell you before your twenty-first birthday because of the way Hunters evolve. We live as humans until our bodies are developed enough to survive the power that comes with being what we are. If you knew beforehand, the memories that would swarm you could kill you."

"What do you mean, memories?" I ask, confusion fully setting in.

"What she means is that unlike humans, Nephilim do not know a true death. We are reborn. Always to the same parents, always as the same family. This is your twelfth life, but as always, you have a choice to make. You can accept who you are, the family legacy, and complete the ritual with the Elders to have all of your memories return. Or you can choose to live this life as a human, without your memories. Though the burden of knowing what you know, and not fighting back, could be great."

"Denny, hush. You know you are not allowed to influence her decision," Maddie scolds my father.

"I mean... I have... You all chose?" My words come

out in a garbled mess, as my world tilts on its axis.

"Wait… Mom…?" I ask and look at my father whose face is painted with guilt and sadness.

"Yes, your mom was one of us too. She died doing what she loved doing. Hunting," Maddie says softly. "I was with her, and I should have protected her, but…"

"It wasn't your fault, Maddie," my father says, patting her hand.

"This is all way too much. Is this why you disappeared?" I look to Colt and Creek, and I can feel the anger inside of me rising. "This is such bullshit. All of you lied to me my entire fucking life. You're telling me my entire family lied to me about who I am, about who we are. About Mom. Lied so much that you two fucking paired up and left without a goddamn word? Fuck this." I stand, and swallow down the rest of my glass of whiskey, thankful for the burn.

"Remington, sit down," my dad says, and I can hear how tired he is.

"No. I will not sit back down and listen to you try to explain how each and every one of you betrayed me. How you lied to me for my own good. Do you have any idea how much guilt I've felt about Mom dying? Thinking she was going out shopping for shit for my stupid birthday just to find out that's not how she died at all! To find out my entire life has essentially been a lie. I don't want this. Any of it." I grab my keys from the counter, leaving the house and everyone I thought I knew better than anything behind. I have to try to process what the fuck I've just been told.

The city is unusually quiet tonight as I patrol, the full moon casts the streets in an eerie glow. It feels like the calm before a storm. Too still. Too quiet. Even Kain's footsteps are as silent and swift as my own. Unsurprising, considering.

"Stop it," he says with a smile. "You keep thinking things are too quiet, and we'll end up covered in more than a little blood and gore."

I laugh at him. "Someone feeling a little superstitious? Even after all this time?"

"Some things are better kept as they have always been. You might call it superstition. I call it knowing that fate's a fickle bitch. You don't live as long as we have without knowing better about these things." The playful smile on his face is one I know that few see, and I consider myself lucky enough to be one of those few.

"I still say you control your own fate." This is a conversation we've had more times than I care to count, but it's what we do. It has been ever since our first meeting.

"How can you say that? Especially considering what we are." He frowns. Even after all this time, he's never been able to wrap his head around my way of thinking.

"Because I get a choice. Each life. I get to choose which path to take. That's not predestined. It's not fated. It's mine, and I own it." I shrug as we hit the next street.

"These new and modern ways of thinking—I fear I will never change to accept them fully. Don't get me wrong, the luxury of these times is something I'd never give up again, but sometimes I wish for the simplicity of life all those years ago. Things today are so complicated. Watching what you say, the fear of offending people. Humans are so… touchy."

"I'll give you that. Got to love this new age seventies shit, though." I start, pausing when I hear it the sound of breaking glass ahead of us. We take off at a sprint, careful not to move too swiftly in case any humans are able to spot us. The smell of blood reaches me before my eyes take in the scene before us.

"Fucking infantile Lycans," Kain growls. He pulls his guns from their holsters and aims them at the two Lycans in the alley. They're cornered, and if there's one thing Lycans hate, it's being cornered. The high wall behind them means their only way out is past us. Unfortunately for them, the human they ripped the throat from is still bleeding out at their feet. Rule number two. Don't kill humans.

"We don't bow to your rule, Hunter," one of them says as I step forward, though he eyes my sword in its scabbard on my back. If only this idiot knew how many different ways to kill him I have available to me right now. My sword isn't what he should be afraid of.

"Well, that makes you a little stupid. I wonder what Roman would say about that." I tilt my head as my words hit their mark.

"You're… You're Remy Bennett?" The quieter Lycan asks, his voice husky from the partial change of his form. The two look at each other before dropping the human.

"How old are you?" Kain asks from my right flank.

"This is our first moon," the first says, his anger is palpable and filtering through his words. I swear. Why the fuck doesn't Roman have these guys locked up? First fucking moon.

"You know I can't just let you walk away from this. You killed a human," I tell them, and fear flickers in their eyes.

"You won't kill us," the first says cockily. "You couldn't, look at you. You're tiny. Even with him backing you up."

"Oh boys, you have no idea," I say, before throwing the obsidian dagger from my hip into his shoulder. I draw my gun on the second in the same breath. Dead shot. He falls to the ground as his brains paint the alley walls.

The first simpers, the coating on my dagger poisoning his blood.

"We never meant to…" he cries. "It was our first moon,

and we avoided round up. Please don't. I won't tell."

"Roman probably isn't going to be happy about this," Kain reminds me. He covers the street for us, knowing that two Lycans isn't something I can't handle on my own.

"His alphas should have a better handle of their wolves. The Alpha of Alphas can come and see me if he has a problem with how I handle things." I kneel down and pull my dagger from the remaining Lycan, his breathing haggard as the obsidian does its job. Blood spurts from the wound. I nicked an artery.

"You have two choices," I tell him. "I can let you die slowly and in agony, the same way I'm sure you did to that human. Or I can put a bullet through your skull."

"Fuck you," he stutters, his breath coming out in shallow spurts.

"Have it your way," I say and stand, putting a bullet through his thigh, and this time I know I got the artery. The shot itself won't kill him, but my bullets are obsidian. Lycans can heal from most wounds, but not those from obsidian. He'll bleed out here, and I'll send a cleanup crew to come and get both of them.

I holster my gun and wipe down my dagger before sheathing it back at my hip.

"The young ones never get any less cocky." Kain grins, death no longer affecting either of us. When you've done what we do for as long as we have, it becomes almost a part of everyday life. Literally.

I notice the blood on my top and sigh as Kain wipes some from my cheek.

"Want to head back and clean up? I'll call my guys to deal with this," he offers, and it warms me. No matter how much people would hate what I have with him, I love him.

"Sure." I smile up at him, and he grins back.

"Want a lift?" he laughs, and I nod. He lifts me into his arms, and I wrap my own arms around his neck, holding tightly as he runs faster than the wind. No human could hope to see or hear us. It's what makes him so dangerous.

"We're here, milady," he chuckles as he plants me back on my feet, opening the door to his one-story home. It's smaller than one might expect considering his status, but I know that no one other than us knows about his place. Well, other than Luc.

"The shower is all yours if you want it first," he offers coyly, shutting the door behind me.

"Thanks. Want to join me?" I take his hand and lead him down the hall to the bathroom. He takes me by the waist and lifts me onto the counter, leaving my head level with his.

"I have no idea how I'm meant to live without you," he says softly before capturing my lips with his. Hard and full of passion, he devours me until I'm breathless.

SIX

It's been two weeks since dinner at my dad's, and I'm still angry. I've ignored every call, every knock at my door, every single attempt at contact. I've even shut out Jack. I don't know how to even begin dealing with any of this, but in my heart, I know it's true. I'd noticed changes before they told me. Just stupid little things that I thought nothing of. Like catching something I'd have never been able to catch before. Being able to run farther, dance harder. Things seemed easier. I thought I was just in better shape.

But it was all a lie.

Am I overreacting about them lying to me? Maybe a little, but give a girl a break. What even is this life? A life of monsters, of all the things that go bump in the night being real? Dracul and Lycans, they said. Nephilim. Thanks to

Google, I got way more information than I could have
ever cared for. Vampires and werewolves. The children of
angels. It's all more than a little unbelievable.

I don't want any of this. I am not strong enough to deal
with this life. No matter what they say. Twelfth life. Are
they insane? And yet, I can feel the truth of it deep down
inside of me, no matter how much I want to cart them all
off to an asylum.

But Dad did say I have a choice. I don't have to be who
they all so obviously want me to be. I can choose the life
I have. The path I've always wanted. To be a doctor. To
marry Jack. To be a mom.

Because I'd be giving all of that up. And I can't give
up Jack. Can I?

I love him.

So what if I am plagued by dreams? Dreams—which
I'm guessing are probably some weird form of memories—
of loving others. Of fighting for more, being more. I am
not that person. Not now. I want too many different things.

My breath speeds up, as if I'm panting. The indecision
of it all rips through me, leaving me almost gasping.

I am not strong enough to be who they want me to be.
I am not a fearless warrior.

I'm the girl who drops bottles at the bar and prays they
don't smash. I'm the girl getting ready to start a career
helping people, to take an oath to do no harm. That girl is

not the same girl who would hunt and kill monsters. It just isn't.

Right?

A knock sounds on my door, and I ignore it the same way I have every other over the past two weeks. I haven't left my apartment at all, calling in sick to each shift at my job and telling Jack I'm sick and he needs to stay away. I don't need an excuse for my family, though. They know why I'm not answering.

I wrap the blanket more tightly around myself and stare out of the window, trying to put my world back together again. Yes, I'm being a little dramatic, but fuck me, I need a minute.

A key turns in the lock. I turn to see who the hell has my spare key when Colt and Creek waltz into my sitting room like they belong here.

"Get out," I tell them, turning my back to them and looking out the window again.

"Remy, come on. You can't ignore us forever," Colt says and comes to stand in front of me, his arms crossed. "We couldn't tell you before now, it would have fucking killed you. Stop being such a brat."

I stay silent, unwilling to be reasonable about this just yet. What hurts the most, more than the Hunter thing, is everything with my mom. Knowing that it wasn't my fault she died. The guilt that I've carried with me since she died was crippling and has affected everything I've done. Every choice I've made. And it was for nothing.

And they knew. Colt and Creek. My two closest confidants. Thick as thieves. They knew how much what happened to Mom fucked with me, and still, they said nothing.

"Is this why you came back? Just for the big reveal? To take part in the loss of my sanity?" I snarl, and Colt throws his hands up in the air, walking away from me.

I close my eyes against the sunlight that batters them once he moves out of the line of the window. A shadow blocks the sunlight again, making the darkness behind my eyes more intense. I open them to see Creek sitting on the coffee table in front of me.

"Remy, we came home for you. Just like we left for you."

"Left *for* me. That's a new one." I laugh.

"Believe it or not, it's the truth," he says softly as he folds his arms. His hair falls into his eyes, but he pays it no attention, his soft and steady gaze focused solely on me.

"We were a danger to you once we turned twenty-one and went through our rituals. New Hunters require training while their memories return. They can be dangerous to younger Hunters who don't know because we're not as used to keeping our damn mouths shut. Why do you think I didn't speak to you while I was gone? It killed me to shut you out like that, but it was shut you out or risk killing you." I can hear his hurt and his frustration in his voice.

"All sounds like a good excuse to me." I shrug.

"Fucking hell, Remy. Stop being such a fucking brat," Colt spits, and I can just see him throw his hands up in the air and shake his head at me. "Neither of us wanted to leave everything we knew, but we did. To keep you safe. To make sure you didn't end up dead. You're the whole reason we left everything behind and went to train with Hunters on the other side of the goddamn world rather than staying with our families and learning from those who know us best."

Colt paces while Creek just watches me intently as if trying to read my mind before he adds on, "We didn't have to worry about Nirvana, she's away at school. All of this was done for you."

I bite the inside of my cheek to keep the words I want to say from falling out of my mouth. I know what they're saying is reasonable. It's more than that, it's everything I needed to hear, to know... But I'm not ready to be reasonable yet. I'm fucking terrified of what all of this means.

"I need you guys to go. Please," I whisper the words, scared that my voice will give away the tears I feel threatening to fall. Creek looks over my shoulder to where Colt has moved into my kitchen.

"We'll go. We'll give you more space, but time is

running out Remy. You're not safe if you don't make a decision. The memories will keep trying to come, and without the ritual, that alone could kill you," Creek says softly. "I know it's a lot, and I know how terrified you are, I can see it. But we'll go. Just know that we'll be here when you're ready."

I nod, not daring to say another word as he stands, squeezing my shoulder before he walks away.

"I don't get why we're giving up," Colt snarls as they leave.

"We're not," I hear Creek answer softly. "We're just doing what we have to for her, just like we always have."

The door closes softly, and the floodgates open. I cry until I can't breathe, grieving for the life I can't have. Whichever choice I make, I lose.

Pulling up in front of my dad's house, I shut off the car and just stare at the front door. The last time I was here, my entire world got tipped on its axis. But I need more information, and while my dad might be gruff, I know he won't sugarcoat the truth. He'll give it to me straight, even if it's not what I want to hear. His mantra has always been that the two most important things in life are family and truth.

The irony of it isn't lost on me, but I guess his truth is

the Hunter truth.

I take off my seat belt and climb out of the car, still trying to convince myself that this is the right thing to do. I've never run from hard things before. I face them, head on. It's how I was raised. I'm not about to change all of that because of this, even if it is the most craptastic thing I've ever heard in my entire life.

As I climb the steps, the front door opens, and my dad meets me on the porch, two mugs of coffee in his hands. He passes one to me and nods toward the swing. "It's good to see you, Remy girl."

His voice is as gruff as ever, but it has a soft wariness to it, and I hate that I'm the cause of that.

"Hey, Dad. Sorry, I just needed some space. It's a lot to process, all things considered." I smile and take a sip of the coffee, strong and sweet, just how I always have it, and he nods.

"I understand that, and we never wanted to lie to you or mislead you, but I need you to know that we had no choice."

I shrug at his words, and he sighs.

"So, what brings you here?"

"I need more information. I can't just make this decision on a whim. I have a lot to lose, no matter what I choose." I pull my knees to my chest, and he sighs again.

"Ask away, you know I'll never lie to you again. I

won't tell you just what you want to hear either, though."

"I know, that's why I'm here. Truth and family, remember? So, first, why twenty-one? It makes no sense to me. I've had so much time to start my life already. Why bring that all crashing down now?"

He runs a hand down his face, stroking his beard as he tries to put the words together in his head. I recognize the look, so I sit as patiently as I can for him to formulate what he wants to say. It takes a moment, but he finally says, "The honest truth of it is that I don't know one hundred percent why. The Elders can probably answer that question better for you... or an angel should you ever come across one. The simplest answer is genetics. The merging of human and angel DNA means taking longer to mature. There is something of a chemical imbalance in us until then, which is why our forms can't take the flood of chemicals and hormones released during the ritual completed to gain your memories."

I sit back, trying to take it all in, but I'm not sure that's possible. How can we not have answers? But I don't ask my questions, I just let him continue.

"Plus, your strengths aren't unlocked until this age. There's no point in ruining the innocence of growth with the knowledge of all that is wrong in the world. Once upon a time, we tried to do it earlier, but the results were catastrophic."

Well, good to know. I guess this is as good of any for them to have ghosted me, but it's probably not going to make me any more reasonable. Again, I stay quiet, because I can't even begin to organize my mind.

"Any Hunter who discovered what they were before this age started recalling their memories without the ritual, and they died. Each and every one of them. Our bodies simply cannot cope with the influx before then."

"Okay, well that was a lot? But I have to ask, Elders?"

"Yes, they're the leaders of the Hunters, our government of sorts, I guess. They're also our police, our lawmakers, our judge and jury. There are seven of them, one from each original bloodline, meaning your grandfather is an elder. I am his proxy, so when he dies, I take his place until he is reborn. Once he takes his memories back, I step down. Each elder rules a territory, and we call the Hunters within the territory a guild."

"Okay. Wow. Erm. Okay," I can't formulate a full sentence as I try to let it all sink in.

It sounds unbelievable. All of it. "So, we can't die?"

"Well, yes and no. We all die, but Hunters, Nephilim, whatever you want to call us, are reborn. It is a gift from the angel blood running through our veins. But we can ask for true death, should we wish it. Some do not wish to continue the cycles. For some, it becomes too much. It is not easy, but it is possible. Though, if a child dies before

81

they reach maturity and unlock their powers, they meet the true death. It is why we protect our young so fiercely."

I blink, unable to find the words I want to say. I've seen my dad worked up, but it's like his entire being glows as he talks about this. I've never seen him believe in something so much.

"And you don't regret your decision, even with what happened to Mom?" I ask softly.

"I miss your mother every damn day, but I'll never regret my decision, and neither would your mom. What we do, it's in our blood. It's a part of us. If you get your memories back, you'll see that."

He says it like it's a good thing, but if our history is just full of death and war, I'm not convinced I want the memories back.

"You'll see that we work toward a goal bigger than personal wants and needs. It's about protecting those around us who have no idea how to protect themselves. To rid the earth of the plague of monsters. The filth that sees fit to ruin our world. Once you remember, you'll see. You'll know what it is to belong to something greater than yourself. To work toward the greater good. To never waver in that belief. Just as you always have." His passion and fire about it all is almost contagious, but I can't help the huge pool of doubt that sits within me.

"Will I remember everything?"

"Maybe, though each person is different each time they are reborn. Some remember everything, though it's rare. We usually remember snippets, strong memories, the ones that matter. Our bodies, somehow, seem to remember better than our minds. If you move forward, you'll start your training, and we'll arrange your ritual; but it will come to you quicker than you can imagine. You've always been a quick study, putting your brothers to shame. The rivalry has been the cause of the biggest headaches of my existence, but no matter what, we always follow the rules of the Hunters."

Rules? Now there's rules? Of course there are rules.

"Rule one, don't reveal what you are to the humans. Rule two, don't kill humans. Rule three, never fraternize with the enemy. Some soft-hearted fools in history have dared to love the filth, have defiled our purity with the animals. We stick to our kind. The only gray area is the Witches, but that's for another day." The disgust in his voice sends a shiver down my spine, I can't imagine hating someone just for being something the way he does, but I guess I must have. Or at least, past me must have.

"I feel like I know so much more, but nothing new all at the same time here, Dad. I don't know what to do." I sigh and put the mug down on the porch. Standing, I wrap my arms around myself. "I am not strong enough for the path you want me to choose. Maybe I was before, but who

I am right now… I'm not who you want me to be."

He doesn't speak immediately, and I cave. "I'm sorry," I tell him as he stares out into the tree line.

"Don't make your decision yet," he finally says, turning his intense gaze in my direction. "You have no idea… If you choose not to go through the awakening ritual to officially become one of us, you have to leave us. You can't be around us if that's the path you choose, Remy. It's not fair, but it is our way. And if you don't leave, we will, and you will not find us."

My heart feels like it's being pulled from my chest at his words. I feel breathless.

"How? How could you leave me like that?"

"You would have made your choice, Remy. It's our way."

I fall onto my sofa and close my eyes. This day. I literally can't even. I don't want to think about it. So much has happened when I already had more than enough to contemplate as it was.

No. I will not wallow. What I need is a bubble bath.

I head to my bathroom and turn on the taps, pouring in a generous amount of lavender and lily scented bubble bath. I pause for a moment to take a deep breath, it smells so freaking heavenly. I shake my head and turn the faucet off as an idea strikes me.

I head to the fridge, pouring a glass of whiskey before picking up the paperback from the coffee table where I left it weeks ago. Back before my life went to shit and reading about Fae royalty was an escape from my mundane world.

A knock at the door stops me in my tracks, and I let out a defeated breath. This had better not be someone coming to talk to me about all of this crazy shit again.

I unlock and open the door, coming face-to-face with some poor guy buckling under the weight of the box he's carrying.

"Miss Bennett?" he asks, sweat rolling down his face.

"That's me. Please, drop it on the counter," I say to him, waving him in.

"Thank you," he groans as he steps forward, struggling a little to lift the box, so I step forward to help him, grabbing one side to place it on the counter. "Can you sign here?"

When he passes me the little tablet to sign my name, I notice his shirt.

Luna's Flowers.

"This is flowers?" I ask, and he nods.

"Only the best, as requested." I sign on his tablet and see him out before staring at the box. I open it quickly. No one has ever sent me flowers.

I open the tall box, and find the biggest vase I have ever seen, absolutely stuffed with purple peonies. My favorites!

SLOANE MURPHY

They're so beautiful. I lift the vase from the cardboard, thankful for my limited but extra strength from this ridiculous Hunter business and discard the box before placing the vase back on the counter. The shade of the flowers is just one lighter than my eyes.

I notice the note tucked in the violet ribbon on the vase and reach for it eagerly.

Happy Belated Birthday, Remy.
Sorry they're late.
I'll see you soon.

I wonder who they could be from. I check the back of the note but find no name. How bizarre, maybe the shop left it off. I grab my phone from the bathroom, and dial Creek.

"You okay, Remy?" he says when he answers.

"Did you send me flowers?"

"Flowers?" He sounds puzzled, and my curiosity grows since it obviously wasn't him.

"Yeah, purple peonies."

"That motherfucker," he growls, and my eyebrows shoot up.

"I'm sorry, what?" I ask since he obviously knows something.

"Nothing. No, I didn't send them," he answers sharply.

"No need to be so pissy, it was just a question. They're probably from Jack, he probably just forgot about them. I'll see you later."

"Sure," he says, and the line cuts off. I wonder who pissed in his cereal.

Fuck it. I'm going to have my bath and relax because I am done with today, despite the vase of beautiful flowers sitting on my counter.

I grab my drink and the book again and head into the bathroom, ready to forget about the world.

SEVEN

I lean down and undo my ballet slippers. Dance class tonight was abysmal, but I'd challenge anyone to try focusing on a plié when you have thoughts of monsters running through your head the entire time. I hoped ballet would distract me from the weird new world I live in, and maybe give me a reprieve from the insanity that has become my new reality. I couldn't have been more wrong.

Instead, I nearly broke an ankle when I landed wrong and then almost took out four other dancers when I barreled into them. I guess some of that newfound strength Dad was going on about came into play as the others flew across the room. I shove the slippers in my bag and shrug into my hoodie and sneakers before heading out into the darkness of the evening.

I never considered being scared of the darkness before. Our little town is so ordinary and so absolutely unremarkable. Nothing bad ever seems to happen here. Except now I know that's because two families of Hunters live here. And because of my awesome DNA and having not done the awakening or the binding rituals yet, I'm a prime target to everything that goes bump in the night.

I put in an ear bud and play PVRIS loudly enough to keep me from freaking out. I hold my bag tighter as I head through the streets, entirely on edge as I walk toward my home. The streets are empty, and I swear I jump at my own shadow.

I stop and shake myself. *Get a fucking grip Remy.*

There's no one out here, and you're overreacting. This is ridiculous. I take a deep breath to get a hold of myself and stride toward the park, where I usually cut through to get home. I've always loved the park at night. There's very little light, so the stars seem to shine brighter. More than once, I've laid in the middle of the field for a while, just looking at the stars and pondering the workings of the universe.

I take a deep breath and slow my pace, enjoying the quiet time and the cool air that hints that fall is on its way. I refuse to be afraid of something that isn't even here.

A noise behind me startles me, my heart races, but I turn to see a group of joggers working their way through the park and release the breath I held. So much for not being afraid.

I turn back to the path and move aside when the joggers reach me, enjoying the peace of the park and the music playing in my earbuds. Looking up at the stars I meander down the empty path and try to spot constellations like I used to with Mom. It used to hurt to do it without her, but I realized a few years ago that she'd love me carrying on the tradition, so now it simply makes me smile.

I'm so distracted I don't see the person walking toward me until I literally crash into them. I fall back on my ass, dropping my bag. That hit is definitely going to leave a bruise. I look up to find the stranger staring down at me.

"I'm so sorry, I didn't even see you," I say, dusting off my hands. I climb to my feet and grab my bag, but the man continues to stare at me. I notice his eyes first, they're so dark it feels like I'm looking into pools of shadows.

My heart races, and I clutch my bag tighter before trying to maneuver around him. He steps in my path, blocking my retreat. "I said I was sorry. Now, if you don't mind, I need to get home. My boyfriend is cooking dinner."

"I don't think so, Hunter." His voice comes out more like a hiss than anything else, though it's just guttural enough to send a shiver down my spine. This is not happening to me right now. I feel sick and like I'm going to cry, but I don't let it show.

"I think you have me confused with someone else," I say, trying to keep my voice steady but failing.

"Just a baby Hunter, out here all alone. Foolish mistake. What a treat you'll be." He licks his lips, and that's when I notice his teeth. Two fangs longer than the others, so long they give him a lisp. I feel my skin crawl, goosebumps covering my arms, and then I make the decision. I turn around and sprint as fast as I can away from him. His laugh rings out across the park, and I realize the mistake I made. Now it's a game, but I have no other choice. I am not cut out for this life.

I scream as I'm yanked back by my ponytail, my bones jarring at the sudden force of the stop. He shoves me, and I crash to my knees, pain rushing through me. He grabs my arm so tightly I can feel his sharpened nails cut deep before he pulls at my hair again, exposing my neck before he laughs.

"Such a pretty little lamb." I feel his breath on my ear as he gets closer. His teeth break the skin on my neck, and pain like I've never known floods me. I do not want to die like this. He releases me and laughs, "So sweet!"

I throw my head back with as much force as I can, and I hear the crunch as the back of my skull connects with his face. I wrench myself out of his grip, and my scalp burns as I jump to my feet and start running. I don't need to go far to get back to Main Street, where I know there are a ton of people. I push myself harder, ignoring the pain that rips through me until I see the lights popping up in the distance. I don't stop until I'm halfway down Main Street, and then fall to the ground again, tears running down my face.

Looking behind me, I don't see him amongst the other people who are looking at me like I've lost my mind, and a sob racks through me. I clamber through my bag for my phone and dial the one person I know who will pick up.

"Remy? I didn't expect to hear from you," Creek's voice filters through from the other end, and it makes me cry harder.

"Help me..." I manage through my tears, trying to catch my breath.

"Where are you?" His voice hardens, and Colt shouts in the background.

"Main Street," is all I manage, and the line disconnects. I pull myself together and get out of the middle of the road. I lean up against one of the storefronts and slide down until I hit the ground again.

The screeching of tires as the truck stops in front of me cuts through the haze. I hear someone cursing, and then look up to find Creek kneeling in front of me. I lost all track of time since I called, but I think they got here pretty quick.

"Remy, are you okay?" His eyes scan my body, taking in the blood, and he swears again.

"Come on, let's get you out of here," he says, tucking one arm under my knees and another around my back before lifting me. I can't find the words to stop him.

"She's still in shock. We need to get her cleaned up," Creek says.

"I've got her. Is all that blood hers?" Colt's voice cracks slightly as he asks Creek. I can feel Creek shrug as he slides me into the back of the truck.

"I have no idea. Let's get her back so we can check her out. She was bitten."

"Fuck!" Colt growls as Creek climbs in next to me and closes the door. Colt rounds the front of the truck and climbs back in, taking off at a breakneck speed, but I don't feel it. I don't feel anything.

I open my eyes when I realize we've stopped moving. I try to lift my head, but my neck screams. As I become more aware, I realize just how much pain radiates through me.

What the fuck?

I groan as I try to sit up, breathless at the attempt.

"No sweetie, you should stay lying down," Maddie says in a soothing voice as she takes a seat beside me.

"What happened?" I ask. I've never hurt like this in my life, and my memory is fuzzy.

"It'll come back, don't worry. The drugs in your system

are likely making things feel a little out of whack. You were attacked last night, but you're at your dad's place now. Creek and Colt went to get you when you called, but as soon as they dropped you off, they left with Bauer to go hunting. Your father and I patched you up and gave you something for the pain. You were lucky. It's rare an untrained Hunter can escape any of the other factions, especially a Dracul once he's tasted you." Worry etches her features, but she shakes her head and smiles back down at me.

"But of course you escaped. You're Remington Bennett, the fiercest of us all. You've always been the strongest, stubbornest Hunter I've ever known. The Shadow Walker." I laugh at her words, then groan from doing so.

"Thanks, I think." I smile, and I feel my lips crack from the strain on them. "Can I have some water?"

I lick my lips, and she nods, rushing away to get me some water. I force myself to sit up because she was right about one thing, I am a stubborn fuck. There's no way I'm staying lying down, even when all I can really think about is whatever the hell she meant by the Shadow Walker thing.

She reappears with my dad behind her, and I know I won't be able to ask her right now.

"Morning, Remy girl. How are you feeling?"

"Like I got hit by a truck. It's fun." I smile and take a sip of the water Maddie hands to me.

"That's my girl. Not letting it get you down." He smiles at me, but the purple under his eyes is thick and deep. It says more about his state than he does.

"Never. Sorry if I worried you guys; you look exhausted," I say softly.

"Oh hush." Maddie waves me off. "Don't ever be sorry. You were attacked. We're expecting to hear back from the boys shortly. It's still dark out, but they'll be back at sunrise."

"This. *This* is why we need to do the ritual. As soon as possible," my dad says forcefully, and Maddie turns with a scowl, a hint of the scolding to come.

"You leave the girl alone. She's barely awake, give her a minute before you start in on her, Denny. Fates help me."

"If she'd done the ritual by now, she'd either have her weapons or be concealed so she wouldn't have been attacked." He growls back at her, and I see her eyebrows lift.

"Oh, is that right? So the factions don't just attack humans at random? Well, I guess we can go put our feet up then, can't we? Our job is done." She rolls her eyes, and I can't help the laugh that escapes me.

"Hey guys, can you not? My head is killing me." The wry laugh catches their attention first, but they both have the grace to at least look a little contrite at my words. "Hilarious as this is, I want to make the most of going back to sleep before my memory of last night comes back and I likely never sleep again."

"Of course, sweetie. Sorry. I'll keep the guys away, we could all use a few more hours sleep. You rest up and feel better. Your Hunter healing is working, so you won't be down for much longer, though it will be slower since you haven't completed the ritual." She smiles at me and shoos my dad from the room. I stop a laugh from rising again and battering my bruised... well, everything.

I lie back down and close my eyes, but then the memories start to come back. A face, and a feeling of fear like I've never known haunt me as I lie there, breathing shallowly.

I stretch out as the sun brightens the room, and for just a second, I'm free. But then the memory of why I'm in my childhood room hits me like a dump truck. I get up and look in the mirror. I gasp at the sight that greets me. No more cuts or bruises, plus my ribs feel fine. Hell, I feel better than maybe I ever have.

What the ever-loving fuck?

"It takes a minute, but you get used to it." I spin to find Creek leaning against the doorframe, a steaming cup of coffee in his hands.

"I don't know that I'll ever get used to this." I sigh and

sit back on the bed, glad to be in at least a tank and some boy shorts with my undeniably male best friend looming over me. He laughs and shakes his head.

"You'll be amazed. Once the memories start to come back…" He pauses and looks at me, a look so penetrating that it feels like he's looking at my very soul. My breath catches, and I hold it until he looks away. "Well, you'll see if you complete the ritual. Though, after last night, and knowing everything… I can't imagine you ever not picking the life of a Hunter. The other factions would rejoice at the infamous Remy Bennett rejecting her heritage." He shakes his head and strides across the room, offering me the mug of coffee.

I take it and close my eyes as I take a sip, unsure of what to even say to that.

"Can I ask you some questions? About who I was, about what you know?" I ask him quietly, and he sighs before sitting opposite me.

It feels strange, looking at this man who almost looks like a stranger but feels like the person I've been closest to my entire life. His eyes are really the only thing that haven't changed. His face is sharper, his hair longer, and he rocks a beard that I never would have believed could have suited him before seeing it for myself. His shoulders are broader, with arms stronger than I ever thought possible. Almost every inch of his skin is covered in ink, telling stories I know nothing about, but I know the man beneath. And I know that he wouldn't have marked himself unless it meant something to him.

He runs a hand through his light hair, and I wait while he tries to find the words.

"I wish... There is so much... But I can't. Not until the process is complete. You need to gain your memories yourself, and only if you have holes after it all can I fill you in. You have no idea how much I want to tell you... to close the gap I can feel between us. Especially when..."

He stops, and I can see how hard it is for him. No matter how angry I am at him, I don't want to cause him pain.

"It's fine, don't. If you can't tell me, I'll just have to wait."

"Does that mean you made your decision?" he says, and I can see him fighting the joy trying to rise at the possibility.

"I think so," I nod, trying to tamper down the emotions waging a war inside of me. Yes, I love Jack, but I know he'd never believe any of this, let alone be on board with any of it. It means giving up everything I've worked toward my entire life. But the idea of letting those things run free, knowing I chose to do nothing about it while innocent people are mutilated and murdered at their hands? That isn't something I can live with. I thought about it when I woke in the middle of the night, and the whole thing plagued my dreams. I could easily have been killed last night. It was fluke and pure genetics that kept me alive, giving me another chance at life. I can't waste that chance by doing nothing.

I also can't give up the people who have always been there for me, even with the lies and deception. I know deep down that they were trying to protect me, no matter how much it still stings.

"I just, I have a lot to sort out. I have my whole life planned... well had. It's just—" I sigh, cutting myself off. "It's a lot. Last night opened my eyes, in the worst of ways, but I know in my heart that I can't just close my eyes to that part of life and keep pretending I don't know it exists. I'd live in fear, constantly looking over my shoulder, and that irks a part of me so deep in my soul that I know this is the right decision."

He leans forward and wraps me in the biggest bear hug of my life, and I let go of some of the rage and bitterness I've been keeping in my heart toward him, hugging him back.

"I missed you," he breathes and squeezes me tighter. He releases me, backing away and heading toward the door. "I know this isn't an easy choice for you. It isn't for any of us, but you're doing the right thing, no matter how much it hurts right now. There's so much more to this, to everything, than you can imagine. I'm going to go start breakfast, but don't worry, I won't say anything."

"I know you won't. Thank you," I tell him, but what I don't tell him is that actually, this was a pretty easy choice.

Is this decision going to break my heart? Blow up my current life? Hell yes it is, but will the other choice be the better one in the long run? Something inside me tells me the answer to all of those questions is a whopping yes, but last night showed me that I am strong enough for this.

Yes, I was scared, but I didn't break, and I didn't die. I survived. I might not have killed the Dracul, but I survived. Without any training, any idea what the hell I was doing, I survived. Something deep inside of me feels like a missing piece of myself that I didn't even know I was searching for clicked into place.

I take a deep breath and get ready for the day. I hype myself up to face everyone at breakfast. But then... then I need to go and face the rest of my life with the decisions I've made.

The smells coming from the kitchen make my mouth water as I finish drying my hair. I throw on a pair of denim shorts, a tank, and a shirt from the limited wardrobe I still have here before heading down to where I can hear several voices talking in hushed tones. Two guesses what they're talking about, and the first definitely doesn't count. I roll my eyes and laugh.

"You guys suck at being stealthy. How you manage to keep the monsters at bay surprises me," I laugh as I head straight for the coffee pot. I pour a mug and turn to face the five people looking back at me. There's a whole range of expressions on their faces. Creek looks amused, and concern colors Colt's face. Maddie & Bauer very nearly look guilty, and my dad? Well, he just looks as grumpy as usual.

"Sorry sweetheart, we weren't..." Maddie starts, and I wave her off.

"Don't be silly, I was playing. You guys can keep to your hushed whispering as long as I get a plate of whatever that smell is." I eye the stove behind Creek. He always could cook, but the scent of meat and herbs from behind him are divine. I flutter my lashes at him playfully, and he laughs before handing me a plate. I take a bite and groan, heading to the table to annihilate the meat, potato, and egg goodness steaming before me.

"Am I missing something?" Colt asks, his eyes bouncing between me and Creek. Creek winks at me, but I only offer my brother a shrug. "I am definitely missing something."

He eyes me almost suspiciously as he sits next to me with his own plate. The others join us, Bauer, Dad, and Maddie chattering away while the rest of us eat in silence. Creek smiles widely at me, I smile back, and I can practically feel Colt's frown growing without even being able to see his face.

"So… I guess you guys should know," I start after I finish eating. The silence that fills the space around us is almost deafening in intensity. "Last night opened my eyes. This Hunter thing—this is a lot. Like beyond anything I could have ever even imagined."

"Remy, you don't have to decide yet," my dad says gruffly, and I shake my head.

"No, Dad, I do. I've already made my decision. I have so much to lose, no matter what I choose, but I can't give this up knowing the truth of what the world really is. I choose to be a Hunter." I finish saying the words, and I feel something settle inside of me, almost like I've just stepped onto a new path of my fate. "There's no way I could have continued living my life, knowing what I know. Looking over my shoulder every day, being afraid of the dark. Giving up my family, my heritage. Knowing that people were dying that maybe wouldn't if I hadn't made the selfish choice to ignore the knowledge that I have."

Maddie's eyes well, and she blinks to wash away the tears that threaten to spill over. I can't tell whether she's happy with my decision. My dad's face barely changes, but he does give me a small smile with a nod. "Well, good. I'll contact the Elders to prepare the ritual."

"Hell yes! Little sis is with us once again. Remington motherfucking Bennett ladies and gentlemen. Factions beware, cause my sister is a badass!" Colt says, and I laugh at his enthusiasm. "You knew didn't you, asshole?" he says to Creek who shrugs and stands, clearing the table.

"Whether I did or not, I'm just glad she made the choice she did," he says with a soft smile before loading the dishes into the dishwasher. I feel a little guilty considering he saved me, stayed out all night hunting, cooked breakfast, and is now cleaning. He at least looks almost content doing what he's doing, so I smile back.

"So, now that you guys know, I have to go blow up the rest of my life," I say with a heavy sigh. I am so not looking forward to the rest of the day. I prop my elbows on the table and glance down at the scarred wood that's seen more than its fair share of family meals.

"I know this is hard sweetheart, and if you need any help, we're all here. For anything," Maddie says, and my dad grunts his agreement.

"Well, first, I need to deal with school, unenroll from everything I just started, canceling my whole life I guess. And then... Well, then I need to speak to Jack." I drop my head in my hands for a short moment before running them through my hair.

"I'm sure I don't have to tell you this, but he cannot know, Remy. He can't know any of it," my dad tells me, and while I know he's not sorry to see Jack go, I can see in his eyes that he's sorry I'm hurting.

"I know, Dad. I won't tell him. I'm certain he'd try to have me committed if I started talking about this stuff in front of him. I just need to figure out how to hide my broken heart while I break his, and that won't be easy." Maddie stands, rounding the table to hug me while Colt squeezes my hand.

"I can't tell you that I know what this is like. I've loved my Nate since I was nothing more than a girl, but I can't imagine how much it would hurt to have to let go of him like you're having to do. Regardless of our feelings about the young man, we know that for you, this decision was harder than it was for us. None of us had ties to the human world like you do."

"Thank you. It hurts, but I don't think it's hit me how much it's actually going to hurt yet. I know this is the right decision." I smile at her as she squeezes my shoulder.

"Will you give me a ride back to my place?" I ask Colt.

"Sure thing, little sis. Are you ready?"

"Yeah, I'll leave my stuff here from yesterday, but I need to grab my bag."

"You ready, man?" he asks Creek.

"Yeah, I'm good to go," he replies, shrugging his hoodie on.

"I'll see you soon Pops. Mads." He hugs them both as

he heads out, with Creek doing the same behind him.

"Let me know if you need anything," Dad says as I hug him goodbye. "Anything, Remy."

"I know, Dad. Thank you." I kiss his cheek before hugging Maddie, grabbing my bag and heading outside toward my new life.

A CROWN OF BLOOD AND BONE

EIGHT

This week has been a shit show.

I've pulled myself from the resident program I joined when I was preparing to move with Jack, I canceled my dance classes much to the dismay of my instructor, and I canceled all of the financial aid I'd secured for school. Basically, I erased all of the plans I've spent the last year making, and now I'm sitting on my sofa, spinning the engagement ring on my finger. I'm trying to work out what the right words to say are even though I know that really, there are no right words for what I'm about to do. My heart feels like I've cut it out of my chest and left it out in the open, exposed to the elements, but I know that the decision I've made is the right one. That this is the path I'm meant to take, the path that I can live happily with.

Jack is on his way. He sent me a text ten minutes ago saying as much. After dodging him for the last few weeks and my lame ramblings about us needing to talk, I know he knows something is wrong. He has to. Right?

When his key twists in the lock of my apartment door, Sushi leaps from the sofa and runs toward my bedroom. He never did like Jack.

Strange little cat.

I take a deep breath as the door opens and Jack comes in. I smile at him, but his face is in a thunderous rage. Awesome.

"Are you sick?" he asks brashly as he closes the door before looking me over.

"No, I'm not sick."

"Then what the fuck is going on? You've been weird for fucking weeks! You've hardly answered your phone except for this morning, and even then it was only a few mumbled words. I've barely heard from you," he says, standing by the door with his arms folded over his chest.

"Maybe you should come sit." I motion to the sofa, and he stomps his way over, opting to sit on the lone chair rather than with me. This sucks, but I guess it's better that he's angry. It'll be easier for him this way.

"So?" he says, and as much as it pisses me off, I swallow it. This is my fault, after all. I can't be pissed that he's annoyed and angry at me already.

"We need to talk. I didn't mean to avoid you, not really, but I needed some time to think about everything," I tell him, trying to stop my voice wobbling. "I know we had all these plans, but this isn't working for me, Jack. Not anymore. The tension between you and my family, us moving away, me becoming a doctor. I feel like I've lost myself to the life you want us to have. I thought it was what I wanted too, but with everything going on, I realized that this isn't the life I want."

"This isn't the life you want?" he says quietly, and I look up to see him staring at me as if he doesn't even know me. I shake my head.

"I really thought it was, and I never wanted to hurt you, but I can't do this anymore, Jack. I love you, I do, but I don't think we're right for each other. I've realized that we want such different things from life, and no matter how much I love you, I can't just leave my family behind. I can't cut them out of my life as if they don't exist because you guys don't get along."

"So, this is about them?"

"No, this is about us, but they are a part of me Jack, and you don't accept them. You can barely stand being around them. I don't want to talk about that, though. I'm talking about us right now."

"Well, it doesn't sound like there is an us anymore, Remy. It sounds like you've made that decision alone already, and it doesn't matter a flying fuck what I think or how I feel about it." He stands, almost shaking, and I can feel the waves of anger radiating from him.

"I'm sorry, Jack. I didn't ever want to hurt you."

"You know what, Remy? Fuck you. If you didn't want to hurt me, you wouldn't be doing this. Shattering our life, all of the plans we built. You should have realized long before now what you really wanted. Or you should have at least had the decency to talk it out with me before you made a decision like this alone. So, fuck you, fuck this, fuck all of it," he spits, holding his hand out to me, and I place the ring in his palm.

"I really am sorry, Jack. This is for the best. For us both, even if you don't see if right now." I tell him as he storms across the room. "Your key is on the counter, and that box on the floor is the few things you've left here."

He pulls his keys from his pocket and wrenches my key from it before slamming it down on the counter, picking up his own along with his box.

"Fuck you, Remy!" he shouts, before storming from the apartment and slamming the door closed behind him.

Tears run down my face, but I know no matter how much this hurts, no matter how much my heart feels like I just shattered it to pieces, this is the right decision.

Now I just need to pick up the pieces of my shattered life and get on with it. But first, I need my best friend and about three pints of chocolate ice cream.

After nearly a full day of throwing myself a massive pity party, I give in and text Fallon to tell her I broke up with Jack. She responded immediately, saying she would grab supplies and head over. That was twenty minutes ago, and I'm still in the same spot I was on the sofa when Jack left earlier.

The lock turns followed by Fallon sauntering into my apartment like it's her own, dropping her bags on my counter before kicking the door shut and turning to me. "You get tonight to throw a pity party, but tomorrow we're back on track, you hear me?"

"But Fal, I just..." I start, my voice rasps from the crying I've done throughout the day before breaking.

"I know, darlin'," she says as she moves toward the couch to hug me tightly. "Tell me all about it."

Before I can start spilling my broken heart out to her, we're interrupted by a knock at the door, and she stands. "That must be the pizza guy, so hold that thought!"

She hurries to the door and takes the pizza from the guy, flirting as she does so and tipping him before she closes the door. I watch as she moves quickly through the kitchen, grabbing glasses and putting more ice cream in my freezer, before grabbing the other bag and the pizza on her way back to me. I feel so pathetic just sitting here like my life is ending, but I can't help it. This might have been my choice, but that doesn't make it any easier. Not really.

The smell of cheese hits me as she puts the boxes down on the coffee table. Fallon pulls out a bottle of whiskey and pours us both a glass, and she hands me mine as I reach for the top pizza box, pulling out a giant slice.

"Let's try this again. Tell me what happened so I know whose ass to go kick."

I sigh and chew the deliciousness that is my cheesy slice of pizza. "I'm not even sure where to begin, but I'm the one who ended it. I told him that what he expected isn't the life for me, that we're on different paths, and that it wasn't going to work. He was so hurt, so angry, and I just... I could see it, his heart breaking at my words, and the rage it created. I never wanted to hurt him."

"So, you made your choice, huh?" she says, and my gaze whips to her.

"What?" She can't know. She *can't*. Dad said humans don't know and aren't allowed to know. Oh shit, did I say something I shouldn't have? My mind races through every conversation we've had since I found out, but her laugh pulls me up short.

"Stop freaking out, there ain't no bees in your bonnet. I've known all about you as long as I've known you. You can be all pissed at me too, Goddess knows Creek was."

"How the fuck? What the... I am so fucking confused right now, Fallon." I open and close my mouth a few times, trying to form the right words, but nothing comes out. I take a swig of the whiskey instead, and the burn comforts me as my world shifts again.

"I guess it's a day for revelations, wouldn't you say? You should probably know that I'm a witch," she says with a small smile and takes a drink of her own, emptying her glass.

"You're a witch?" I ask, stunned. How is this even my life right now?

"Surprise!" she says, throwing her hands in the air, making fucking jazz hands, like this isn't a big deal. "But I'm what you guys would call a good witch, none of that wicked witch of the south shit. My family's worked with yours since the beginning of our line."

"So everyone else knows? I have so many questions, Fal. But I can't find the fucking words to ask them. So everyone in my life has been hiding stuff from me?" I ask, my mind blown. Was I keeping the Hunter stuff from her? Sure, but I probably would have caved at some point and told her anyway. Her being a witch makes a lot of things make more sense, but holy fucking shit.

"I know it's a lot, girl. Especially after everything that's been thrown at you in the last few weeks, but we can't reveal ourselves to humans either, and if you'd made the decision to reject your Hunter heritage, you'd have left me behind too when you left with Jack. I couldn't of told you, no matter how many times I would've tried. It's a spell. It keeps us from telling who we are to people who aren't part of the factions, or to those who don't know or make the choice to not live this life. It sounds a hell of a lot more complicated than it is, and I didn't mean to just dump it on you like this. I know you got a lot going on, but I hated keeping secrets from you." She smiles sadly at me, and I realize that all of these secrets must have weighed heavily on those around me. They suck for me, but it couldn't have been all fun and games for them either.

"Wow. So, you're a witch? You can do magic and shit?"

"Yeah, I can do magic and shit," she laughs, shaking her head. "But there's limits and restrictions on what all we can do. There are others, who don't abide by the rules of the coven council. Those who fell on the side of the Dracul and the Lycans, and then there are those who go to whoever pays them the most money, those who have no respect for the power we wield or its consequences. But yeah long story short, I can do magic and shit."

"This is... it's so cool, and yet, kinda terrifying that I have been walking around blinded all this time and not having any real idea of what was happening in the world around me."

"I know, but no more blinders for you, Remy. Now,

how about we eat our own weight in pizza and get drunk to high heaven to soothe that broken heart of yours? We talk about all of this tomorrow, when the hangover is banging around in our heads." In true Fallon fashion, she pauses before offering me a huge, overdone wink. "You know I got a little something, something to ease them hangovers, though."

"That sounds kind of amazing," I say with a small sniffle as I think about Jack's face again when I told him we were over. "It hurts, Fal. I didn't want to hurt him, but how could I make any other choice?"

"I know, sugar, I know. It'll get better sooner or later. Love is the one thing that rules all of us, faction and human alike. Matters of the heart are one thing no spell can fix. But you did the right thing. If the stories I've heard about the fearless Remy Bennett are anything to go by, you might have just turned the tide of the war we're facing in our favor."

"There are stories?" I ask, shaking my head, because how is this my reality right now?

"There sure as hell are. But it's gonna take a while to get your memories back, and I can't say shit until you do. Sorry."

I shake my head and wave at her nonsense. "It's fine, you're not the first, and you won't be the last to have to keep your mouth shut around me. I don't understand it all, but I'm so glad that you know, that I have someone other than the guys to talk to. Because all of this is just so freaking much!"

"Oh, I know, and you don't know the half of it yet. Now, how about we put on Dear John, stuff ourselves with pizza and throw one hell of a pity party?" She laughs and takes a giant bite from the slice of pizza in her hand. I laugh at her, knowing I made the right choice asking her to come over. There's no one quite like your best friend to help heal a broken heart.

NINE

"Remy, for fuck's sake, this isn't hard. You just need to relax," Bauer huffs as I bend over, trying to catch my breath. Eight hours I've been at his place, which I'm now renaming Hell, because this place isn't his house, it's a fucking torture factory.

"Just because this is easy for you doesn't mean it is for everyone else, you jerk. You've been doing this for a lot longer than I have," I pant.

"Actually, no. You've lived more lives than I have, so you've done this a hell of a lot more than I have. You just need to give in to it. Your instincts will kick in if you let them, but you have to stop overthinking!"

I glare at him and drop to the floor.

"I don't know how to do that, Bauer. I get that you're

frustrated, but so the fuck am I! This might not be weird to you, but you have your memories back, and you've had years to adjust to it all. I've had a few freaking weeks, and I still don't have any of my memories. I have fragments, but I'll be fucked if I can tell the difference if I can between dreams and memories at this point. But this, the fighting? This is all new to me right now. You can't treat me like some honed warrior, even if that is what I was before, because that's not who I am right now." I raise my head and stare at the ceiling of his basement torture chamber and try to even out my breathing.

I'm a dancer, and I run most days, but this kind of training, this is a whole new world. Circuits, skipping, cardio... and that was just his goddamn warm-up. Then he gave me a stupid wooden staff and attacked me, hoping my instincts would just kick in. When it was obvious that wasn't happening, we tried all sorts of combinations. While I'm better than I was when we started, I'm not learning as quickly as he hoped.

As in, I'm not an instant fucking badass.

The urge to roll my eyes at his obvious disappointment is real.

"Remy, I never expected you to be the warrior you've always been from the word go, I don't know what I expected." He sighs and runs a hand down his face before sitting opposite me on the floor.

"It's weird. I'm always the eldest, and yet you taught me most of what I know. Where you've had like twelve lives, I'm only on my sixth. You're the best of us, at least any of us that I've ever met, and you've always just picked up where you left off. I can't say much more than that, because it could still be dangerous, but something feels different this time. You're different."

"Of course I am, jackass. I had a whole life that I had to up so I could be this person. From what Maddie said, that's unusual. But this life has shaped me. Losing Mom changed me. I don't know if we lost her this early in other lives yet, so I can't say for sure. I'm positive I'll get there once my memories are back, but for now, treat me like an absolute moron with this stuff. Please, I freaking beg you. Eight hour workouts are not usually part of my life." I laugh and lie back on the mats covering the floor.

"Oh, believe me, I can see that, and despite the ritual not happening for another few weeks, you'll thank me for this beforehand. Your body is already starting to change, the angel blood is awakening. You're stronger, faster, more lethal. Honing your skills, even with just the basics before the memories come back, will be good. It means that when you remember how to do what you used to do, your body won't be working against you. Unfortunately, the muscle memory isn't something that carries over. Just the knowledge, so you still need to train."

SLOANE MURPHY

"Ugh, this sucks, why can't I just wake up a total badass?" I groan, and he laughs at me.

"Because that would be much too easy, and a Hunter's life is anything but easy. That was the first rule you taught me. That this life is hard, but there are so many things that make it worth the insanity it brings." He stands and smiles down at me, offering me a hand up. "That being said, get your ass up off my floor. You caught your breath, so now we start again."

"Sadist. You're a goddamn sadist," I hiss as I take his hand and he helps pull me to my feet.

"Yes, yes I am. Which is why I'm the best teacher you'll have. Dad doesn't have the patience, Colt would baby you, and Creek, well, he's Creek. It's why I always train you when I'm around. You're just as much of a sadist as I am, Remy. You'll see." He winks at me and throws the staff back at me. "Now get yourself into the starting stance. We're not leaving here until you disarm me or pin me. Time to up your game."

I take the stance he showed me hours ago and prepare myself. Taking deep breaths, I steady my heartbeat and try to focus on the new things I discovered I have, like the sharper sight, the insane hearing, the ridiculous speed. I can't always tap into them, but it's sure as hell helpful when I do.

I hear him take a breath a second before he launches

124

toward me, and I do what he asked. I don't think, I just do. I raise the staff as he brings his in an arc over his head, and I meet his blow. The force of it shakes my arms, but I grin at him before pulling back and trying to go on the offensive rather than on the defensive like I've been all morning.

He laughs as I parry back, using the movements he taught me, with a flair of my own that comes through when I quiet the voices in my head. Who would've thought he'd be right? Maybe I should pay more attention to him. I laugh when my offensive flurry makes him take a step or so backward before a lethal smile graces his face. I see the exact moment he decides to stop pulling his punches.

Apparently, even though he wants me to be trained, my big brother doesn't want me to beat his ass, at least not yet. Not that there's much risk of that, but I know I got too cocky, and now I'm going to hurt. A lot.

Faster than I thought possible, he strikes, and despite my new speed, I have absolutely nothing on Bauer. I end up on my back, winded, with the end of his staff grazing my throat.

"Nearly." He winks at me and pulls back the staff. "Definitely an improvement. I could almost see when you stopped overthinking."

I sit up and try to catch my breath again. "You have a severely unfair advantage."

"Humbling, isn't it?" he laughs. "Come on. Again."

"Slave driver," I grumble and get to my feet again.

"You're damn straight I am. I told you, we quit when you pin me or disarm me. The rest is up to you."

I almost growl as I drop into the starting stance, holding the staff a little differently than how he showed me, it's more comfortable, and I feel confident. "Bring it, asshole."

He laughs at me, and for a second, I think I've bitten off more than I can chew, but I see him feint right as I drop and swipe at his ankles with my staff. He jumps backward before I can make contact, but the hesitation is enough that I have time to catch him with a blow to his ribs, dropping him to one knee. I lunge again, hoping to win, just once, but I should have known better. I jump into the air, but get pushed backward by a powerful force and fly back into the padded wall before I slide down to my ass.

"Don't get so cocky, Remy. Cold and calculating is what keeps you alive in this world of ours. Cocky and hotheaded will get you dead real quick. You had a dozen other ways you could have attacked, but you tried to showboat. This isn't a competition; this is life or death. Yours, mine, our family's, hell every family alive." His voice shakes, and I'm not sure if it's anger, disappointment, or adrenaline. Regardless, guilt and shame floods me, leaving me feeling contrite. He's right. I just wanted to win, to make it stop. I wasn't thinking about anything else, and considering what was at stake, I was being a foolish child about it.

Maybe I'd be better off not knowing all of this, but this is my life now. I'm going to embrace it if it's the last damned thing I ever manage to do.

After the hardest, albeit most thrilling workout of my entire life, I'm sprawled out on the floor in Bauer's basement, trying to work out what my new life is going to look like. How it's even going to work. I'm going to need a new job because fates knows that working in a bar every night probably isn't going to work. My excuse of being sick isn't going to work much longer either. I'm sure they're already trying to figure out a way to fire my ass.

Bauer left me to my aches, pains, and musings about twenty minutes ago when Colt called him. I didn't bother asking what it was about because the look on Bauer's face was more than enough to shut my mouth. My biggest brother isn't exactly the most talkative of people on a good day, though knowing what I know now, that makes a lot more sense to me. He's way older than me, which means he's had to tread carefully with his words around us all for a while now. I can't even imagine how hard that must have been, how alone he must have felt being the only one. I know that he had Dad, Maddie, and Nate, but when we were younger, Bauer, Colt, Creek, and I were almost inseparable. Then Bauer grew up and left the three of us, which meant that Colt and I were thick as thieves even at home, with Bauer on the outside.

My heart hurts a little for him and how lonely that must have been. Though, I have no idea if there are other Hunters around here, people his own age for him to train with, to talk about stuff with. I can't imagine having found all this out and not having everyone I love around me to help me deal with it, even if I didn't want their help to start with.

"There she is, the badass extraordinaire. Bauer beat you bloody yet?" Colt's voice rings out across the room, laughing as he descends the stairs into the basement.

"Not quite," I call out, not moving. His shoes squeak against the mats as he moves closer, and then he's looking down at me with a wicked glint in his eye.

"Maybe you should train with me instead. I learned a whole host of new tricks traveling around the other side of the world, you know." He holds out a hand to help me up, which I take, barely standing on my aching legs once he has me on my feet again.

"Don't be ridiculous," Bauer says, joining us as he practically bolts down the stairs. "You know as well as I do that when she has her memories back, she'll kick both our asses all over the place, at the same goddamn time. She's trained with the best of the best in every goddamn life. She always learns something new to put us in our place. Don't give her a reason to break you when she's back to her old self."

Colt laughs at Bauer's warning but shrugs. "You're not wrong. I swear my arm still aches from—"

"Colt, shut up!" Bauer rolls his eyes, and Colt looks at me guiltily.

"Sorry, I just got caught up. Don't want to break you."

"Don't sweat it, Bauer's been breaking me all damn day." I laugh. "So, what secrets did you spill to make our biggest brother look like someone pissed in his cornflakes this morning?"

Colt starts laughing as Bauer stares at me like I have two heads. "Holy shit, she really is starting to come back."

Bauer shakes his head and laughs under his breath. "That she is."

"Anyway, I didn't tell him anything." Him? Him, who? My mind barrels through the possibilities, but the only other person I can think of is Creek, so I stare at Colt expectantly, waiting for him to continue. He offers me a secretive smile as he says, "I asked him if I could come over. Since you're training now, I thought you might want your old friend back."

"I have no idea what you're going on about." I roll my eyes at him as he backs up and heads toward the stairs up to Bauer's kitchen.

"Come on, you'll see," he beckons. I glance at Bauer who shrugs his shoulders, shaking his head at the same time.

"You don't think I should see whatever it is yet?" I ask softly.

"I think he's pushing too much too quickly because he misses hunting with you. He means well, but he seems to keep forgetting you're still vulnerable. That said, I do think that what he has might help your training." He shrugs again and heads up the stairs, leaving me to decide whether or not this is a step I want to take.

I know this is going to take time, but I'm also the nosiest person to ever exist. I just like to be in the know. But could that impulsivity be my downfall right now?

Bauer didn't seem to think it would be too dangerous, and since he's the most experienced of us all right now, I decide to just go and see whatever it is that Colt has for me.

What's the worst that could happen right?

I push the door from the basement to the kitchen open to see the two of them lounging in the room. Bauer sits on the counter by the window, and Colt is sprawled in a chair at the small kitchen table. The light from the windows floods the room, and as much as I love the light the summer sun brings, I'll be happy to see fall descend fully and experience the beauty of the colors it brings with it.

"Okay, so what is it that you've brought for me?"

"First, do you forgive me yet?" Colt looks me dead in the eye, pleading with me. I don't know what exactly he sees in my eyes, but he's quick to go on. "For disappearing on you, I mean. It sucked, and then I stole Creek away, for both of you, but I know how much that must have hurt you. It was the last thing I wanted to do, but I didn't see any other way to keep you safe."

"Honestly, not yet, but I'm working on it. This is a lot. I'm just trying to push through it all, and push down anything that distracts me from what I'm trying to do. The pain, the heartache, it all sucks, but that's what I have right now. What you did hurt me, and while it might have been for my own good, it stings," I tell him as honestly as I can.

This isn't what I had in mind when I climbed the stairs. I've tried to focus as little as possible on all the hurt and bitterness roiling around inside of me. The pain would drown me if I let it, so I stuff it down every single morning when I wake up just so I can breathe. The pain of splitting up with Jack, of him leaving a box of my stuff outside my door and not even bothering to knock, will sting for a long time. The pain of Colt and Creek disappearing out of the blue is still there. Yeah, I'm dealing with it badly, but I'm doing better than I thought I would.

I'm getting there, and somehow with Creek, it's easier

because Colt had already left me. I'm trying to let go of all of my anger since my mom always said holding onto it was like drinking poison and expecting the other person to die. Useless and disappointing. So, I'm trying, but I'm only human after all. Or well, not.

"I can understand that," he says, some of the pep gone from his voice. I don't miss the flash of disappointment in his eyes before he looks away from me. It takes him a second, but he looks back at me and says, "Okay, anyway, the reason I'm here. I'm way too excited for this, and you won't even have a real clue yet, but there is no way I'll last until the ritual. Plus I know you'd probably kick my ass if I waited."

He rambles as he moves into the other room before reappearing with a case.

He places it on the table before me, and it feels like all the air is sucked from the room. I can barely breathe as I reach forward to undo the locks on it. I lift the top, and sitting in the old and worn violet velvet, the same color as my eyes, sits a sword. I reach forward to touch it, but a pain unlike anything I've ever experienced stabs through my head. I grab my temples and try not to scream at the pain as I feel myself falling from the chair. I can barely hear as Bauer wraps himself around me, lifting me and walking me back down to the basement, where he places me on the floor, I think.

My eyes are clenched tightly closed as I struggle against the white-hot pain in my head. It's so overwhelming I want to throw up. I curl up into a ball, instead, trying to fight the pain back, but it's useless. I feel Bauer at my side again, before something cold brushes against my lips. I open my mouth, and he pours the foulest liquid I've ever tasted into my mouth. I can only barely make out the sound of him urging me to swallow through the pain. I swallow, trying not to gag.

I feel the cold liquid as it hits my stomach, which rolls in response, and I curl back up into the ball, praying to whichever gods exist to free me from this pain.

After what feels like forever, the pain starts to ebb away. I feel my mind start to drift, and I give in to the wave of darkness and emptiness that washes over me.

I open my eyes, still surrounded by darkness. I lift my head slowly, and I can just make out the dim light filtering in from the top of the stairs, indicating that I'm on Bauer's couch in the basement. I lower my head, taking stock of the aches and pains I know should be racking my body. But other than the throb in my head, every other part of me feels fine. Although I am tired and nauseous. As I sit up slowly, the world tilts a little, and I realize the pounding in my head might just be a little worse than I first thought.

"Bauer? Colt?" I call out, my voice hoarse. I guess I screamed more earlier than I realized. I can hear footsteps moving across the floorboards above me, before coming quickly down the stairs.

"Oh, thank the Fates, you're awake," Bauer says softly as he hands me a bottle of water. "Sip it slowly, Remy, I mean it. You scared the absolute shit out of me."

"Sorry," I rasp before taking a sip from the bottle. The icy cold feels so good that I want to chug the whole bottle, but knowing Bauer, he'd rip the thing away from me before I got the chance. "What happened?"

"Too much too soon is what happened. The exact reason we don't tell Hunters about their lineage until they're of age. But even then, you're still at risk until you've completed the ritual. Seeing that sword before your birthday would have killed you. I was scared it still might."

"How long was I out?" I ask, trying not to focus on the fact that I could have died. Because holy fuck. And that pain... if this is why everyone lied to me for so long, I forgive them. Fuck feeling pain like that ever again.

"A few hours. I called Dad, and he contacted the Elders to initiate the ritual earlier. They're all on their way here now. We'll do it this weekend because it's not worth the risk of waiting any longer." His eyes wrinkle with concern as he looks over me again, making sure that I'm really okay.

"Okay," I tell him, I'm not going to fight him. That sucked ass.

"Good. Now, you're staying here tonight, I've made up the spare room. I need to call Colt, so let's get you upstairs so I can update everyone that you're awake."

"Oh Fates, Colt. Can I call him? Or will you at least tell him that I don't blame him?" I look up at him, and he shakes his head.

"You're not calling him, you need to rest, but I'll tell him. It won't make much of a difference, but I'll tell him." He picks me up off of the couch, and he's so much bigger than me that I feel about ten again. I'm so woozy that I don't fight him over it, though.

"Thank you for looking after me," I say with a sigh, closing my eyes as he carries me up the stairs.

"That's what family does, Remy. I might not have been around that much the last few years, but now that you're back, that's going to change. I'm always here, no matter what okay?"

"Thanks, Bauer," I sigh before letting sleep take me away again.

TEN

This is it.

Today's the day of the ritual, which is why I'm lying in my bed under my covers, pretending that the sun isn't rising. Pretending that today isn't the last day of the life I've led until this very moment. After today, everything changes, and there's absolutely no going back.

My phone rings on my bedside table, and I groan. Last night, Jack drunk dialed me about a dozen of times, leaving me a myriad of messages, with everything from "I love you", to, "you ruthless bitch, you ruined my life". So, yeah, that was fun and exactly what I needed before today.

My phone stops ringing before starting right back up, so I give in and throw the covers off. I pick it up to see Creek's face looking back at me as I answer the video call.

"Morning, Sleeping Beauty," he laughs, and I give him the bird.

"Screw you, this is not an appropriate time for humans to be awake." I stick out my tongue at him and laugh at the ridiculousness of it all.

"It's a good thing you're not human then, isn't it?" he laughs back at me, and I can't help but roll my eyes at him.

"It's still super weird, though. Like I might have made this decision, but the fact that monsters actually exist? That I'm not human? Yeah, haven't exactly wrapped my mind around that yet. Probably won't for a while." He pulls a face at me, and I laugh at him. I missed this. I missed him.

"Yeah, it took me a while too. I'm so glad we can talk about this now, and that we'll be able to talk more freely after today. It felt like half of me was missing these last few months without you, Remy. I can't... I don't want us to ever have to be like that again. Not in this life."

"Well, I don't plan on going anywhere anytime soon, so hopefully we won't have to." I smile at him, trying to disguise the torrent of butterflies kicking up in my stomach. "I need to get my shit together before I head to Dad's, I should probably get going, but thank you for being my alarm clock."

"That's why I was calling. There's been a slight change in plans. I'm going to swing by and grab you, and then we'll head to the chambers. Your dad and my mom were summoned there early, your brothers are heading there together in a bit, which leaves me to come get you." He looks almost awkward, and it hits me how much he's changed, how much we've both changed since he left. Nothing used to be awkward between us. But then, before he left, I didn't have to fan myself after seeing him. I honestly don't care about *how* he turned from my cutesy best friend to this beautiful, hulking man. But sweet Jesus, how can he still be so ridiculously hot when he's being awkward?

"That's fine. Do I need to wear anything in particular? I probably should have asked this already."

"No, but I'd wear something, erm…" He blushes, and I adore the look on him. It doesn't happen often. "You'll be stripped down to your underwear during the ritual, so something suitable for that, I guess."

I can't help but laugh at him.

"Something that won't scandalize the Elders, or my dad or brothers. Got it."

"I missed this," he murmurs so quietly I think I might have misheard him. I can't help but smile at him when he softly continues, "I missed you, us. I just wanted you to know that.

"I haven't completely forgiven you yet for ditching me without a word, but I missed you too. And I'm glad you're back—that you'll be with me today."

"Me too, Remy. I better go, but I'll be over soon. I'll text before I leave."

"Okay, see you soon." The screen goes black, and I sigh. I can only hope that things go back to the way they were with us. Fates know with all this crazy shit happening I'm going to need my friend.

I climb out of bed and put the coffee pot on before jumping in the shower. I keep it cold enough to shock me into alertness. Alert is not a state I'm living in right now, and I can't afford to not be on the top of my game today. I pull out my least scandalous underwear followed by the least smart-ass t-shirt in my closet along with a pair of decent jeans. I pull my long hair into a high ponytail so it's out of the way and drift back to the coffee machine that is practically screaming my name. My phone buzzes on the counter and a quick glance lets me know that Creek is on his way. The anxiety hits me sideways, and I sink to the floor, cradling my coffee.

I made the right decision.

I know I did.

Right?

Fuck my life. I made the right decision. The words become my mantra until a knock at the door breaks my train of thought. It opens seconds later, and Creek finds me sitting on the floor in my kitchen, hugging my coffee cup. He doesn't say a word. He just comes and sits next to me, putting an arm around my shoulders and pulling me close to his side. We sit in silence for a few minutes until I feel like I can breathe properly again, and I lean my head on his chest.

"Thank you."

"Any time. I didn't realize your anxiety still got you like this," he says, concern coating his words.

"It hasn't for ages, but I guess with everything that's been going on, it just crept up on me. I haven't been running like I usually do, which probably isn't helping. You know how that helps me clear my mind." I shrug, and he squeezes me again before jumping to his feet and then helping me up.

"I guess we better get this show on the road," I mutter with a sigh.

"I'll be there every step of the way, Remy. And if you need a minute, just signal like we used to. I got you."

"Thanks, Creek," I say and hug him again.

"Always," he murmurs into my hair before I pull back.

I slip on my chucks and grab my leather jacket and keys. I roll my head on my neck and square my shoulders.

"Let the madness begin."

We pull up in front of an ominous looking building, and I glance at Creek. Surely this isn't the place.

"Ermmm…"

"I know, Remy. It's weird and creepy, but that's kinda the whole point. It keeps people away. Prying eyes aren't exactly what we want around here. Though, if anyone did try, they'd have a hell of a time trying to get through the security."

"There's security here?" I ask, shocked because this place looks like a rickety hellhole that's one strong gust of wind from falling down.

Creek laughs at me and shakes his head. "You should have learned by now that when it comes to this new world, nothing is what it seems."

"I guess you're right."

"I guess I am, and I guess we should stop procrastinating and head in before your dad or one of your brothers comes out here to drag us inside." He smiles at me, and the rising storm inside of me settles a little. It's always been this way between us, and I'm glad it still is. He's my anchor, keeping me rooted when my world starts to feel like a little too much.

"Yeah, wouldn't want to start today off in an embarrassing way. Not like these guys aren't going to see a whole lot of me soon anyway." I roll my eyes. "Is there a reason for the nakedness?"

"I'm sworn to secrecy, and you shouldn't even really know that bit, so keep quiet. The walls around here literally have ears."

I laugh and unbuckle myself, but take his words to heart. He joins me in front of the truck before leading the way to the building. He glances up to the top right before lifting his arm to a small box to the right of the door, which scans his wrist.

So freaking bizarre.

"Told you security was tight," he laughs, seeing my face.

I shake my head as a buzzer sounds and the door opens. "Into madness we descend," I say, to myself more than anything, but he chuckles as he enters through the door. Creek heads down the ominous stairwell that greets us, and I follow behind him quietly. My head is on a swivel as we descend, taking in the candlelit lamps that line the walls on the way down.

When we reach the bottom, we're faced with a long corridor that's lined with doors. At the end of the hall stands a set of huge double doors, looming down upon us. Creek doesn't have to say anything, I just know that's where we're headed. I follow him down the dusty hall, the ground no more than packed dirt.

"Ready or not," Creek says as we reach the doors. He pushes them open, and I stop in the doorway to take in the sight before me. I'm met with a windowless, domed room that's lit by dozens of candles scattered around the space.

The flickering candlelight highlights the symbols etched into the stone walls. Directly opposite of me is a raised platform, with seats spaced equally across, and I assume they're the seats of the Elders. What gets me, though, is the altar in the middle of the room. It looks so out of place here, the sleek black shininess stands out amongst the dirt and plain stone of the room. Similarly to the walls, symbols are etched all over the altar.

A shudder runs down my spine, and I clamp my lips shut to stop from uttering a word.

"Where is everyone?" I ask Creek quietly.

"Probably in the antechamber at the back. Let's go to the preparation room, you can change in there," he says and spins on his heel back down the hall. I follow him to the third door down and into the room beyond it.

"You can get changed here. There's warm water in the taps, so you can clean up if you need to, and you'll find a robe on the back of the door. Strip down to your underwear, and put on the robe. You'll be collected when they're ready."

"You can't stay?" I ask, taking in the foreboding little room.

"I can't. This is meant to be a time of reflection. To come to peace with the decision you've made, to accept everything that is to come on the new path you have chosen. I imagine Mom will be here soon to walk you through it all properly. I'm not your guide, but you'll meet them soon too."

"My guide?" I ask and he shakes his head.

"I'll see you out there, okay?" he says, disregarding my question in favor of hugging me tightly again. It centers me and stops the shudder that threatened to rack my body. I don't want to be afraid. I made this choice, and regardless of the chaos it brings and the pain caused by it, I know that I was meant to do this. I was meant to be here. So, I take a deep breath and release him.

"I'll see you out there," I say to him, and shut the door as he leaves. I'm left with nothing more than my thoughts.

I sit in the dark room, illuminated only by the weak, flickering light of the candles. I have no idea why there are all these candles when there's obviously electricity here for all of the security. It must be a tradition thing. It's so quiet, I almost don't dare to make a noise.

My thoughts are going a million miles a minute while I try to prepare myself for whatever is about to happen. A guide Creek said. What the hell is a guide?

I'm pulled from my thoughts by the door opening, and I stand just in case I need to move. Maddie's smiling face appears, and I feel my muscles let go of the tension I wasn't even aware I was holding.

"Oh, sweetheart!" she says, rushing in to hug me. "I can't believe the day is here already! Your mom would be so proud of you. I'm sorry she can't be here to help you with all of this, but I will be here for you every step of the way, okay?" She brushes some of the hair from my face that's fallen from my ponytail and sighs.

"Thanks, Maddie. It's all a little daunting," I tell her, and she laughs.

"It's so funny to see how you are without the past influencing you—I've always thought that. Don't let the past change you too much, okay?" She doesn't give me time to fixate over the sentiment of my new self and old self mingling. Rather, she rushes on, getting out as much as she can in a quick moment. "Your guide is on his way; he's one of the Elders, and he will complete the ritual. He'll be the one to guide you through your memories and help get them in order, at least the ones that appear in the beginning. After the initial flood, when memories come back, they seem to automatically make sense and slot themselves into the right places. It's a funky process, but Ben is an old and dear friend of our families, and he asked to be the one to guide you through this."

"Er, okay," I say, not really sure what to make of it all. I shrug because the who of it all doesn't really make a difference to me at this point.

"He's just outside, so I'll go grab him. Then he'll walk

you through some stuff before we get started, okay?"

"Sure." I smile at her halfheartedly.

She opens the door and waves in an older man who instantly strikes me as kind. His smile is soft as he enters, glancing over me.

"Good morning, Remy. I'm Ben. It's a pleasure to meet you again," he says before shaking my hand. The rough calluses on his hands are like sandpaper against the soft skin of my own.

"Hi," I say, unsure what else to say because this feels awkward as hell.

"I'll see you soon. Love you, Remy," Maddie says and waves, leaving the two of us alone in the small room.

"Come, child, I know this must be a lot for you to take in. Before we complete the ritual, I want to go through some things with you. I know your family will have started to explain the process to you, so why don't you tell me what you've got a grasp on so far, and I can expand from there." Ben's thoughtful, kind eyes make me feel better in all of this madness. The Elders, for the main part, seem kind of terrifying, but he's a good guy. I remember he would visit when I was a child, and he always had so much patience. I guess that's why he's a guide.

"This honestly all still sounds ridiculous inside my head, and even more so when I try to say it out loud. But essentially, monsters are real, and I'm a monster Hunter."

Heat creeps up my neck as I blush, the words still feel absurd, even though I know they're the truth.

"Do not worry, child, in these modern times when the fear of the supernatural is merely something for the movies, you are not alone in your hesitance to believe. Both of your brothers and your friend, Creek, struggled with accepting the reality we live in." His voice is warm and smooth, and his words help me relax. I try not to smile at the thought of Bauer trying to accept this as truth. He's only eight years older than me, but I remember when we were kids, he'd ridicule me and Colt for watching scary movies, berating us for being scared of something so obviously untrue. He was so certain that we were only afraid of our own imaginations.

"Thank you." I smile at him.

"Let's start from the beginning, shall we? As I'm sure your father told you, we, the Hunters, are Nephilim— of angel blood. Our people have been around since the beginning of time, protecting the humans and ensuring they never become aware of the true world.

"Our faction is governed, if you will, by the Elders, and each Elder looks after their own territory, which we usually refer to as a guild. We are not immortal, but we are pretty hard to kill thanks to our blood. Even if we are killed, we are reborn. You, I believe, are on your twelfth rebirth, and in each life you have chosen the life of a Hunter, so you will have many memories coming to you.

"You may not regain all of your memories of your past lives, which is why we do this fun little explanation bit in each life, so you have the facts. You may regain all of your memories, but usually the process takes around six months. After that point, anything that is missing is unlikely to come back." He pauses and watches me as it all sinks in. Twelfth life. I mean, I know my dad told me that already, it just hadn't really sunk in until now. Well shit, maybe that explains all the fucking sex dreams recently. My heart skips a beat as I think of Jack and the look on his face when I broke off the engagement; my ring finger still feels bare.

"The reason you're finding out now, rather than when you were younger is because of the power of the memories and the steps of the ritual. Your powers as a Nephilim do not awaken until near your twenty-first year. I'm sure you've noticed some things already, more strength than you had before, maybe better sight or hearing, being faster and more graceful than you once were. That is your body finally accepting the power in your blood.

"We must wait until your power is accepted because otherwise the memories, the sheer intensity of the power, would kill you. Do not be too hard on those around you." He looks at me knowingly. "They left to protect you, as new Hunters are less on guard, and they have a lot to learn.

Once our memories are fully restored and we can be sure of our words and actions, it is safe to be around our young again. I understand you had a small taste of what happens when knowledge is given too soon."

He looks at me, and I blush a little. He's not wrong; I swear I can still feel a ghost of the pain in my head.

"Any questions yet?" he asks, and I shake my head. My mind hasn't stopped whirring since I found out what I really am, so I just want to listen and soak it all in. While training has been one thing, I haven't given myself the chance to focus on the fact that monsters are real, and I'm training to hunt them. I've always been great at compartmentalizing, and I'll be fucked if I didn't shove that little nugget in a box far down in the depths of my psyche.

"Okay, so now you know more about us, I'll explain a little more about the other factions. There are our enemies, the Dracul, who you would associate with vampires as the modern world has deigned to call them. They are not sensitive to sunlight as the myths describe, but they do prefer to hunt at night, so they are essentially nocturnal. Also garlic, wooden stakes, crosses, all of that is utter nonsense.

"The Lycans, again, you would probably know them as what cinema has called werewolves. You've got to love the modern spin on everything." He shrugs with a smile and a sparkle in his eye, as if he's teasing me. "Again, not sensitive to silver as the myths would have you believe, but a lot of the rest is correct. They're a patriarchal system for the most part, led by alphas, and are stubborn and pigheaded."

Leaning back, I try to process his words. This is still all a fucking *lot*.

"These two factions are a drain on our world. They prey on the weak, the humans. They feed on them, kill them for sport, or keep them as pets. Both factions can be made as well as born, but those who are made, if not done properly, are even more dangerous. They are the scourge of the earth, and the filth must be destroyed." His warm voice, now cold and venomous, shocks me. His eyes bleed with pain, and I imagine that when my memories come back, I'll feel the same sort of hatred he does. How dare these factions treat humans this way!

"And then... then there are the Witches. They are a torn faction, some work with us, some for the filth, and others will simply work for whoever pays the most. They are rarely a loyal bunch to anyone outside of their coven, though that isn't always true, as you yourself will come to remember. We do occasionally need their gifts." The venom in his voice lessens, but I can tell that he doesn't like the fact that Hunters must rely on the Witches for anything. One thing I have noticed is that Hunters are a proud, stubborn, egotistical bunch. None more so than the Elders. Though, considering what Fallon told me when she announced she was a Witch, this little bit of information isn't something I don't already know. Though I'm not going to interrupt him when he's obviously working toward something that he feels is big.

"The Dracul and the Lycans are not impossible to kill, though it can be tough. We have blades and bullets made with materials that are deadly to them. A Dracul's weaknesses are different to those of the Lycans, but you will garner all of this in your training and from your memories as they come back to you," he tells me and pats my hand, gone is the angry cold warrior, and his warm, soothing demeanor back. It throws me off that he could be these two very different people, but I guess with many lives lived, and with the many different people you are, personality whiplash should be expected.

"Have we known each other before?" I ask hesitantly, and he smiles.

"We have. When we are reborn, it is always to the same lines, and our eyes or birthmarks tell us who we are. Your eyes have always been the same bright violet color, and in your first life, you were almost condemned by the humans to be a witch because they are so unusual. But your eyes are how we always know that you are Remington Bennett, along with the birthmark on the inside of your left wrist." I gasp and look down at the strange star there that has always been on my wrist. "It is the sign of the Bennett line, each of your family has one, and then they each have their own differentiating marks too."

"This is so weird, so my brother is always my brother?"

"I can see how it could be that way, but yes, if your brother is reborn in the same life cycle as you, then he is always your brother. Sometimes new lives are born, for example, in your first life, it was just you and Bauer. Colt didn't appear until your third life. But you don't all always appear in the same cycle. So, for some of your cycles, you've been an only child, some had all three of you, and sometimes it's just two of you. There isn't an exact science as to how or why it happens the way it does, it's more about the need of the time. Anyway, as I was saying, Creek isn't always reborn when you are. He didn't show up until your fourth life I believe, but when he is reborn, we always know that you are coming. The two of you have been friends for centuries. The fates play a very strange game with us all."

"So, you mean fate makes us friends?" I rub my temples, because this is all a lot.

"Something like that, but as your memories return, you'll see what I mean." He pats my hand reassuringly.

"So, the ritual? Is it painful?" I ask hesitantly, almost not wanting to know.

"Not necessarily, but it does depend on how much

comes back to you at the beginning, whether it's one big hit or just a trickle. It is different for each of us each time. Fate is a bit of a minx like that." He winks at me, and I laugh, some of the tension leaving me.

"Thank you, I needed that." I smile.

"Of course, my dear, it is what I am here for. Now, speaking of the ritual, if you have no other questions, and since you're dressed, we shall begin." He stands and offers me his hand. I take it and stand beside him. Ready or not, I guess.

A CROWN OF BLOOD AND BONE

ELEVEN

I follow Ben back into the main domed room that Creek showed me earlier. This time, all but one of the Elders' chairs are full, and my family and friends are dotted around the edges of the room. Even Nate made it back. I smile at him, and he winks at me, setting me a little more at ease.

I pull the robe closer to my body as we walk across the room to the altar, and my hair floats around me, free from its binding. Ben takes my hand.

"I present Remington Elise Bennett to the Elders, ready and prepared to take her oaths as a Hunter," he says, and they all murmur their acceptance.

"Do you, Remington, swear to uphold the Hunter laws, our way of life, and vow to protect our faction against all odds, at all costs?" the man in the center chair of the platform asks, and I gulp. I don't even really know what I'm agreeing too. But I clear my throat regardless.

"I do," I say clearly, trying to hide the nervousness I feel.

"Then let us begin," his voice booms around the room, and it's as if a blanket settles over me, a weight I didn't feel before. Ben motions for me to remove the robe and to lie on the altar. I do, and holy motherfuckers, this shit is cold. I can't help the goosebumps that cover my skin as I lie down, trying not to squeak as my bare skin comes into contact with the dark stone.

"*Fata vocant, ad hanc adducere nos ut in venator nobis,*" Ben says as he stands at the head of the altar, placing his hands on my temples. "*Rogamus autem vos, Angelus scientiam, ut restituat in aedis dedicandae se unum ex memoria vobis.*"

I lie still as the room begins to glow, and heat rises from the altar below me. The symbols carved into the stone walls around me begin to glow, and I just know that the symbols beneath me are glowing too.

"Close your eyes," Ben whispers to me, and I do, unsure of what is to come.

"Remington Bennett, your body is marked with the symbols of the angels, one for each life you have had, for each life you have dedicated to the cause." His voice rings out, and I feel the symbols on my body. They almost itch, as if they're coming to life with his words.

"Angelus autem ducibus nobis dona puer hic noster de quo in suis bonis quasi unus accipit vera semita."

His voice grows distant as the marks on my body heat to a painful degree.

"Ut rogatus est, et illud fieri."

The Latin becomes nothing more than a whisper as pain racks my body and my mind. I feel tears stream down my face as the pain grows to be too much.

Pictures inside of my mind hit me, feelings, faces, and so much more. My mind screams at the flood of memories until I can't hold it any longer, and then the screams tear from my throat. I try to move, to escape the heat and the pain, but my body is held in place, trapped. And then a warmth washes over me, and the pain subsides. The warmth grows at the base of my neck, pressure building warmer and stronger until I think I can't take it any longer. I'm at my tipping point when it releases, and I hear an intake of breaths and groans in the room around me. I open my eyes, sitting up slowly, to find the others in the room sitting on the floor, either groaning or holding their heads.

"What the hell was that?" one of the Elders asks, looking to Ben who is sprawled on the floor at the head of the altar. I jump down and go to him to see his nose bleeding. I shake him gently, and he moans while slowly opening his eyes.

"Are you okay?" I ask, and he laughs.

"I'm quite fine," he replies, sitting up with a groan.

"You need to explain," one of the Elders demands, a woman with gaunt skin and a swath of blue-gray hair. "This is quite unusual."

I glance around the room just to be met by the bewildered looks of my family. Of course, I get to be the weirdo amongst the freaking monster Hunters.

"It was the power of the Angel. Apparently, Remington here was Angel-blessed in one of her past lives. Because the flood of memories was more than I have ever known, possibly because of her age span, the angel's protection kicked in to keep her safe."

The others in the room all look at me, a mixture of shock and awe, with a hint of suspicion from some of the Elders too.

"Angel-blessed? Well, I'll be damned," Dad's voice echoes across the room, and I look at him as I slip the robe back on from where it pooled on the floor.

"Erm, are you sure it worked properly? I don't feel any different," I say quietly to Ben as I help him stand.

"Yes, dear, it went almost exactly as planned. It will take a few days, and then all that was restored today will become a part of you fully. You may feel a little disoriented for a few days, so I suggest resting. But, let me be the first to say, welcome to our faction." He bows slightly, and I cringe a little, though I try not to let it show. Why the hell would he bow?

"Thank you," I say to him before turning to my dad, who has moved to stand at my back.

"Thank you, all of you, for receiving us, and so quickly," he says, meeting each of the Elders' eyes.

"You are welcome," Ben tells him with a warm smile, and I feel my dad's hand settle on my shoulder.

"Let's get you dressed, Remy, and then we can head back to the house." His gruff voice reassures me—he's still my dad, and I'm still me, even with everything going on. I nod and walk from the room, leaving the noise of the chatter that starts behind me as I leave.

Hurrying into the small room I was in before, I discard the robe and throw on my jeans, t-shirt, and chucks, slinging my jacket over my shoulder before hauling ass out the way we came in. I don't want to be here longer than I have to be. This place creeps me out.

"Where are you running to?" Creek calls out behind me as I reach the stairs to climb out of here.

"I need some air, you coming?"

He nods and jogs toward me, joining me as I almost run up the stairs, pushing open the heavy door with a thud. I suck in deep breaths of the fresh air and simply breathe until my heart stops racing.

"You just always have to outdo us all, don't you?"

Creek teases, nudging me with his shoulder.

"What can I say, I'm just that awesome." I laugh and walk toward the car. "I suppose everyone's going to want to know about the Angel-blessed thing, huh?"

"You could say that," he laughs. "I've never, in all my lives, heard of anyone being Angel-blessed, so I'm going to guess that, yes, people are going to have questions."

I groan, and he laughs again as he climbs into his truck.

"Want to grab donuts and coffee on the way back? Give yourself some more time, some space, before the madness at your dad's begins?"

"Yes. Hell freaking yes, even. You are a godsend, Creek Winchester!"

"Technically, angel sent, but eh, details," he laughs, and I shove him playfully. "Buckle up, angel-girl. Donuts are calling to me!"

We pull up onto my dad's drive, and I groan. I just shoveled my way through three raspberry glazed donuts, and I don't feel even a little guilty about it, but my stomach feels so bloated that I feel like I need to unbutton my jeans.

"I told you that you shouldn't have eaten that last one," Creek gloats, and I give him the bird.

"You don't get to donut shame me. I needed them. Every single one." He laughs and shakes his head at me before his face turns serious.

"How's your head? Has anything filtered through yet?" he asks, almost eagerly, and though I hate to disappoint him, I still shake my head no.

"Other than the itching on the back of my neck, I don't feel any different at all really." I shrug, unsure if that's a bad thing or not.

"Let me see your neck?" he asks, so I unbuckle as we pull to a stop, and turn in the seat. I lift my hair off the back of my neck, and he gasps.

"Holy shit, Remy. You're marked by Leviathan." he says, the awe in his voice startling me. "Your Angel mark is bigger than usual, it goes all the way down under your top, but sitting above the Hunter's usual marking is Leviathan's sigil. I'm going to take a stab in the dark and say that's who blessed you, and holy shit."

"Who the hell is Leviathan?" I ask, dropping my hair back into place.

"We should go inside, your dad will know more than I do," he says before jumping out of the truck, and grabbing the boxes of donuts from the back seat.

I sigh because that isn't what I wanted to hear, and I'm sure that when my memories come back, I'll know who the bloody hell Leviathan is. For now, I'm clueless. Climbing out of the truck, I try not to scratch the back of my neck, though the feeling has started to descend over my shoulder.

Shaking it off, I close the door and follow Creek into the house, where I can already hear mingling voices.

Oh, the wonders of Hunter hearing. I try to shut the voices out, but it suddenly makes a lot more sense that my parents bought this place. It's so secluded that there aren't other houses within miles, so there isn't any extra noise to filter out either.

I pull my jacket tighter as I head inside, and Colt meets me at the door with a stupid grin on his face.

"Hey, little sister. Welcome to the clan, for reals."

"You're such a goofball, Colt." I push him out of the way, and he laughs again.

"Yeah, but you wouldn't change me for the world!" His voice follows me as I walk through the house and back to the kitchen where everyone else is undoubtedly congregated. It's been the same way for as long as I can remember.

I enter the room, and it goes quiet, except for the sound of Colt laughing as he walks up behind me.

"So, that was fun," I say with a shrug and take off my jacket. It's hot as hell in here. I look around the room and take a seat at the table, grabbing another donut and ignoring the fact that I'm going to practically burst. Emotional eating is a real thing.

"Remy," my dad starts, but Maddie interrupts him.

"Now then, her memories won't be back fully for the

next few days, so no questions, from any of you." She pins everyone with a look that says not to give her shit, and Nate laughs next to her.

"My wife, badass, mother extraordinaire, and layer-down of the law." He takes a sip from the mug in his hand, his eyes still dancing with laughter.

"Don't you start," she rolls her eyes at him, but the rest of the room murmurs in agreement.

"Remy is marked by Leviathan." Creek drops the bomb unceremoniously, and all their gazes shoot toward him before turning back to me.

"Leviathan? That isn't possible," my dad says as Bauer leaves the room. The stairs creak under his weight as he climbs them, and I assume he's going up to the library. Because as much as my eldest brother loves cars, he is also a total book nerd. "Remy, will you show us your mark?"

"Sure, I just showed Creek. I don't understand what the big deal is, though?" I stand and turn my back to them, pulling my hair up.

"Erm, Remy, it's still growing," Creek says, and Maddie shushes him.

"Growing?" I ask warily.

"Yes, sweetheart," Maddie says softly, closer to me than I realized. "I've never seen anything like it, but it's beautiful. It's on the back of your neck, and from what I can tell, it's growing across your shoulder."

She pulls the back of my T-shirt from my neck and hums. "Just as I thought. Your Hunter mark is there, in the middle at the base of your neck, but it is surrounded by the mark of Leviathan, and then something else that I don't recognize. It's like roots, or vines, with bursts of color and symbols. I imagine Bauer will want to start looking into this straight away."

"Will I not just remember what it means?" I ask, puzzled.

"Not necessarily," Bauer says as he re-enters the room with a book bound in brown leather. It looks older than anything I've ever seen. He sits across from me at the table and opens the book.

"This is the mark of the Hunter," he says showing me an image on a page surrounded by text that I only half recognize.

"Is that Latin?" I ask and he nods.

"It is the old language," Dad answers from across the room.

"Once your memories return, you'll be able to read it, write it, and speak it as well as the rest of us. And anything that's missing, Bauer can help you with," Nate says reassuringly.

"Okay. Can I see that?" I ask Bauer who nods and spins the book so I can look at the image. It looks so strange, and yet at the same time, so familiar. It's a circle, wrapped in vines with a sword through the middle, and the hilt above the circle, as if the sword is piercing it.

"Every Hunter has one," Bauer says and lifts his arm to show me his on his wrist, surrounded by tattoos so that it's almost hidden. "We tend to disguise them when they're in an obvious place, so it's not a beacon to the other factions. They appear in different places in each life, but your old mark will be represented by a constellation, which people just assume are weird birthmarks, just as you always have. The more marks, the more respect a Hunter is given in the community. Unless they have been cast out as rogues for whatever reason."

"We can be cast out?" I ask, my head whipping to my dad, Nate, and Maddie. Creek and Colt are unusually quiet, but then, they've always been the most in tune with me, so I guess they're trying to give me the space Maddie called for.

"We can," Nate says. "It is unusual, though. If a Hunter breaks our laws, depending on the crime, there are two punishments. Banishment, which is being cast out of the community, or death. Upon rebirth, if killed, Hunters are usually not given the choice to join the faction again until they have cycled at least twice as a human as part of their punishment."

"Holy shit," I say, wide-eyed. "Nice of you all to have left out these wonderful snippets of information until there's no turning back."

"Remy, you have never been cast out or killed for breaking laws," my dad says, but I catch the look Nate casts in his direction. I can't read it, but it's as if I'm missing something, a silent conversation between them. My dad shakes his head subtly, and I tuck that away because now I know I'm missing something. Maybe my memories will reveal the full truth, but if not, I'll need to circle back to that. "I'm sure you have nothing to worry about."

"What exactly are the laws?" I look back to Bauer who's scanning the book again. "And is there a picture of Leviathan's mark in there, or am I going to have to do a weird mirror jig later?"

"I'll find you a picture of Leviathan's mark," he tells me, "but your mark is more than just that, hence the book. As for our laws, there are a lot, and most will likely come back to you in time. The most important ones are: do not betray your faction, do not allow humans to become aware of any faction, and under no circumstances, no mixing of the factions."

"No mixing of the factions? What the...?"

"There have been Hunters in our history who thought the monsters were more than the filth that they are," my dad says with disgust. "They thought they could be saved, that they were not so different to us. Fools."

"Oooohhhhh." My dad's disgust is matched on every

face before me. I guess it's because I don't have my memories, but I don't get it. Love is love, right? But I think I'll keep those thoughts to myself; I don't think this is the crowd for it. And who knows, maybe I'll change my mind once the memories come back.

"Exactly. But for now, try not to worry about all of this. You just need to focus on staying rested and letting the memories come back to you."

"Well, actually, I was thinking we could have some fun, see how much is back subconsciously," Colt says with a devilish glint in his eye. "Throwing competition anybody?"

Nate and my dad laugh as Bauer and Creek roll their eyes.

"Really, Colt? You just don't want Remy to beat you," Maddie sighs with a smile.

"Hey, I'll take what I can get for as long as I can. I'm all about playing the odds to my advantage."

"What do you mean, throwing competition?"

"Knife throwing," Creek informs me with a grin. "It might be a stupid competition, but it's fun as shit. Plus, you used to kick everyone's ass, almost every time, so it might be nice. Treat you to some humility in case everything comes back before you need to hone your skills."

"Is this a good idea? I've never thrown knives in my life, and if my skills of throwing so much as a ball are anything to go by, this could be dangerous."

"You'll be fine, we're Hunters. We're made of tougher stuff," Colt says cockily.

"Or at least we heal quickly," Creek says with a shrug.

"Why not?" Nate asks with a shrug, and my dad shakes his head.

"Fine, come on. Let's get the targets set up. Colt, your idea, your responsibility, so you get to help me and Nate haul everything out of the shed." He strides across the room, giving me a small smile, and heads out the back door into the back yard, with Nate, Colt, and Creek in tow.

"I will never understand men, no matter how many lives I live. Their incessant need to compete for everything never changes," Maddie says, sitting next to me. "How are you doing?"

"I'm okay, I think. I'm a little freaked out about the weird blessing and my freakazoid mark that's apparently growing, but otherwise, I'm okay. I mean, I'm sure there's going to be a point where I have a complete meltdown, but that's future-Remy's problem. For right now though, I'm dealing."

"I'm glad to hear it sweetheart. I know none of this is easy, but I must remind you that you can't say a word to Nirvana," she urges.

"I know, I would never endanger her. She's going through enough as it is, she doesn't need any of this on top of it." I smile at her, and she returns it.

"She told you?" she asks, and I nod. "It figures, she's always seen you as a big sister more than anything else. I'm glad she has you to confide in. And I'm glad you'll be there when it's her turn for all of this."

"Me too, I can't imagine going through all of this with no one around to answer questions and to stop my general freak outs. I can't imagine how hard it must have been for Bauer."

"There's a reason that boy always has his nose in a book when he's not hunting." she says with a sad smile. "Your mom was great with him, though. Your dad and Nate, they can be a little draconian with their methods, so be thankful it's Bauer training you. In the lives where you were the only child, yours and your father's arguments when training are almost legendary. Your mom would lose her mind."

"I look forward to remembering," I sigh wistfully. It will be nice to have all the same memories that everyone else already seems to have.

"Just remember, you might not remember everything. It is rare for a Hunter to regain all of their memories. I've only heard of it happening once in all of our history, so there might be holes, or stories someone tells you that you have no recollection of. You'll learn to embrace it. Don't forget that it also takes time, so try not to get too frustrated.

With as many lives as you've lived, I can tell you, there are always things you'd rather not remember."

I hug her as shouts carry through the house from outside. "I guess we better head out there."

"Oh no, I'm not getting involved. They're all such sore losers. You go, I'm going to whip together some food for lunch, I have a feeling everyone's going to be hungry after this," she chuckles and shoos me out of the door.

I cross the yard until I find the four of them about half a mile from the house, with five targets set up, each one farther back than the one before it. The fifth one is so far back I can barely see the black dot in the center.

"This doesn't look impossible at all." I roll my eyes, and they all chuckle.

"It'll be good practice. You can always have a few practice shots at the trees if you want. Seems fair," Colt says cockily.

"Hand me the stupid knives," I tell him, jutting my hand out toward him. He hands over five blades, and I put four of them on the ground at my feet to get a feel for the one that's left. The weight and balance of it feels so familiar, and I hide a smile as I watch each of them take a turn at the first target.

Everyone hits the yellow ring. Some land knives close to the black bullseye, but no one quite hits the mark.

I step up to the mark on the ground and palm the knife

until it feels just right. Reaching back, I throw the knife forward, watching in awe as it hits the yellow ring. Not quite where I was aiming for, but for a first go, I'll take it. I whoop, and Colt grumbles behind me.

"Beginner's luck."

"Don't be sore, Colt," Nate chuckles as my dad makes a note of who came closest. We get points, one to five depending where we hit. I earn two points, having come in fourth, with only Creek below me. He offers me a smile that lights up his whole face, and I know he's not pissed I beat him. It's only the first go, anyway.

The second target goes much the same, yellow ring all round. This time I get third, and Nate grumbles about stupid girls and beginner's luck while I do nothing but smile. Something about this feels so right, like something I've done a million times before. Like this is my thing, when I've never really had a thing other than dancing. I'm not going to lie, it feels kind of epic.

"This is why you have the Archer's mark," Creek whispers to me from behind, closer than I'd realized he was standing.

"I have what?" I ask, not moving away from him, leaving barely any space between my back and his front.

"The Archer's mark. One of your constellations. You've always been an excellent marksman. Your constellations represent parts of you from each life. Colt knows this, so I don't know why he always thinks he'll beat you, but with each life, he tries. I just like watching him eat his words." His breath warms my ear, and I shiver.

"Your turn, Creek," Nate says, eyeing us with another look that I can't read. Creek steps away from me toward the mark for the third target. He hits the red ring with a shrug. I see my dad and Nate's knives in the yellow, my dad's closer than Nate's, but still no bullseye.

Colt swaggers forward and throws, but his frustration is clear before he even releases the knife. It builds further when his knife lands, riding the line between red and yellow. "For fuck's sake."

"It's okay, you might still beat me," I goad, and he gives me the finger, making me laugh. "It's all just good fun, you big baby. Suck it up."

I step forward and take the spot he was just in. Taking a deep breath, I focus on the target, filtering out the world around me in a way I didn't think possible. Without thinking too much, I release the knife and wait, holding my breath as it hits its mark. Riding the line of the yellow ring and the black dot.

"Well, hot damn!" My dad whoops, and I laugh. "She's still got it." I clap my hands and grin at his praise while the others just grumble. "That's my girl," he says, giving me a high five as I walk past him. I haven't seen my dad this loose and happy in forever. It's a nice change.

"You showing them how it's done?" Maddie calls as she reaches us, protecting her eyes from the sun.

"She sure is," Nate shouts back, and she laughs.

"Lunch is nearly done, so don't take too much longer."

"Yes, ma'am," Nate tells her with a salute, and I laugh as she blows him a kiss. I wonder if my parents would still be as happy as they are if Mom was still alive.

I watch as they each throw at the fourth target, closer this time than last, but I still take top place when I graze the center dot again.

"Last chance, Colt. You're third. Your sister is winning. You think you can take her? There's only a point in it." My dad goads him light heartedly as Colt steps up to the mark.

"Shut it, old man. I've got this." He rolls his shoulders and stretches out his neck.

"Get on with it, stop delaying the inevitable," Nate calls out with a laugh. Apparently they don't mind losing as much as my brother does.

He throws, letting out a yell as his knife hits the center of the target. "Hell fucking yes. Now you can go eat crow, old man."

Nate waves him off and goes to retrieve the knife. "Only fair that we clear the board for everyone on this one."

The others take their turns none coming as close to the central dot but not seeming to mind. I step up to the mark and Creek appears behind me again. "You've got this, I've seen you make this hit without even thinking about it more times than I can count. Your mind is remembering, even if you can't tell. Don't think, just let go."

I take a deep breath and try to focus like I did before, filtering out the noise, letting go of everything, and focusing on nothing but the target and the weight of the knife in my hand. I line myself up and close my eyes, letting my instincts take over as I release the blade.

"Holy shit," I hear Colt say before I open my eyes and see my knife, embedded deep in the target, dead center.

"Woooooooo!" I cry out and Creek laughs, lifting me up and spinning me around.

"I knew you could do it," he says as he puts me back down, and Colt groans.

"Come on, this is so unfair!" he whines, and I can't help but laugh.

"Better luck next time? It was only one point, who knows, maybe it was a fluke." I wink at him, and my dad and Nate laugh.

"Something like that," my dad says shaking his head. "Colt, get this shit packed up, we'll meet you inside."

"Come on, man. I'll help you," Creek says to him as I head inside with my dad and Nate, to find a grinning Maddie flitting around the kitchen, laying the table, and humming to herself.

"You show them how it's done?" she asks when she turns and sees us.

"You know she did," Nate says with a wide smile. "Colt was as pissed as ever. Poor guy, you'd think after this many years, he'd have accepted it."

"He'll never accept it, he's a Bennett," Bauer says as he appears in the room. "I found your Leviathan mark, Remy."

"Enough of that," Maddie interrupts. "It can wait until after everyone eats."

"Yes, ma'am," Bauer says with a smile as she clucks at him, and he takes a seat at the table. I sit down opposite him, in the seat I've been sitting in all my life. The others join us in time, as Maddie lays out a feast before us. How she whipped this up while we were outside fucking around astonishes me. Cooking is not a skill of mine. The eggs, ham, cheeses, and pastries make my mouth water as she adds potatoes and other meats too.

"Dig in!" she announces, and it's like feeding time at the zoo. Luckily, I grew up like this, so I'm used to practically fighting for my food. I guess that's part of the fun of eating like this, with the ones you love.

I stuff my face, despite the donuts earlier, and content sighs and groans ripple around the room as Maddie smiles from her seat.

"I'm glad that you all enjoyed it." She beams. It's so

hard to try and imagine her out killing beasts and kicking ass when she's always seemed like such a homebody to me. She excels at the things I know I never will, she's such a mom. That's something I don't think I'd be that great at, and considering this life, I'm not sure it's something I'd choose either.

It hits me then, that I don't know if I've ever had children, and I'm not sure that I want to know yet, so I tuck the question away for another time. Maybe once my memories are back, I won't have to ask.

I stand and start to clear the table, and Bauer joins, helping me load the dishwasher while the others all talk around the table.

"So, you found the mark? What does it mean?" I ask quietly, hoping that the others' conversation will distract them enough from my question.

"I did, but I don't know yet, there isn't much information about it, or about being Angel-blessed. At least, not that I could find yet. I'll keep looking though."

"Thanks, Bauer. I appreciate it."

"Anything for you, Remy. Now you should probably go rest, it might not feel like it right now, but the ritual takes a lot out of you, and the next few days are going to suck." He gives me a sad smile, and I worry about how much he's not telling me.

Bauer wasn't wrong. I went up to my old room yesterday afternoon and fell straight asleep. The strangest dreams haunted me, and when I woke up this morning, I felt like death. Genuine death. And fuck my fucking life, I had to rush to the bathroom to hurl the second I opened my eyes, so that was fun. So much for the all powerful, kickass Remy Bennett my brothers keep going on about. I feel like shit.

After the excitement of waking up hurling, I shoved some dry toast down my throat and passed up on coffee in favor of coming back to bed. I've tried to go back to sleep for the last few hours, but I just can't. The headaches that keep assaulting me are devastating. Each time I come out of one, I feel a little different—like I'm a different person, but only kind of. It's the weirdest sensation. But there is an upside. I'm remembering things.

Like the names of the constellations that make up my birthmarks, or old angel marks, or whatever the hell it is. I can't remember why I got those specific ones yet, beyond the archer that Creek told me about, but I have the weirdest snippets. I feel so shitty, I haven't even taken a second to look at the marks on my back. I've seen hints over my shoulder, but Bauer says it's still growing, so I'm just going to wait till I don't feel like my eyes are going to fall out of my head to try to catch a glimpse of myself. Especially with everything hitting me like it is right now.

I have memories of moments with people I don't know, like the dreams I was having weeks ago. I know that Kain is someone I've worked with a lot. I also get the feeling he isn't someone I should mention to my family, but I have no idea why. Instinct tells me to keep my mouth shut though, so that's what I'm going to do. Not everything is meant to be shared. My mom used to tell me that when I was younger, and it's never made more sense to me than it does now.

I also know that I'm meant to have the sword that Colt tried to give me before. Now that my memories are starting to filter through, I feel like I'm missing a limb without it. I've had the sword forever, it's been with me through everything. That much I know.

I also remembered about obsidian, how it's a Lycans greatest weakness, and that iridium in any form is enough to kill a Dracul, but you're still better taking their heads. Apparently, my film references are completely wrong, because sunlight, garlic, holy water, and mirrors are all big myths. They don't sparkle either. They look exactly like humans, except more ethereal. One of the differences that gives them away is the copper ring around the outside of their irises. Not exactly the most obvious detail, but thank the Fates for Hunter eyesight apparently. I don't remember much about Lycans yet, though I'm pretty sure that will come. It was the Dracul that haunted my dreams last night.

"How are you feeling, Remy?" Colt pokes his head around the door of my bedroom, letting in a dim light, which still manages to make my eyes water.

"I'd be better in darkness," I tell him, pulling the comforter up over my head. I hear his chuckle and a click as the door closes.

"That better?" he asks as the mattress dips under his weight. I pull the comforter back down and find him sitting cross-legged at the end of my bed. Seeing his hulking form at the end of my queen bed is amusing as fuck. He looks so out of place, but I swallow the laugh because my head hurts enough as it is.

"Much, thank you."

"How's your head?" he asks, and as I sit up properly, I get the feeling he needs to talk. It's not often he looks this serious.

"It's been better, stuff is starting to come back to me. It's a bit of a jumbled mess, and I feel more confused than anything; but I could be worse, I guess." I shrug. "Is it always like this?"

He nods, looking solemn. "Yeah, it sucks ass. I was in bed for a week, but then, my ritual wasn't as dramatic as yours. I didn't get all of my memories, even after the six month mark, so there's still gaps but most stuff has been filled in. The important stuff anyway." I smile at him, and he shrugs. "I think you might get it all back."

"Yeah?"

"Yeah. Being Angel-blessed is no joke. It's like a fairy tale to us Hunters. A story from generations before us. All the way from the beginning. Of those who managed such spectacular feats that they became Angel-blessed with great powers, beyond those of a normal Hunter. And, I mean, you were kinda beyond anyway. If I'm honest, it kind of scares me, Remy.

"It's going to make you an even bigger target, and not just to the other factions. Not all Hunters are what they seem, so just be careful, okay? Once it's safe to fill you in completely, I will. I trust you, you're my blood. I know you wouldn't betray us or the faction. You've always been about the greater cause. Just trust me, but outside of the people you know closest, trust no one. Not even the Elders."

"I'm not scared, Colt. I mean, look at how the mark tried to protect me at the ritual. And something inside of me tells me that was just a tiny warning hit. But if it makes you feel better, I'll be careful."

"Thanks, Remy. Bauer asked me to check on you and your mark. Get some pictures." He waves his phone in front of his face. "That okay?"

"Sure," I nod and move so my back is facing him. I lift

A CROWN OF BLOOD AND BONE

my hair out of the way and close my eyes as the flash lights up the room.

"So, this is weird, but, can you lift your top?" I can practically hear him squirm behind me, and I laugh.

"Colt, it's just my back, it's not like we've never been swimming together." I roll my eyes and lift my tank top, his intake of breath makes me pause.

"It's grown, hasn't it?" I sigh.

"You could say that, yeah." He snaps a few more pictures, and I pull my top down. "Do you need anything else before I head out? I'm hitting the gym with Creek for a bit before our patrol tonight."

"No, I'm good thank you. Just tell Bauer to let me know what he finds. Oh, and can you send me those pictures? As soon as I can stand the light, I want to take a look." He nods and my phone buzzes on the nightstand. "Thanks."

"Anything for you, little bit. Catch you later."

"I'm not going anywhere." I sigh and lie back down, wondering what Colt meant about the Elders. I close my eyes and decide not to worry about it. Fates know I have enough to worry about right now as it is. My head starts pounding, a low thrum, and I know what's coming, so I get comfortable and pray for sleep.

The branches of the trees whip my face as I tear through the forest, running faster than I can remember ever running. I hear them behind me, the rogue Lycans from the nest I found tonight. Of course, I'd insisted on coming alone, one little Lycan nest is nothing. I'm a fucking idiot.

I pause, holding my breath and focus on listening to their steps. The thuds of movement become rhythmic, and I realize they've shifted. Motherfuckers.

I debate climbing the tree since wolves and climbing are two things that typically don't go together. That seems like the easy way out, though, and Remington Bennett has never taken the easy way out. Never.

I take a deep breath and start running again. I head west to the clearing I found on the way here, knowing that I have a better chance of surviving if I have the space to fight, rather than darting through these goddamn trees.

Howls ring out around me as the wolves notice the new hint of fear in my scent. The pounding behind me grows closer, and I push harder. This is not my night to die.

I reach the clearing, and it's completely empty, lit by the glow of a full moon. If Lycans could only shift with a full moon, it would make the rest of the month so much easier.

"Hunter," a half-shifted man growls as he breaks the tree line.

"You guys should have gone on your way rather than chasing me. That was a very stupid idea."

"You slaughtered our mates!" a woman who just broke the tree line screams.

"You shouldn't have left the safety of your pack, I guess. Rogue wolves are easier to track. Easier to put down." I shrug, faking the nonchalance I wish I felt.

I draw the swords from my back, only one of them lethal to the Lycans emerging from the trees. Considering that there's six of them and only one of me, I'll take my chances on any injuries at all. I already took out six of these shitheads, and I have no idea how so many rogues banded together. Usually they travel in pairs or four wolves max.

I spin slowly, making eye contact with each of them, taking note of the markings on those who are half turned or still in their human skin. There are twelve packs on this continent. All led by the Alpha of Alphas, Roman Knight. But some of these markings don't belong to the American packs. I don't even recognize some of them, but I can't focus on that right now.

"We are pack," the first man who spoke growled, his voice more wolf than man. At his word, two of the shifted charge toward me.

I raise my swords, ready for their attack. They come at me from opposite sides, and I don't even think. I just feel. I raise one blade and drop one knee as the first jumps for my throat. My blade pierces their chest, and I drag downwards to the stomach. Blood sprays around me, covering me, but

I barely notice it as the other charges straight for me. It knocks into me, throwing me backward. I groan as I roll, but I end up crouched as it charges me again. The half-turned woman runs at me too. I sheath the iridium sword, and pull the gun from my thigh holster.

"Fuck this shit." I aim and fire, the woman almost looks stunned as the bullet hits her in the heart, and she drops as the other wolf bites down on my shoulder. I grit my teeth as it locks on. This isn't my first bite, but Jesus Christ, this shit hurts. I swap my gun between my hands and shoot the wolf between the eyes. The whine as it releases my shoulder and falls to the ground barely registers as I shoot two others who start moving toward me.

"Really? Do you have a death wish?" I shout to the others, but I can tell that with their rage, the blood lust has taken them. Fucking rogues.

"Guns are for the weak, Hunter. And here I was thinking the great and legendary Remington Bennett was more of a Hunter than that," the leader goads, but I roll my eyes as I feel the holes on my shoulder starting to close.

"Guns are for the clever, moron. But if you want to do this the old way, I am more than happy to kill you that way." I smirk and sheath my sword and gun.

"That ego is going to be the death of you," another man on the edge of the clearing says quietly, but it still reaches me like he knew it would, and I shrug.

"I earned my ego, pup."

"Don't say I didn't warn you," he mutters, and moves quicker than I've ever seen a Lycan move. I duck but still feel his fist glance off of my wounded shoulder rather than my face where he was aiming. I don't manage to escape the second fist to my ribs. I grit my teeth and pull a throwing knife from my hip.

Fuck this.

I jab at the Lycan, quick, fatal hits. Throat, thigh, chest. So quick he doesn't register the blows until it's too late. I feel movement behind me and throw the blade backward, listening for the moment it hits its mark in the other man's throat.

"I tried to warn you. I was even going to let you live, give you the chance to make better choices, but you fucking morons just couldn't take the out. Couldn't just go back to Roman. Now look at you." I shake my head and wipe some of the blood from my face, feeling it smear.

"You will regret this," the wolf at my feet utters, his breath labored.

"I don't think I will," I say kneeling down to him and putting my hands on either side of his face. I twist, and the bones crack. It's not enough to kill him, but it is enough to knock him out while he bleeds out. I'm a Hunter, not a sadist.

The gurgled breath of the other wolf reaches me, and I

sigh. I turn and head over to him, removing the blade from his throat, wiping it on my leather pants before tucking it away. He grabs my ankle and his claws tear through my pants and Achilles' tendon. I bite my lip to stop from screaming but grab my gun and shoot the motherfucker between the eyes before falling backward onto my ass.

"Fuck!" I shout into the silence of the forest. There's no way the wound will heal quickly enough for me to get out of here on my own.

"You need a hand?" the voice echoes around the clearing, and my head droops.

"You couldn't weigh in before now?" I bite out.

"You know I couldn't."

"Fucking bullshit faction politics."

"It is what it is."

"Are you going to help me or not?" I clench my teeth as I try to stand but fail.

"I will. I'm just cherishing this moment, where the great Remington Bennet needs my help." His dark hair reflects the moonlight, and his laugh does things to my body that it has no business doing. He sniffs, my arousal hitting his nose as it peaks. *"Needs more than just my help,"* he says, practically purring.

"Roman, I swear to the Fates."

I wake up in a pool of sweat, panting. What the fuck

was that, and why was the Alpha of Alphas helping me?

TWELVE

Four days have passed, and I finally feel like I can breathe again. My memories aren't even remotely close to being fully back, and I'm more confused than I've ever been in my life. I'm keeping everything to myself until I understand more—like why the hell I was working with Roman Knight, who the hell Kain is, and how the latter factors into everything. Other stuff makes more sense, of course. I remember more about what we are and our ways, but it's strange. Because I see the old me in my mind, and it's like she's a different person. I don't feel like her, and I don't even look like her, except for my eyes. I mean, maybe we look related, but it's the violet eyes that always give it away.

I shower and dress for the first time in days, and that

alone makes me feel a ton better. On my way down the stairs, I hear banging in the kitchen followed by Bauer cussing. I guess he's trying to cook. It never was a skill of his. Of any of ours, other than Mom really.

I laugh when I find him covered in what I'm assuming is egg from the looks of it. The glass bowl lies on its side on the floor, with the rest of the mixture pooling at his feet.

"Having fun?" I smile, and he looks up and groans.

"Barrel of laughs. Can't you see this is my favorite thing?" he mutters as he bends down and picks up the bowl.

"How about I clean that up while you change, and we go out for breakfast? Molly's still does the best breakfast stack on this side of the world." I smile, and the smile he gives me in return warms my heart. I haven't always been close to Bauer, but with some of my memories back, I know that isn't always the case with us. Sometimes, he's like the other side of the same coin.

"I'm glad to see you're feeling better, and yeah, that sounds great. We better check to see if the others want to come. If we go to Molly's without them, heads will roll," he laughs and heads upstairs to change while I clean the gloopy mess up.

Once it's dealt with, I pour myself a coffee and just enjoy feeling more like myself than I have in a while. The cloud of the breakup with Jack doesn't seem so dark and heavy anymore. Fates knows I've dealt with worse heartbreak than that. In this life and in others. Even if I don't remember the specifics, I can feel it. That this isn't going to break me. The weight of all things Hunter weighs down on me, but it doesn't feel crippling. It's as if I know that my memories are coming back, and with them comes the knowledge that I can deal with the burden it brings like I have a dozen times before.

I smile into my coffee cup as Colt bounds into the kitchen with a huge grin. I guess it makes more sense to me now that my brothers never moved out of here. Safety in numbers, out in the middle of nowhere, so should anything happen, no innocents get caught in the crossfire. If they think I'm giving up my apartment, they can think again.

"You're back!" he says as he slides into the chair beside me. "And we're going to Molly's!"

"You're very excited for this time of the day." I laugh.

"It's Molly's. Of course, I'm excited! I've been gone a long time. There were no Molly's out there on the other side of the world. I miss that place, *hard*. I texted Creek, he's going to meet us there. I swear he was more excited about that than going on patrol last night," he says, shaking his head before leaning forward and pulling something out of his back pocket. "Your keys. Your cat is a menace, but he's been fed, watered, let out, and let back in. I have the cuts to prove it. Little shit."

I laugh as he rolls up his sleeves, though the faint lines

that are obviously from Sushi are almost healed.

"Big, bad Hunter can't even take on my poor little pussy cat. How on Earth do you survive out there?" I tease.

He shoves me gently, and I laugh again as Bauer joins us. "Dad's not coming, he's working on something this morning, but he asked us to bring him something back."

"Sounds good to me," I say, standing as my stomach growls.

"I call shotgun!" Colt shouts and bounds out of the house. I swear to all the fates, he has Peter Pan syndrome.

"I guess you're driving," I say to Bauer since my car is still parked at home.

"Fine by me," he says with a grin. "Better than letting you drive."

"Hey! I am not a bad driver."

"Whatever you say!" He shakes his head as he chuckles, and I follow him out of the door.

Breakfast was amazing as ever and being around those three as they gossiped away about this and that felt so natural, so right. They were talking about a night from about a hundred years ago, and I laughed with them as they told the story, right before it popped into my head. It's still the strangest sensation, but with each memory that comes back, I feel more myself. More confident in the decision I made. And yet, my heart still hurts, even though it's been broken before. Being around everyone makes me feel like

I'm home, but a part of me still misses Jack, and the chance of a normal life. That same part of me still misses dancing and the pressures of my job.

Bauer dropped me off at home twenty minutes ago, and I've been puttering around, trying to figure out what to do with myself ever since. I have so much weird, nervous energy.

My phone rings, startling me from my ponderings. Creek's face stares up at me from my phone, and I smile.

"Hey, what's up? Miss me already?" I joke as I answer the phone.

"Hey, I was just deciding what to do for the day, and I wondered if you were up for a drive?" Creek's gravelly voice filters through the phone, and I tamper down the wistful fluttering of my heart. Not only is it way too soon since everything that happened with Jack, but Creek is my friend. He always has been, and that's it, at least as far as I can remember. The last thing I want to do is ruin that.

"Sounds fun! Can we take my Mustang?" I plead. I miss driving her. The last time I did was when I picked them up from the airport.

"We could, except where we're going might just kill her, so probably best to just take my truck." I can hear the smile in his words.

"*Fine!*" I concede. "How long till you're here?"

"Well, I mean, I'm kinda downstairs already."

I laugh at his words.

"Of course you are." I shake my head. "Give me two minutes, and I'll be down."

I grab my jacket and pull on my chucks. My jeans and t-shirt should be good for wherever we're heading, so I pull my ridiculously long hair up into a messy ponytail and grab my keys, scratching Sushi behind the ears before I head down to where Creek is waiting.

Parked just outside of the main door, Creek's huge truck idles, and I can see him grinning down at me. I pause, the truck is identical to Colt's, and I flash back to the other week when the Dracul attacked me. His face is all I see, and I'm rooted to the spot.

"Remy, you okay?" Creek's voice pulls me from the memory, and I shake it off.

"Yeah, I'm good." I walk to the truck and pull myself up into the cab. "Just having a moment."

"You went pale as fuck." Concern laces his voice as he looks me over.

"I'm fine, really. So where are we going?" I ask, and he takes the hint to drop it.

"Well, that's a surprise. Don't want to ruin it."

"Of course not." I shake my head with a smile and buckle myself in. "Come on then, off on the adventure we go."

We drive for what feels like ages, catching up on

everything he's been up to since he left. The guilt he feels about ghosting me is obvious, so I try not to be too prickly about it and try to enjoy just having my friend back and hearing about his globetrotting adventures. About training with Hunters on the other side of the world. "Wait, the Van Helsings exist?" I ask because... No freaking way!

"Yeah," he laughs. "The ones I met were absolute pricks. They were so far up their own asses, as if their name meant something other than the fact that one of them obviously slipped somewhere and let a human know the truth. Even if it's spun as a myth."

"No freaking way." I sit back and reel. "Dude, they're like famous."

He laughs at me and shakes his head. "Maybe, but you'd hate them. So freaking arrogant, and really not all that great Hunters. Now, the Nagasaki family? Them, you'd love. True Samurai, and they still honor the codes of the old times. I learned a lot from them. Colt, though, he was *way* too Colt for them." He laughs, and I join him because I can only imagine.

"That doesn't surprise me at all."

Creek pulls off the road we've been on for a while, turning onto a smaller dirt road. "Nearly there."

He looks over at me, and while I can't get a read on him, it still feels like I'm missing something. We sit in comfortable silence while we finish the drive, pulling up to a hidden lake. A house sits far off in the distance, the white painted wood gleaming in the afternoon sun, but it's obviously rundown and abandoned.

Birch trees circle the lake and lead a path toward the house, and the whole place just feels peaceful.

"This place is beautiful," I sigh, and climb out of the truck.

"It really is," Creek says as he joins me at the front of the truck, a soft, cool breeze wrapping around us.

"It feels so... It feels almost like home." I sigh because something about this place resonates deep inside me, and Creek smiles at me.

"Something like that. Come on, I need to do some work up at the house, but I brought a picnic for after. I figured you'd be up for helping, keep you busy and all that. Besides, you always were a sucker for being by the water."

"Sounds like fun. Is this place yours?" I ask as we start the trek up to the house, enjoying the sounds of the birds and the ripples on the water.

"Kind of," he says with a shrug. "I know you said earlier you were feeling better, but how has it been? The memory dump, I mean. Have you gotten much back?"

"I mean, I've gotten a lot of weird stuff back. Feelings and moments, but nothing monumentally life changing. I remember rituals, every single one of them. I remember training, and my love for the fight. I've had a few dreams, which I think are other memories, but not much about my actual lives. I've remembered a lot of Hunter lore, random as fuck information, but not much about who I was, if that makes sense?" I shrug.

"It does, it'll come. At least, that's what Ben thinks, and he's not usually wrong." He smiles down at me, towering above me now. It's still a little strange, him looking like this, so different yet still the guy I've always known.

"You've spoken to him?"

"Yeah, he's been around. He usually stays for a bit after, even when the other Elders return to wherever they're stationed. He's always the guide for us. We've known him a long time."

"Oh," I say, unsure of what else to say.

"He thinks something is happening within the Elders, though... something he's being kept out of," he tells me, and I sigh. It's not unlike what Colt was talking about.

"Yeah, Colt mentioned something about it."

"Well, just keep your guard up, okay? Even with Ben. We might have known him a long time, but a lot can happen in between cycles." His smile is tight and doesn't reach his eyes. "Anyway, enough of that. I hope you're ready to get messy."

We stop at the back of the house, where he reaches up and plucks a key from the door frame before opening the door. "Mind your step."

I follow him in and gasp at the sight before me. The inside has been completely gutted, the brickwork is exposed on one side of the room, and the other walls are all whitewashed. The majority of the downstairs has been opened into one space, with the kitchen to my right and the rest stretching out around us. Something about the room feels so damn familiar.

"You've been working pretty hard, I see."

"I haven't been home long, but I wanted to get a start on it. The vision for this place never really got realized, so I wanted it to be right. It's huge, so huge, so I decided starting down here was a good idea. There's still the sunroom and the library separate down here, plus the utility room. There are stables outside that need patching up too, and that's all before I can even think about the next two floors. I'm happy with what I've managed so far."

"Can I look around?" I ask wistfully.

"Sure. What's mine is yours." He smiles at me, and it warms me. It feels like I've swallowed a whole swarm of butterflies with the way my stomach's twisting. "Just be careful where you stand."

I nod and take off to explore, leaving him to get started on whatever it was that he brought me here to help with. I'll help, but first, I want to look around.

I discover seven bedrooms, four baths, and what looks like a game room over the next two floors. The place is huge. I make my way back to Creek and find him topless, paint roller in hand.

Holy freaking cow.

Like, I knew he got ripped while he was away, being a hulk of a man and all that now, but holy freaking ovary explosion. I clamp my lips together to keep the word vomit from spilling out—because nope. I can't start drooling over my lifelong best friend now, but that doesn't mean I'm not going to ogle the fuck out of him while his back is to me. I might be his friend, but I'm not fucking blind.

"You want to come and help, Remy?" he asks without turning around, but I can hear the laughter in his voice. Shit. Stupid Hunter hearing.

"Yeah sure, just getting my bearings," I say with a blush. "Where do you want me?"

He looks over at me with a heated stare, but I look away and take off my jacket. "There's another roller on the counter. These walls need another coat of white before I start on the floors. White paint on gray carpet isn't the easiest to get out."

"Sure thing!" I say, almost too eagerly and go to grab the roller before joining him again.

"Did you enjoy exploring?" he asks, looking me over again.

"This place is phenomenal, Creek. I'm almost jealous it's not mine." He smiles at me, but disappointment clouds his eyes.

"Thanks. It'll be better once it's finished." He shrugs and starts painting again. I pull my phone out of my pocket and press play on my music list, *Wildwood Kin's "Steady My Heart"* pours through, and I smile before I start painting too.

The silence isn't uncomfortable, so I don't think. I just lose myself to the physicality of painting. It might not exactly be strenuous, and with my new Hunter strength, I don't tire, but it's more than I've done in a long while.

We finish the room in almost no time, and I look around, trying to envision the place when it's finished, when a memory hits me. I've been here before. With Creek. I see the room, not as it is now, but what it was. Before. In another time. He looks different, but I know it's him. He looks so jaded, and yet, so at peace. The vision flickers before disappearing, and I come out of it to find him staring at me.

"We've been here before," I say, my voice barely more than a whisper, and he nods, still looking sad. "It was so different. We were so different." I chase the memory, but nothing else comes. "I only saw us, in this room, in a different time. I don't know when, or why, but..."

"It's strange when they hit you like that." He smiles softly and comes toward me. "But sometimes they show you exactly what you were missing."

He stands so close to me, and it feels like all of the breath has been sucked from my lungs. My eyes meet his, and it's like I'm stuck. Fixed in place, unable to move. His hand lifts and brushes the hair that's fallen from my ponytail behind my ear. His thumb strokes my cheek so softly. My breath hitches as I lean into him.

"Yo! Where you guys at?" Colt's voice reaches us, breaking whatever spell we were under. I step back from Creek, trying to steady my racing heart.

"We're just in here," Creek calls out, walking toward the sound of Colt's voice.

Holy shit, what the hell was that?

"I figured I'd find you guys here. I brought something for Remy. I figured she shouldn't be without it all for much longer." Colt says as he enters the room, a black duffel slung over his shoulder. His gaze bounces between us as if he's trying to read the room. "It's looking good in here, man."

He claps Creek on the shoulder, and they do that weird bro hug thing they do. I shake my head. They're such dudes.

"What did you bring me?" I ask once I feel back in control of myself.

"Well, I mean, I tried this once already, but you've done the ritual now, so we should be good to go." He shrugs with a carefree smile, letting go of whatever tension he felt in the room as he entered.

He eases the duffel onto the floor and kneels down to unzip it. He pulls out the box he showed me all those weeks ago at Bauer's, and I sigh, my heart skipping a beat at the sight of it.

"You brought my sword," I sigh, rushing over to him.

"Swords." He smiles. "And your guns. Dad had them all in the armory back home, but a Hunter shouldn't be far from her weapons once she's been awakened. It's like an itch in the back of your brain that you don't notice until it's gone."

I look at him and realize he's right. There was a buzzing, dim enough to dismiss, but with my sword within touching distance, it's silenced.

"Thank you, Colt. How did I get these?" I say as I drop to the floor and lift the boxes. I move them to the counters in the kitchen, eager to open them, yet hesitant at the same time.

"Well, the black hilted one with the obsidian blade was a gift from Creek here. Your old sword was shattered after a particularly gnarly fight with some pissed off Lycans. But the iridium one—the one in the box—I don't actually know. You didn't have it during one life, but when I cycled back, you'd had two lives without either of us, and you had it. You could ask Bauer, but I'm not sure that he knows either." He shrugs without a care. I open the box, and it's as if the blade sings. As if it's happy to be reunited with me, and I'm flooded with a sense of joy and peace as I lift it from its violet velvet setting and unsheathe it. The sword is perfectly balanced, and it's the perfect length, as if it was made just for me. The decorative hilt glints in the sun filled room. I twirl the blade cautiously, getting a feel for it, and I feel the stupidly big grin on my face.

Hello, old friend.

I re-sheathe it and place it back in its box, not wanting to get too carried away. I know that the blade isn't going to leave my side for long from now on. The guys both watch me, grinning like it's my birthday and I'm surrounded by a pile of gifts. I try the other sword, the gift from Creek, and again, the metal sings as I slice the air with it. It's not as intricately decorated as the other, but the mark of the Hunter is etched into the top of the blade just below the hilt.

I move to the smaller boxes and find two guns. Small, but perfectly sized for my hands. One black, one silver, and both with symbols carved into them. I recognize the symbols from the altar at the chambers, but I'm still unsure of their meaning. "The black is for obsidian bullets, the silver for iridium. Keeps things simple, and the markings help keep your shots true. Not that you need the help," Colt says with a shrug, while Creek stands in the corner with his arms crossed, silently watching, his face unreadable.

"Thank you, Colt." I sigh and put the guns back in their boxes, before hugging him.

"No worries, little bit. They're yours, we've just been keeping them safe." He shrugs as I let him go. "You guys need any help here?" he asks, looking at Creek, who shakes his head.

"Nah, we were about done."

"Okay, cool. Want to head to the range? Give our girl a whooping before all of her skills come back? Let her play with her toys?" Colt asks, waggling his eyebrows, the piercing bounces, making me laugh.

"Thanks, but we actually have plans," I tell him and stick out my tongue.

"Without me?" he asks, staggering back with a hand on his chest. "You wound me!"

I laugh at his dramatics, and even Creek cracks a smile. "Sorry, bro."

"It's all good, I get it. The dynamic duo is reunited." He pretends to wipe a tear from his eye, and I swipe him in the gut.

"Shut up, dummy. You two have been off having the greatest bromance of all time for over a year."

"Yeah, yeah. Everyone wants a bit of me, I get it," Creek laughs, whatever was up with him seemingly forgotten.

"What can I say, man, I miss your sweet, sweet lovin'. It's been too long." Colt laughs, and I giggle because they're each as ridiculous as the other.

"I missed this," I say. This is exactly how it used to be before they both up and left, making their choice to become Hunters. I can't begrudge it, because I wouldn't want them to be any different. If they had chosen differently, we wouldn't be here now, but no matter how much I try to let it go, it still stings a little. I try not to think about it. Because if I do, I'll think about Jack too, and that's a whole well of hurt that I don't want to dive into today. Or any day soon.

"Aww," Colt says, wrapping one of his barbarically big arms around my neck. "I missed you too, little bit, but I'll be on my way. Don't forget we're patrolling again tonight," he says to Creek.

"Looking forward to joining us this weekend, Remy?" he asks me, and I gasp.

"I'm hunting this weekend?" I say.

"Yeah, didn't Bauer say? You'll be going out with the two of us, giving Dad a night off. The old man is slowing down, just don't tell him that because he'll still take your head off your shoulders." The excitement bubbles up inside me. The restlessness I've been feeling is finally getting the outlet I've been looking for.

"He didn't say a goddamn word, but hell yes I'm excited." I grin at them both. Colt's grin matches my own, but Creek just looks grim.

"Right, I'm off. I'll catch you later, man. Don't get up to too much trouble you guys," Colt says, grabbing the duffel and throwing it over to me. "Be careful where you keep that shit."

"I will. Stay safe," I tell him as he turns to leave.

"I always do." He winks at me before bumping fists with Creek and leaving.

"Well, hurricane Colt has officially left the building," I sigh.

"That he has. You hungry? Ready for that picnic?" Creek asks with a small smile.

"I sure am. I just need to clean up."

"Use the bathroom on the next floor. The water is all still running, might be cold, but it's there," he says to me. "I'll get this stuff put away, and then we'll head back down to the truck."

"Sounds good, and thank you for today. I needed this. Just something normal." I hug him tightly.

"Anytime, Remy. If you ever need to escape, just say the word, and we'll run away, however far and for however long you need."

.

.

THIRTEEN

I strap the swords across my back and fasten the gun holsters to my thighs. I take a look at myself in the mirror and laugh. I knew my love of leather would have its time. My black crop top, and leather under bra waistcoat show my midriff, the tattoo on my hip peeks up over the top of my ripped black skinny jeans, and the fishnets under them peek through.

I pull on the chunky heeled boots that I found in a sale years ago to complete the look. My mark has started to creep round my shoulder and down my arm, and having looked at the pictures Colt sent me, I have no idea what it's building to. I can't help but love it. The Hunter's mark is topped with the mark of Leviathan, a crown, with one single drop of blood hanging from it, but the unknown part is the vines that seem to grow from the base of my Hunter's mark. The thorny vines that grow over my shoulder and down my arm intercede with symbols, some from the altar that I recognize, with others that no one seems to know what they are.

I'd be worried, but it hasn't caused me any harm up to this point, so I have no reason to fear it. Especially with the Leviathan mark. I know it's a protection of some sort—I just wish I remembered how I got it and why.

"Are you about ready?" Creek calls out from the main room of my apartment.

"Nearly!" I shout as I grab the cloak Dad gave me this morning. Apparently, it's been mine since my first life. It's made of a material discovered by the Hunters, almost impenetrable, yet supple and soft.

It's matte black to help me hide in the shadows, and honestly, it kind of makes me feel like a badass. I slip it on and lift the hood, which paints my face in shadow without restricting my vision in the slightest. The clock might be my new favorite thing other than my swords. Well, not new, but yeah. I drop the hood back and take one last look at myself in the mirror. Walking to the main room of my apartment, I find Creek and Colt sitting on my sofa with football on, eating my pretzels.

"Just make yourself at home, why don't you?" I ask with a laugh, all the while shaking my head. "And here I was thinking you guys wanted me to rush."

They both turn to look at me, and Colt has this stupid grin on his face—his mouth is full of pretzels, and he looks like a total dork. Creek's eyes darken with heat as he takes me in, his eyes roving my body inch by inch. Goosebumps cover my arms at the intensity of his stare, but I shake it off. Creek is my best friend, and that isn't a line I want to cross. If we haven't crossed it before, it's definitely not a line I'm going to take a run at now. Maybe when we were younger, but it just doesn't seem like a good idea, all things considered.

Right?

I bite my lip as Colt turns back around and elbows Creek in the side. Creek groans, but his eyes dart back toward me, and I'm pretty sure he's showboating for Colt's sake.

"You ready?" he asks, and Creek grunts at him. "Let's head out then."

"Where are we going?" It's an important question since my swords aren't exactly inconspicuous. Maybe a hundred years ago no one would think twice about the sight of them, but in this time and world, people are definitely going to look at us sideways.

"We're just doing a patrol through the abandoned blocks of warehouses a few towns over. Nothing too extreme for your first hunt," Creek tells me, and I roll my eyes.

"So much for the fun of the hunt."

"There's plenty of time for the fun of your hunt, Remy." Colt sighs like I'm an impetuous child, and I resist the urge to stick out my tongue at him to show him how childish I can really be. "In the meantime, this still has to be done. We've found more than a few rogues in similar places since we've been back. It seems as if the Lycans and Dracul have been drawn to this place in the last few months, but no one seems to know why. Activity is definitely up, so we're going."

"Oh, okay then. Well, after you guys, I guess." I grab my phone and keys from the counter and slip them into my back pocket.

I follow them out of the apartment and down to the waiting truck. Colt climbs behind the wheel, and Creek follows me into the back. We drive in silence, the anticipation building in the air around us, and I can feel the adrenaline pumping through my veins. We leave the city lights of Salem's Bay behind as we head down the dark, quiet roads to wherever it is they're taking me.

The silence sits somewhere directly between comfortable and uncomfortable, and I find myself picking at my nails. The adrenaline pumps steadily through my veins, and while I've remembered enough to know that the thrill of the hunt is one of my favorite things, I can't help but feel the teeniest bit of nerves over the upcoming chase. The drive isn't terribly long, so I'm not lost to my thoughts for too long. Colt pulls off of the road, and I spot dim lights not too far off. We pull all the way up to the gates of the complex before stopping.

"Ready or not," Colt says softly, and we all climb from the truck. I stretch my arms to the side, shaking out the tension of underused adrenaline, before joining my brother and Creek at the gates.

"Okay, so we're going to stick together tonight. Remy, if anything happens, please don't jump in the deep end. It's your first night back, and you're not one hundred percent back to your old self yet."

I sigh at the pleading tone in Colt's voice but nod anyway. "Sure thing, Dad."

Creek shakes his head at me but stays silent. He signals for us to be quiet and then indicates to his ears. I focus my hearing, pushing the Hunter gifts to spread out around me. I don't hear much, other than the scurrying of animals in the fields behind us, and it seems as if the guys are met by silence too. They move forward, almost in perfect unison.

Colt scales the gate first, heaving himself over the top and dropping down nearly silently on the other side. He waits a second, checking to make sure it's clear before motioning for me to climb over. I step up to the gate, reaching for the railing before Creek's hands find my waist, helping me over the gate. I swing my leg over the top and then hang down the other side, landing as quietly as I can manage. Creek follows quickly and silently. How two guys as big as them can move that quietly absolutely baffles me. I shake it off with a quiet huff. I guess it's all part of the Hunter toolkit.

A woman's laugh tinkles in the distance, and the hairs on the back of my neck stand up. Silence falls for a half a second before a breeze tears through the complex, ruffling the leaves of the trees on the outskirts of the perimeter. I must be distracted as hell—definitely not at the top of my game—because I don't realize a man is approaching until he appears before us.

Dracul.

"Dinner's here," he says, his head tilted to the side, eyes manic as he takes us in. "It's been far too long since I last tasted Hunter."

"You guys talk too much," Colt says and pulls his gun, aiming straight for the Dracul's heart.

"Maybe that's because I'm just the distraction."

I duck on instinct, and a blade flies over my head, landing in the heart of the Dracul before us. I spin to see another three Dracul striding in our direction.

"Oh goodie," Colt says, spotting the Dracul as he and Creek turn. "And here I thought tonight would be quiet."

He steps forward at the same time as Creek, both

offering me slight cover from the three approaching Dracul. I turn my back to them and focus on the Dracul that appeared first. I watch, little better than disinterested, as he pulls the blade from his chest with a gleeful grin.

"Pretty little Hunter, I think you'll taste good. Maybe I'll hurt you just enough that I get to keep you for a while," he says, and Creek growls from behind me.

"Aren't you just a big ball of crazy?" I smile at the Dracul, and my fingers itch to take action. "We'll see which one of us is bleeding at the end of this, won't we?"

A calm sweeps over me. It feels familiar and comfortable. A killing calm. Instinct rules me as I pull my sword, shutting out the other two and focusing on the creature before me. I smile at him and lunge forward at the same time he does.

The motherfucker is fast!

I swing the sword and glance a blow on his arm, and I laugh as I hear him hiss.

"Not so pretty anymore, am I? And you thought this would be easy," I taunt. The sound of the fight behind me threatens to distract me, but I focus, knowing that Creek and Colt will look after themselves and one other.

"You little bitch. You'll pay for that," he says, throwing the blade he took earlier at me. I dodge it, but not quickly enough, and it embeds itself in my shoulder rather than my throat where it was headed.

Holy crap that hurts.

I sheathe my sword in the holster on my back, knowing I'll be useless with it now that my shoulder is fucked up and quickly grab my gun. In a blink, the Dracul becomes frenzied. I chance a glance at Creek and Colt, only to see that their Dracul are distracted by the scent of my blood.

"I was right, such a tasty little Hunter. So sweet. You don't smell like the rest. What a treat, what a treat indeed!"

He rushes at me again. I lift my gun to shoot him, but he crashes into me before I can get the shot off. Fuck, I'm rusty. His claws tear into my arms where he holds me against the ground, and I feel the warmth of my blood spilling from the wounds.

His saliva drops down onto my chest as he stares at the blood. I wrestle to get him off of me, but even with my Hunter strength, this Dracul is beyond strong. He releases one of my arms and licks the blood from his claw.

"Such a tasty little Hunter," he sighs, his elongated teeth making him lisp his words.

I try to reach for my other gun, but he still has me pinned. Suddenly there's silence, and wetness rains down on my face.

I blink through the blood obscuring my eyesight and see that the Dracul above me is headless. A very pissed off Creek looks down at me as the body drops partially on top of me.

"Shit, Remy," he exclaims as he kneels down, fingers hovering just over the wound on my shoulder. "Colt, she's bleeding badly."

"Fuck!" Colt shouts and runs over to me. "All three of them are down. Grab her, I'll get the gate open, and we'll get her to Fallon. She can help heal her."

"Can't I just heal?" I sigh as Creek pushes the Dracul off of me and scoops me up into his arms.

"Not this time, Remy. The Dracul around here have started coating their claws in a poison that seems to slow our healing. You could heal easily from the knife wound, but we need a Witch for the rest."

"Fuck."

"Yeah, fuck." He jogs, and I try to stay as still as I can as the motion jostles my body and irritates the wounds. The blood loss makes me feel dizzy, so I close my eyes.

"Hurry, Colt," I hear, but it sounds muffled as if far away. I drift closer toward a calm slumber as the doors slam shut, and we move.

I try to breathe in, but I cough with blood sputtering from my lips.

"Fuck, no, Remy, you don't get to leave me like this. Not now." Creek's face appears in my line of vision, and I feel his arms wrap around me. He scoops me up from the ground, the warehouse where we just emptied a Dracul nest silent as the cold seeps in.

"It was a lucky shot," I say, coughing.

"We're going to get you healed. You just need to hang on. The witches' shop isn't far from here."

"Creek, it's too late," I sigh and rest my head on his shoulder as he runs with me, not listening to my words.

"Just hang on, Remy. We're so close."

"Creek," I say, my breath rattling. "Stop."

He halts, the night closing in, and the only light for miles comes from the moon above us. "It's too far," I say with a smile. He looks down at me, tears on his face.

"I can't do this without you, Remy. It's too soon. This is so fucked up. I'm not giving up," he starts to run again, as quickly as his Hunter speed can carry us across the terrain back toward the city where the Witches reside. I close my eyes, accepting my fate. This is not my first life, and it will not be my last. Though I wish it hadn't been ripped away from me so soon.

Not when we barely had the chance to explore what we finally discovered.

"Just a little longer. Hold on, Remy," Creek's voice filters through my ears, bringing me peace, and I smile. I have known love in many forms, but the love Creek gifted me with is possibly the purest I've ever felt. Unyielding, unfaltering, and all encompassing.

"I love you, Creek," I sigh, as my heartbeat slows. The blade that sits in my heart destroys me with each passing beat.

"I love you too, Remy. In this life and all others to come. Please don't leave me," he pants, and his tears splash down onto my face. "It's not fair, I only just got you."

"I'm sorry. Tell my family I love them, and that I'll see them soon."

"No, Remy, you'll see them soon enough. We're almost there. Just another minute." His movements grow faster, more erratic. And then we stop, a smash of glass filtering through the air before Creek calls out.

"What on earth!" a woman's voice reaches my ears as the darkness starts to close in around me. "Quickly, bring her over here. There's not much time."

We move again, and I hear the sound of crashing around me before Creek's warmth leaves my back, and I'm laid down. "We may be too late." The woman's hushed voice sounds afraid.

"Heal her," Creek growls and takes my hand.

"I love you," I whisper. "It's okay."

"Shut the fuck up, Remy."

I scream as the blade is pulled from me, to be replaced with a deep pressure. The darkness closes in further, but then a warmth floods me. Witch Light. The heat grows to the point of making me want to scream out at the burning sensation, but I have no voice as the magic holds me in place.

As quickly as it began, the heat recedes, and I take a deep breath.

"Thank you, thank you!" Creek utters above me, but I can't speak. I can't even move.

I feel warmth and pressure against my lips as Creek kisses me.

"Don't you ever do that to me again, Remington Bennett. I will always catch you, I will always be by your side through anything, but fuck you for cutting it that close."

expected."

I glance around the room, locking gazes with Creek. The worry and the pain I see in his eyes floods me with a whole barrage of emotions I'm not ready to unpack. The memory, or dream, or whatever the hell it was, comes to the forefront again, and I avert my eyes quickly as awkward tension coils in my belly. Holy shitballs. Maybe it wasn't real, right? It could just be a hallucination. I was dying. Shit like this happens all the time, right?

But I chance a quick peek at him again, and I feel it all the way to my core. There's truth in the memories, and the newest parts of me, the reemerging parts, yearn for him. My heart falls as quickly as it soared at the realization that I've loved my best friend in past lives. I might have immersed myself in my new reality, opting out of my old life, but I'd be lying if I said I didn't still miss Jack. It hasn't been very long, and despite everything that happened between us, I did really love him.

I shake it off as I push myself into a sitting position. There's a time and a place, and this sure as hell isn't it. Besides, if Creek remembers anything about our past selves, he hasn't said anything. I'm sure as hell not going to be the first one to bring it up. Not yet anyway. It's too soon. Plus, I have way too many other things I need to focus on right now.

"Thank you, Fal," I croak, swinging my legs off the

table. I'm still a little lightheaded, but I do feel stronger than I did when I first opened my eyes.

"Anytime, sugar. I was going to swing by and find you guys tomorrow anyway, so honestly, this saves me the trip." She winks at me and beckons me to follow her toward the living room as I laugh. I can always count on Fallon to find the silver lining in literally any situation.

"What's up?" Colt asks as he and Creek follow us into the living room.

"I could use your help getting something back that was stolen from me," she starts as she settles onto her sofa. She fixes me with an intense stare, and I feel the weight of it all the way to my core. I perch on a chair near the sofa, leaning toward her as her gaze swings to the guys. "I'd do it myself, but it was stolen by a Dracul."

Shit.

"How the... Nope, never mind. What did they take?" Colt asks, shaking his head.

"My witch's talisman. It's been in my family longer than you can imagine, passed down from a great, great, great something grandma. It's old as dirt, y'all—like it's literally been in the family since the beginning. Simone Laveau created it, and she was one of the most powerful witches of all time. I can't express to y'all how powerful this thing is. Goddess only knows what those beasts want with it, but it sure as hell can't be anything good."

Fallon wrings her hands in her lap as she continues, telling us how it was stolen from her mother's store. From the corner of my eye, I can just make out the skeptical glint in Colt's eye as she explains that she'd taken it off to clean up after a spell had messed up. When she came back, it was gone. I clench my jaw as she tells us she traced it with a spell to a Dracul nest, but she wasn't willing to try to get it back alone, knowing that her power would be limited without the talisman.

"We can get it," I tell her, and Creek nods his agreement from where he stands next to my chair. I get the feeling he'd probably agree to anything I asked of him, and the thought makes me shift a little uncomfortably. "It's the least we can do after tonight."

"We are not your errand boys, though, Fallon. You'd be wise to remember that," Colt snaps, and I whip my gaze around to him. What on Earth?

"Trust me, I know all about how you Hunters rarely deem yourselves low enough to help mere witches," she snaps back at him, and my eyebrow shoots toward my hairline. Where is this coming from? "Y'know, despite the fact that our factions are allied. And don't get me started on all that expected obedience crap y'all require."

I'm slack-jawed as my eyes bounce back and forth between my brother and my best friend. He glowers at her words, she rolls her eyes, and I realize that I've missed something big between the two of them while I've been all wrapped up in my shit. I settle my gaze on Fallon, but she shakes her head subtly. I don't say anything, but I give her a look that tells her we're talking about whatever the hell this is.

"Guys, I'm super tired; we should get going," I say as I stand. Creek follows suit, but Colt and Fallon seem to be locked in a silent battle. My eyes narrow as Fallon crosses her arms over her chest and Colt's jaw clenches. I'm definitely getting to the bottom of this, but now isn't the time. "Colt."

He looks at me, and the fire in his eyes dims as he shakes himself out of whatever silent power struggle he was in with Fallon. "Sure, let's get you home."

He turns on his heel abruptly and marches out of the room. Weird."

"I'll see you soon, Fallon," Creek says with a small smile before following Colt out of the room.

"Thank you again, Fallon."

"Oh girl, shut up. There's not a whole lot I wouldn't do for you. That brother of yours, though..." she almost growls the words, and I shake my head bemusedly.

"We are going to talk about whatever the hell that is soon," I promise her, and I don't miss the way her shoulders stiffen. "I'm going to fall asleep where I stand if I don't go home and get to bed, so we'll leave that conversation for another day, yeah?"

"Go, rest," she concedes, some of the tension leaving her shoulders as her eyes rove over my body as if she's getting one last check in. "Be careful, Remy. Maybe ask one of those idiots to stay with you tonight, just in case. Even for a Hunter, blood loss isn't a joke." I roll my eyes at her mothering, but she smiles at me. "Love you, girl."

"Love you too," I tell her with genuine love in my heart. Fallon's my person, and she's stood by my side through everything "Text me that address, and I'll drag that pair out tomorrow to check it out. We'll get your talisman back."

"Thank you. Really."

"Anytime," I say as I hug her. She offers me one last smile as I turn to leave the room, heading for the truck. I'm met with two surly Hunters sitting in silence.

"I don't want to hear anything about nearly getting myself killed," I say as I slide into the backseat of Colt's truck, ignoring the small stain of blood coloring the seat as I settle in. "Can you please save your lectures for tomorrow? I really just want to go home and sleep."

"I'm staying at your apartment tonight to keep an eye on you. Blood loss..." Creek starts before trailing off, and I try to ignore the haunted look in his eyes.

"Is no joke. Yeah, Fallon gave me the speech already, don't worry. It's fine by me, you can take the spare room. But no lectures," I insist, and he nods. Colts is noticeably silent, but I let him stew over whatever's going on with him. One hurdle at a time.

We drive in silence until Colt pulls to a stop in front of my apartment. "See you tomorrow, Colt."

"I'm not around tomorrow, little bit, but I'll see you in a few days. Try and stay out of trouble?"

I roll my eyes and hug him around the seat. "I'll try."

I smile at him, climbing out of the truck as he and Creek fist bump. I wait for Creek to join me before heading into my building. I try to shove away the awkward feelings that intrude at the thought of being alone with him in my apartment. Stupid fucking memories. What use are they when they just make my life harder?

"Are you okay?" Creek asks softly as he shrugs out of his jacket and kicks off his boots. I perch on the edge of the sofa and undo my boots, ignoring the way my stomach insists on flipping as Creek roams through the living room.

"I'm fine, just kicking myself about tonight." I shrug, only half-lying. Leaving the cloak in the truck because I was too hot was *stupid*. I'll suffer the heat in the future in exchange for the protection.

"Remy, don't. This was your first hunt in this life. Your memories aren't back completely, and we weren't really expecting there to be anyone there. Especially not three older Dracul; remember, the older the Dracul, the more skilled they are. They're faster and stronger, usually more ruthless, and almost always more battle worn. Those three felt old—not ancient like the original family lines but still old. You have nothing to berate yourself about, Remy. You handled yourself way better than I did during my first hunt." He smiles down at me warmly, and I try to not read anything into it. I make a studious effort to ignore the way my name sounds falling from his lips. Just because that one memory said he loved me... When he kissed me...

My thoughts are a jumbled mess. I bite my lip to stop the tingling I feel in them as I get a little lost in the memory from a past life. I should really be listening to him rather than staring at his mouth, especially since I'm pretty sure I just heard him mention that most of the ancient Dracul lines are extinct or in hiding. Did he just say something about the head of the Dracul? I give myself a mental shakedown and force my attention back to what Creek's saying.

"On my first hunt, I froze and nearly got the Hunter with me killed. We came across a mated pair of Lycans in a killing frenzy, and I froze. It happens. Knowing these things exist and facing them are two very, very different things."

"Thanks." I smile at him, and Creek nods, his eyes roaming my body. There's an instant of heat in his eyes, and there goes my stomach again. I have to pull myself together. It's definitely time for a cold shower. I stand and stretch before saying, "I'm going to grab a shower, and then head to bed. You know this place as well as I do, help yourself to whatever."

His slow perusal of my body continues, and I fight the flush that threatens to creep across my body. As suddenly as his gaze heated, it cools when he glances at the dried blood on my arms. There's a hard set to his jaw as he says, "Night, Remy."

"Night, Creek."

"Remind me again why we're heading into a known nest of Dracul with no backup and no idea of how many there are?" Creek hisses, and I smile coyly at him. We're hidden in the shadows as we creep toward the abandoned hotel.

"Because Fallon asked us to. Plus she saved my life— we sort of owe her one." I roll my eyes at his bitching. He's been grumbling about our quick little heist ever since I mentioned it to him this morning. He's insane if he actually thought I'd just forget Fallon's request.

"We should have come with Bauer, especially with Colt out of town..."

"Bauer had his own shit to deal with, and I'm not going to leave a powerful witch's talisman in the hands of some Dracul." I shrug and move forward, pulling myself over the wall at the perimeter.

"Yeah, yeah, but it's still stupid. Mom or Dad could

have come with us," he grumbles, but I ignore him.

"I'm sure we'll be fine. We're not here to kill anyone. In and out."

"Yeah, I know. No killing unless necessary," he says rolling his eyes playfully, but then his look hardens. "They're not rogues, but they're still Dracul, Remy. Don't think you can trust them."

"I'm not an idiot, Creek. Stop treating me like a child. You don't have to come in with me." He grunts at my declaration, but I'm so, so close to leaving him outside anyway. I've had enough. "Well then shut up and back me up already."

"Fine. Let's go," he says, waving forward. I take in the building before me. I studied the old blueprints for this place at the library earlier today, learning all of the exits and as much as I could of the layout. There's always the chance that any of it could have been changed by its inhabitants, but I doubt it.

Creek glances toward the sky, and I can practically feel his reticence rolling off of him. "We don't have much time before they awaken. They might have already, which would make this suicide."

I nod at his words, taking the warning seriously as I creep across the lawn as silently as I can manage. I know there are risks, but time is paramount. We work our way around the building, finding a broken window on the first story to use as our entry point.

"I don't like this, Remy. Something feels off."

"Shh!" I glare at him.

I pull myself though the window and drop into the dark room before pausing to let my eyes adjust to the pitch black surrounding me. I pause as Creek breaches the window and listen for movement beyond the room. Though the darkness is thick, it is not so late in the day that the Dracul should stir. But after yesterday, I'm not taking chances.

I step farther into the room, and Creek follows quietly, standing close to my back. He's so close I can feel the heat coming from him, and I find my mind wandering to the old memory of his lips on mine once more. I shake myself and force my traitorous brain to concentrate on the task at hand.

He taps my shoulder, making me jump slightly, before signaling the way he's going. I take the opposite side of the room, searching as quietly as I can for the talisman. While I don't think for a second it would just have been abandoned in an easy to access room, I'm not going to leave an empty room unsearched. I think back to the picture Fallon sent me of her wearing the talisman. It's a necklace made of dark metal, twisted with intricate filigree, with a yellow gemstone laid beneath it as a pendant.

I clear my side of the room quickly and meet Creek at the door. He signals to me, indicating that he's heading just outside of the room. I nod and tilt my head to tell him I'll go left, heading to the front of the hotel while he heads further into the depths of the hall.

I watch him go, silent in the darkness, and try not to worry about sending my best friend into a pit of our enemies alone. He wouldn't have gone if he didn't think he could handle it, and I know that deep down. I trust him not to get himself killed, so I take a deep breath, exhaling slowly as I creep toward the entrance hall of the hotel.

I hear voices as I get closer, and I pause. Hunter hearing is good, but the Dracul senses make ours seem almost human in comparison. Their sight, hearing, sense of smell, speed, and brutality are almost unrivaled.

I tread carefully as I move forward, trying to work out what they're saying without being detected.

"They will come for this, Alex. Why on Earth would you take a witch's talisman, and why the hell would you bring it back here? We'll have to move the entire family now. They'll know about this place, you fucking idiot." The woman's voice, full of rage, makes me shudder. I'm glad I'm not Alex.

"We can use this," the male insists. "We have witches who rally to our cause. We've been viewed as vermin for too long. We can rise with the power of their line on our side. This talisman could help us turn the tide of the war! Lift the veil obscuring the truth, make people see what once was!"

"You're nothing but a fool!"

"Lysandra, that is enough." A dark voice ripples through the emptiness. There's a velvety sort of quality to the voice that brushes over me like a gentle caress, and I realize I know that voice. I hold my breath as my mind struggles to place the voice.

"Alexander, she's right. Taking that talisman does nothing but give the Hunters more reason to come after us. It is a beacon to the Witches; they have already traced it. Hunters are here." My stomach drops at his words. He knows we're here, and now so do the rest of them.

"We must leave!" Lysandra's voice is shrill, "They cannot get the little ones."

"We must fight!" Alex cries. "There are more of us than there are of them."

Footsteps rush into the foyer, but I struggle to focus on them when goosebumps erupt over my arms. I can feel the weight of a stare on me from behind. I turn, and my breath catches when I see a man from my memories.

"Remy?" his voice is barely a whisper, but my body reacts viscerally. I jerk at the sound of my name, and it feels as if my heart has been torn from my chest. "You're back."

"Kain?" I stutter, and his eyes shine.

"You remember."

I shake my head. "No. Not really." My stomach flips at the pain swimming in his eyes.

"You must go. Quickly. Your partner is on his way back, unharmed. I ensured it."

"Creek," I utter his name, and pain paints the man's features again.

"He is here this time?" I nod, though I still do not understand fully what's going on.

"There is no time, you must go." He pulls me close, quicker than I have a chance to react to, but my body melts against him in his arms. "I have missed you, more than you could ever imagine. But you must go."

He releases me, and my legs almost fail me, my body not wanting to leave him behind.

"The talisman..." I whisper.

"I will ensure its safety, and I will find you. I will always find you."

"But how?" I ask, my eyes widening as I finally pick up on a detail I missed before. He has elongated fangs, and a circle of amber around his iris. It can't be...

"Because a love like ours can never be broken," he says, pulling me closer and kissing me with a bruising sort of passion. It's a quick kiss, but the heat behind it steals my breath. "Now go, Remy, please. I will distract them as long as I can."

I'm numb as I circle quickly and quietly back to the

room where I entered, trying hard to not look back at the man—no, the Dracul—who made me feel so much, so quickly. I shake my head to clear my thoughts. I have never felt so confused, and I don't have time to not be on the top of my game as I spot Creek in the distance, heading toward me.

"We need to go. Now," I tell him.

"Did you get the talisman?" he asks, and even though I shake my head no, he takes my warning seriously. We slip out of the hotel and run the distance back to where my car is parked a few blocks away. We dive into the car, and I suck in deep lungful's of air, catching my breath.

"What happened?" he asks, looking me over to make sure I'm in one piece.

I somehow manage to keep my breath steady as I respond, "I heard them talking. One of them, named Lysandra, wasn't happy it was taken. I have a feeling it'll be returned. They argued, but one of them realized we were there, which is when I hauled ass back and found you."

"That's so fucking weird," he says, looking at me like he knows I'm not telling him everything.

"I'm just glad we're out of there unscathed." I smile awkwardly as I try to quickly brush past the topic.

"Are you okay?" he asks, watching me closely.

"Yeah, I'm fine. It was just a close call." I shrug and start the car. Silence descends between us, and I find myself clenching the steering wheel tightly as I think about the Dracul's kiss. It's probably the only thing that distracts me from Creek's brooding the entire drive back to my apartment.

"Are you staying again?" I ask him before we get out of the car.

"I might as well. The house feels a little weird with Dad home."

I nod at him with a smile before heading toward my building. The silence between us is a little less awkward as we climb the stairs to my apartment, and I'm glad for that at least. Still, I can feel his gaze on me as I unlock the door.

"You want something to eat before we crash?" Creek asks as I close the door behind us, shrugging off my cloak.

"I can always eat, you know that." I spin and come face-to-face with him. There's barely an inch between us.

"Remy..." his voice breaks, and I suck in a breath.

He reaches up, cupping my chin gently and forcing me to look into his bright blue eyes. I shiver at his touch, and the world falls away as he leans forward, pressing his lips to mine, so softly that I think I might have imagined it. He pulls back and sighs, before kissing me again with a hungry sort of insistence. I wrap my arms around his neck, my hands in his hair as his arms lift me, cupping my ass to bring me to his height. He pushes my back against the door, and I moan at the intimate contact.

He pulls back, catching his breath and resting his forehead on mine. "I don't know if you're ready, but I couldn't not kiss you. It's been too long, and after everything that's happened between last night and tonight..."

He trails off, and I sigh as he releases me, letting my feet drop back to the floor.

"It is too soon, but I do remember. A little at least," I tell him, and he nods, a look mixed of resignation and acceptance on his face. I am definitely going to need another cold shower after this.

"I can wait," he intones solemnly. "I'll always wait for you,"

My heart beat a little faster as he turns away. He heads toward my spare room, leaving me alone to try to figure out how the hell I can react so strongly to two different men. My heart tells me I'm not ready to face those questions yet, but I have the distinct feeling that I'm not likely to let either of them go either.

"How is it possible that you are nothing like what I was taught to believe?" I sigh, cradled in his arms, and he holds me tighter.

"Because men have long twisted our story for their own gains. I am only glad that you could see through it. That you can see the truth of who I am."

"I will always know who you are. I will always see you. I do not care what you are, just who you are. That is what matters to me. You fought for me against your own kin, and you saved me. Even though it might have hurt you. Even as their leader, you sacrificed for me. That shows me more than words from bitter old men." I lift my head from his chest and nip his jaw playfully.

"You are more than they realize, Remington. Your path will be littered with pain and sorrow. I only hope I can help light that path for you in your darkest moments."

I sigh at his words and kiss him again softly. I refuse to acknowledge that this man is meant to be one of my greatest enemies. He's a monster, they tell me—but they do not know him. They do not understand, and so, they can never know. Even those closest to me will never know to whom my heart truly belongs.

"I have something for you," he says, and the fire that roars at our feet dances in his eyes. He stands from our pile of blankets, naked as the day he was born, and I try not to stare. I fail. He walks from the room, chuckling softly and shaking his head as if he knows all about my struggles.

I wait quietly for him to return, but it doesn't take long. He flashes back in front of me with a devilish grin. "Nearly got you," he laughs, and I join him.

"Nearly." I smile, but his smile turns serious as he draws my attention to the box in his hands. "This has been in my family for generations, passed down through the line to the warriors. It's a stark reminder that even our own kind are not always our allies."

He sits opposite me and opens the box, revealing a sword, sheathed in black, laid in violet velvet that matches my eyes. "I want you to have this, Remy. It will protect you, even when I cannot. It should serve as a reminder of what you mean to me. A reminder that I am with you, even when I'm unable to reach you—in this life, and the ones to come. I know that this is not your first life, but you must know that I will follow you to the ends of the Earth in every life I am blessed to be a part of, and I will always defend you, even in those that I am not."

My heart races at his declarations and I'm speechless. I never thought that I could feel so much love for another being, and yet, I feel like my heart is going to burst. I hate that others don't see him the way I do, but I know that makes our time together even more precious.

He lifts the sword from the velvet and pulls the blade from its sheath. "My family crest sits here in the hilt, hidden from those who might hold it against you but known to those who most need to know."

He places the blade in my hand, and I'm awestruck by its beauty. "This is iridium?"

He nods at my question, and my heart soars at his trust in me. Such a blade could end his existence, and yet here he is, giving me something that is not only dear to his heart, but something that will help keep me safe from his own kind.

"Kain, I cannot accept this," I sigh as I hand it back to him.

"You can, and you will," he says, his tone brokering no argument. He places the sword back in its sheath before setting it gently on top of the violet colored velvet in the box. "You will do so to ensure that I know you will always be safe against those of my kind who wish you harm. So that I know I am protecting you, even when I can't be there myself. Please, take it for me, even if not for yourself."

His plea makes my heart skip a beat, and I nod. "For you, I will do anything."

He kisses me again, softly at first, laying me down as his body frames mine. I run my hands down his sculpted chest and sigh into his hungry kiss. I will never get enough of him. Not in a million lifetimes.

I pant as he kisses lower, dragging his teeth over my throat. "Please," I beg as my heart beats furiously in my chest.

His laugh vibrates against my skin, making me shiver. "Patience."

My chest rises and falls with every shallow breath he steals from my lungs as he maps a trail down the line of my throat and over my collarbone. I can barely think, my primal instincts taking over, with lust and love dancing together in a whirlwind of passion. His lips move to my breasts, and I gasp as he flicks my nipple with his tongue. His teeth scrape against my skin, and he cups my other breast in his hand, toying with it as I gasp. My back arches into him, and he smiles.

"Kain," I cry his name breathlessly as he works my body, stoking the fire in my core and making me slicker than I thought possible.

He kisses his way down my flat stomach, his hands sliding softly down my body to push my knees apart as he trails down. When he reaches my navel, his tongue circles the sensitive spot, teeth nipping and slightly breaking the sensitive skin there.

The sensation is overwhelming, and my body reacts instinctively. As he trails lazy kisses down to my mound, I grip the blankets with both fists, eyes tightly shut in hope of regaining some semblance of control. It's all in vain.

Kain is playing my body like an instrument, owning it as though it is his birthright. My hips push into him, pleading for more, so much more.

I know he's hard, his need is a powerful thing for his kind, yet he's taking the time to make me beg. The stories of old never give his kind any credit, yet here he is, putting my needs before his own.

"Kain, please." I do beg. For him. For me. For us.

"Not yet," he growls, "I need to taste you, and I want to watch you lose yourself."

The feel of his tongue sliding along my folds conjures a cry that surely shakes the walls. I feel him on my pussy but also in my heart and mind. I feel him everywhere, touching and loving me, worshipping every inch of me with his tongue.

I moan again as his fingers enter me, hooking them just right; but when I feel his teeth bite around my clit and his tongue lavishing that greedy little nub, I lose all semblance of control. Thrashing and begging. There could be tears falling down my cheeks as the pleasure overrides every other sensation known to our kind.

"Please, Kain. Please, now," I cry, choking on my own words as my desire takes on a life of its own.

His lips brush against my skin as he smiles. He takes one last taste, and his hard body slides its way up mine until he thrusts into me in one long, powerful stroke. His teeth break the skin of my neck as he thrusts, and I cry out. The pain heightens the pleasure, and his need mixes with my own as he gives as much as he takes. His hips move setting a lazy pace, and I lift to match it, the sensations within me building with each movement. His hands pin my wrists above my head as he takes what he wants from me, his pace increasing, his control slipping as we lose ourselves in each other. I writhe under him, hissing at the restraint and wanting to touch him. He releases me and claims my mouth in the same manner that he claims the rest of me. He edges me closer to the brink.

His kisses trail back to my breast, where he bites me again, and I cry out. I drag my nails down his back, drawing blood of my own and awakening the most primal parts of him. He thrusts into me even harder, faster, claiming me as his own. His teeth release me, and he flips us, so he is beneath me.

I kiss him till I'm breathless, and he meets me, thrust for thrust. His hand moves to my clit, and it's all I can do to stay upright. He works me to the edge of the abyss, and I bite down on his shoulder, stopping the cry as I fall over the edge. Pleasure floods my body until I can barely see, and he finds his own release.

"I love you, Remington Bennett," he whispers to me before kissing me again softly.

"I love you, Kain Michaels." I sigh as he moves onto his back beside me and gathers me onto his chest. I practically purr at the contact, sore in the best sort of way. I sleep, more soundly than I have since I discovered what I am.

FIFTEEN

I pad into the kitchen, my pajama shorts and tank barely enough to protect me from the chill, but coffee calls to me like a siren, so I find it hard to care. It's still early—early enough that the sun has barely risen—but my mind has so many thoughts running through it that finding sleep is nearly impossible.

I move to the kitchen and find the coffee pot full and a note leaned against it.

Remy,
Dad called, so I headed home. Nothing to worry about. I wanted to talk, but it will have to wait. Don't overthink it.
I'll wait for you forever.
Creek

Well shit.

I let out a sigh and pour myself a cup of coffee. After the kiss with Kain yesterday followed by my intense dream last night, I don't even know what to do with myself. I've never felt more conflicted. Because there are two men haunting my thoughts now, and my body responds viscerally to both of them. I have memories of loving them both. The fact that Kain is meant to be one of my greatest enemies? Yeah, I'm not ready to process that quite yet, but I guess my thoughts about love being love are ones I've always had.

I falter at the thought. If Kain is that different from what we're told, are all of the Dracul that way? Have I, have we all been killing innocent people? I sit on my couch and wallow in the possibilities and implications.

How is it possible that all of this is happening to me? The mess I find myself facing in this life is the culmination of my actions in my past lives, but surely I knew how I felt about Kain when I loved Creek before. Was I as conflicted then as I am now?

A low ache throbs in my head, and the pain makes me close my eyes.

This is all too much.

I just wish I could remember. Remember everything. To have everything make sense to me.

I sigh and rest my head on the back of the sofa, and

Sushi jumps into my lap, purring as he circles and lies down.

"Things used to be so simple, Sushi. Why can't things still be simple?" I mutter.

I sit in quiet peace for a moment, but it's interrupted by a knock at the door. I lift Sushi from my lap, his hiss at me a sign of his displeasure, and move to the door. I peek through the peephole and, seeing no one, open the door cautiously.

I glance down the hall, again finding no one. I start to close the door, but I notice the box at my feet. I bend to lift the dark box, fingers flitting over the violet ribbon it's wrapped with. I close the door quickly, hurrying back to the sofa and placing the box on the coffee table to stare at it in wonder.

Who the hell would be leaving gifts at my door?

My mind flickers to Jack first. This is something he would do. But if it is him, whatever is in this box probably isn't something I want to see.

Curiosity eventually gets the better of me, and I pull the black envelope from the top of the box. The back is sealed with wax, the symbol matching that of the hilt on my sword.

Kain.

My darling Remy,

I am sorry our reunion was cut short last night. Our time always feels too short. Meet me in three days at dusk. I will be where you found me. The others are gone.

Yours Always,

K

I sigh at his words, and my heart clenches at the thought of seeing him again, especially after my exquisite dreams of him. Will seeing him trigger more of my lost memories?

I pull the ribbon from the box, and it falls open beneath my touch. My breath catches as I catch sight of a black dagger, the hilt topped with a violet gemstone. Shaking my head, I lift it to inspect it. The blade looks as if it's made from the same material of the symbol-covered altar in the Hunters' headquarters. His house crest is engraved on the blade, just under the hilt.

It's beautiful.

I place the blade on the table and glance into the box, seeing Fallon's talisman peeking out from black tissue paper. I can't help my smile. He returned it, just as he promised he would.

I know I'll have to find an excuse to not be around in three days because I've made my decision. I'm meeting him, but I need to talk to Fallon first.

"Wait, wait, wait." Fallon practically squeals from her perch on my sofa. "You're telling me Creek kissed you? Twice! And you have memories of him telling you he loves you, and you haven't mentioned that to him yet? What the hell! Mind blown, Remy. Mind. Blown. I need all them dirty details, girl!"

I shrug at her outburst. It's nothing less than what I expected from her. After all, she was the one encouraging me to leave Jack and hook up with Creek. I chew my lip as I consider my next words for her. I haven't told her about Kain yet, and I don't know if I even can.

"Can I ask you a really out of this world question?"

"Out of this world is a specialty of mine, so shoot." She grins at me, which is how I know she has no idea of what's coming.

"Are all of the monsters really as bad as my family makes them out to be? Or are there exceptions? Dracul who actually feel true, human emotions? Lycans who don't just want to dominate the world?" I wrap my arms around myself, preparing for the worst.

"No, they're not all that bad." She sighs. "Just don't tell your dad I said so. Hunters are... well usually they're pretty biased. Once upon a time, all of our factions lived in relative peace. Hunters were created, essentially, to police the factions and to keep the rebels in line. At least, that's what I garner from my ancestors' journals."

"Woah." I lean back against the arm of the sofa, facing her. "Why don't I know this?"

"You honestly might, but you don't remember knowing it or whatever. It's also this CIA-level secret in the Hunter world. And let's be real, if the Dracul or Lycans were to say anything, it's not like any Hunter would believe them. They'd take it as myth or lies. Witches, we always ride the line. And you keep in mind that I'm only telling you because you asked, otherwise I'd keep my mouth shut. Goddess knows what sort of trouble I could get into for telling you this." Fallon shakes her head as she sighs.

"Have you ever... You know...?" I trail off awkwardly, and she laughs.

"Have I ever what? Fucked a monster? You're damn right I have. Like I said, Remy, they ain't all bad. There's a reason y'all hunt rogues when you first start out. That way you see the worst their kinds have to offer, so when you come across someone different later, you think it's just another lie to draw you in and get you killed. What makes you ask anyway?"

She watches me closely, and I try to keep my face straight. I try to not squirm under her gaze.

"What happened?" she asks, and I shift in my seat. So much for not squirming. I don't know about old Remy, but current Remy has never been any good at lying.

I snag the box with her talisman in it from the coffee

table and hand it to her. "Open it."

She unties the bow I redid and lifts the lid.

Her eyes go wide at the sight of her talisman nestled in the tissue paper.

"You got it back?" she asks, awe in her voice as she fingers the heirloom. "But I don't get it... What's with the box? And why the hell is it so big?"

"I wasn't technically the one who got it back." I sigh, running a hand through my hair.

"You're as nervous as a senator in church, girl. Your eye is practically twitching." She watches me closely, taking in my fidgeting form as her eyes narrow. "You tell me what happened, Remy Bennett, or so help me Goddess..."

The idle threat hangs in the air, and I clear my throat. I wring my hands in my lap before answering, "I took Creek to the address you gave me to get your talisman. And there were Dracul there, but it wasn't some rogue nest. It was a home—a vampire clan lived there. There were children and families, but they discovered we were there."

"Oh shit." Her eyes go wide, and she clutches her chest like some kind of dramatic southern belle.

"Something like that, yeah. But someone helped us escape. He delivered that, or had it delivered here, this morning."

"What the ever-loving fuck? A Dracul helping a Hunter... I've never!" She looks like I just dropped a nuclear warhead on her, and guilt ravages me. I should have kept this to myself, I knew it. It was selfish of me to want some help navigating the craziness I keep finding myself in the center of.

"I know. I mean, I have no fucking idea, but I know," I say with a small shrug.

"Who was it? Did you know him?" she eyes me, like she can sense I'm holding back the most important details.

"Do you really want to know?" I sigh, fully aware that once she knows about it, she can't unknow it. I don't want to put her in a shitty situation because of me.

"Oh, fuck off. I'm your best friend. If you're in a pile of shit, I'll be there with my waders on. Goddess only knows how your family would react. But I'm Switzerland, baby. I'm not gonna judge." She pats her black curls. I wonder if she has any idea, but I know she doesn't. She can't.

"Does the name Kain mean anything to you?" I ask her, and she stares at me, mouth opening and closing over and over again, her eyes wide. She looks like a Japanese Koi at feeding time, and I almost laugh at the sight. But only almost. Shit's too serious to actually laugh right now.

"I... Kain... Surely... Holy shit," she mumbles, struggling to find her words. She pulls herself from the couch and paces the floor in front of the large windows in the living room.

I sit silently, letting her process. Apparently, she knows

more than I do about who he is, and I've just dropped another bombshell on her. Guilt gnaws at my stomach, but I swallow down the sick feeling that floods me. This is Fallon—she would never betray me. A small weight lifts from my shoulders knowing I'm finally not alone.

She slides down the wall, sitting on the floor. Sushi jumps into her lap, purring as she absentmindedly strokes him.

"What did he look like? Because it can't be..."

"He was... beautiful, in a strange way. He had dark hair, longer on top, so it kind of fell in his eyes, which were the brightest blue I've ever seen, even with the amber ring around them. He was tall, definitely well over six foot. He was broad but not in the same way as Creek. He was more lean beneath the black shirt and pants he wore. There was just something about him. A sense of confidence in every word, in each of his actions." She's practically gawking at me.

"Did he have a ring? A silver ring with a black stone? Did you see any markings on his skin?" she asks, and I shake my head.

"I didn't have time, it was so quick." I contemplate telling her about my sword, about the dagger, but I hold it back for now. Something tells me that she's not really ready to know the whole story just yet.

"Okay, well holy shit. I think that was Kain Michaels,"

she says, and I nod, recognizing the name from my dream.

"Who is he?" I ask, and her gaze snaps back to mine.

"Wow, your memories really aren't back yet. I'm real surprised your brothers haven't given you the low down yet. You gotta ask them for a history lesson. Because holy shit, man." She runs her hands through her hair, and I notice the slight tremor. Her words are barely more than a whisper when she answers. "Kain Michaels is the last known living Dracul of the old times. Back when the factions were at peace, the Dracul were ruled by three royal families. Rumor has it that most of the old lines have been killed or are in hiding.

"Kain... is a man of legend, literally. He fought in wars that are nothing better than myths now. He's destroyed entire empires and brought down kings and dictators. He is an absolute force. The King of the Dracul is what they call him now, the last hope the Dracul have to bring peace back to their kind. To bring back the old ways. To let the other royals out of hiding.

"Legend has it that he was always the general of the Dracul. His father was a great mind, but no one could plan, strategize, and execute like Kain, which is how he became the protector of the Dracul. The other royals looked after the politics of it all—keeping the relationships up with the other factions, keeping their people fed, keeping them in line. Kain was the one who always went to war with our factions, against humans, alongside humans, whatever it took to make the world a better place."

"Sounds like you're quite the fan." I wink at her, tamping down the jealousy that flickers in my heart, and she barks out a laugh.

"The things I've read about him... It's hard to see him as the monster everyone wants to make him out to be. Then again, I've never met the guy. I only know secondhand stories. But knowing what I do about the Dracul and the Lycans, compared to the stories the Hunters spout off, I kind of admire him a little.

"Giving up everything for his kind. Rumor has it that he had a great love once, and the Hunters killed her. That's what sparked the war between the two factions, and what spiraled down to the world as we know it today. There aren't firsthand stories of it in the journals, so it could be nothing more than a story. But the romantic in me likes to believe it's true." She shrugs, a bit more relaxed.

I hum in the back of my throat, considering her words carefully. She just offered me a hell of a lot of information, and I don't know what to do with it.

"If it is him, Remy, you gotta be careful. I don't know why he'd help you. And even less of an idea as to why he would help you help me."

"It's not like I'm going to go out hunting for him, Fal. Well, I mean, you know what I mean." I laugh, hating that

I'm choosing to not tell her about his note and my dream, but something inside me tells me to guard those secrets with my life. I'm going to trust that instinct.

"Good, I wouldn't want you biting off more than you can chew. That's more than enough talk about magic and monsters. You owe me all the dirty details about what's happening with Creek! I need something a little stronger than this soda first, though."

"Help yourself." I wave toward the kitchen as she stands. Fallon plants her hands on her hips and cocks her head in my direction.

"I know you are not going to make me drink alone, Remington Bennett." She eyes me, her eyebrow raised, and I can't help but laugh.

"Fine, but I'm only having one. I'm training with Bauer again tomorrow. Apparently getting my ass handed to me this week means I need to step up my training."

"Yeah, makes sense. But more importantly, whiskey or tequila?" she asks as she opens the door to my freezer.

"Dealer's choice." I smile at her as she moves around my kitchen like it's her own, and I feel lighter, even if I am a little disturbed at the new knowledge about the man in my dreams. But I'm still left with questions because I still don't have any indication of who the man from my first dream all those weeks ago was. His voice... I can still hear it as if it were yesterday, and that voice doesn't belong to anyone I know or anyone I've met since the ritual.

I shake off the thought because Fates know I have enough to deal with right now as it is. Fallon hands me a glass before sitting opposite me on the sofa again.

"Spill..." she says with a wide grin. I sigh, ready to spill my guts about the one thing I know I can actually tell her everything about.

"We started off the same as always, with the exception of me being pissed at him for leaving. And before you start, I know he had a good reason, but you tell that to my stupid girl hormones." She snorts, and I take a sip of the liquor. It burns going down. "Anyway, things started getting better, and then there was this moment that I thought he was going to kiss me, but Colt happened."

"Fucking Colt," she grumbles, and I laugh.

"Right, and don't think I'm not going to ask more about that by the way."

She waves me off. "Don't change the subject!"

I laugh at her impatience and continue to tell her everything, all the way from the beginning. I enjoy the down time with my best friend, where I can pretend we're nothing more than two human women and that trouble with men is the biggest worry we have in the world.

I pull up to Bauer's house with a sigh, ready to enter his

hellish basement again for a day of getting my ass handed to me. I wish I had more of my memories back. I yearn for a way for me to get them back faster, to trigger a waterfall of knowledge so I could understand more. So, I understood what led me to fall in love with the king of the Dracul. Because that's what the memories I have are telling me. Could it have been a ploy? Some sort of trick? Could I have been sent to infiltrate enemy lines, to get on the inside to bring them down that way?

Or was I a traitor to my faction?

I can't imagine being a traitor, betraying my family in a way that would cause them such devastation if they were to find out. But I can't ask. Because if I did betray them and it wasn't a ploy, the fallout would be catastrophic. And if I'm being honest with myself, it didn't feel like a ploy. Not in my dreams or when Kain kissed me.

And yet, the memories I have of Creek make everything so much more confusing. The lines are so blurred, and I want to go back in time and kick past me. Because that bitch is causing me some serious headaches in this goddamn life.

I rest my head on the steering wheel and try to gather my thoughts, so that Bauer doesn't suspect something is wrong. The last thing I need is him prying, trying to work out what's wrong with me.

I push it all down into a box that I visualize chaining

up and shoving into the very back of my mind. It probably doesn't do a damn thing, but it makes me feel better. I gather myself and climb out of my car to find Bauer opening his front door. I briefly wonder why he has this place, considering he still lives with Dad, but I guess everyone needs their own space sometimes.

"You okay?" Bauer asks as I approach, looking concerned as he leans against the doorframe, arms crossed.

"I'm fine, just tired. I guess nearly dying will do that to a girl." I shrug, but immediately regret my words as the look on his face grows stormy.

"Well, I'm going to see to it that that doesn't happen again We'll be training hard, and a friend of mine from the other side of the world happens to be on his way here for business, so he's going to help us out too." He steps back, letting me into the house and then shuts the door. He joins me in his kitchen after a moment.

"Who is he?" I ask, curious because Bauer having mysterious friends isn't really something I expected. He's always been a bit of a loner.

"He's someone I trust with my life, and yours too. I met him when I first became a Hunter. We trained together, went hunting together. Traveled a lot. You thought I was off at college, but I was off seeing the world and killing the filth." I hold in the wince at his tone, his words, and smile at him.

"Oh, wow, yeah I totally didn't link you being at college with this craziness I've been so wrapped up in my own stuff, it hadn't even crossed my mind. Sorry. So, who is this friend?"

A car pulls up outside, and Bauer smiles, heading back to the front door.

"Bauer, man it is good to see your ugly mug." The laughing voice reaches me, and I watch out the window as a man who looks roughly the same age as Bauer walks up to the house.

"It's been a while, Archer. Come on in." I hear the smile in Bauer's voice and lean on the counter as their footsteps move down the hall.

"Archer, meet my pain in the ass little sister, Remy. Remy, this is Archer Doturo," Bauer says as he walks in, Archer in tow. The stranger studies me from across the room. He's as tall as Bauer, so around six foot four, but not quite as broad. The look suits him. The main difference is the air about himself that he carries. My hackles rise, and my internal warning bells go off. This guy is bad news. How does Bauer not see that? I smile through my panic and wave.

"Nice to meet you, Archer." He nods back to me, and I can see him trying to measure me up with his stare. Seriously though, how does Bauer not feel this tension?

"Likewise, I'm sure." His British accent comes off as

blunt, so I'm sure Bauer doesn't think anything of it, but his entire facade puts me on edge.

"I'm training with Remy today, I figured you wouldn't mind helping out. Two minds are better than one," Bauer says with a manly tap on Archer's shoulder, and Archer looks me over again.

"Training the legendary Remington Bennett. I'm sure the honor is all mine," he says. "We've not had the pleasure of meeting, in any lifetime, but I have heard more than a little about you, Remy." His smile doesn't reach his eyes.

I try to smile at him again. "Well, let's hope I don't disappoint the legend of my past."

My snark rattles through, and Bauer looks at me funny, as if telling me to stop being so rude. But I can't seem to help myself. He's already under my skin, and he's barely been here five minutes.

"Let me go change, and I'll join you."

"Awesome man, we'll be down in the basement. You're staying in the room up the stairs, at the end of the hall on the left. Make yourself at home."

"Thanks, I slept a lot on the flight over here, so I'm ready to go." Archer nods at me before leaving the room, and only a second passes before Bauer storms over to me.

"What was that?" he asks, his voice an angry whisper through gritted teeth.

"Something about him isn't right, Bauer. I can feel it."

"He has saved my life more times than I care to count, Remy. Your instincts are all over the place at the minute while you adjust to Hunter life and your memories fall into place. Keep yourself in line. This is the one and only time I'll say it." I step back, unused to his anger being aimed in my direction. I get the feeling I don't know the whole story here.

"I'll try," I say, not willing to promise anything just yet.

"Good. Let's go," he grits the words out and stalks over to the door that leads down to the basement, nearly ripping it from its hinges. Jeez, he's touchy today, and I get to train with that now. Yay me.

I lie on the floor and groan. Since training with them one-on-one hasn't apparently broken me enough, they want to try and train me together. Their reasoning? Dracul and Lycans rarely travel alone. How fun for me!

They're currently conferring in the kitchen, talking about how they're going to continue my torture... sorry, training. If I wanted, I could use my Hunter hearing to find out what bullshit they're planning, but honestly, I'm too kind of exhausted. I'm suddenly grateful that my speed, hearing, and sight upgrades were something I just took to. I didn't have to learn to switch them on and off. Running around like the Flash probably would have created some questions somewhere along the line.

My body shouldn't ache this much. Hunter strength and healing is meant to make me feel amazing, or at least, that's what Colt told me. Either he lied or Bauer is just trying to prove to me that I can still hurt, I can still die, and I need to learn how to fight properly. I need to know how to keep myself alive and not ache like I just went eleventy-billion rounds with Tyson.

I groan as I sit up, crossing my legs and bowing my head. I feel the stretch on my spine as I pull forward, teeth gritting with the low ache there. I go through the motions of the stretches I used to do after a hardcore dance session, and loosen my muscles, preparing myself for the next onslaught.

Their voices grow louder as I drop into the splits and lean my body down my right leg, enjoying the burn of the stretch. "You about done?" Bauer asks, and I turn my face toward him, leaving my forehead resting on my knee in the stretch.

"Just about," I smile sweetly, knowing it's going to piss him off more. I find it hard to care after he's been such a jackass all morning. I sit up and twist, mirroring the stretch on the opposite side and feel their eyes on me.

Surprisingly, Archer wasn't as much of an asshole this morning, a pleasantry he left fully to Bauer. But something about the set of his jaw as he watches me makes me think that's all about to change.

"I hear you've had a few run-ins with the Dracul so far?" His voice floats across the room to me as I pull out of the stretch and stand.

"Yeah, Colt said their activity has been up lately, that there's been more gathering near here, so I guess that's why." I shrug and grab my water bottle, guzzling down the cold nectar.

"Well, something is happening, because the Alpha of Alphas is here. We tracked his movements from Europe, though we've lost him in the last few weeks. But we know he was traveling in this direction, so Bauer wants us to try some other techniques in case you come across Dracul and Lycans together."

"That could happen? I thought factions kept to themselves for the most part?" I ask, my gaze bouncing between them.

"So did we," Bauer says with a grimace. "No one seems to know what the fuck is going on, but we need you to be ready for whatever is coming. Our family holds this territory, and I'll be damned if we let the monsters overrun our home."

"Okay, I guess we better get to work then," I say with a nod. Despite the panic rising in me over my broken memories, I can't let it show. I can never let it show.

"After this, we're heading to the gun range, and you're coming with," Bauer orders, and I shrug. It's not like I have anywhere else to be today.

"Whatever you say." I bounce on the balls of my feet as I track their movements. They separate, circling me on the mats.

I barely have the chance to take a breath before they both lunge for me, and I relax into the calm I've noticed that settles over me when my adrenaline and fury runs high. My thoughts shut down, and my body takes over as I dodge fists, ducking and rolling, hoping to pit them against each other, though I know that isn't likely to happen.

Bauer throws a fist toward my ribs, and I jump back into the waiting arms of Archer. His hold tightens, and I struggle to escape. I bring my elbow back into his gut and swing my fist down into his crotch. I stomp on his foot and then charge at Bauer as his friend falls to the mat.

I spar with Bauer, but he's faster, stronger, and better trained than I am. We parry, but I don't get a chance to land any decent shots before Archer roars behind me, running toward me. I don't hesitate and jump as he reaches me, flipping backward over him as all of his speed and rage crashes into Bauer. They fly backward into the wall.

I smile from my crouching position on the floor. Holy shit, I can't believe that just happened.

Laughs and groans come from the pile of limbs across

the room, but I stay planted, waiting, wondering if they're going to attack again. Adrenaline floods me, and I feel a spark, the joy of the hunt, and I'm glad Bauer isn't letting me train with my weapons yet. My fingers itch for a throwing blade. To finish the job. My instincts can't quite make out the fact that they don't actually want to hurt me.

"That's enough, Remy," Bauer's voice calls across the room as he and Archer approach me slowly. "Pull yourself out of it."

His voice is calm, soothing. They both watch me, eyeing my stillness as I calculate their movements. "Come back to us, Remy."

I close my eyes and shake it off, remembering where I am and that they are not the threat my body is telling me they are. I take a deep breath. I sit back down on the floor, and they start to come closer, still slowly enough to not trigger whatever it was that was driving me.

"I've never seen it. I thought it was nothing but some make believe tied to the legends," Archer says, almost in shock as they sit opposite me.

"Seen what?" I ask, tilting my head at them.

"When you fight, when you truly give yourself over to it, you get what legend calls The Wild. You slip out of yourself, and you become little more than your instincts with the ability to tear through legions without a second thought. What just happened was just a very, very small hint of it. I've rarely witnessed it, but those times you slipped into it, using it in battle, both against human and monster, have helped change and shape the course of history," Bauer says cautiously.

"You make me sound like an animal." I roll my eyes. Everyone keeps talking about my past; and since I have no idea about it, it does little more than make me cringe.

"Not an animal. A weapon, one of the greatest in the Hunter's arsenal. And now with your angel mark..." Archer's voice trails off, but his eyes almost glow with the possibilities. The alarm in my head goes off again. I don't want to be a weapon for the Hunters. I want to be myself.

"I am not a weapon," I tell him gruffly. "I am a person. And how the fuck do you know about my angel mark?" I cross my arms and shoot an accusatory look at Bauer. He has the decency to look guilty. I purposely didn't put my hair up to keep it covered, and I have a long-sleeved crop on to hide my arm since the vines now dangle toward my elbow. The mark appears to have stopped growing, but that's beside the point.

"Word has crossed the globe about what happened after your ritual. Yet another myth that appears to be true. What is it about you, Remy, that makes you so special?" he asks, and the calculating look on his face sends a shiver down my spine. Bauer seems to catch on to my unease and stands.

"My sister always has been a little different, but she's just the same as you and me. I'm going to throw some food together, I suggest you guys shower and change, then we'll head to the range." He holds out a hand to pull me up, and I take it while Archer gracefully stands.

"I don't have anything to change into, I'll just go like this." I motion to my workout gear. Leggings are truly a girl's best friend. "I am definitely up for food first, though." My stomach rumbles at my words, and Bauer laughs. Archer still just seems to study me.

A CROWN OF BLOOD AND BONE

SIXTEEN

I close the door to my apartment, wanting nothing more than to fall face first onto my bed. This day has been the absolute longest. Between the training, the gun range, and dealing with Archer being creepy, I don't think I've ever been so exhausted. He was quiet at lunch, and left me and Bauer to it at the range. I worked my way through so many different guns it was hard to keep track. While I do have my own guns, I need a good range of knowledge. And it turns out that so much has changed with the weapon since my last life, I need the training regardless.

I also signed up for a Krav Maga class that Fallon emailed over to me. I mean, why the hell not? At least it won't be my brother kicking my ass.

Sushi wraps himself around my ankles as I lean against

the door. My muscles protest as I pick him and his bowl up to feed him, and he meows. I bury my face in his fur as he purrs, and finding comfort in my cat makes me feel more human than I have in a while. I laugh at how ridiculous I sound in my own head and fix his dinner before looking in the refrigerator to find something for myself. I scan the bare space and sigh. Takeout it is, I guess.

I rummage through the junk drawer that holds the Holy Grail, the takeout menu stockpile that I've managed to collect. It's not that I eat out often, but sometimes, takeout is the only thing that's suitable.

I dial for the local Chinese, because Ming's is by far the most superior Chinese food of all time and try not to drool as I place my order.

I drop my phone on the counter after ordering and pad toward the bathroom. Looking in the mirror, I notice how tired I look, and yet my skin almost glows. I lift my top over my head and pull my hair to one side as I try to take in my new marking. It looks like a freshly inked tattoo. No wonder the boys are completely covered; The marks aren't exactly inconspicuous. Maybe I can get my whole arm done, work something into what's already there to hide the rune-like symbols that intertwined with the vines. The more I look at them, though, the more familiar it looks, almost like a map I think I've seen somewhere before. A memory tickles at the back of my brain, but no matter how long I look at it, nothing comes to me. Sighing, I turn on the shower and finish undressing before stepping underneath the hot water. Breathing in the steam helps to clear my head.

I don't think about anything as I stand under the stream and just be, letting the water wash everything away. A bang pulls me out of my stupor, making me jump. I dash out of the shower, wrapping a towel around myself confused. My food shouldn't be here yet. I rush to my front door, peeking through the spy hole to see the back of someone. I open the door, keeping the chain engaged considering my current state of dress, and peer through the gap.

"Sorry, I totally spaced. You guys were super quick tonight," I ramble, but when the man turns, I realize he's not holding my food.

"You're not the delivery guy," I say warily, wishing I'd put on more than my towel.

"No, I'm not." He smiles at me, the look almost feral.

"Can I help you?" I ask, and he looks through the gap, his smile growing at my state of undress.

"I'm sure you could." He winks at me, and I try not to gag. No thank you. "But that isn't why I'm here. I'm here to give you this."

He reaches into his leather jacket and pulls an envelope from it, handing it to me through the crack in the door. I'm reluctant to take it, but I reach for it anyway. To be offering something so small, the man opposite of me seems so menacing.

"Nice to see you again, Remy," he says before turning and walking away, leaving me wide-eyed at my door. I come to my senses and slam the door shut, my heart racing.

What the actual fuck?

I throw the envelope on the counter as if it burned me. Who the hell was he, how does he know me, and how the fuck does everyone seem to know where the hell I live? I run my hands through my wet hair and pace, contemplating opening the small envelope.

"Fuck this," I mutter, and turn all of the locks on my door, understanding why Bauer insisted on installing so many now. I check the windows to make sure they're all secure and head back to the bathroom. I finish my shower, and dress, coming back into the main room as another knock sounds at the door. My body stiffens, still on high alert, wondering where the next threat is coming from. I move to the door, as quietly as I can manage and look through the peephole again. A spotty teenager waves a bag of food in front of the glass greets me, and I roll my eyes.

Way to overreact, Remy.

I undo all the locks and open the door, smiling at the kid as he hands me my food, and I grab my wallet from the counter, paying and tipping him much faster than usual. I slam the door shut and click the locks back in place, no longer hungry.

I contemplate calling Creek or Fallon. Even Bauer, but I have no idea what's in that envelope, and knowing my luck, it's something else that I won't be ready to share with everyone yet.

Fuck my life.

I sigh and plonk myself down onto the sofa, trying to ignore the envelope on the counter. Is one night of peace really too much to ask for? Flicking over to Netflix, I put on The Vampire Diaries, laughing at the irony of it all. I settle in to binge watch the show, trying not to focus on the shit storm that is my life until I fall asleep.

The light flooding through my windows wakes me, and I groan at the crick in my neck. That's what I get for falling asleep on the sofa, I guess. I stretch out before lying back down. Sushi makes himself comfortable on my stomach.

The envelope from last night flashes across my mind, and I sigh. Of course I couldn't rest, why would my mind let me have even a moment of peace? Though I'm not going to lie, binge-watching television last night was a great distraction. I can already tell it's definitely going to be a new coping mechanism of mine. Apparently, vampires on TV aren't anywhere near as terrifying as they are in reality. Though that Elena chick seems to have as many issues in her life as I do right now. I roll my eyes at the amount of drama it all equates to.

I almost miss my simple life with Jack. Just for a second, regret fills my heart at the decision I made. It leaves almost as quickly as it came, but I let myself wallow a moment longer.

This would all be so much easier to navigate if I just had all of my memories. That's when I remember I'm supposed to meet Kain tomorrow evening.

Shit.

I wonder if he will tell me more about my past.

Or will he try to protect me from it all? My skin heats at the thought of his kiss, at the memory of my dreams of him and our time spent together in them. The pieces I've stitched together in my mind tell a story of a passionate, all-consuming love. The type of love you see in movies, but all I have are pieces. I struggle to make my mind believe what my heart tells me—that I've loved him for a long time.

Conflict wars inside of me between my heart and my mind. Between what I feel and what I've been told. The thought haunts me that I might have lied to my family and betrayed my faction. And yet I was the one who said love is love. What if everything I've been told is all lies, like Fallon hinted at? What if the Dracul and the Lycans are more than what we are told to believe? Even in my first life, I was led to believe that the war between the factions had been going on for ages. Can history really be changed so easily? And why would we want to change the truth of our past?

I close my eyes against the intrusive thoughts. How can I possibly begin to comprehend the enormity of it all without all of the information? But I fear that there is no way to get all of the information. Even if the knowledge exists, who would risk the wrath of the Elders of the Hunter faction to tell me the truth?

I might hear a version of the truth from Kain if what Fallon read is true, but can I trust him?

My mind feels like it's going to explode with all of the questions running through it.

Fuck this.

Knowledge is power, and I do know one place that might have the knowledge I crave. My dad's library. Even if it doesn't have everything I seek, maybe I can learn more about myself, about the mark I carry, and who the hell Leviathan is. Maybe that will at least give me some idea of where to begin.

I jump up, and rush to change and brush my teeth before grabbing my keys, my new mission at the forefront of my mind.

I pull up at my dad's place, but the house is dark, which is weird. There's almost always someone here. But then again, Colt is away doing Fates only know what, and Bauer is busy with his asshole friend. I guess Dad is out, so as I slide out of the car, I'm thankful I still have my own key.

The porch steps creak as I make my way up them, which makes me realize just how unnaturally quiet it is here. I listen harder and realize there's not even the sound of insects. A strange sense of foreboding fills me, and I rush into the house. That's when the smell hits me.

Blood.

I race toward the smell, trying not to scream when I find him lying on the floor in the kitchen, blood pooling around his prone form. I pull out my phone, dialing Fallon's number with shaking hands. She answers on the first ring as I kneel beside my dad, checking for a pulse. It's there, but it's weak. What the fuck happened here?

"Fallon, I need you to get to my dad's. Now. Hurry." I disconnect the line without further explanation. There's no time. I call Bauer on speakerphone as I tear my shirt to create a tourniquet for the wound on his thigh.

"Remy, what's up?" Bauer asks, the noise around him is so loud I can barely hear him.

"It's Dad. You need to get here. Quickly. There's so much blood."

"I'm coming, Remy." The panic I feel rushing through

my body comes out in his tone as he continues, "I'll call the others."

"Fallon is already on her way."

"You did good, Remy. Just hold on." The line goes dead, and I turn my attention back toward my dad's prone form. I try to assess where the other blood is coming from.

"I've got you, Dad," I say, for him as much as myself. I tear open his shirt and find two bullet wounds. I place my hands over them, trying to stop the bleeding as much as I can, and pray to every god I don't believe in that help arrives soon.

Memories flash through my mind. There's so much blood. So much death. I try to focus on my breathing, try to focus on keeping my dad breathing. It feels like a lifetime until I hear the screech of tires followed by footsteps thundering toward me.

"Holy shit," Fallon gasps as she kneels next to me, blood coating her knees as she does so. "There's so much..."

"Fallon, take over for Remy on that stomach wound. Remy, you press just as hard as you can on that shoulder wound, you hear?" Fallon's mom, Marie sweeps into the room, and I can almost feel the power rolling from her. Relief fills me, because if anyone can help my dad, it's Marie Laveau. She kneels on my dad's other side and places a hand on my shoulder.

"This thigh tourniquet might just have saved his life,

Remy. Well done." She undoes the tourniquet, and blood spurts from the wound. "Whatever hit him got an artery."

She places her hands on top of the wound and starts muttering under her breath, the words foreign to my ears. Light fills the space beneath her hand, and I feel the power in the room. My neck heats in response to it, itching and burning, but I try to ignore it and keep my hands on my dad's shoulder.

"Remy!" Bauer's voice calls out, and two sets of footsteps race toward us. When Bauer and Archer find us, my shoulders slump. I've never considered myself the damsel in distress type, but I don't know that I've ever been happier to see my brother. He kneels on my other side, placing his hand on top of mine. "I've got this, you can let go. You did good."

His voice is so soothing, and I feel someone at my shoulders peeling me away while Bauer takes my spot. I glance up to find Creek behind me, Maddie and Nate standing in the doorway. Creek pulls me into his arms, and I give in to his embrace as the shock sets in. He leads me to the kitchen, Maddie following behind us, and they help me clean up as best I can.

"Do you know what happened?" Maddie asks softly as Nate appears from the other room.

"He's healed, but he lost a lot of blood. Marie got the bullets out, but they're not a metal I recognize." Anger coats his words, but it's worry that lines his face.

"What does that mean?" I ask.

"It means that the tides are turning. Someone found a material that Hunters aren't resistant to. If it wasn't for Marie..." His words filter away as he shakes his head against the unspoken implications. "What happened?" He pins me with a stare, and it burns into my soul.

"I don't know," I tell him truthfully and hang my head as Creek runs his hand up and down my back, trying to soothe me. "I came over to dive into the library, to try to encourage my memories to return. When I got here, it was deathly still and quiet, and I just knew something was wrong. I rushed in and found him like that, which is when I called Fallon and Bauer."

"That was quick thinking, and you must have remembered something from your training because that tourniquet saved his life. Whoever did this must have left just as you got here—otherwise it would have been too late."

Marie and Fallon join us in the kitchen, cleaning up their hands before joining me and Creek at the table. Marie regards me with a solemn look before saying, "His wounds were grave. We've gone and healed them the best we can, but the strain on his heart from that much blood loss... Only time will tell if what we managed was enough."

"You can't heal his heart?" I ask, confused.

"We are not healers, though we have some healing ability. A true healer may be able to help, but depending on how long it takes one to get here..." Her words trail off as Bauer and Archer join us in the room.

"He's in his bed. We cleaned him up and sorted out as much as we could," Bauer says, his eyes not leaving mine. "Did you see anything?"

I shake my head, wishing my answer were different. That I could help in some bigger way. "Do you think this was one of the factions?" I ask, the words barely a whisper.

"Of course it was." Archer scowls.

"But what about…" I start, but Archer cuts me off.

"Those filthy, mangey animals did this. Why on earth would you think otherwise?" The venom in his voice is unmistakable.

"I just wonder how they got their hands on a new weapon?" My words hang in the air, and silence surrounds us.

"I guess we'll have to wait for your father to wake up to tell us what happened," Nate says, calling an end to the conversation. "Thank you for your assistance, Marie, Fallon. As always, you have our gratitude."

"It was our honor." Marie nods to him. "Our family have long been friends to the Bennetts and Winchesters. We will always assist when we can."

She stands, Fallon mirroring her pose. "We're headed

out, but if you need anything, just call."

"We will," Maddie says, hugging her tightly. "Thank you."

"I'll call the Elders to let them know what has happened," Nate says and heads outside.

"Are you okay?" Creek asks me softly, drawing small circles on my back.

"I don't know," I tell him honestly.

I want to be strong. I want to be this legendary person they all expect me to be. But I'm not the person they think I am, at least not right now. Right now, I'm scared, terrified that my dad isn't going to survive, scared that I might have been the cause of this somehow, and scared that if they discover the truth, I'll lose everything.

Eventually, everyone leaves except for Creek, who helps me clean up the blood from the wood floors in the kitchen. I scrub as if each stroke can undo what happened. As if it can take back the fact that my dad is upstairs, fighting for his life and there's nothing I can do to help him.

"He's going to be okay," Creek says softly, looking at me as I sit back and huff, blowing a stray piece of hair off of my face.

"I hope so," I tell him, and my voice croaks around the words. "How do we deal with this so often? So much death?"

"You just do, and after a while, you get used to it. Once your memories settle, you'll understand."

"And what if this wasn't one of the other factions? You and Colt both said something about shady shit going on with the Elders."

"The Elders would never do something like this. There aren't enough Hunters in the world as it is. It's hard enough to keep afloat above the flood of Dracul and Lycans. They would never dare give our enemies the weapons they need to win the war we've been fighting for a millennia."

"But how do you know?" I press, hoping for any hint that this could be something else.

"I don't," he says, shaking his head. "But until your dad wakes up, we won't know the truth. I need you to not focus on the who right now. What were you looking for when you came here?"

"I was searching for answers. About my past, at least. I always see Bauer pouring over so many books, so I wanted to try and find some stuff out for myself. Did I ever keep journals?"

His eyes go wide at my question, and I shake my head.

I guess that's another question I shouldn't be asking.

"Never mind." I sigh. "I'm going to head up and grab a shower, then head to bed. You don't have to stay. I can keep an eye on Dad," I tell him as I wring out the last cloth.

It finally comes out clear rather than pink.

"Don't be stupid, Remy. I'm not going to leave you alone. Not now, not after everything that's happened. You don't have to be this strong in front of me. You can lean on me like you always have. You can trust me," he says, the sincerity in his eyes is like a punch to the stomach. Because if he knew everything, I'm sure he'd turn his back on me too.

"I'm not trying to be strong, Creek. I'm just coping the best way I know how. You can stay if you want to." I sigh, standing up and stretching out after being on my knees for Fates only know how long.

He stands up and steps toward me, so close I can practically feel him brushing against me. "Remy, please. Don't shut me out. Even if nothing else, we have been friends our entire life. Even if you want nothing more from me, let me be your friend."

I look up into his eyes and find nothing but compassion and understanding. My guilt overwhelms me, and the tears I've been trying to hold back spill over. He wraps his arms around me, holding me tight.

"He's going to be okay, Remy. Your dad is a tough son of a bitch." His words only serve to make me cry harder. Why did past me have to screw present me so hard? Why did I have to see Kain, and why is Roman here?

There's so much I don't understand, and what happened

here tonight just adds to a pile that feels like it might topple at any moment.

I pull away once I've steadied my breathing and have my tears under control. "Thank you," I tell him, and he smiles at me before kissing my forehead.

"I'm always going to be here for you, Remy. Even when you don't want me to be. Even when you think no one else has your back. I will be here."

Why does he have to be so damn sweet? I hug him tightly one last time before heading upstairs to check on my dad, who is still sleeping deeply. I jump in the shower, trying to wash away today as much as I can, and the sounds of Creek puttering around downstairs comfort me. Deep down, I'm glad he didn't leave. Exhaustion so deep I can feel it in my bones sets in, but I know I wouldn't sleep if he wasn't here.

A CROWN OF BLOOD AND BONE

SEVENTEEN

Morning comes, and despite my exhaustion, I barely slept. The fear of something going wrong with my dad, or whoever was here returning and hurting him or Creek, kept me up. I yawn as I descend the stairs, jumping when I crash into Creek at the bottom.

"Sorry, half dead here," I murmur as he steadies me, his hands on my waist. My cheeks heat at the realization that all I have on is a nightshirt that comes to just below my ass. "Erm... I need coffee... yeah, coffee."

I see the moment he realizes what I'm wearing, my words barely register with him. His grip tightens slightly as his eyes take me in slowly, inch-by-inch. My nipples pebble under his intense, heated stare, and his sharp intake of breath tells me he noticed. My blush deepens. Nope, no matter who we were, the thought of him and me like that still seems so confusing, no matter what young teenage me dreamt of.

"Remy." My name sounds like a plea on his lips, and my body tells me that I want so much more than settling for just being friends. I learn forward and brush my lips across his cheek. It's the gentlest of kisses, and he stiffens under my touch.

"Morning," I whisper before pulling back from him. While my body might be ready, my treacherous mind is still whirring about a million miles a minute trying to make sense of everything else. I remember that I'm meant to meet with Kain tonight, and it steels my resolve to not make anything messy here. There's too much left unanswered for me to give into my baser urges.

"Morning," he rasps, letting go of my waist and taking a step back.

"Thank you for staying last night." Pretending that nothing just happened might be the only way to keep my sanity in this situation. I make my way into the kitchen and pour myself a coffee. I put some bread in the toaster as he follows me in.

"It's fine, you guys are family, and you needed me whether you wanted to admit it or not. I checked in on him this morning, and he's still asleep. He has a slight fever, but otherwise he's okay. Bauer called; he'll be over in a bit so you can head home for a while."

"Thank you. I have to head to the bar later to pick up my stuff after my Krav Maga class, but I can come back after." I smile as I take a sip of my coffee.

Oh, hello sweet nectar.

"Okay, Colt is on his way home. He wasn't due for another week; but with everything happening, he cut the trip short."

"Where is that brother of mine?" Nobody has said much about it, which only makes me more suspicious.

"No idea. But it has to be pretty far away if it's taking him a few days to get home."

"Makes sense. I wonder what on Earth he's up to."

"Who knows? The Elders obviously have him chasing something down and will likely be furious if he hasn't retrieved it even with the circumstances. He has a knack for tracking stuff down, so that would be my best guess." He shrugs and grabs my toast as it pops up. I slather it with butter and groan as I take a bite.

"Something about toast in the morning is just freaking orgasmic." I sigh, before demolishing the rest.

"You need to look after yourself better." Creek eyes me with concern. "When did you eat last?"

"Just now." I roll my eyes at him. "I'm fine. I'm going to check in on Dad and then go head first into the library. Are you sticking around?"

"No, Dad wants me back at the house. I'm guessing he wants to find out who did this sooner rather than later. We both know he won't wait for an official investigation. He doesn't have the patience." He runs his hand through his long, dirty blond hair, gathering it and putting it into a man bun. That particular look, combined with his beard and his ink, makes me squirm. Why, oh why, does he have to be so damn hot these days?

He smiles, like he can read my mind, and I stifle a laugh.

Nope. Not today.

"I'll see you later then?" I ask as I head back toward the stairs.

"Sure, let me know when you're back here, and I'll swing by to keep you company again."

"Thanks. Oh, what do you know about that Archer guy?" I ask as an afterthought, and he raises an eyebrow at me.

"Not too much, why?"

"No real reason. Guy gives off major asshole vibes, and something about him seems off. I don't trust him. Plus, he shows up out of the blue with almost no warning, and then this happens to Dad... I just, I don't know. Something doesn't add up to me. It feels wrong."

"Trust your gut, Remy. It's never steered you wrong before. If you don't trust him, I believe you. I'll ask my dad about him later, see if I can get any details on his family."

"You're the best." I smile as he reaches the front door.

"I know. Catch you later, Remy." The door closes behind him, and I sigh as his footsteps leave the creaking porch and crunch across the gravel in the front yard.

If life were simpler and there weren't so many strings left to unravel, it would be nice to indulge in the feelings growing between us.

I make my way up the stairs and pop my head around the door to my dad's room. He's still out cold, and he looks so pale and fragile. I check his pulse, just to settle my nerves, then leave him to rest. I know he wouldn't want me hovering and fussing, even though he nearly died. Stubborn old goat.

I throw on a pair of jeans and a t-shirt before heading to the third floor. The entire floor is nothing more than a library and a bathroom, and I used to get lost in here for hours at a time when I was younger, reading about adventurers, slaying dragons, the Fae courts, and people with magical powers. If only little me had known what I do now, she'd have wondered less at the magic of it all.

Adult me? She's just trying to survive the process.

I head to the back corner where Bauer usually hides and pull random titles from the shelves. I have no idea where to start, but any knowledge is better than no knowledge at this point. I flip through the pages of some, and skim the contents, trying to trigger something inside of me to remember.

Finally, I pick up an old leather-bound book. It's soft to the touch and looks as if it's been read more than a few times. Untying the leather strap that keeps it closed, I open it and realize this is a journal. I scan the page, and I realize it's one of Bauer's.

I close it since reading it would be such an invasion of privacy. But at the same time... Maybe it will tell me something about myself?

No.

I shake my head and put the journal back where I found it. I won't do that to him because Fates knows I'd lose my shit if someone did it to me. I just wish I knew where I kept mine. I pick up one of the other books, *The Myths and Legends of Angels* it reads, and the mark of the Hunter is stamped on the front beneath the title, but there's nothing else. I open it, to find yellowed pages and handwritten script, though there are many styles, as if several people have added to the book to pass along the growing knowledge.

I lose myself to the book, taking in the stories, the adventures and the battles of old, including the story of the creation of Hunters. It started with the fall of the Archangel of War. A great general of the angel legions, Leviathan. He betrayed their laws for the good of his people and was punished for it. Those who followed him, who believed in his actions fell alongside him and were left to roam the Earth, unable to return to Avalon, the realm of angels.

My heart hurts for the general. He did what he knew he must, no matter the cost and regardless of the consequences, to save the ones he loved.

I sit back and close my eyes. What happened to the angel, and why do I bear his mark? Did I pick up his cause, betray the laws of the factions for a greater cause? I sigh and rub my eyes. I need to find out how to trigger more memories, yet I dare not ask the Elders. With all the warnings from Colt and Creek and what's happened with Dad, I don't trust them, even though I'm told I should. I wish Mom were here, she would know exactly what to say. I like to think she wouldn't condemn me for my past choices too. She'd understand that the heart does what it wants. She always said that your heart was your greatest tool, the best guide, and the most trustworthy of advisors. That to follow your heart was the right path, no matter the obstacles you face.

I rest my head on the table, wishing she were here with me, and my heart is heavy. She would have been the best at helping me acclimate to this world. Patient to a fault, she would have explained everything, answered all of my questions, and been the best guide when I needed it. She would have picked me up when I faltered, no questions asked.

"Remy, you here?" Bauer's voice echoes through the house, and I sigh.

"In the library," I call out, knowing now that I don't have to shout for him to hear me. The stairs creak as he makes his way up to me, finding me in his corner with books scattered around me and my head on the table.

"You okay?" he asks, sitting opposite me. "This is some heavy reading."

He lifts the books, chuckling at some of the titles I pulled out.

"I just wanted to find a way to possibly trigger some memories. I hate not knowing everything—being in this limbo. I feel like I'm trying to do a jigsaw puzzle but half of the pieces are missing," I groan, and I hate myself for it. I've never been so whiny.

"I get that. Fates know we've all been there, but sometimes there is no way to trigger them. They either come or they don't. Is there something specific you're trying to unlock?" He looks at me, sincere, and I'm positive he doesn't suspect the truth.

"Kind of, but I don't know exactly what's going on, so I don't even know where to go to trigger it," I half-lie, deciding that tonight Kain is getting a whole barrage of questions, whether he wants them or not. Even if he can't answer everything, hopefully filling in the gaps will help some things make more sense. Even if it's only a little, it might nudge me closer to the truth of things.

"Well, if there's anything I can do to help, just ask; and if I can answer, I will." He smiles at me and pats my hand.

"Do you know where I hid my journals?" I ask him, hopeful, but not expecting an answer really.

"I don't, sorry. You were always very protective of them. We even tried a treasure hunt once when we were bored to try to uncover the truth, I honestly have no idea. Sorry."

"It's okay, it was worth a shot." I shrug with a smile.

"How's Dad?" he asks, standing with me.

"About the same," I tell him as we head back downstairs. I've been up here for hours barely moving, and I feel it. Sitting, pouring over books is not something I do very often.

"Well at least he's no worse." He breathes a sigh of relief, and I feel a tinge of guilt that I've not been more concerned, yet again wrapped up in my own drama.

"I'm going to head home for a bit and then to my class. I have to swing by the bar and pick up my stuff after, but I'll be back tonight, okay?" I say, echoing my earlier words to Creek.

"Yeah, that's fine. I've cleared the next few days so I can be here. You don't need to worry about coming back if you have stuff going on." He smiles and pulls me in for a bear hug. I sink into him; the comfort and safety offered by my big brother has always been the same. Always my protector. Always looking out for me.

"Thanks, Bauer, I'll text you and let you know if anything changes; but if not, expect me back." I grab my stuff from beside the door, along with a bag of laundry I found by the washer. "I'm taking the laundry with me; I'll get it done at the apartment and bring it back later."

"Thanks, Remy." He smiles at me, and I wave as I leave.

I wonder if he'd be so thankful and understanding if he knew where I was really heading tonight.

EIGHTEEN

The shadows wrap around me like a second skin. While Kain said to meet at dusk, the sun was hidden today so darkness came in quickly. Having checked the perimeter, I walk toward the abandoned hotel straight up the front steps. I slip in through the huge wooden doors as quietly as I can.

The entry hall is a big open space with stairs on either side of the room. I realize this must be where I heard the Dracul when I was here before. I step forward, and the wooden floor creaks beneath my feet, making me flinch.

"You came." Kain's voice echoes through the room, and I look up and see him standing on the first-floor mezzanine. My heart races upon seeing him, and I wonder how I didn't remember him fully. I know I recognize him on a deeper level.

He moves slowly as he walks down the stairs, meeting me in the middle of the room. I gasp as he caresses my cheek, cupping my chin as he joins me. He's so close to me it's hard to figure out where he ends and I begin. My hands reach for his arms almost instinctively, his muscles jump beneath my touch and his eyes almost glow.

"I did not know if you would." His words caress my skin, and I sigh as he lowers his head and kisses me softly, just a whisper of his lips upon mine. "I missed you, *mon amour*. It feels like it has been forever since my heart last felt yours."

He rests his forehead against mine and pulls me tightly into his embrace. His scent fills my nose, and memories of our time together flood me. The laughter and the love, but the darkness too. The secrets, the hiding, the fear.

"I remember," I gasp. "So much... and yet..." Words escape me. There are still so many holes, but one thing that is perfectly clear is that loving Kain was not a choice. Loving him was something that swept me up and carried me away. Loving Kain made me realize that so much of what I was raised to believe wasn't right.

"My first life... you were there... You showed me the truth."

"As I will always do, my love. You brought me back to life. Our meeting in Paris is one of the fondest memories

I have, and I will cherish it for my entire existence. I have searched for you every life you've lived since then. I have always found you, and I always will." He kisses me again, and I feel it in every inch of my body. My toes curl at the tidal wave of love that sweeps through me, and I tangle my fingers in his hair.

"You cut your hair." I smile. "It was longer when I saw you last."

"It was, but these modern times called for a change. Much about you has changed, but you are still my Remy."

"I don't understand... There is so much still missing." I've just gained a whole load more new memories, and yet I'm more confused than ever.

"I know, and I wish I could answer all of the questions I know you have, but I cannot. You always told me that I should not. Not until it was time, and not enough time has yet passed."

I frown at his words, but I can feel the truth of them. "Past me is a pain in my ass."

He chuckles and pulls me into his arms again. "You say the same thing in each life, *mon amour*, but each time, you are thankful for it. Eventually, at least."

"How did you find me?" I ask, hopeful that he can at least answer that. He pulls back and leads me over to one of the sofas in the corner of the room, sitting, but keeping contact with me, as if unwilling to let me go again.

He loosens the collar of his shirt and pulls a necklace from it that looks suspiciously like the talisman of Fallon's. The only difference is that the gemstone is red. "This was made for us, by Antoine Laveau. It contains your blood, and it heats when your life is started anew. It always takes me time to reach you, and sometimes your life is at a point where I cannot make myself known to you, but I am always there, even if only in the shadows to guide you. To help where I can." His eyes are sad, and it breaks my heart. "At least I have found you now before it is too late. This life, I will not let you go as easily as I have before. I have missed you too much and searched too hard. Darkness is coming, and I will not let you be taken away by it."

I sigh at his declaration. Sure, this explains the dreams, but the feelings I have for Creek do not make anything any easier for me. I'm also curious about what he means by *darkness is coming*, but that's something else for future Remy to deal with.

"I know your heart does not belong solely to me, and I made my peace with that long ago." It's uncanny the way he can read my thoughts. I shudder against him, and he pulls me close. "But if you will let me be a part of your life, let me back into your heart, I will love you and treasure you with all I am. Protect you with every tool at my disposal." He kisses me again, and I lose myself in him, forgetting any and all questions I might have in this moment. I barely take a breath when he lifts me, so I straddle him. His hands roam my body, lighting a fire in their path.

"I have missed you so much I cannot say, but you cannot stay here, Remy. It is not safe for us." His words brush against my lips between kisses, and they bring me back to reality. I sigh. "Believe me, I dislike this as much as you do."

His hardness beneath me is proof of his words. He cups my cheek gently, eyes searching as he says, "I have somewhere unknown to those who would betray us, but you should know that has Roman arrived here. I know you and he... have history." His face shutters, unreadable, and I realize that there must be more to my history with Roman than the dream suggested. "I should not say anything, but I do not know why he would risk coming here. Not with the Elders still gathered and with my clan having declared the territory. It is highly unusual. I am still waiting to hear from him, but I want you to be prepared if you come across him or his kind."

"Thank you," I tell him with a small smile. "My brothers told me the Dracul hold a substantial presence here at the moment. Is that you too?"

"It is not. I came here because of rumors, ones that I hope cannot possibly be true. It was a happenstance that we crossed paths, but I have never been so thankful to the fates for it."

I frown, because rumors that strike fear in the heart of the King of the Dracul—the warrior who built civilizations as easily as he tore them down—is certainly a threat to be afraid of.

"Is there anything I can do? Can I help?" I ask. His blue-eyed gaze meets mine, and his eyes soften.

"Not yet, my love. I do not wish to put you in any more danger than you're in until you are ready. You will kick me at that point for protecting you, I'm sure, but I will take the punishment. You are my heart, and I will always protect you, even from yourself." I sigh, and lean forward, my head on his chest.

"We must not linger here, but I couldn't go any longer without seeing you. Can I see you again?" He strokes my hair, and I melt against him once again.

"Of course, but I need to tell you, that Creek... he and I... it is complicated," I mumble quietly. I can't quite get my words out in complete thoughts.

"It is always complicated, *mon amour*. I do not wish to share you, but if the only way I can have you is to do so, then I will."

I shake my head, the thought of it seems impossible. To love them both. To be able to have them both. I mean, as far as ideas go, it's not the worst I've ever had. But Creek would never... he would never accept that I could love someone that he hates so much. Right?

I say nothing, just taking comfort in his arms for the small amount of time we have left together tonight.

"We must go, Remy." He sighs, though his arms tighten around me.

"Okay," I agree, but I have never felt more unwilling to leave. "How will I see you again?"

He smiles down at me as I lean back, and he pulls a cellphone from his jeans. "Modern technology is a wonderful thing."

He passes it to me, and I put my number in. My phone pings seconds after handing it back to him.

"Now you can reach me whenever you need." He smiles before leaning forward and kissing me softly once more. I sigh as we part, and he lifts me with ease to my feet, standing swiftly as he does so.

"I will leave first to ensure it is safe. Wait two minutes before you leave behind me." He runs his thumb across my lips, and his eyes flash with heat. Then in an instant, he is gone.

My heart thunders as my brain swims with this new knowledge, the love, the pain, all of it. It threatens to overwhelm me, but I take a deep breath and shove it down. Later. I'll deal with it later.

I'll find time so I can sift through everything, but for now, I have to get myself together. I wait the two minutes he requested before I leave, walking on silent feet back to my Mustang. I pull the keys from my pocket and unlock the car. A breeze rushes past me, his scent hits my senses, and I know that was his goodbye. That he kept me safe even when I didn't realize. Just as he promised he would.

I pull the car to a stop in the driveway at my dad's house and rest my head on the steering wheel. So much happened tonight, even though it felt like so little actually transpired. Chunks of my memory still float just out of my reach, and I can't help the frustration I feel over it. The guilt from my selfishness reaches up and hits me as I realize I haven't thought about my dad once since I left here earlier in the day. I groan and shake off what I've learned tonight. My dad needs me, even if he's still unconscious. I need to get a grip on myself. My family has always been there for me, helping me even when I didn't want or need it. The least I can do is be here and be present, rather than being wrapped up in my own shit.

I climb out of the car, taking a deep breath as I do and head into the house. I can just make out voices in the kitchen, so I head that way. I find Bauer and Creek sitting around the table, talking in hushed voices.

"Remy," Creek says, seeing me first and giving me a heated look that would make any girl swoon. Bauer's head flicks in my direction, and he gives me a taut smile.

"What's wrong?" I ask wearily. "Is it Dad?"

"Oh, Fates, no. Dad's fine," Bauer says quickly. "But we did just get news from Archer. Roman Knight has been spotted in the city, and nobody seems to know why."

I feign shock and sit beside them. "Roman Knight, Alpha of Alphas, right?"

"The one and only," Creek says, and fear flickers in his eyes. It disappears a second later, but I tuck it away to look into later.

"Have you guys met him before?" I ask, looking between them. Bauer shakes his head, but Creek nods.

"Just once."

"And he still lives?" I ask, knowing that the opportunity for any Hunter would have been too great to pass up on.

"It's complicated." His voice strains before he empties the rest of the glass in front of him.

"I won't ask," I say, and he relaxes a little. "Besides, I get the impression that questions are not the way forward." I laugh, and Bauer shoots me a look. I stick my tongue out at him, and he shakes his head at me as I continue, "What? Every time I ask a question, I get told to wait. So, I'm waiting, kind of."

"Only you would hear that Roman Knight is in town and shrug it off like I just told you what's for dinner," Bauer says while rolling his eyes at me.

"Well, I mean, he hasn't caused any trouble yet, or

you'd have said something. And since the Dracul activity is up in town too, it's pretty obvious that something is happening. Maybe we need to dig a little deeper. Maybe I can look into it?" I offer, shrugging my shoulders as if I'm doing this for them and not just making an excuse to meet Roman. I mean, it's definitely for both reasons, but they don't need to know that. Plus, Dad seems to be okay, so I don't see how offering my help could hurt.

"Not a chance in hell, Remy," Creek says, gripping his glass so tightly I'm afraid it might shatter. "You're still going through your awakening. He'd chew you up and spit you out."

"Oh, shut the fuck up." I roll my eyes, and they both gawk at me. "What? He doesn't know that I don't have all of my memories back. And it's not like I was suggesting I just walk up and knock on his door, announcing myself. I was just going to poke around. I want to be useful, and you guys keep pushing me back. I get it, you want to protect me, but did you ever think that maybe I don't need you to protect me? I've heard stories and remembered even more at this point. I might not have everything, but I know for sure that I'm not some goddamn helpless freaking fairy princess who needs to be locked in a fucking tower."

I hadn't realized how much it was getting to me, everyone trying to protect me. As much as I appreciate where they're coming from, I'm starting to feel stifled.

Like they're trying to clip my wings.

"Well, I guess more of the old Remy is back than I realized," Bauer says with a frown. He stands from the table and leaves the room without so much as a backward glance.

"What crawled up his ass?" I ask Creek, who's looking at me like he doesn't know where to start.

"Remy, Bauer has seen you rush into things more times than he can count, and while you're literally a legendary figure to the Hunters, you're still his little sister. He's nearly lost you too many times. He might have only been around for six of your twelve lives, but he feels the loss of you each and every time. He's the cautious brother. He thinks before he acts, unlike you and Colt who act first, consequences be damned."

"Oh." I don't know what else to say, especially when he seems so disappointed.

"Yeah, so maybe try not to rush into danger so much before you *really* remember. I know it goes against your nature and against the very grain of who you are, but with your mom gone, your dad already riding the line, and Colt not here, Bauer is really struggling. Even more so now with this new Hunter killing material that no-one seems to have a clue about."

"I didn't know," I say quietly and reach over, finishing the whiskey Bauer left behind.

"I know you didn't. You have a tendency to get a little wrapped up in your own head, and that's fine. We love you, and we wouldn't change a thing about you. Usually, you're wrapped up because you're trying to keep one of us out of the line of fire, but just for now, take it easy? Don't go rushing off into the night, okay?"

"I can do that." I sigh. Fuck my life. Poor Bauer. I'm such a selfish bitch right now, and I kind of hate myself for it. "Is there anything I can do here?"

"No, Bauer has everything handled. Just be here for him, especially until Colt comes back." I nod at him and slump in my chair.

"Sorry."

I sigh again, and he puts his hand on my thigh. "Don't be sorry, Remy. Just know that you have people counting on you and watching out for you, even when you don't want it."

I nod, taking him in as we sit in the dimly lit kitchen. He looks so, so tired, and I ask, "Are you okay?".

"I'm fine, I've just been helping Dad look into the material in the bullets we pulled out of your dad. No one's heard a whisper about it, and its composition is so strange."

"I'm sure your dad will work it out." I smile and squeeze his hand.

"I hope so because the other factions are deadly enough as it is. With this at their disposal, they could wipe us all from the Earth and wreak havoc until we begin to cycle back." His head droops, his chin resting against his chest, and it hurts me to see him so harrowed.

I stand and wrap my arms around his shoulders. He turns, burying his face in my chest, his arms tight around me. A shudder runs through me, and I wonder again how I can care so deeply, react so extremely, to both him and Kain.

Despite Kain's declaration that he would share me, I know I will have to give one of them up. I'm not sure I could ever choose, and I sure as hell couldn't be with them both and lie to them. The lies and secrets I carry are bad enough already.

I stroke his hair and hold him until the tightness in his shoulders subsides. Creek has always been a sensitive soul. So strong and willing to carry the burdens of others, but he's always been unwilling to let others carry the weight on his shoulders. It's a privilege that he still lets me be that person for him.

"You should sleep," I tell him softly, and he pulls back from me. My heart flutters as he looks into my eyes.

"I could say the same about you."

"I will, once I check on my dad and Bauer."

"Fine," he says, pushing his chair back and standing with a groan. I follow him up the stairs, trying my best not to over appreciate the man in front of me when it seems so inappropriate. But Fates above, I only have so much strength.

"Stop checking out my ass," he laughs softly, and I swat it.

"Shouldn't have put it in my eye line if you didn't want me to ogle." I match his laugh with my own, smiling at his back.

He walks down the hall to the bathroom, and with one final glance at him and that ass, I go the opposite way to my dad's room. The door is already ajar.

I walk into the silent room to see my dad with more color in his face than he had this morning. I smile, thankful that he seems to be healing quickly. With the bullet matter unknown, we're not sure how long it will take for him to heal fully, but I have hope that it won't be too long. My dad is a fighter. He won't let something like this keep him down for long.

I take his hand and sit with him in the silence for a while, enjoying the peace of being able to be here with him.

When I feel myself drifting toward sleep, I put his hand back by his side and make my way to Bauer's room. I knock but snores answer me. I sigh, sorry that I missed him. I'll apologize tomorrow for being such an ass.

I head to my room, not bothering with the light when I enter. I kick off my chucks and strip down to my tank and panties, undoing the ponytail in my hair and sighing at the relief that simple action brings. I slip beneath my sheets before I realize I'm not alone. I hold my breath, but I realize it's Creek, and he's already asleep on top of the comforter. He must have been waiting for me.

It is not the first time he's slept beside me, and I don't want to disturb him. He looks peaceful for once, so I turn over and close my eyes, the soft sounds of his breathing lulling me into a deep sleep.

NINETEEN

When I wake, the heat is stifling. I groan, remembering that I'm not alone. Creek is the source of the heat, wrapped around me like my own personal cocoon. I smile, even if I am uncomfortable from the heat. I try to lift his arm to get up, but he groans and pulls his arms tighter.

"Go back to sleep," he murmurs, burying his head into my neck. I shiver at the feeling of his lips on my skin, goosebumps covering my entire body.

"Maybe I don't want to sleep," I whisper back to him. He pulls me even closer, and even with the comforter between us, I can feel his hardness digging into my back.

"Do not tease me, Remy." His voice, full of sleep and all gravelly makes my pussy clench. I might have told him I wasn't ready and implied that it was too soon, but my traitorous heart seems more than ready to move on from Jack. I realize then that what I felt for that man wasn't true love. It felt nothing at all like the way I feel for Creek. For Kain.

I shift in his arms, turning to face him. He maneuvers so that he is under the sheets with me. I run my hands up his bare chest, feeling the muscles below tense at my touch. I leave them there to rest between us, and I can feel his heartbeat beneath my hands. His eyes close at the contact, and he leans his head toward mine, so close I feel his breath on my cheek.

"What are we doing?" His words are so soft, almost a plea. I answer him with a kiss, and his lips devour mine. He moves us, so that he is above me, and kisses me with so much passion, it steals my breath. He traces kisses to my neck as he grinds down into me, and I bite my lip to stifle the groan that threatens to escape. His hands move upward, lifting my tank, and I pull up slightly so he can remove it. He throws it to the floor before his hands and lips are back on me.

"Creek," I gasp as he marks a path down to my breast— kissing, licking and sucking, and I know he's marking me. Laying his own claim, in a place few will ever see. His mouth moves to my nipple, and I tangle my fingers in his long, wild hair.

His hand moves slowly, softly down to my wetness,

and I gasp as his fingers stroke my clit as his mouth sucks on my nipple.

"Holy shit." I can't help but grind against his hand at the sensations his ministrations pull from me. His fingers work me into a frenzy, not relenting until I topple over the peak he led me to. He quiets my release with his mouth over mine, swallowing my screams.

He pulls back and looks down at me with a panty-melting smile. "Morning," he says softly, and there's a tenderness in his eyes that makes my heart stutter.

"Morning," I mumble with a blush. He rolls off of me then and pulls me into his embrace, leaving head resting on his chest. I lie there, not knowing what to say, since we just blew past the line I'd tried to draw in the sand to keep anyone from getting hurt. To keep things from getting even more complicated than they already are.

"Stop overthinking it, Remy." Creek laughs underneath me. The sound rumbles through his chest, and I smile at how well he knows me. Maybe it will be okay. Just maybe it will all work out, and so for now, I'm going to push the worries away and enjoy this.

I reach down and cup him. He's hard as steel beneath my fingers, and his sharp intake of breath only serves to widen my smile.

"You don't have to, Remy. That's not what this was."

"Hush," I say, kissing him gently again. I trace my

fingertips back down his chest and slip my hand beneath his sweatpants.

Commando. Interesting.

I tease the tip of his cock, hard and warm beneath my touch. I love the way he feels, the way he reacts to me. I slip from his grasp, and pull down his sweatpants, revealing him to me. And holy mother of all that is right with the world. He felt huge beneath the material, but to see his dick up close and personal.

Just wow.

I move down the bed, sitting between his legs. I lean down and swipe my tongue around the head, stroking him as I do. His breath hitches, and he groans as I take him into my mouth, his sounds encouraging me.

He holds my hair and guides me further down onto him until he reaches the back of my throat, making me gag before letting me up for air. My eyes water, but the shudder that runs through him excites me enough to do it again. I let his hand guide my head down as his hips thrust up, and I delight in how lost he seems. I look up at him because I want to see him as he comes undone, and I find his hooded eyes staring back at me like I'm his queen.

"Fuck, Remy." He tries to lift my head, but I keep sucking his thick cock until he empties himself down my throat with a shout. I swallow and lick my lips, smiling up at him. He sits and pulls me up to him until I'm straddling his waist, and he kisses me again so softly.

We sit in comfortable silence until I hear movement downstairs.

"I think we woke your brother," Creek says, and I can feel his awkwardness already.

"If we did, so be it. I'm pretty sure my brother isn't a saint." I shrug but pull myself away from the comfort of his lap.

"I'm going to jump in the shower, want to come wash my back?" I ask with a cheeky wink.

He groans and rubs a hand down his face. "You little temptress."

He looks conflicted, looking to the door and then back to me. He seems to make up his mind as he leaps from the bed and scoops me up into his arms, making me squeal.

"I will never get enough of you."

As is par for the course lately, this day has been exhausting. After my extremely nice wake up this morning, my day spiraled. Not wanting to leave the house, Bauer had us all running drills and circuits on the land behind it. I don't remember the last time I sweated that hard without it being fun.

My body is now sore and not in a good way. I slip down onto my sofa with a sigh. Colt texted us all earlier to let us know he'd be back tomorrow, but with no more information than that. He still didn't offer a reason as to why he up and left, either.

My mind whirrs as my body sinks further into the cushions below me. I kick off my shoes and curl up, despite knowing I need to move. There are things I need to do, especially since Nate and Maddie have been the only ones patrolling since my dad's accident, but I can't muster the energy to worry about it.

My phone vibrates on the table, and I groan.

Please don't be important.

I lift my phone and see Kain's name. Maybe I should have been more discreet with his contact info, but no one really pays attention to my phone except for me.

I miss you, mon amour. Not long until I will see you again, however Roman's arrival is causing problems. A gift for you, to remind you of me until we meet again.

K

The text makes me smile even if it doesn't all make sense. I drop my phone onto the cushion next to me when a knock sounds at my door. I stand, stretching my sore muscles as I move toward the door. I open it just to come face to face with nothing but air. I look down and see the small black box wrapped with violet ribbon sitting on my doormat. I reach down and claim it, shutting and locking the door behind me.

My phone buzzes again on the couch, but I ignore it and look down at the small ring box, my breath shallow. I untie the soft ribbon slowly, drawing it out, unsure if I actually want whatever is in the box. I lift the lid and gasp at what sits there. My fingers trace over a black obsidian wishbone ring that has a pear-shaped amethyst set in its center.

It's beautiful. I lift it from the box and slide it onto my index finger, and the fit is perfect. It's such a thoughtful gift, with elements that represent us both. The obsidian represents his greatest weakness, and the amethyst for my eyes. I go back to the sofa and pick up my phone to thank him just to find another message from him.

A treasure for my treasure.
One I have kept for a millennia and gifted you a dozen times. I hope you like it as much in this life as you have in your others.

K

This ring has been mine longer than I remember. The fact that he kept it safe for me makes my heart burst with sudden emotion. It's such a small thing, but it's representative of so much. I lie down, my mood suddenly plummeting.

How on Earth will I choose between Creek and Kain when the time comes?

I take a deep breath, deciding that now is not the time to worry over it. Fates only know how many other things I have to juggle right now as it is. I head to bed, leaving the window open for Sushi to return when he sees fit.

I run through passageways so dark that I can barely see my hand in front of my face, but I let my instincts guide me. The sound of steel on steel rings out in the distance, and I push harder. If I don't get there… I don't want to think of what might happen.

The air whips past me as I move as fast as my body will carry me, barely more than a shadow to mortal eyes. That's when I hear the roar, and I fear I am too late. Lights flicker in the distance, and I know that I am so, so close.

I hurtle forward and crash into the room, finding the two of them locked in battle. Their movements are equally fast, and I know that each is as strong as the other.

I can't let them kill each other; my heart couldn't take it. I watch, waiting for an opening to bring an end to the madness. I rush forward, knowing this will be the end of me in this life, but I also know it's a sacrifice I would make time and again.

I reach them and in seconds feel the blade pierce my heart. For a moment, everything stops. Not a soul breathes as they realize what has happened.

"Remy, no!" Creek catches me as my knees fail and falls with me, cradling me in his arms.

"What did you do!" Roman roars, pulling at the dark locks of his hair.

"Stop, please." My words pierce the air as blood trickles from my mouth. "Stop this madness. You cannot kill or blame each other. The choice was my own."

"I don't understand," Creek says as Roman paces in front of us before crumbling to the ground on my other side.

"My mate…" his hushed cries cause tears to well in my eyes. Creek's gaze snaps to Roman.

"That isn't possible," he grits out, before looking back down at me. "Tell me this isn't true, Remy."

He pleads, and I know he doesn't understand. He couldn't possibly, and yet I beg him to try with my eyes.

"Nothing is impossible in our world, Creek," I say and rest my hand on his cheek as tears stream down his face.

Roman lifts me from Creek's arms and cradles me against his chest.

"Where are the Witches? We must get her to one," he growls. "Your foolishness and bigoted hatred will be the death of her."

"There are none. They fled when your kind came to the town. Her death is on your hands." Creeks words are laced with venom, and I wince.

"Stop it, please. Just stop. You both live in my heart, and I could not choose, so I chose myself. Either of your deaths would have broken me, but you're both stronger than me. Try, please, to mend the bridges that were burnt by our ancestors. Learn, as I have, the truth of it all." I try to breathe, but my heart stutters in my chest, failing me.

"Remy, no." Creek's voice breaks as Roman kisses my forehead.

"Go now, my mate. Suffer no more. I will find you again."

A CROWN OF BLOOD AND BONE

TWENTY

The call came in as I was brushing my teeth. The message was simple. Get my ass home.

Fucking pushy asshole men.

Sure, I might have woken up on the wrong side of the bed this morning with the red mother dropping by to say hello. Yeah, I'm cranky. I don't appreciate the summons or the dictation of my movements, especially when I had plans. Those plans included getting real cozy with my couch, getting a little closer with the ice cream bucket in my freezer, and streaming the latest season of Vampire Diaries. How *dare* they summon me.

All of this just because Colt is home. It's not about Dad, he's the same as he has been. I checked first thing this morning before I planned my perfect day. But *no*, Colt, the freaking douchebag, stomped all over my plans.

Am I whining? Hell yes, I am. Am I going to apologize for it? Abso-fucking-lutely not!

I rinse my face and shut off the taps before pulling my mop of hair up into a messy bun on the top of my head. They should be thankful I got dressed and put a goddamn bra on today. Makeup can suck it.

I feed Sushi and grab my phone and keys before heading down to the car. The smell of the vintage leather when I climb in calms me a little, but I still feel the irritation, burning like bubbles beneath my skin. I love this car. I close my eyes and rub the steering wheel while taking a deep breath. I am not willing to sacrifice my baby because I'm in a shitty mood and end up rear-ending some asshole on the way over to my dad's.

I swear, if they don't have breakfast waiting...

I put the car in gear and ease out of the spot, cranking the music up so loud I can barely hear myself think. It's the only way to spend this journey because the more I think about the summons, the more pissed off I'm going to get. PVRIS fills my car with their haunting melodies, and it's almost enough to lift my mood, especially with the hint of fall just beginning to peek through. The leaves are finally turning to those beautiful shades of brown and red rather than just green.

I wind down the road to my dad's house and turn off

into the drive, slowing as my tires crunch on the gravel. By the time I reach the front of the house, I notice the three other vehicles already parked there. All trucks big enough to tout the masculinity of their owners. Bauer. Colt. Creek.

Awesome. A full house.

I park and take a minute to tamper down my irritation as much as I can. Don't get me wrong, there's no doubt that if they piss me off today, I'll fly off the handle. Considering all of my fun new skills, it definitely won't end well. So, I try a breathing exercise from my new meditation app and try to visualize the unreasonable rage draining from me.

After a few minutes, I climb from the car and head inside the house, only to hear more voices than the three I expected to find. I stroll through the house to the kitchen but don't find anyone in our usual spot, so make my way toward the family room. When I step into the room, the voices stop.

"Holy shit, it's my Remy girl!" The man, with skin so dark it almost glows, practically runs toward me and lifts me into his arms spinning me in circles. I hold on tight, not willing to be flung across the room. What the hell is this madness?

He lets me down, squeezing me in a tight hug before noticing how stiff I am.

"She's only two months into her awakening, Gabriel," Colt says behind us.

"You don't remember me yet?" he asks with a pout, and I shake my head.

"Nope, sorry." I shrug and take a step back, noticing several other faces that I don't recognize in the room. "What's going on?"

"What's going on is my bestest, baddest, bitch doesn't remember me," he huffs. "Rude. Well, I'm Gabriel. Nice to see you again, I guess."

I laugh at him because he's outrageous but obviously amazing.

"Obviously, I'm the freaking worst. But seriously, what's going on?" I look at Bauer who's standing at the front of the room, wondering why no one let me know what the hell was going on before I rocked up in here.

Colt moves his head, motioning for me to meet him in the back yard. I leave the room, leaving everyone in there still looking at me like I'm some show clown.

"What on Earth is this, Colt?" I hiss.

"This is a gathering because the faction activity in Salem's Bay is getting out of control. These are people our family have trusted for an eon. I thought Dad would be awake by now, that it would be okay to bring them here to help."

"Is that why you left?"

He shakes his head and runs his hands through his hair.

"No, I left because we have reason to believe that two

faction leaders are coming here, and the Elders wanted to know why. No one seems to know, and that dickbag Archer is here now tracing the Lycans. There's too much going on, and no-one seems to have a fucking clue why." I gulp at his words but shake off my unease.

"This is insane, you know that right? I thought I was meant to tread lightly these first six months, so that I don't seize and die in an overabundance of memories or some other crap. And yet, you bring all these people here. People who obviously know me, or at the very least know of me if their stares are any indication. And all the while, I'm in the middle of my freaking awakening. Great idea, Colt."

"I didn't have a choice, Remy. There are too many of them, the Lycans and Dracul, gathering on the outskirts of our city. We needed a force in case things get bad. Especially with Dad out of action. There aren't enough of us here to go up against these sorts of numbers." He paces on the porch as I lean against the house. I roll my eyes.

"And what about the Elders? Are they concerned about helping us right now? Or are we just disposable to them?" The words are sharper than I intended, but the resentment in them rings true. Colt's head whips up to meet my gaze and he rubs the back of his neck, picking his words carefully, and I realize I'm getting more of my old self back.

"Remy, we've had this conversation more times than I can count. The Elders explain their actions to no one."

"Just because that's the way it's always been, doesn't mean that's the way it should be. How much more are they keeping from us? What else are they hiding?"

"Enough, Remy," Bauer says sternly as he steps out onto the porch. "We will not go through this again. Not right now. We have more than enough to deal with."

"Fine. I'm going to check in on Dad," I say, and move past him and into the house, trying to keep the rage that's simmering just below the surface in check. As I climb the stairs, more things begin clicking into place. My inherent dislike of the Elders, my impatience over no one ever questioning what we're told. I begin to understand why it was so easy for me to fall in love with Kain, and with Roman if last night's dream was a true memory, which they so often are these days.

I sit on my dad's bed next to him. I wish I could just talk to him about it all. But the problem with remembering is having memories of how he didn't believe me. Or how he wouldn't listen to me, refusing to believe there was anything wrong with our ways or our unyielding laws and belief systems. They're out of date and just wrong, but I've never been able to make him see that.

Yes, some of the Dracul and the Lycans were out of hand. Yes, some of them attacked humans, hunted them, and kept them as pets. Those are the ones I would hunt to the ends of the Earth. But the others, the ones who just wanted to live their lives with their families, experience the ever-changing world in all its wonder, are the ones I refused to hunt. If not outright to the Elders, then at least in my own way. Would I find them? Of course, I'm good at what I do. I'm one of the best. But would I slaughter them when they have done nothing more than be born or made into a faction that wasn't my own? Not a chance.

I pushed for us to be better, trying to bring others to my way of thinking without risking a blade through my heart or the true death. But so many refused to see the truth, even with the world as accepting as it was among the humans in that lifetime, I could see it still in the Hunters I met. That unwavering faith, the belief that the monsters are nothing but filth, pests to be exterminated to create a better Earth. It's a belief that persists to this day, with my brothers, my father, and even Creek.

In this instance, I'm glad the Hunters struggle to conceive. Our numbers don't grow much or quickly, which might be the only thing keeping their ideal of extermination from becoming a reality. I'm positive the council of Elders, with their barbaric ways, would push for it if they had the opportunity.

It hits me then, the reason for the extra Hunters.

It is not a precaution but rather an opportunity for extermination. I scramble to pull my phone from my pocket and pull up Kain's number. I try to call but am unsurprised when it goes to voicemail.

You need to get your people out. Quickly. Hunters are gathering.

R

I send the message and pray that his pride doesn't get in the way of protecting his people. I don't understand why he would bring his clan with him on a hunt. The warriors, yes, but the women and children? Were they as fierce as the men, yes, but so many would be put at risk. Maybe my thoughts are draconian, but having lost my mother, I can't think of a worse fate for a child to exist without their own, regardless of who or what they are.

It changes you.

I take a deep breath and try to calm my racing heart.

"Remy?" I open my eyes and gaze at my dad at the sound of his voice.

"Dad? You're awake! Holy shit. I'll get you some water, hold on." I jump from the bed and rush to the bathroom, grabbing a glass of water. "Bauer!" I shout as I rush back to the room. I help my dad sit up and then hand him the glass.

"Sip it," I scold him when he takes a gulp, and he glares at me over the rim but changes to sips of the water regardless. I might have issues with my dad, but that doesn't mean I'm not glad he's awake.

Footsteps bang up the stairs as Bauer, Colt, and Creek barge into the room.

"You're awake," Bauer says, stepping forward.

"Have I been out long?" he asks, his voice still croaking after being asleep for so long.

"Not too long, a few days," Bauer answers him. "What happened?"

My dad's eyes harden, and his entire body shudders with rage. "We were betrayed."

After Colt got the other Hunters settled in a hotel in the center of Salem's Bay, he came back with Nate and Maddie in tow. While he was gone, Bauer helped Dad about, getting cleaned up, while I sat and talked with Creek. I didn't mention the dream. Because if it wasn't a dream, if it was real, then I'm sure he already knows, and I have no idea how to tackle that. I don't know if we've ever discussed it before, in lives between then and now, and it's making me feel anxious as hell.

"Are you okay?" Creek asks me, watching me closely as I nurse my cup of coffee.

I let out a huff and blow some hair off my face. "I'll be fine."

I hope the answer is enough, but I don't have to worry

because Dad and Bauer appear in the kitchen, where the rest of us sit, waiting. Being watched and analyzed was not on my to do list today, hell none of this was, but I can't be anything other than happy that my dad is finally awake.

He makes his way across the room, shrugging off Bauer's helping hand. Bauer moves behind him like his shadow, just in case.

"I am not decrepit, boy. I can walk," my dad scolds, but Bauer rolls with it.

"I never said you couldn't, old man. But you've been out cold with no food for days, the likelihood of you falling is real, and considering how long you've been healing, I'm pretty sure you don't want to be sidelined again because you fall and break something." Bauer bites back, and I catch my dad's smile before he wipes it away and sits down at the head of the table, exactly where he should be.

Creek jumps up, and starts rummaging through the fridge, as if he knows the greatest help he can offer at this time is keeping us fed. The room is quiet for a few moments, with the exception of Creek's movements in the background, while everyone waits for my dad to speak.

"Have you found out what they used to injure me?" His gaze roams through the room, meeting each one of ours in turn until settling on Nate.

"Not yet, but I'm working on it. I've been using limited resources, keeping everything on the downlow because I didn't know who attacked." My father nods at his words, and now that I know more, it makes sense that we kept this mainly in house. I also understand why Colt was touchy about Dad still being asleep with the other Hunters here.

"I brought the Bellos back with me from Africa. We need more manpower here with the recent surge in numbers, and I thought they would be best. Abel agreed to come," Colt tells him, and my dad nods.

"Good idea. They have been friends of ours for many years, I do not believe they would turn against us now."

"You said we were betrayed?" I ask since no one else seems to want to say it.

"I was attacked by a Hunter. I do not know who, the coward attacked from behind with the shots before I disarmed him, but his face was covered. I only know he was human from his eyes. No amber ring. No silver flecks." He bows his head as if ashamed before straightening.

"Do you know why?" I ask, the rest of the room deathly quiet, and he shakes his head.

"I have no idea, but for it to happen so soon after the knowledge of your angel mark spread leaves little doubt in my mind that it wasn't coincidence." I suck in a breath at his words.

"This is my fault?"

He looks me in the eye, hesitating before shaking his head. My stomach tightens. The hesitation was enough.

"It is no one's fault but those who sanctioned it and those who carried it out. There has been unrest in our faction for many years now, but the splintering only continues to grow. The Elders do not seem worried about it, but warring amongst ourselves while our enemies grow in strength and number is not what we should be doing. That said, I want to know more about the bullets and the blades he used. Maybe if we can find out what, we can discover who and why."

"I'm working on it," Nate says.

"I'm glad you're okay, Denny," Maddie says softly. "But how about for a change, instead of storming off to the depths of battle, we celebrate that you're back with us and healthy. Creek is already cooking enough to feed an army, so how about we bring Abel, Celeste, and Gabriel back, and invite Marie, Fallon, and Rebel over. Make a night of it."

"Maybe he should rest," Bauer inserts, but my dad shakes his head.

"I think a night with my family, including our extended family, is exactly what I need." I read between the lines, knowing full well that my dad intends to speak to Abel, Celeste, and Marie about what happened to him. Find out if anyone has heard anything. How better to disguise a meeting to our enemies than as a revelry?

But a spark of hope ignites in me, and I hold on to my

father's words. Dissent in the Hunters, while terrible, could be exactly what I have hoped for so long. Maybe others have discovered what I have, that not all is as it seems, that things do not have to be the way we have been told they always were. The lies of the Elder council poison us, and while no one seems to know why the change happened, I know that it did.

Another thing for me to think about later.

Colt leaves the room, his phone to his ear, most likely calling Gabriel, while Maddie calls Marie. I pick up my own phone and see a message from Kain.

A war is coming. We will not flee, when all we have dreamed of is within our grasp.

K

I steady my reaction, careful not to portray anything but mild disinterest at the screen, before I tuck it back away in my pocket. Hope swells in my chest, but I school my emotions.

"Who's patrolling tonight?" I ask, since it's been so long since I've been out. The opportunity to get out and talk to Kain feels just within reach.

"Some of the Bellos' cousins volunteered. After being stuck on a plane for way too long, they jumped at the opportunity to be outside," Colt says as he walks back into the room, and my heart sinks a little.

"You're heading out tomorrow, so get your rest tonight. Your first solo hunt." He winks at me, and I smile, feeling far more confident in my abilities than I have since my ritual.

A CROWN OF BLOOD AND BONE

TWENTY ONE

I leave my apartment on foot. I'm heading out of the city, but with the harvest festival coming up next week, parking here has been impossible. The colder air stings my cheeks, but I relish it. I've always been a fan of colder climates.

My swords are tucked under my cloak; and considering the crowds, I feel relief over my decision. Even if it is closer to Halloween, costumes aren't considered normal on adults around here. I make my way through the crowds of people for the four blocks it takes to reach my car before jumping in and cranking the heater full blast. The cold I like. Freezing fingers? Not so much.

I set the location of the warehouse district two towns over on my GPS before starting the slow drive through heavy traffic out of the city. With the increase in activity in the area, our patrol borders have widened. We're apparently the only Hunters on this half of the continent, which definitely explains the amount of camping trips Bauer and Dad used to take, leaving Colt and I alone at home. Not that I was ever bothered. I am not a camping kind of girl. Can I slum it when needed? Yes, but would I choose to? Not in this life, or any other.

The roads clear, and the lights fade away. Darkness creeping in, only broken by the lights of my car.

A flash to my left just catches my eye, and I slow the car to look. I have to ensure I'm not being tailed. I look forward a moment too late and see a man in the middle of the road. I slam on the brakes, but I know the collision is coming. My poor Mustang. I brace myself best I can as I hit him, and my car spins, hitting something else which flips it up into the air. The car rolls, and I struggle to keep myself tucked in, but I fail with the force of the movement. The car skids to a stop, and I groan. I'm suspended upside down with blood running up my face, and my shoulder feels like it's been dislocated. I touch it and grimace. Yep, definitely dislocated.

I hear cheers around me and shake my head. I must have hit it harder than I thought. I clamp my teeth as I pop my shoulder back in, whimpering as I do.

I try to reach for my phone, but the seatbelt pins me

in place, and of course I can't reach the blade in my ankle holster either.

Fuck.

The cheering grows louder and shadows appear on the ground as the light grows around me, flickering like firelight.

I see feet at the window beside me before their owner crouches down and smiles at me through the space where there used to be glass. The smile chills my bones, and I try not to panic.

"Pretty little Hunter we caught here, boys. I think we should have some fun. Her blood smells delightful." His eyes glow silver before he stands, and the door is ripped away.

Lycans.

Hollers and whoops cry out into the night, and I wonder how they traced me. Or maybe it was sheer dumb luck on their part that I was headed out this way. They don't seem to know who I am, only that I'm a Hunter, but I know my blood would give that away. My vision blurs as the world tilts, but I force myself to focus. Hands reach in and pull at the seatbelt, snapping it and grabbing me before I drop. I'm wrenched from the car, the motion jostling my throbbing shoulder and aching head.

Dazed and injured, I struggle against the man carrying me. It hurts to breathe, though, and I realize I've likely broken some ribs. I just hope I haven't pierced my lung.

I stop fighting, trying to reserve my strength and take in my surroundings. The light I saw must have been the bonfire that sits in the middle of this field in the middle of nowhere. I look around and realize this isn't just a few Lycans. There are at least a dozen. What the fuck are Roman and his alphas up to, letting a cluster of rogues grow to this size? Hunters are not the only ones who were meant to police the factions.

"Fancy trying to find dinner and stumbling across a Hunter, boys. The huntress must be with us tonight," the man roars, and the cluster roars back. This is just what I need. To be dinner. A few more steps, and the man holding me drops me to the ground. I groan as my bones rattle with the impact.

I try to stand, and managing to get to my feet, I rush the Lycan closest to me. I grab the blade from my ankle, hoping to do as much damage as I can before I start to run.

Running from a cluster of rogue Lycans is probably the most idiotic thing I could do. They enjoy the chase just as much as the kill. But if I'm going to survive, I need to get the hell out of here.

So I run, and my breaths stab with each lungful of air I suck down. I push through it. I am miles from the edge of Salem's Bay, and there's no traffic on this road. Which is likely why the Lycans chose to set up camp here.

I tune into my hearing as I run, my eyes already scanning my surroundings, checking for further traps as I sprint. I hear them, too close behind me, so I push harder. Their speed typically is faster than mine, but only if they're shifted, and the time it would take to shift would definitely give me the chance to get away. I just have to hope they don't decide the shift is worth it.

When lights appear in the distance, relief floods me, but then a blade buries itself in my thigh, and I fall to the ground. The Lycans get closer, so I try to stand again, but I can't put any weight on my injured leg. Fuck.

A roar, louder than any other I've heard tonight, tears through the night, and I wince. The rushing footsteps behind me slow to a stop, and there's a rustle in the grass in front of me just before I see him.

Roman Knight.

He runs straight past me, half-turned, and barrels into the group behind me. Two fully shifted wolves follow behind him quickly. Screams cry out behind me, and it takes everything inside me not to sob.

I put a leash on my emotions and shove them down as the screams and cries begin to die down. I do not have time to panic.

The two shifted wolves appear at my sides, scenting me before howling.

"You're bleeding," Roman says roughly as he appears

at my side, kneeling beside me. He pulls the blade from my thigh, and I clamp down on the scream that threatens to tear from my throat. I hear, more than see, him take off his T-shirt and wrap it around my thigh. "It hasn't hit anything important, but it is deep. You will need to see a Witch."

"Thank you," I say shakily and roll to a sitting position, careful not to jostle the material on my leg.

"What the fuck are you doing out here alone?" he roars down at me, and it makes my hackles raise immediately.

"Who the fuck are you to shout at me about being out here! You don't own me, and you sure as hell don't get to dictate my actions."

"Who the fuck am I? I swear to the Fates, Remy." He paces in front of me and pulls at his hair. His chest heaves as his anger rolls off of him. "Who the fuck am I... Do you not remember?"

I just look at him and cross my arms, raising an eyebrow. I'll be fucked if I'm going to tell him. He might have just saved my ass, but he does not have the right to speak to me like that.

He rolls his eyes at me as he continues to pace. "You must remember, otherwise you wouldn't have let me help you. Who the fuck am I... really? I'm the guy who just saved your pretty little ass."

"Are you going to tone down your inner asshole, or do you want to get the hell out of my face?"

He barks out a laugh, and the two wolves beside me whine, lying down and putting their noses beneath their paws. I'd laugh if I wasn't so focused on the man in front of me. He's the bigger threat, no matter our history.

"Tone down my inner asshole. You nearly get pulled to pieces by twelve fucking Lycans, but I'm the asshole." His movements slow as he paces, as if he's working through the anger roiling around inside him. He must be settling his wolf as if tearing the other Lycans apart wasn't enough satisfaction for his inner beast to know I'm okay. His languid pace does give me the opportunity to check him out properly, which is probably the last thing I should be doing right now. I have more than enough to deal with as it is, and I mentally scold myself for potentially making things even more complicated than they already are. I curse past Remy yet again. "Fucking woman. She doesn't understand. Sure, she's alive and safe, but fucking hell."

He pulls at his hair, his musings quieting before he stops and stares at me.

"You remember me?" he asks, his eyes no longer glowing. He's finally calmed himself. "Who you are to me?"

"I remember," I tell him, unwilling to be the one to break eye contact. He laughs before walking away.

"The only woman in all of history who refused to look away." He shakes his head but smiles nonetheless. "Why are you out here?"

"I was meant to patrol two towns over. Your arrival, and the surge of Dracul, has the Hunters on edge."

"I had a feeling Kain would be here, too." He frowns. "You met with him?"

I keep quiet, not yet trusting him with that information. I may be his mate, but the wolf inside of him is a tricky beast. It would do anything to protect me, even from myself.

"Of course, you have. Your bleeding is slowing."

I roll my eyes at his ability to switch topics at the drop of a pin.

"Why was there a rogue cluster so big?" I ask him, pinning him with my gaze.

"The same reason there are issues in your own house. War is coming," he tells me, his face unreadable.

"And where do you fall in this war?"

"Wherever you stand," he says, and the wolves beside me howl their agreement, loudly enough to make my ears ring. "Did you get my flowers?" he asks, and I look back at him, puzzled. "For your birthday," he sighs, exasperated. "Purple peonies."

Oh, holy crap. "That was you?"

"It was me. They used to be your favorite."

I smile at him. "They still are. Thank you."

"Are you ready to head back?" he asks, and I nod as I

reach out for him to help me stand. He moves toward me and rather than simply helping me stand, he scoops me into his arms.

"I can walk," I tell him with a huff.

"I know you can, but let me do this. For me, not you. The wolf will not settle until the bleeding stops. Keeping you close makes him happy." I sigh at his words but don't argue as he begins the walk back toward my city.

I limp across my apartment to let Fallon in. I texted her once we were close to the city limits. Despite my protests that I was fine, Roman wouldn't put me down until we reached the apartment building. Growling and grumping about his stupid breakable mate the whole way.

Fucking Lycans.

"Girl, I don't know what the hell you've yourself into, but you and I... we need to talk." Her voice is shrill as she storms into the room. "I swear I only hear from you when you're broken."

"I'm sorry. Yes, we'll talk, but I'm still kinda bleeding. Can you help? I mean, it's probably basically healed by now, but... you know." She waves me onto the sofa, so I close the door and limp back to where she's perched on my coffee table.

"Pants down," she insists, and I roll my eyes but do as

I'm told. I lie down so she can access the wound on my thigh.

"It's nothing too major, you lucky bitch. A few inches the other way and this could've been dangerous. What happened, and why the hell did you call me for something that would have healed itself in a few hours?" She quirks a brow at me, and I roll my eyes.

She presses against the wound, and the heat of the healing power she's pouring into me burns across my skin. I grit my teeth and answer, "I was ambushed by a cluster of rogue Lycans—twelve of them. They destroyed my goddamn Mustang. I want to kill them all over again just for that."

"Holy mother of Fates, twelve? That's not a cluster, it's a goddamn rogue pack!" She sucks her teeth and makes a disapproving noise. "How'd you get out of that with only this and a few other scrapes and bruises?"

"Are you sure you want to know? Because it's a whole thing, and well, it could get me killed," I answer her honestly. Fate knows she deserves the truth, and I already know she's more liberal than the Hunters. The Witches just are.

"How much trouble are you in?"

"At the moment, not too much," I answer with a sigh as she removes her hands from my thigh. "But if people find out the truth, then I'll be in a whole pile of shit."

"You're all fixed. I have a feeling we're going to need pants and tequila for this conversation. You pants up, and I'll grab the booze." She shakes her head, a little wide-eyed. She grabs two glasses and the bottle of Cuervo from the kitchen while I put my pants back on. She raises the glasses toward me as she makes her way back into the living room, and we settle back on the sofa.

Fallon pours us a shot and throws hers back before giving me a tight smile and pouring herself another. "Alright, let's hear it."

"Honestly, I'm not sure where to begin, and I still don't know everything."

Fallon levels me with a look that says she won't leave without the entire truth, so I run my hands through my hair as I try to figure out how to best answer her. "So... I told you about the whole thing with Creek already…" I pause, taking a deep breath as she nods her understanding. I look her square in the eye and continue, "Past Remy screwed me, Fallon. It turns out past me was as open and loving as I am now and just as open-minded as the Witches. I know that the Hunters' stories, their ways, don't make total sense, and I know that because Kain Michaels was my lover. No, that's not right. He was my love in my first life and many others since then. I've always known the rocky truth, just not the whole story behind why things are the way they are."

"Holy shit! Kain Michaels... Damn girl, that vampire is one fine piece of man meat," she exclaims, her eyes wide. I can't help but laugh at her. "Keep going!"

"Well, it turns out Kain wasn't my only dalliance into other factions. I'm not sure which life it was, but in one of them, Roman Knight recognized me as his mate. I don't know how or why, or even much more than that yet, but *that* is how I got out alive tonight. He found me and tore the Lycans to pieces with two of his pack members. The overbearing asshole made me call you on the way back. He literally wouldn't put me down until he heard you agree to come over and patch me up."

She lets out a whistle and fans her face, looking more excited than disgusted, which is honestly what I half-expected. What even is this life that I've led?

"I don't know how it all fits together, but I know that Creek knew, in whichever life it was, that I was Roman's mate because he killed me."

"He did fucking what!!" she screeches half out of her seat, chest flushed from the tequila.

I shake my head and pull her back down onto the couch. "He didn't intend to; he was fighting Roman."

"And I'm sure you barged in there like a woman possessed. Holy shit, Remy, you idiot."

"I know, I know... And then there's Creek. And now they're all here. Together. In my goddamn city, in this one life. Each of them wanting a piece of me." I shrug and tip the tequila she poured down my throat. "That's essentially it in a nutshell."

She sits there, blinking at me and looking a little shell-shocked. I give her a minute to process and pour us both another drink.

"What are you going to do?" she asks me, sipping her drink.

"I have absolutely no idea. I mean, what can I do? I can't ask my family for help. They'd probably kill me, literally. I can't be with all three of them, but I have no idea how I'd choose between them because my stupid heart belongs to each of them. Plus, I have no idea what's still missing from my stupid memories. I'm hoping that past me had a goddamn plan, some way of working out where the hell she was going. Because the path she's leading me down is murky at best and straight to the true death at worst." I gulp, before swallowing the contents of my glass, finally feeling a light buzz, but it does nothing to help the impending dread that fills every inch of my body.

"Girl, I say have some fun. Have a little harem. Why the fuck not? The boys can learn to play nice, maybe even nicer than nice if you're lucky." She winks at me, and I burst out laughing.

"Could you imagine the looks on their faces?" I giggle, and she laughs with me.

"I would pay to see it, sugar. Pay to see it!" She claps her hands in time with her words making me laugh harder. I wipe at the moisture at the corners of my eyes, and her laughter fades away. "Uhm, excuse me, what is that on your finger?"

I offer her the simplest explanation. "It was a gift."

She eyes the ring on my index finger, and I suddenly glad the other men in my life haven't paid any attention to it. "Is that obsidian? Oh my fucking Goddess, is this from Kain?"

She gasps as her gaze whips up to meet mine, and I nod. "Girl, I need me a Dracul King, this is beautiful." She fans her flushed face making me laugh more.

"I mean, you can't have him, he's mine." I stick my tongue out at her and she laughs right back at me.

"Territorial already, I see."

I sigh, chewing my lip before swigging from my drink. "Honestly, I don't know. When I'm here in my normal life, not really. But when I'm with him, with any of them, I don't even really want to test the theory..."

"I can only imagine. Let's get real for a second, if Creek knew once, maybe he'd be more open to helping you than you think? And Colt is more open-minded than people realize too," she says, and her dark skin almost glows as his name falls from her lips.

"What on Earth does that mean?" I ask, and she

narrows her eyes at me. "Looks like I'm not the only one who's been keeping secrets."

"It doesn't mean much," she sighs. "Honestly, I don't know what any of it is, but when things make more sense, I swear I'll explain."

"Just not in too much detail." I laugh, and she rolls her eyes.

"With the amount of dick in your future, you won't have to live vicariously through me, so don't you worry that pretty little head of yours about it. Where are all of your many men anyway?"

"No idea. Roman left begrudgingly after he carried me here."

"He carried you here? Oh damn," she practically swoons.

"Kain is holed up somewhere. He said he'd come for me when it was safe, and Creek is probably off with my brothers somewhere up to Fates only know what."

"Honestly, I don't know whether to be jealous of you or feel sorry for you." She smiles sadly, and the sincerity in her gaze makes my heart wrench. "Whatever you choose, someone is gonna get hurt, and I know you don't want that. Just follow your heart, Remy. It hasn't steered you wrong yet. Jack being the exception, of course."

"Jack was..." I take a breath. "Jack would have been good for me if I was human. If I was human, my family probably wouldn't have disliked him as much either. Things would have been easier, that's for damn sure. And yet, as much as I want to throttle past Remy, I can't find it in myself to regret my actions in my previous lives. My heart is so full, I just wish Mom were here. She'd know what to do."

Fallon nods at my words and offers me another sad smile. Yeah, your mom would have been on board and on your side to the end. You wanna talk to my Mama? She's always felt the same way as you—that love is love regardless of your faction. She hates the racism and bigoted nature of our kinds, and I'm pretty sure she plays with the other factions as a big fuck you to those who look down their nose at us. It's just the way she is. It's why I was always surprised that she and your dad worked so well together. She was so close to your mom though, so I guess it makes sense."

"Thanks, but I don't think Marie would be able to help me out of the mess I seem to have created for myself. One advantage to the swell of Lycans and Dracul, plus everything with my dad, is that people seem to have forgotten about my Leviathan mark." I shrug, trying to find the silver linings where I can.

"Small wins." She smiles.

"I've just tried to keep it covered as much as I can. I think it's stopped growing now, but I don't understand the symbols intertwined with it."

"Maybe ask one of your lovers. Creek obviously doesn't know much, otherwise he would have said so, but one of the others might." She shrugs, and my eyes widen. I hadn't thought of that.

"Fallon, you're a genius."

"Oh, girl I know. People just underestimate me because of the accent." She winks at me and finishes her glass. "Right, I better get back, Mama's gonna be waiting up for me. You'd think I was twelve, not twenty." She rolls her eyes and stands. "If you need me, I'm here. For anything, even facing off against your family."

"Thank you, Fal." I hug her tight. "You're the best."

"And don't you forget it," she says with a wink before releasing me. "You lock this door behind me, you hear? You might have a harem of protectors out there, but there's way too many beasties out there that you seem to be pissing off and attracting without even trying."

"I will. Are you going to be okay getting home?"

"Yeah, I ordered an Uber. It'll be here any minute."

"Okay, stay safe, Fallon. Call me if you need me."

"Ditto, girl. Ditto."

I close the door behind her and lean against it with a sigh. That went better than I thought it would.

TWENTY TWO

Patrols and training. That's all my life consists of anymore. Creek is out with Colt and the Bellos, hunting. I try not to hope that they aren't successful, but I can't help myself, not with the knowledge I now carry. The guilt they will carry when the truth becomes known will be bad enough as it is.

Revealing the truth is the one thing I am focused on. I can control it. I can research it with the goal of making the world the way it once was again. So many other things are outside of my control, but this is something I can try to make happen. I try not to think of the fallout that may come along with it, convincing myself that it can't be worse than the chaos we're currently facing.

My dad and Nate have been working around the clock

with Maddie to figure out what the weapons that were used against my dad are. Roman has apparently fallen off the face of the Earth; no one has seen or heard anything of the Lycan alpha and Kain… He says he's staying away for my own good for the time being, though not for long.

I shake my head as I throw another fist at the punching bag in front of me. The boxing gym is old and smells like men and sweat, but thankfully no one pays much attention to the girl beating the crap out of a bag in the corner. It turns out this has been the best outlet for all the new rage filtering through my being. I stumbled across the gym this morning and decided to take a peek. This place is a hidden gem that I plan to keep in my ever-growing vault of secrets.

Sweat runs down my back as I take out my frustration on the bag in front of me. I punch until my arms are so heavy I can barely move them. I grab my water bottle and gulp it down, groaning as my phone pings inside my bag.

I ignore it, trying not to focus on the new Hunter killing weapons, the rumors that made Kain stiff with fear, and the war that's simmering is on the brink of actually breaking out. Top that off with my disastrous love life, or what little of it exists right now, and I'm understandably on edge.

My phone continues to ping in my bag, only adding the rage I can't seem to let go of. I rip off the gloves that I borrowed from reception and root through my bag for my stupid phone. Four missed calls from my dad, another two from Maddie, and a handful of messages sit waiting for me.

Remy. Call me when you get this. Colt

You need to come to your dad's. I hope you're okay. Sorry I haven't been around much. Creek

Something is happening. Whispers grow louder, and I worry for your safety. Please let me know you are okay.

K

And then one from an unknown number.

Meet me. Tonight. R

Roman.

I respond to the first two, telling them I'm on my way. I take the time to let Kain know that I'm perfectly fine and not a freaking china doll.

I don't know what to say to Roman, so I say nothing and tuck my phone back in my bag instead. I wipe my face with a towel before heading out of the gym, stopping long enough to return the gloves as I leave. I try not to stomp my feet and act like a brat as I make the walk out and call for an Uber to my dad's. Roman had my car towed, but no one else knows that it's totaled yet. I try not to think about it, adding it to my ever-expanding list of Future Remy Problems.

How it's only been a little over two months since my awakening is beyond me. It feels like a lifetime already, though I realize that could be because of all the memories.

I clear my mind on the ride over, letting go of some of the worry and trying to breathe deeply to settle the turmoil inside of me. I pull out my phone again as we head down my dad's driveway and bring up Roman's text.

I can't tonight. Something is happening.
Are you back?

It doesn't take long for his response to come through.

I never left. Just sorting business out.
If not tonight, when?
Saturday?

I mull it over. Without a job, it's been hard to keep up with the days, but my phone tells me it's Tuesday. I try to not get too caught up on the no job thing—thank the Fates for my Hunter savings. I won't have to work for this lifetime, nor many others.

Saturday works. Where?

I will pick you up. Be safe, you never know what lurks in the dark.

His response sends a chill up my spine. Not only has he been here the entire time, but now he's giving me some cryptic warning. Awesome. I try not to think about the fact that one of the world's deadliest predators can disappear from the face of the earth and move around in the shadows without anyone realizing it.

The Uber stops in front of the house, and my stomach drops. There are so many cars here.

Great.

I thank the driver and climb out, pausing to watch as he leaves. I'm desperate for another moment of peace before I face whatever waits for me inside the house. The voices reach me before I even get to the door, and I realize they're in the back yard.

I walk on the wraparound porch to the back of the house, and the laughter and squeals of children reaches my ears. The smells hit me before I even get back there.

A cookout.

They harassed me for a cookout.

I roll my eyes but wave as people spot me. Still, I turn on my heels and head into the kitchen.

"Remy, sweetheart, you made it!" Maddie exclaims with a big grin. "We thought we should celebrate your dad's recovery. And with Bauer's birthday next week, it seemed like something fun to do since we had everyone here."

"You realize they made it seem like someone was dying to get me here, right?" I tell her.

"Of course. they did. They didn't think you'd come otherwise. You've been distant lately."

"What..." I interrupt, but she waves me off.

"You've been present in body, Remy. But your mind... like I said. Distant. We understand. We've all been there, but we didn't know if you'd come for this. Just know that you can talk to us. We've all been through the awakening. Your struggle isn't new to any of us, even to you, but you won't understand that until it's complete. I am always here for you, you know? No matter what." She squeezes my shoulder before turning back to the cutting board in front of her. Salad bowls galore are scattered across the kitchen. I shrug off my jacket and hang it over the back of a chair.

"Can I help?" I ask, guilt coloring my words because she's right. I might have been here, but I haven't been, not really. Other than my stolen moments with Creek, my mind has been whirring, trying to make sense of the mess I've landed myself in.

"You sure can, after you shower." Her raised eyebrow

as she looks me over makes me laugh. "The potatoes should be cooled by now, so you can make the potato salad once you're finished," she says with a warm smile, and I can't help but wonder if her words of *no matter what* would still be true if she knew my deepest, darkest secrets.

Running upstairs, I grab the quickest shower I've ever taken and throw on some fresh clothes before joining Maddie back in the kitchen. I grab the potatoes and everything else I need from the refrigerator before losing myself in the motions of it. I seize the serenity of the moment, enjoying the quiet comfort Maddie's presence offers, and I vow to at least attempt to be present for my family.

The laughter of the Bellos' children makes me feel lighter as I help Maddie carry everything from the kitchen and lay it on the tables that have been set up. My dad, Nate, and Abel are all manning the grill, beer in hand, while my brothers and Creek mess around with the kids, playing what I think is meant to be football.

I smile, wider than I have in a while, as the sun shines down on us. There's not a cloud in the sky, and I take the moment to appreciate everything that I have.

"Grub's up!" my dad yells and like a swarm of cicadas, everyone descends on the tables Maddie and I just laid out, while Dad brings over trays of burgers, chicken, and steak. Creek comes up behind me, wrapping his arms around my waist and hugging me. A flush stains my cheeks as he kisses the top of my head while both our families watch.

Shock covers their faces momentarily, but they brush it off quickly, smiling as they turn back to the food.

"About time." Colt smiles cheekily. "Maybe now he'll stop brooding."

"Shut up, man." Creek laughs and squeezes me tighter. I try to not let panic overrun me. I'm stunned at his declaration to everyone without us having spoken about it. I guess after the other morning, with our history, he just assumed. He couldn't know how complicated everything in my head and heart is.

"You okay?" he asks, and I try to let go of the tension that made me stiffen in his embrace.

"Yeah." I smile up at him, and he kisses me softly. I sigh into the kiss. It's gentle but hot enough to make my toes curl. Good fates.

"Let's get you something to eat." He smiles down at me, and I nod. He takes my hand and leads me to the other side of the table, passing me a plate before starting to fill his own. Maddie catches my eye, making a heart sign with her hands, and I shake my head with a grin, trying not to blush again. I add some food to my plate, and Creek adds extra helpings while I roll my eyes. I am never going to eat this mountain.

"When did this happen?" Dad asks as we sit down near

him.

"This time you mean?" Nate laughs next to him.

"She hasn't regained all of her memories yet, this could be dangerous," my dad says to him, concern evident on his face.

"I'm fine, Dad. I've remembered some. Not all, but I'm okay. We're okay." I say as I squeeze Creek's hand, realizing the truth of my words as I say them. We will be okay. Even if he rejects me for my choices, I know I have to tell him. And if he does reject, it'll hurt, but I'll still be okay. I think.

"Hmmmm," he gripes, but goes back to eating his food.

"Took long enough, especially after last week," Bauer says as he sits opposite us, and I just shake my head. My family has all the subtlety and tact of a freaking sledgehammer.

"Shut up, Bauer," I whisper angrily, glancing around at our family members closest. Thankfully, no one else is paying any attention to us.

My brother smirks, and it takes everything I have to not flip him the bird. Instead, I sit with my hand in Creek's eating and enjoying the company around us. Enjoying the momentary peace because I'm afraid there won't be much of it in the next few months.

TWENTY THREE

I find myself back at the abandoned hotel, thankful that there are enough people on patrol tonight that I don't have to be. I hope to see Kain, but I know it isn't likely. All I want is to trigger another wave of memories. If Kain's the one who told me the truth about the change in the relationship between the factions, surely he's the one who will trigger the memory of *why*. Unless he never really knew.

I don't know what I'll do if that's the case, but I head into the abandoned hotel anyway. I'm not really paying attention to my surroundings, too lost in my own head.

"What are you doing here, Remy?" I spin and come face to face with someone I don't recognize, but that voice... I know that voice.

I stay quiet and still while he watches me, and I realize he was the Dracul I heard in here before Kain found me a few weeks ago. "Who are you?"

"You wound me, Remy. You don't remember me?" he says, a hand on his chest. He takes a step back as if truly wounded by my words, and I laugh.

"Always the joker, my friend." Kain's voice echoes through the hall, and my stomach leaps. "She is only two and half months into the awakening. It is lucky she remembered me, otherwise we might have all been dead the other night."

The stranger looks back at me eyes wide. "You were hunting us?"

Kain's footsteps draw closer until he stands between us, and I shake my head. "I was searching for my friend's necklace."

He nods, piecing it together.

"Luc is my second and a dear friend. You can trust him as you would trust me," Kain tells me as his arm wraps around my waist, pulling me close to his side.

I smile at him, and his grin grows wide. "Oh, this is going to be so much fun."

He rubs his hands together at his words, and Kain laughs. "Do not tease her, she might not be awakened fully, but she will remember eventually."

"Oh, the fun we three had," he sighs reminiscently.

"The adventures we had. Do you truly not remember?"

I shake my head, and his smile falters.

"So be it, if it doesn't come back in time, then we shall regale you with the tales of the past while making new memories!" he says with a glint in his eye.

"I'd like that," I tell him honestly. "But until then, we have a problem."

"What is wrong, *mon chérie*?" Kain asks, and I pull away from his side.

"Roman is here. I ran into him a few nights back, and I remember..."

"Love, I know of your relationship with Roman, as well as the others. I told you I didn't always find you in time."

"But the three of you are all here now. All at once. What am I supposed to do with that? Creek basically paraded me around as his in front of the Hunters today. I can't lie to him, but my heart can't let you go either."

"I will say it as I have said before. I will share your heart, so long as you will have me. Mine belongs solely to you, always and forever. I will take whatever piece of you I can."

His words make my heart swell, knowing that no matter what, he will be at my side.

"I couldn't ask that of you."

"Sure you can," Luc says with a laugh, and I roll my

eyes at him.

"You do not ask, my love. It is offered willingly. I will not let you go again."

I nod at his words, unsure of the words to use to properly express my gratitude.

"I cannot promise the others will be as willing, but I have seen how they love you. I think you may be worrying about things that do not matter... or will not matter once you are honest with yourself and with them." Would having all three of them really be a possibility? Would it make me selfish to want more than one, but not allow them to find another? Because fate knows that the more I remember, the worse my jealousy grows.

"Thank you," I say and walk back into his open arms. "Now that's all cleared up, do you want to come with us?"

"Where are you heading?" I ask, knowing I will say yes regardless.

"Quiet," Kain says sharply, and I practically hold my breath. They both go so still, sensing something beyond my Hunter capabilities.

"Shit," Luc hisses. Kain looks at him, sharing a look the way that only people who have known each other lifetimes can. Luc nods subtly, before moving closer to us.

"What's going on?" I ask quietly as Kain lets me go and flashes away from us.

"Rogues. So many rogues," Luc says. "We need to get

you out of here."

"I will not run from a fight, Luc. Not when you both hurl yourselves toward it. That is not who I am."

"I know, but I had to try. He will kill me if anything happens to you under my watch." He hands me a sword from his belt, before palming the other.

"It's not what you are used to. It will probably feel a little heavy, but since you are practically unarmed, this will have to do."

I curse myself for not arming myself before coming here. The idea of it is still foreign to me, though I don't think I'll forget again in a hurry.

"How many?" I ask quietly as I follow him up the stairs to the next floor as swiftly as I can.

"At least fifty," he hisses. "They must have scented him."

"Why are they attacking him? He's their leader."

"Not everyone appreciates the way of the Dracul. Some people rebel against the Hunters' tyranny, blaming Kain for its longevity. They think he is unsuitable to lead, despite his history, because of you. That his feelings are tainted and that his duty to his own kind comes second." He shakes his head. "It is ridiculous, but the murmurings of mad men have raised riots and rebellions throughout history. It is why there are so many rogues right now. The house numbers are shrinking. We are still a force, but they are gathering, much like your Hunters."

He's barely through his explanation before he darts forward as a Dracul rushes us. He grabs the rogue by the throat and tears with his claws, blood pooling on the floor beneath him faster than I can blink.

"They are coming." It's the only warning I get before the front doors burst open and the hall floods with bodies. Half rush forward, off into the direction that Kain fled, and the rest rush up the stairs toward us.

I shut down all thoughts in my mind and give myself over to the Hunter instincts that guide me, slipping into the killing calm. I rush forward to meet them, the sword an extension of my arm. I cut through one of them, and two more surround me. I cuss myself again for not having brought my own weapons.

They charge at me, but I fly backward from a force at my back. It takes a second to realize that Kain now stands where I was only seconds ago, and the two Dracul are already headless. I blink, watching as if mesmerized as the man who has been so gentle with me becomes the man legends speak of. In the time it takes Luc to dispatch the two Dracul harassing him and join me, Kain has torn through the rest of them, like a man possessed. Covered in blood from head to toe, he faces the last standing rogue.

"How dare you come here, to my home, and attack me!" His voice bellows, the foundations of the hotel practically shaking at the force of the sound.

The Dracul almost curls in on himself at the shout, but Kain does not stand down. He grabs the rogue by the neck and lifts the man into the air. I watch as he squeezes the rogue's throat, cutting off his air supply. Not enough to kill him but enough to make him hurt.

"They said you had betrayed us, sided with the Hunters. That's why so many of us are disappearing." The words come out scratchy as he tries to speak around the lack of air.

"Kain." I sigh, and his eyes dart to me, the amber ring circling his irises having overtaken most of the blue. He turns back to the rogue, squeezing tighter before throwing him back.

"Go back to whoever they are and tell them that I was merciful with you tonight *because* of a Hunter. It is she who saved your life. As for the missing Dracul, I am here searching for them. Why would I be here if I were stealing them away? Fools!"

The rogue nods, on his knees cowering. Kain snarls, "Get out of my sight."

The man scampers down the stairs and out of the hotel.

"Well, this was messy." Luc laughs, and I shake my head.

"Much as I appreciate your brute strength, you didn't have to pull me from the fight," I tell Kain, hands on my hips, as I try desperately to not lose my cool.

"Uh-oh. You're in trouble again." Luc laughs and leaves us in a flurry. I can only assume it's to get someone in to help with this mess.

"I know you can fight with the best of us, *mon coeur*. But I could keep you from harm, and so I did. You have not yet awakened fully. I could not risk you so casually."

I huff at his words.

"What is it with all these stupid alpha egos telling me I'm not ready to fight?" I grunt, and he walks over to me slowly.

"I am sorry, Remy. I did not mean to offend you."

"Fine, it's fine. I'm being a brat, I know it, and you know it. Hell, Luc isn't even here, and he knows it." I hear his laughter ring out, and it makes me smile a little. "I'm just sick of always being in this in-between place."

He moves to hug me but seems to realize his filthy state and stops. I laugh at him, the Dracul who needs blood to survive, not remembering he is dripping with it.

"We should get out of here," he says, and I nod.

"Luc, do you have things sorted?" he asks, and Luc's voice reaches us from wherever he is in this infernal place.

"I do. Have fun kids." I laugh at his words and shake my head.

"Would you like to come with me, Remy? We are staying in a hotel not far from here. I can get cleaned up, and then we can talk."

"I would like that." I smile at him, and he shrugs out of his suit jacket, using it to wipe the blood from his hair and face.

"That will have to do for now." He smiles at me and lifts me into his arms, and I try not to think about the gore.

"Close your eyes. It's been a while," he says with a wide smile, showing his fangs. I close my eyes and hold on tight. Wind wraps around us, with enough force that I think it might collapse my lungs. It only lasts a few minutes, and when the sensation lessens, I open my eyes to darkness. Kain puts me down, and then with the click of a light switch, the room lights softly.

"I'm going to go get cleaned up, make yourself comfortable," he says with a smile in my direction. His eyes are back to the bright blue I've come to associate with him. I nod, and he strolls across the suite and into a door on the opposite side. I shrug out of my cloak and kick off my boots. Some people would say heeled boots are no good for running or fighting. To them, I say two words, fight me. I strip off my jeans and tank. The blood is basically dried now, but it's still pretty gross.

I head to open the door closest to me, hoping to find a closet, and smile when I come across neatly hung clothing. I grab one of the white shirts and slip it over my shoulders. It's so long it covers me just below my ass. I smile at my reflection and run my fingers through my hair to detangle it as much as I can.

I sink into one of the chairs that look out of the window. The city is lit up below us, offering a pretty view of so many lights against the black of the night sky. Anticipation builds in me as I listen to the sounds of the shower in the background. A low burn in my stomach builds as I wait for him.

He pulls open the door to the bathroom, revealing his flawless figure as steam pours out behind him. The contrast between his pale skin and dark features, coupled with the hazy mist from the steam, gives him a mystical air. He's truly a presence from beyond this realm. He's fascinating and delectable, mouth-watering and mysterious. And he's all mine.

My legs are unsteady beneath me as I push myself to my feet. I sway across the room to him, stopping just beyond his reach. I can't seem to stop my lazy perusal of his body from top to bottom.

"I think you have some drool, just there," he jokes, pointing to the corner of his lip.

I cross my arms over my chest, pulling the hem of the shirt up a couple inches. He double-takes, as if just realizing I'm wearing his shirt and not much else. I quirk an eyebrow in his direction and smirk as I say, "You try coming face to face with all of that and not drool a little."

"I prefer the view I have, thank you very much," he says, the bulge under his towel twitching. In a fraction of a second, he pulls me against him, his tongue licking my lips before his teeth capture my bottom lip, slowly pulling it away before releasing it. It takes every ounce of my self-control to not moan in response.

"Well, I suppose I shouldn't drool too much." I shrug, playing it cool, knowing very well that I'm about to light a fire under his domineering ass. "I'm surrounded by bodies like yours all the time."

I barely take my next breath before he slams me into the nearest wall, his body flush with mine. His naked chest heaves with desire.

"Is that so?" he asks, his gaze roaming my face before traveling down my neck. His eyes linger on my chest. "You know, you look rather tasty in my shirt," he croons, his fingers nimble as he meticulously unfastens each button, "I'm suddenly starving for you."

As he pushes the shirt from my shoulders, it falls off my arms and pools at my feet. He hooks his thumbs in my lace panties, and he snaps them off without a care or a thought. He's not rushed, eyes heating as he takes in the way his actions make me squirm with need. He enjoys the slow burn, the game of anticipation and aching as my body burns with need for him. He loves the way it makes me lose my mind.

"Do you know what happens, Remy, when you try to tease the beast inside me?" he asks, as quietly and calmly as though he were asking about the weather.

"I think I might," I sass back, knowing full well he's going to fuck it right out of me.

I reach behind me, unfastening my bra and letting it fall to join the rest of my clothes on the floor. I stand before him, at his mercy, naked and trembling with need. "I think I like it when your beast comes out to play."

His hand is suddenly at my jaw, tightening and holding me prisoner to his lust. The beast within him dances in the pupils of his eyes. The bite of pain as his fingers dig into my skin sends a rush of arousal through my body. It calls to my inner wanton, the woman inside of me who needs to be fucked like her life depends on it.

"Oh, Remy, the things you say…" He trails off as he runs his hands down my sides, resting them on my ass before he jerks me up. He turns us, stepping into the steamy bathroom, and sets me on the countertop. I can just make out the feeling of the mirror at my back through the haze of my arousal.

"Lie back, little minx," he whispers, already pushing me down. I rest on my elbows, my head pressed against the mirror and my ass on the ledge of the countertop. I spread my legs open wide for him, so that he sees every inch of my hungry pussy. "You will watch me while I punish you with my tongue," he commands, dropping to his knees with one fluid movement.

Punishment?

In what world would him eating me out be considered a punishment?

I don't have time to ponder that question as his fingers dig into my thighs and his mouth attacks my lower lips like a starved man. My head tilts, and all I can see in the reflection of the mirror is the movement of his dark head rhythmically bobbing up and down, mimicking the sensation of his tongue licking from bottom to top. The barrier of the mirror makes the sensations more erotic somehow. The view seems much more sensual.

His thumbs separate me, and I hiss at the sensation of his fingers on me, opening me up for his viewing and tasting pleasure. Every touch, every breath is in his control. Every sensation is of his making. When he reaches my clit, his fangs drag over my skin as they extend, the pinch making me tremble with anticipation. Taking a gulp of air as his tongue laps up my hard nub, I'm certain nothing could have prepared me for the intensity of his first bite on my engorged clit. My entire body lifts from the counter, and if not for Kain's hold on me, I might have fallen to the floor. My entire being feels as if it's melting as the orgasm rips through me.

"Holy shit, what was that?" I ask, breathless. His only

answer is biting down again, drinking this time.

My orgasm hits all over again, lights and sounds and electricity ravaging my entire body as he sucks in my blood and my juices.

"If that's punishment, Kain, I might be a naughty girl more often," I pant, my whole body on fire from the never-ending orgasm.

"Now," he says, standing and looking down on me with eyes colored with the heat of lust, "I'm going to fuck you until you're too tired to sass me anymore."

The towel wrapped around his waist falls to the floor along with my jaw. He isn't just big; he's long and silky with a vein that makes my body scream desire and want.

"Don't worry, little minx, it'll fit nice and snug." And before I can catch my breath or argue, he picks me up and carries me into the shower. The cold of the floor makes me shiver as he places me on my feet. He reaches behind him, turning the water to a steady stream, and I look up at him. He brushes my wet hair from my face before bending down to kiss me again. I lose myself in the feel of his lips on mine as his hands wander over my body. His hardness digs into my stomach and I smirk, pulling away from his lips, kissing down his chest, lowering myself to my knees. I look up at him, the amber taking up most of his eyes again as I lick from the base of his cock to the tip. His groan rattles through him, and he clenches his fists at his sides, not taking his eyes from mine. I cup his balls softly and take him into my mouth as far as I can take him before hitting the back of my throat.

"Fuck, Remy," he groans, and I smile around his cock, repeating the movement before swirling my tongue around the head. I bring my other hand up and wrap it around him, moving it with my mouth, drawing snarls and moans alike from him.

"Enough," he barks, and pulls me to my feet before taking my mouth with his, bruising my lips with the intensity of the kiss. His arms lift me, and I wrap my legs around him. He backs me up against the tile wall of the marble shower and slams into me. I hold onto his shoulders as he pumps relentlessly into me, his movements hard and dominant. His groans are an echo of my own with each thrust he delivers. I am nothing more than my wanton need as he drives his dominance into me over and over again.

"Do you know how much I desire you, *mon amour*? How much I have fantasized of you?" His tender words are in complete contrast to the bite of his tone and violence of his thrusts.

I nod, incapable of forming words.

Digging his fingers into my ass he demands, "Say it."

He thrusts in and grinds against my tender clit, stealing my breath and my words away from.

"Y-yes," I stutter, his cock working its magic on my

brain and body.

"Do you know how much I love you, *mon amour*?" he continues, pulling out quickly and pushing in just as fast.

"Y-yes, oh Fates, yes!" I cry out as another orgasm starts to build from deep inside my belly. My heels pushing into his sculpted ass, begging for more.

"Good girl," he murmurs at my ear. "Now, come," he commands and as he thrusts inside one last time, his fangs latch onto my neck and both of us fly into an orgasm that has me seeing stars. Our bodies convulse as he pumps his seed into me all the while sucking my life source for his own. He gives and he takes, and I will happily give and take as much as he is willing to offer.

"I love you, Kain, so much," I sigh as my climax finally relents, our bodies slowly coming back to earth as Kain licks up the errant droplets of my blood, leaving me breathless.

"*Moi aussi, je t'aime. De tout mon coeur.*"

"What does that mean?" I ask, my voice nothing more than a murmur.

"I, too, love you. With all of my heart."

Slowly and carefully, Kain releases my thighs, putting me back on the ground so I can stand my own. It's not an easy feat when your legs feel like jelly.

With one arm, he secures me in place and with the other, he lathers me up with a loofah. His movements are gentle and slow over my body as he worships my skin. We both rinse before turning the water off. He carries me out of the shower and onto the plush carpet. With one thick, soft towel, he dries me off. He offers me no words, only our breaths and thoughts accompany us as he repeats the action on himself before carrying me to the bedroom and laying us down on clean sheets.

We're both in a haze of love, our fucking still buzzing in our veins.

"That was..." I don't know how to finish the phrase; it was so much.

"That was us, *mon coeur*. And that was only the beginning."

TWENTY FOUR

I walk through the forest barefoot, at one with the nature around me. Everything is so green and lush, and I can just make out the sound of wolves playing in the distance. The air here is muggy, and the smell of rain from the night before permeates the air. The canopy of leaves and branches above keeps the beating sun from my already-tanned skin.

We've been here for months, enjoying the freedom that comes with the forest. Hunting and foraging for our food, reveling in the outdoors. Just being pack. After a rough few weeks of establishing myself within the pack as Roman's mate, things have finally settled down and we've almost established a routine.

Four wolf cubs' barrel toward me in the undergrowth,

their black and white pelts that are usually so soft caked with mud. Their silver eyes glow, their excitement and joy palpable. One jumps up at me, and I catch her in my arms, scrubbing the space between her ears as her tongue lolls out of her mouth.

"Come on you guys, let's head back for dinner," I say to them, and they yip and howl back at me. The pup in my arms wriggles before jumping down and rushing ahead of me back to our camp. I take my time, walking languidly through the trees on the path that we've worn into the ground since we've been here.

As much as I love the pack, and I wouldn't give it up for the world, sometimes I need some time to myself. If you'd have told me a year ago that I'd be here, I'd have laughed in your face. But meeting Roman Knight changed my entire life. I already knew that something was amiss. There was a hole in my memories that clawed at me, pleading with me to understand. And then I met him. The most domineering asshole I've ever met, though with a heart of gold. I've never met anyone like him, not in this life or the five before.

My lives have been peppered with moments of joy but ruled mostly by death and torture. At least, for as much as I can remember. For some reason, my memories barely came back this time, and with my mother and father refusing to fill in the gaps for me, there is no one else I can turn to. No siblings, no cousins, or other Hunters my age, at least none *within the Hunter families we deal with. Life was lonely before Roman. It was nothing but duty. Following orders I didn't believe in, from a man I was starting to resent. My father is a hard man, his beliefs resolute. When I began to question the ways we live, he threatened to have me cast out, and so I left, traveling halfway around the world by sea, running as far from him as I could.*

That's when Roman found me.

Or well, that's when Roman tried to kill me.

I still take pride in the fact that I was the first person in existence to pin him. Female or not, I pinned him, and then he claimed me as his mate. Marking me and taking my blood before I even really knew what it meant. The beginning was hard as he adjusted to the fact that I wouldn't just lie down and take his word as law. It was hard for him that I had my own opinions, and that I wasn't afraid to voice them. I was not a woman typical of our time. I refused to cower, to bow down to his every whim. It's the reason he claimed me, and I secretly think he gets off from the conflict.

We moved the pack deep into the forest when rumors of wars ravaging the world began. Conquerors wanting to claim lands that were not theirs to take. Slaughtering humans in droves. If this were another life, I might stand up and fight alongside the humans, but it isn't. I am pack, and that means I protect them first, above all costs.

I break through the tree line into the clearing where

we made camp in this humid, sweltering place. I do not know the name of this place, and we are hidden so deep in the forest, we have not seen a human for much time. I spot Roman on the far side of the clearing, close to the pool at the base of the waterfall. Pups climb all over him, and his laugh booms across the space.

My heart warms seeing him so carefree. It is so very rare that he gets to be this way, but life has been easier, simpler since we came here. The outside world is less of a threat. I make my way over to the fire where the cooks are preparing dinner and offer my assistance before being waved off. Cooking for the pack is deemed a privilege, and no one wants to sacrifice that.

Roman sees me from across the clearing and stands. I can hear as he tells the children he'll play more tomorrow before striding toward me. He captures my lips with his hands buried in my hair as he claims me, not caring who can see. I hold on to him, my hands clenching his biceps, which twitch beneath my touch. I stand on my tiptoes, giving as much as I get from his mind-blowing kiss.

"You've been gone longer than usual," he murmurs when he breaks the kiss, his silver eyes studying me. "Are you unhappy here?"

I shake my head at his question and smile. "No, I just wandered farther than I have before, so it took me longer to return."

"You should not wander too far; you do not know who travels this place. It could be dangerous." His concern warms me. It's not his dominance steering his words, but rather his love for me.

"Then it is good that I am not just anyone and capable of looking after myself." His hand grips my throat, not tightly enough to steal my breath, but enough to keep my attention on him.

"You are mine, and while I acknowledge that you can look after yourself, you will not put yourself in such situations needlessly." He growls, kissing me again, his hand still on my throat. I melt into him, the pressure only making me want him more, and I know he scents it when his chest rumbles.

"Later, you and I will finish this," he says with a heated look, releasing me and storming back to the cold pool and diving in.

I wake in my room, sleep still clinging to me and groan at the sunlight filtering through. I haven't had a good night's rest since the night I spent with Kain earlier this week, and even that was my first restful slumber since I spent the night with Creek in my bed. I'm beginning to think I'm only ever going to sleep well with one of my men in bed. When I started to think of them as *my* men, I've no idea. My dreams are full of memories. Some of them haunt me with the things that I've seen, others make me squirm when I wake up, practically setting my pussy on fire.

I huff, nervous about seeing Roman after putting him off earlier in the week. With more of my memories coming back to me, the thought of seeing him practically makes my ovaries explode. Underneath it all, like a stone sitting heavily in my stomach, is my guilt. Because Creek still doesn't know. He offers sweet kisses and soft words— not quite declaring his love for me, but the actions are close enough that I know it's coming. The guilt eats at me because I know I can't say it back. Not because I don't feel it because I know I do. But because of the others. I slept with Kain after Creek told our families I was his, and I've barely been able to look him in the eye since. Until he knows about the others, about everything, I can't tell him because I can't hurt him more than I know I'm already going to.

The fact I'm going to meet Roman tonight, rather than see Creek again deepens the pit in my stomach, but I need to find out more.

I will tell Creek, I will. I just... I need to see what this is with Roman, if he even wants me as his mate in this life too. I've noticed that I've only been with him in two of my lives. I know one was my sixth from Kain, who found me in the life I was with Roman. Even though he kept his distance, so as not to dampen my happiness. The other though, I have no idea about. I have no recollection of any others, so I can't help but wonder how the pack handles that. How he deals with it. If he even wants that again or if he's moved on to another and is simply here to tell me that.

Yes, his wolf was protective of me the other night, and he sent me beautiful flowers for my birthday. But he's made no other move toward me, and I feel as if I hang in the balance, waiting for the axe to fall.

He told me he would come and collect me, like a prize, but I swallow that thought. He wasn't always such an asshole. Sometimes he was sweet and caring. The domineering side of him is always present, but what else should I expect from the Alpha of Alphas? I'm just happy that he always seemed to accept that I would not bow to his every whim. I hope he's still the same with this in particular.

Because even if he doesn't want me, if he has moved on, a piece of him is still mine. And while it might make my life easier, a piece of my heart would leave with him.

I throw off the sheets and head toward the bathroom, not bothering to dress because I have nowhere to be just yet. I turn on the shower to let it heat up and walk to the kitchen to start the coffee pot, yawning as I go through the motions.

"As much as I love the view, I'm surprised to find you

naked." I scream as I spin to see Roman sitting in the chair by my window with Sushi in his lap, purring under his hand.

"What the ever-loving fuck are you doing here, and how the hell did you get in?" I refuse to cover myself in my own home, so let him get an eyeful.

"I told you I would collect you, did I not?" He raises his eyebrow, his only movement apart from stroking my traitorous cat. To be honest, I'm kind of jealous.

"Enjoying stroking my pussy?" I quip, and his eyes darken.

"I suggest you shower quickly, and do not test my patience, Remy." His eyes glow, and I know I've pushed his buttons enough.

"Fine, but don't think this is over. This," I wave my hand around the room, "is not okay." He glowers at me but doesn't say a word as I stomp to the bathroom to get ready for the day.

I take the world's quickest shower, realizing belatedly that he'd have smelled my arousal. I groan at the thought of so many missed opportunities. I fight to get my hormones under control, refusing to be led by them and dress as quickly as possible. Thankfully, my waist length hair sits in natural waves, so after running a quick brush through it, I'm ready for the day. I slip a hair tie in my pocket just in case.

"Are you almost done?"

I spin at the sound of his gruff voice. He stands in the open doorway, filling the space with an arm above him, leaning slightly through the frame. His muscles bulge, and I cuss myself for being so easily distracted by him. I'm blaming it on the dreams and the memories.

"I am glad to see your patience is as lengthy as ever."

He grins lazily at me, but his look is entirely predatory.

"I'm glad I do not disappoint."

I stand before him, hands on my hips, refusing to back away or to look away first.

He belts out a laugh and steps back from the doorway allowing me to pass. "Better view back here anyway."

I roll my eyes at him as I pass. I stoop to grab my boots from where I left them near the couch and begin putting them on. "Those aren't going to work, princess."

I glance at him, and as much as I want to wipe that smug grin from his face, I'm also not stupid enough to wear the boots just to spite him. "Fine. And don't call me princess. Is pissing people off to this extent a skill you were born with or one you learned?"

His eyes flash, and he gives me a predatory grin. "Ah, the age-old question of nature versus nurture... I guess you'll have to stick around long enough to find out, won't you, princess?"

I sigh and flip him the bird. I swear his chest rumbles

in response, part laugh, part growl.

I remove my boot and grab my chucks from under the coffee table and slip them on instead, trying to ignore his snickering. "Any chance of telling me where we're going?"

"Not a single one. Oh, but you should probably take these." He reaches into his pocket and throws me a set of keys. "Your car, fully restored."

"How on Earth did you manage that so quickly?"

"I am a man of many talents."

"Thank you, Roman." I smile softly at him.

"Guess I'm more than just an asshole, huh?"

TWENTY FIVE

"**I**'d have thought you'd miss the great outdoors." Roman snarks as we walk back up to my apartment. "I wanted to show you the place where our pack will gather once they arrive."

"Roman, you took me on a two-hour drive and a four-hour hike, just to show me a spot in the woods. If the pack had actually been there, I could understand it. Otherwise, why?" I practically growl as I yank the door open from the stairwell to the hall.

"Maybe I missed you. Maybe I wanted to spend some time with you," he says, and I glare at him.

"Or maybe you wanted to see if I could still keep up with you even when you're in shifted form," I snark back, stopping only long enough to open my door. It swings open with the force of my push. "Maybe you wanted to see if you could piss me off with all your little digs and taunts."

"If I did, it obviously would have worked," he says, grinning at me as he grabs a bottle of water from the refrigerator.

"Oh, of course just make yourself at home," I huff, because his presence is too much for this space, and I feel like I'm on edge in the place that is usually my retreat. "But really, what was today about?"

I drop onto the chair by the window and watch him as he prowls around the place, taking in each and every detail.

"It wasn't about anything other than your time," he says so softly I almost miss it. I realize that beneath the domineering, alpha mask, is a man that very few actually get to see. The man who loved me enough to risk his pack and accepted our bond as mates.

"Roman, I…" My words are interrupted by the sound of a key in the lock of my door. Before I can move, it swings open and Creek stands in the doorway. Roman stands between us, growling.

"What the fuck!" Creek shouts, pulling the gun from his shoulder holster and pointing it at Roman as he steps forward and closes the door.

"Creek, I can explain." I move forward, but Roman snarls, keeping me behind him. "Roman, he's not going to hurt me."

I gulp, hoping my words are the truth.

"It wouldn't be the first time." The words tear from Roman's throat, more animal than human.

"That was your fault, you fucking animal," Creek hisses, and I ease my way between them.

"Remy, you need to start talking. What the fuck is Roman Knight doing in your apartment?"

"You already know," I say quietly but firmly, meeting his gaze. "I know you do because I remember."

He looks gutted, like I just drove a blade into his core, and lowers the gun. "I thought that we…"

"We need to talk," I say to him, moving closer before turning to face Roman, making sure I'm fully between them. "Roman, can you give us some time? I can call you later or something."

He growls again, and Creek's hand comes to my waist, but I plant my feet so he can't move me.

"If he hurts you, Remy, I will kill him."

"I'm not the one who would hurt her. That was your fault, and you fucking know it!" Creek snaps from behind me.

"Enough. Please." I push Creek backward, into the kitchen and free up the pathway to the door for Roman, whose eyes glow so brightly I fear he might shift. "Wait here," I say to Creek and move slowly toward Roman.

"I will be okay," I say, putting my hands on his chest,

before placing a soft kiss on his cheek. "Please trust me."

He stands tall, before reaching down and kissing me hard, as if claiming me as his own before ripping away and leaving without another word. The door slams behind him as I turn back to Creek. My stomach plummets at the look on his face—a look mixed of brokenness and a hint of betrayal.

"You need to explain, Remy."

"I know," I sigh. "Maybe you should sit."

He shakes his head and crosses his arms. He leans against the counter, jaw clenched as he stares at me through narrowed eyes.

"You want a drink? Cause I sure as fuck need one." I move around him and pour myself three fingers of whiskey and throw it back before pouring another. I grab a glass for him, and he takes it.

"So, I guess, I need to start from the beginning..." I say, and dive into the tale of how my memories came back about them—all three of them—and how I pieced together that I loved all of them in different lifetimes. It's hard to explain how having all three of them existing in the same lifetime threatens to tear me apart since they each hold a piece of my heart. All of them willing to take me, however they could have me, if only I would love them too.

"I love you, Creek. I always have I think, even when we were kids. It's like I just knew. I wanted to tell you everything before now, but I was afraid. Terrified that you would reject me. That you'd hate me."

I watch him, on edge, as he takes everything in. I try to not let my emotions get the better of me, but I can't take the silence.

"Creek, say something. Please…" I trail off, insecurity that had never been present before rearing its ugly head. I've never felt insecure with Creek. But now he knows, and it could change everything. I couldn't lie to him—not anymore.

"Remy," he breathes, his voice soft, gentler, calmer than I expected. "Come here." His request is part command, part plea. As though me being this far away from him is a travesty.

He walks us to the sofa, pulling me down to straddle him with my arms around his neck. "There is nothing you could say to me that would change the way I feel about you." Fisting my long hair in his fingers, he pulls me back exposing my neck. I think he's going to kiss me but instead, he runs the tip of his nose along the column of my neck until he reaches my jaw where he leaves a tender kiss. Repeating the same action on the other side of my neck, he again kisses me gently on my jaw.

"Even this. Did you fuck the Lycan yet?" I shake my head as much as I can, my scalp stinging from his grip. "The Dracul then?"

"Yes," I breathe, not used to seeing this side of him.

"Did he bite you here?" he asks as he kisses my pulse point, his hand keeping my head held in place.

"Did he make you bleed?" His words aren't harsh, but there's an edge to them that instead of scaring me, turns me on.

"Yes," I whisper, grinding my core on his ever-growing thickness.

His mouth moves to my collarbone and nips a path from one side to the other. "Did you enjoy it?"

"Fates yes." I'm panting now, remembering the way Kain licked up the droplets he'd caused with his bite.

With my eyes closed, I see nothing, but I feel every single one of his moves. Every swipe of his tongue over my skin and every pinch of his teeth. I know he's comparing himself to Kain, but he shouldn't.

"I am going to show you how much I love you, no matter what you tell me. I am going to make love to you until you forget anything but us." Make love to me... Because that's what this is. He looks at me like wants to worship my body and my mind, like I'm the reason for every breath he takes. I practically drool as he takes off his t-shirt; the man is like poetry in motion.

"Every day for the rest of my life, if you'll let me." Instead of pulling my hair, he pushes my head closer to him, just shy of our lips touching. "Don't you know,

Remy? I would destroy the world and create a new one if you asked it of me."

Slowly, deliberately, he brings our lips together. First gliding from side to side, taking his time, breathing in our scents and listening to our shallow breaths.

"Kiss me then, Creek. If you'll have me, knowing everything that you do, then I am yours," I whisper, and our mouths finally breach the space between us. Our tongues dance to a song of our own making. With my hands on his bare chest, I dig my nails into his colorful skin. My pussy begs to be filled, to be loved by this man.

The sound of ripping alarms me at first but I can't bring myself to look, my attention fully on his kiss. It's only when I feel the cool air touching my back that I realize Creek just destroyed my tank top. Hopefully my jeans won't be as easy to discard.

"Take them off," he demands, biting my bottom lip before putting his hands on my hips and pushing me into a standing position.

I do as he asks, shimmying out of my pants like a cat in heat, my purple eyes fixated on his green ones that are bright and almost luminous with lust. I'm starting to pull down my underwear when he stops me with a gentle touch to my hand. "Let me," he says, scooting up and pulling me between his parted knees.

Placing a kiss on my stomach, he licks a path from my

panty line to my navel, circling it before placing both of his hands on my ass and lifting me up to his face as he lies back on the sofa.

My pussy, though covered by the thin material of my underwear, is at his mouth. His hot, wet mouth. His tongue pushes the material inside me and rubs it against my clit. It feels so fucking divine, and I moan from the pleasure of it.

Another ripping sound meets my ears, and this time I know what it is without the need to see it. My ass is bare and soon my core will be at his mercy. "Oh Fates, Creek, that feels so good," I cry out as his tongue spears inside me, licking up every drop of my juices. Reaching my clit, he sucks the nub into his mouth working me into a fever pitch. The orgasm builds, and I'm toppling toward the edge when Creek pushes two fingers inside of my pussy from behind. I'm done, soaring over the edge of pleasure like a madwoman. I don't recognize the cry that bursts from my lungs; I only know that it belongs to Creek.

Before I regain my senses, Creek stands, shucking his clothes with practiced movement. His cock stands proud and ready, jutting out with the need to make me his.

Sitting back on the sofa, he spreads his legs and lets me straddle him once more. We're both finally naked, both filled with undeniable lust for the other. Both feeling the love emanating from our very pores.

"You may love them, Remy, but know this," he pulls

me close, the tip of his thick cock resting at the entrance of my hungry pussy, "you will love me too. Because I," he enters me, slowly, deliberately, painfully filling me one torturous inch at a time, "belong," he grips my hips and buries his cock so deep I can feel him in my heart, "to you."

My hair falls on either side of us, our eyes locked as I take control of our lovemaking, rising and falling in tempo with our breaths. I ride him, faster and deeper with every second we come closer to paradise. Purple eyes to green eyes, man to woman, Hunter to Hunter. We are one soul, one love. The faster I fuck him, the deeper his nails dig into my skin. The louder I cry, the further I fall for him. Finally, with our bodies joined to the hilt, I halt at the promise of an orgasm beyond anything I've ever felt.

Creek slides his hands up the length of my spine and hooks his fingers at my shoulders. He pulls me closer, grinding his long, hard cock deeper still and suddenly we're falling over the edge together.

We cry out, our heads falling back, our mouths parted on a gasp and our souls intertwined by our very essence.

"I love you, Remy, now and for always."

"I have no idea how I let you talk me into this," I huff as Colt pulls the chair out for me. "I can get my own chair, asshole."

"Come on, little bit. It's been forever since we hung out just the two of us. Your birthday wasn't exactly a celebration, and then there's everything that's happened since... I wanted us to do something nice. Especially since I missed your birthday last year, too." He smiles that cheeky smile at me again, and I cave.

"Fine, fine, I'll play nice." I laugh and take a seat. He pushes me under the table before sitting down opposite me. "I don't even remember the last time I came here."

"Franco's is the best Italian on this side of the world, and I'll fight anyone who says otherwise." He grins, and I laugh at him.

We fall into a comfortable silence for all of two seconds, but I just can't help myself. "So... you and Fallon, huh?" I ask as I waggle my eyebrows.

"No, Remy. Just no."

"Oh, come *on*. She's been so tight lipped, but I know, I *know* something is going on," I tease.

"Remy, please just drop it. She's not a Hunter, so nothing can come of it." He smiles, but it doesn't quite reach his eyes.

"Does it matter that much to you?" I ask, for myself as well as him, and he shakes his head.

"It doesn't, but it's not just my opinion that matters. The Bennetts are a respected Hunter family. An affair within another faction, even with one that's an ally, would devastate the people closest to us," he whispers and picks up the menu.

"The people closest to us should love us, regardless of who we're with." I frown but pick up my menu too, because he doesn't seem to want to talk about this anymore.

"You and Creek though, that's a good match. That's exactly what people expect." He says with a tight smile. "I'm happy for you."

I reach over and squeeze his hand. "I hope you find happiness, Colt. No matter who it's with."

"Thank you, now enough of this crap. Let's eat some good food, and then I'm thinking laser tag." He grins again, and I laugh at the childish glee on his face.

"I haven't been to laser tag in *forever.* Hell yes!" We order when the waiter approaches and just shoot the shit until our meals arrive. After eating the most beautiful chicken Alfredo and garlic bread that's ever been placed in front of me, I am bloated as hell.

"I have no idea how I'm going to run around for laser tag right now." I puff up my cheeks, and he snorts a laugh at me.

"You look like a hamster," he giggles, rubbing his own stomach. "But we'll just walk there and take care of some of these carbs. Plus, you can't back out. Creek and Bauer are on their way back from dropping douchebag Archer at the airport, so they're going to join us."

"You don't like him either?" It feels like the most important piece of information from his little diatribe. Or at least, it's the only piece of information I really latch onto.

"That guy is so far up his own ass, I can see his eyes in his mouth. He thinks he's better than the rest of us when he's a subpar Hunter at best. He's a damn good tracker, though. I'll give him that; it's why he was sent after Roman, but that's literally the asshole's only redeeming quality."

"I'm glad he's gone. Bauer was weird with him around."

"You noticed that too, huh?" he asks, leaving cash for the bill and standing. I follow him out of the restaurant and onto the brightly lit sidewalk.

"It's hard not to notice. It's like he's a harder, colder version of himself rather than the Bauer we know and love."

"I think something happened a long time ago, and Bauer just doesn't want to let his guard down, even if he says he can trust Archer with his life. He won't talk about it—he just brushes me off, but yeah. It's weird." He shrugs, and we fall into a quiet cadence of footfalls.

We stroll in comfortable silence to the laser tag warehouse and sit in the sun waiting for Creek and Bauer to show up. A few minutes later, Bauer's truck pulls into the lot, and they climb from it. My mouth goes dry as I take Creek in, his hair is down and wild, like he's been running his hands through it. Not to mention his white t-shirt is tight as sin on his arms.

"Down girl," Colt laughs, and I shove him gently, rolling my eyes.

We play-wrestle as they approach. They pull to a stop a few feet from us as I victoriously get Colt into a headlock before bouncing around to celebrate my victory. Bauer bursts out laughing while Creek shakes his head. "You guys never change."

"I don't ever want to." I laugh as I release Colt and give him a hug. "You guys ready to be annihilated?"

They all laugh at me, shaking their heads, but we head inside. I feel giddy, like a kid again. We haven't done anything like this in years, and with all of the stress and headaches of everything happening recently, this is exactly what I need.

We pay the woman at the counter and then gear up. I'm glad I wore chucks, shorts, and a vest with a shirt today. I don't have any hindrances to hold me back from absolutely kicking their asses. I can't stop the huge grin from forming on my face as I pull my hair back into a ponytail. Creek walks toward me, somehow rocking the bulky, electronic chest piece, and his eyes dance as he reaches me. He pulls on my ponytail, and I sigh, falling forward to rest my hands on his chest as I kiss him softly.

"Hey you."

"Hey." He smiles. "How you doing?"

His voice is gentle, and his smile is soft, and both melt my heart equally. That he can still look at me like this, love me like this, knowing what he knows makes me soft for him I feel so much lighter, closer to him, now that he knows.

"Shouldn't I be asking you that?"

"I told you, beautiful. Nothing in the world could change what you mean to me or how I feel about you." He cups my chin and kisses me softly. I melt against him.

"I guess the love birds are teaming up." Colt laughs, and I roll my eyes as I pull away from Creek. He keeps me close, his fingers intertwined with me.

"It's us four versus the team that's already in there according to the girl who gave me the gear." Bauer says. "Poor fuckers."

"Yes!" Colt whoops, and I laugh at them both.

"Is that even fair?" I ask, and Bauer shrugs.

"Nothing is fair in love and war. You'd do well to remember that, Remy," he says, looking at me funny. Whatever emotion it was disappears, and he smiles. "Let's get this done."

He slaps the laser gun against his shoulder and heads into the dark room, Colt bouncing right after him, and I lead Creek in behind them.

"I was right, not even close to fair." I laugh as we hand the gear back to the girl behind the counter, who just looks at us wide eyed. After a few hours of decimating any team that came up against us and barely taking a hit, we decided to call it a day.

"So much fun though," Colt says, his eyes glittering, still riding the high from all the wins.

"It's been a while since I had that much fun," Bauer agrees, looking more carefree than I ever remember seeing him.

"Oh, Mom will kill me if I forget to tell you," Creek says suddenly as he hugs me from behind, and I crane my neck up to look at him. "We're throwing a surprise party for your dad this weekend. At his house since it's bigger than anyone else's. Plus, Dad knows we'll never get him out otherwise. It's going to be Saturday morning. Be there by ten or prepare to face her wrath."

"Dad hates surprises," Bauer says, eyebrows raised.

"You tell my mom that. It's his fiftieth, there is no way in hell she's letting that go."

"Didn't Dad say he just wanted a quiet night?" Colt asks Bauer, who nods.

"Yep. I'll hide in the back. I'll make sure to stay there

Friday night, so I'm not late," Bauer says as he leads us out of the converted warehouse.

"I'll do the same," Colt agrees.

"Maybe I should too. We can make him a small dinner?" I ask, and they murmur their agreement. "Awesome, I'll shop before I head over."

"You guys need a ride?" Bauer asks Colt and me.

"Sure, but just to Franco's. We walked here from there earlier," I say and climb into his truck. The drive to Franco's doesn't take long, and it's only a few minutes until I'm climbing back out of the truck, Creek at my back.

"Can I come back over tonight?" he asks quietly, and I smile up at him.

"Yup. You can come over with me now if you like?"

"Not expecting any other visitors?" His eyes darken a little with the question.

"I'm never expecting visitors. They tend to just appear out of thin air, but no," I reassure him. While he might be okay with me being with them, he is still a Hunter. I don't expect him to just get over his prejudices overnight.

"Then yes, I'll come with you now." He kisses me before turning back to my brothers. "I'll catch you guys in a bit. Safe patrols tonight, boys."

"Be good, you two. Don't do anything I wouldn't." Colt belts out a laugh as he climbs into his truck, and Bauer just waves before he drives off. When we get into my car,

Creek drops his hand on my thigh, fingers stroking the soft skin there as I start to drive. I bite my lip and fight the urge to clench my thighs.

"You better be ready to finish what you start," I purr. My eyes are focused on the road ahead, but my body is completely attuned to the man beside me.

"Don't I always, beautiful?" Creeks asks, licking his lips as his hand squeezes my bare thigh. I'm suddenly much more happy with my decision to wear shorts today. My apartment isn't too far away, but if he tries hard enough, maybe he can get an A for effort.

"Yes, but this will cut it close. There's barely ten minutes left before we reach my building, I doubt you could make me come in that sort of time." I shrug because we could always play catch up once we get home, but the thrill of it all makes goosebumps erupt over my skin.

"Is that a challenge?" he asks me, determination in his tone.

"It is what it is, Creek. You can't…" One long finger slides up the leg of my shorts and breaches my entrance without hesitation, making me lose my grip on the steering wheel.

"Holy shit, warn a girl before you do that," I moan as he drags my juices from the opening to my clit and rubs in deliberate circles until my legs begin shaking.

"Still think I'm at a disadvantage, here? That I'm

not up to the challenge?" He doesn't wait for an answer, pushing two digits inside me instead. My eyes lose their focus while my legs spread wider still to accommodate his movements.

"I—no—um..." I'm an incoherent mess by the time he pinches my clit and leans in to suck on the column of my neck. I close my eyes for the briefest of seconds, but it's just enough to make us swerve. Luckily, Creek has better reflexes than I do and brings us back to the correct side of the road.

With less than five minutes before we get home, Creek has a thumb on my clit and two fingers inside me. He pumps steadily in and out of me, sucking my neck and urging me to pull over.

And I do it because I don't want to die in the middle of an orgasm. Though there are worse ways to go, I suppose. Once we're safely parked on the side of the road, I let my head fall back and give Creek more room to maneuver.

"Fates, that feels so good," I moan, my hands gripping the steering wheel like my life depends on it.

With a quick flick of his thumb on my clit and two pumps of his fingers inside me, I arch off the seat and let out a cry of pleasure. Creek doesn't relent, riding out the orgasm along with me with measured strokes of his fingers.

I can't breathe.

My chest heaves, and my breath comes in hard, broken

pants. Meanwhile, Creek watches me, slowly circling my clit and spreading my juices all around my pussy. There's a self-satisfied grin planted on his lips.

"Gloating is not a good look on you, Creek," I tell him, barely able to speak. Clearly lying right through my fucking teeth. There's no look he can't pull off, but that isn't the point right now.

Bringing his cum-covered fingers to his mouth, he licks them, one by one, with a glint of pride shining in his beautiful green eyes.

"Like I said, beautiful, I always finish what I start."

TWENTY SIX

Dinner last night was full of love and laughter, and it hurt my heart to see that beneath it all, Colt was hurting. It makes me so angry that the Hunter's ways are the way they are. That no one believes in what once was or sees what could be if we just stopped fighting each other.

Do the rogues still need to be dealt with? Of course. But the rest? Imagine how much more peaceful life would be if we could all live together harmoniously like our ancestors did before the Hunters decided to change it all up. We're the villains in this story.

I vow, here, for him, for me, and for any others who have fallen short because of this insanity, that I will find a way to end it. Even if it takes me another twelve lifetimes.

I climb out of bed and open the curtains, stretching as

the sun creeps high into the sky, painting it pink. I consider my dreams from the night before as I stare into the back yard at my dad's house. I feel settled, for once. Last night's dreams were an onslaught of memories. Fights, love, travel, happiness, and more sadness and pain than I care to think about, but I'm finally starting to feel like my old self again. More confident, more self-assured. The knowledge that no matter the enemy, I have people on my side, and the skill set to keep us alive, even if I need a little help sometimes. I know I still don't know everything yet, but I feel like I know enough that I can finally start to be a help, rather than a hindrance. I have no doubt Bauer will be more than pleased for me to stop pestering him with questions.

I throw on shorts and a cropped t-shirt, wanting to enjoy some of the last heat of the year. With fall finally here, the weather could change at any moment.

I pull my hair back, preparing to be pulled into the kitchen with Maddie. I know she loves it when she can gossip with us, and I know how much she misses my mom too. I'd rather be in there with her than dealing with the guys anyway.

Another barbeque she said. With even more people this time.

I roll my eyes but smile. Her hearts in the right place at least. My dad is going to be grumpy as shit, though. He was bad enough that the three of us were making a fuss last night, cooking him steak and giving him presents. Apparently, he's too old for presents, but I still saw how much he liked the Desert Eagle that Creek helped me source for him.

I bounce down the stairs to find Creek, Maddie, and Nate already down here. I guess I got up later than I realized. "Morning beautiful," Creek says as I approach and pulls me in for a chaste kiss.

"Morning yourself." I smile up at him, kissing him on the cheek again before heading over and hugging Maddie and Nate.

"You're in a good mood this morning," Maddie coos and steals another hug, making me smile.

"I am! What's not to be happy about?"

"Indeed," Nate says looking between Creek and I. "Bauer and Colt have taken your dad out for a bit, so you're on set up duty with us. Creek and I were just about to head out to my flatbed and pull in the extra tables and chairs, so you're helping Maddie in here."

"Fine by me," I say, then he and Creek head outside.

"I'm so happy that you're happy, sweetheart. It warms my heart to know you guys found your way back to each other again. Your mom would be happy for you guys too." She wipes at her eyes, and I refrain from rolling mine.

"Maddie, did I ever have kids?" I ask, and she looks at me wide-eyed.

"I don't think... Oh, screw it. No, you didn't sweetheart. You always put the faction first, and with it being so hard to conceive for our kind, you always said someone who desperately wanted children should be the one to have a baby. It's why we were so shocked when Nirvana came along. We've always been happy with just our boy, but I'd always dreamt of having a little girl. She was a surprise, I'll tell you that! I can't believe she's growing up so quickly."

"This is her first life?"

"It is, which makes me worry. It's so much harder the first time. She won't have memories to fall back on, and she'll be so reliant on the rest of us and so much more at much more risk because she's so very untrained."

"Then it's a good thing she'll have all of us. It will be nice to have another woman out there on patrol with me." I wink at her, and she laughs.

"I imagine it will. Your mom and I used to love it. I'm a bit too slow these days, I'm afraid, but I keep the archives up to date, and I keep the other families up to date and in the loop with the Elders."

"I wondered why you hadn't been out. What are the archives?"

"They're our most treasured possession, though few outside of the Elders get to see them. They hold a full and detailed history of our kind, all the way back to the beginning with Leviathan."

"Oh wow, I bet that's an interesting read," I say, trying not to show my excitement. This could be exactly what I need. The proof needed to show the other Hunters the truth.

"I imagine it is, but the only people who read the histories are the Elders. The scant few of us others that have access only get to update it."

"That's a bit strange, isn't it?" I ask, my disappointment leaking through.

"Maybe a little, but the Elders govern us, and their word is law. It makes sense that they are the ones with the histories," she says with a smile. "Now then, why don't you get started with the decorations while I preheat the oven?"

"Of course," I agree, trying to tuck the archive information away for a later date. "Where are they?"

"There's a bag or six out on the porch, sweetheart. Thank you!" she calls after me as I stalk toward the porch, mind tumbling over the implications of the information she inadvertently shared with me.

I push the thoughts away, reminding myself that I'm here for the family, and I spend the next hour blowing up balloons, putting out tablecloths and decorations, and hanging bunting. Maddie sure went all out, and just the thought of my dad's face when he sees all this makes me giggle.

Voices grow louder inside the house in the brief moment before people start spilling out into the yard. Abel, Nate, Creek, and Gabriel each carry speakers, which they put around the yard. Fallon, Rebel, and Marie bring out a ton of string lights and start stringing them around the trees that line the space.

Maddie bustles out of the house and instructs people where to put things down, like a true dictator at work. I lean back against the table I just finished setting and enjoy the sun on my face as well as the hubbub of people rushing around the yard.

Creek and Gabriel head toward me, laughing. Creek stoops and pulls me up, tucking me against his side as if he can't stand the distance between us. Gabriel grins.

"I knew it wouldn't take long!" he exclaims, clapping his hands. "Girl, you and this fine piece of man meat would make the most beautiful babies!"

I laugh at him, but Creek looks down at me lovingly. "Maybe one day."

I shake my head at him but don't say a word because it's not something I've really thought about. I'm not sure I'm cut out to be a mom, not with the life I lead. And with all the men in my life, who would be the one I chose to father my child? Would the others be happy with that kind of decision? I haven't even managed to get them in a room together yet, let alone started thinking about those sorts of things.

My phone pings, and I look down to see the message from Colt.

"They're two minutes out," I tell Creek who kisses the top of my head and leaves to tell Maddie.

"Remember me yet?" Gabriel asks, watching Creek's ass as he walks away.

"Kind of, I remember drinking. Lots and lots of drinking," I say, and he belts out a laugh.

"There always was a lot of drinking after a hard night. We had so much fun when we were stationed in Romania with stories of the vampires around every corner. Those people still know how to drink, you know."

"It's all coming back in pieces, but it's still so jarring to see parts of the world that I don't have any recollection of going to. There are so many places I've always wanted to visit, and it turns out I've been to some of them a dozen times over."

"I feel you, but it does get easier. After the awakening period, you know that whatever isn't already there won't come back, so it's easier. Plus, people can fill in some of the holes for you without risking too much. These first six months can be as dangerous as the first twenty-one years. It's less risky, but the risk of death is still there."

"I think I'd rather just know everything all at once, rather than in snippets. It's driving me insane."

"Yeah, but you'd lose yourself. We're each a little different in every life, and as we remember, those previous lives of ours merge—our old habits, phrases, moods, all of it comes back a little and merges with who you were before the awakening. Imagine waking up being little miss sunshine, then having all your memories dumped on you at once and turning into a walking rain cloud. It would be too much."

"I guess you're right."

"Oh, girl, I am. Now come on, Maddie is waiting, and that woman terrifies me."

I laugh at him as he pulls me to where everyone's gathering around Maddie. She hushes us all, expecting both silence and perfection, with Dad and my brothers so close.

Less than a minute after we're silenced, the squeak of brakes, and the slamming of doors announce their arrival, but there are more voices than I expected. I stifle my laugh as I hear Bauer trying to maneuver Dad and his grumpy ass to the garden.

"I don't understand why you couldn't just get it by yourself," he says as he steps into the yard.

"Surprise!" everyone yells.

Dad spins, grumbling instantly when he sees us all. "I hate surprises."

I laugh, as do most other people around me.

"Stop being such a cantankerous old man and come down here, Denny," Maddie demands. He makes his way toward her, still grumbling as she pulls him into a hug. My focus is pulled back to the door where my brothers appear, and I'm surprised to see Ben behind them. I make my way toward them, but Fallon grabs me, pulling me into a hug.

"Where have you been hiding, missy?" she asks, and I relax, the confusion of seeing the Elder in our garden momentarily forgotten.

"I've been busy with my little harem," I whisper to her, and she bursts into laughter.

"Well, that's the best excuse I heard all year."

"Creek knows," I confide, and her eyes go wide.

"Holy Goddess, Remy. How? When?"

"Not here," I tell her. "Later."

"I'm going to hold you to that!"

"Fine by me. I'll see you in a bit, I just want to grab my brothers," I tell her, hugging her quickly before trying to spot Ben in the crowd. I can't see him, so I head for the kitchen, knowing that's where Maddie will be, and likely Ben too.

The wave of cool air hits me as I enter the house, and I almost shiver.

"Remy, just in time! The brownies have just finished cooling. Can you cut them up and put them with the others?" Maddie asks as she whirs around the kitchen, taking advantage of her Hunter speed to get things ready in time.

"Sure thing. Hey, Ben." I smile at him as I grab a knife from the drawer and start cutting the brownies into smaller squares.

"Good to see you, Remy." His warm smile reaches his eyes, and he steps closer to the counter to avoid Maddie's flailing. "I hear you're doing exceptionally well with your training."

"Thanks, my brother is something of a slave driver, but I've been trying to keep up as much as I can, despite a few hiccups here and there. I've been doing lots of reading too, looking into our histories to make sure I understand the bigger picture."

He quirks a brow at my words but doesn't say anything, as if he knows what I'm thinking. "Indeed. And your memories?"

"Coming back thick and fast each day. There's plenty of stuff that I'm missing, but I remember quite a lot," I tell him, and the truth of my words hits me. Between the constant dreams, things coming back to me as I read, and as I spend time with my guys and family, I remember more than I thought I did.

"I'm glad to hear it. Our memories are our most powerful tools and our most powerful weapons."

His words trigger me, and I feel myself falter as it hits

me. We've had this conversation before, and before that… Ben knows. He knows everything, and he's on my side. He wants to help me. My eyes go wide as he nods at me, as if aware of what just happened inside my head. He raises a finger to his lips, and then points to his watch.

"Later." He grins and then heads into the garden with the others.

Holy crap. I try to tamper my excitement at the possibilities presented by having an Elder on my side and focus on enjoying the day with my dad. The door opens, and the man of the hour walks in.

"Hey, Dad, what's up?"

"So many people," he grumbles, but he's smiling. "You know how much I hate surprises."

"Oh, I know, but it's your birthday. You can't just let it pass you by." I hug him quickly because hugging is not a thing Denny Bennett does.

"I could have quite happily let it pass by, thank you very much."

"Denny Bennett, you will stop your whining this instant," Maddie scolds, tossing the towel in her hands down onto the counter. "Emily would have done it, and she would have wanted *me* to do it. You know that as well as I do, so you are going to go back out there, socialize, and enjoy your birthday, dammit."

I look at her wide-eyed before looking at my dad, who

looks as shocked as I feel. Maddie never loses her cool.

"Yes, ma'am," he says, swiping a brownie, making her roll his eyes.

"Denny?" Nate asks as his head pokes in the door and takes in the room. "Erm… maybe you should come back outside, Den."

"Already on my way," he says, grinning wider than I've seen in a while, and I laugh. The two of them look like scared little boys as Maddie stands with her hands on her hips, looking one hundred percent like the wrong person to mess with.

"Men. I swear, they don't grow up. Their toys just get more dangerous." She rolls her eyes as she huffs. "Now then, sweetheart, why don't you start taking this stuff outside and grab those brothers of yours to help?"

"You got it!" I say with a grin and grab as many trays as I can without running the risk of dropping them and back out of the kitchen into the yard. Music is playing, the sun is shining, and everyone looks so carefree. I don't remember a time when everyone looked this relaxed. All the kids are with sitters, so everyone is able to just let loose and enjoy the company of their loved ones.

Night falls and the string lights glow, lighting up the space gently. People are dancing, drinking, and just enjoying themselves. The night feels free, the people freer without a care in the world, but I can't help but feel on edge. Seeing the glances between Colt and Fallon all day, my heart hurts for them. I know there isn't anything I can say to make a difference to my brother, but it didn't make me any less sad when Fallon and her family left earlier. If I was her, I wouldn't be able to face all of this—hide how I feel and hide my resentment alongside it. The Witches are an ally to our faction, thus there is no reason for them to be kept apart and yet they are.

"What's wrong?" Creek asks as he sits behind me on the bench seat on the picnic table, wrapping his arms around my waist and resting his chin on my shoulder. "You seem tense."

"I can't shake this feeling. It's like we've missed something." I don't mention Colt and Fallon to him. Their business is their own, and it's not my secret to tell.

"I've always trusted your gut, but maybe it's because we've been working so hard since your awakening. We haven't had much opportunity to do this sort of thing. Usually things aren't as crazy as they are right now, or at least that's what Dad told me. The increase in the other factions' numbers around here have people on edge, but things have been quiet since the Lycans attacked you. I can only assume those two have finally got their people in line, even if only because of you." His words sound true enough, but something still doesn't feel right.

Kain and Roman have always had a good hold on their factions. Either directly or through those beneath them, but it's the rogue activity that made them both come here. It's the rogues who have been banding together in a way unlike anything I've ever seen. It isn't me.

A shudder runs down my spine with the first scream. The lights go out, and we're thrown into pitch darkness.

"Shit," Creek says, standing but keeping a hand on me. Our eyes only take a second to adjust, and when they do, I see Dracul and Lycans surrounding us. Some filter through the tree line, and others pour from the wraparound porch. There must be at least fifty of them and no more than twenty of us.

Silence hangs in the air and time feels like it's stretching out before us. Hunters gather, creating a circle of sorts, and we move to join them as my dad's voice rings out in the dead space around us. "What is the meaning of this?"

There's no response other than the snarls of the rogues as they attack. I shut everything out, thankful that I've had time to regain enough memories since I was last attacked that I barely even feel fear. A killing calm sweeps over me as I rush forward and join the fight around me. Weaponless, we're at a disadvantage, but sheer force of will pushes us forward.

I use my opponents' speed and strength against them,

using it to snap their bones before twisting their necks. It might not kill them, but it will put them down for long enough that we can work through them to get to our weapons. Or at least that's what I hope.

I try not to think about the people around me—people that I love and hold dear—instead focusing on taking out as many of the rogues as I can. A Lycan dives for me, and I dart backward only to feel the teeth of a Dracul tear into my shoulder.

When the fuck did they start working together?

I shove my elbow backward into the Dracul's gut, and he releases me from his bite on instinct. I throw my head backward, shattering his nose, but that gives the Lycan an opening to attack. His fists rain down on my ribs, winding me, but I refuse to give in.

"Maddie!" Nate's cry comes from behind me, the fear for my surrogate mother giving me the boost I need. I place my hands on the Lycan's head rather than dodging his blows and twist as hard as I can. The bones shatter, and he drops to the ground. Before he even hits the ground, I spin to face the Dracul, my blood running down his face. The pain of my shoulder barely even registers as I dart forward and begin the dance again. He's too distracted by the scent of blood, so I put him down easily too.

The sound of a shotgun cracks out in the air, and my gaze whips in the direction of the noise. My dad and brothers emerge from the house, weapons in hand.

It doesn't take long before the rogues who are still standing start to flee. Not all of them make it out, though, as my faction rains their anger down upon them. Soon, silence fills the air once more, and the disabled rogues are shot. The threat is gone, but my gut aches at the sounds of crying that occasionally punctuates the silence.

"Celeste," Abel cries, dropping to his knees, and I turn to see him cradling her head in his lap. Both her throat and heart were ripped from her body.

"Is everyone else okay?" I ask my dad as I reach him, but he shakes his head. I follow his line of sight to see Gabriel on the ground lying next to an unmoving Ben.

"No," I gasp, and my feet move on their own accord toward the fallen Elder. I don't bother checking for a pulse. The hole in his chest tells me he's not getting back up. The matching one that nearly dissects Gabriel breaks something inside me.

"How the fuck did this happen?" I look to the Hunters around me who are still standing. My anger is reflected on their faces, but I know that deep down, my rage burns a damn sight hotter. "How the fuck did we not know about rogues banding together in these kinds of numbers?"

No one says a word, and I look back down to Ben's face. "This will not go unanswered," my dad says, fiery rage heating his words. "We will mourn and give the fallen the respect they deserve in passing, but then... Then we hunt."

TWENTY SEVEN

It's taken us two days to get to this point. To contact the loved ones of the fallen and make the necessary arrangements. The faction is up in arms about the loss of an Elder, and my dad has been asked to step up in the interim.

To cover and look over our territory on this continent.

In those two days, both of my brothers, with their emotions running over, have bitched about me being too calm, too still. What they don't know is that the anger is there, deep in a pit inside me, but I hone it. Same as I always have, keeping it in check until it's time to unleash it when most needed. That time will most certainly come when we hunt.

Bauer's already started putting feelers out, trying to get some intel on when the rogues from those factions started working together, who leads them, and whether it was planned by the heads of those factions. He doesn't know what I do. That Roman and Kain would never put my life as at risk as it was at that barbeque. But still, the question remains. If not them, then who?

I didn't tell either of them what happened, and yet, they both still knew. They've been blowing my phone up day and night for the last two days, while I've focused my time talking arranging Hunter memorials for them all. Which hasn't been easy all things considered. All while the others bitched and moaned, getting very little done.

Maddie looked as exhausted as I felt when I left my dad's last night. I finally called it a day around midnight, nearly crawling back to my apartment and into my bed. Which is exactly where I find myself now, trying to not mourn everything I lost when Ben's life was taken. All those possibilities squandered. I don't want to be a selfish, heartless bitch, but my friend is gone. I know I will see him again, but it won't be in this lifetime. Of that, I am sure.

The memorials are tomorrow, so I'm taking today for myself. A day away from everyone, to just… be. To embrace the fact that I survived and take care of myself. Just for one day. So, I climb out of bed and head to the bathroom and start to run myself a lavender and lily bubble bath.

Sushi appears at my feet, so I pick him up and pet

him, enjoying his quiet company. "I better get you some breakfast," I say softly and pad my way through to the kitchen, going through the motions and almost feeling like I'm in the past, long before I knew about Hunters, and monsters, and magic. When I'm finished with Sushi's breakfast, I pop some bread in the toaster, then turn on the coffee maker, enjoying the stillness of the morning.

I eat my breakfast while I wait for the tub to fill, and once it has, I sigh as I sink into the hot, steaming water. With my hair piled on my head to keep it as dry as I can, I lie back and let the water relax the kinks in my tense muscles.

Closing my eyes, I let myself drift off as I think of happier times. Trudging across Europe with Kain. Exploring ruins buried deep in the green forests with Roman. Living the life of luxury with Creek in England, among the royals we befriended on the battlefield.

So much time, so many memories, and so much love. I wonder how I'll manage to keep them all in this life. If they can learn to tolerate each other, possibly even befriend one another, because of their love for me. To keep me happy.

I lose track of time, lost in my memories and enjoying the peace they bring. I try to not grow frustrated at the things that are missing, all of the numerous things I still don't know.

The water cools, and my skin starts to prune, so I climb

from the serenity of the water. I wrap myself in a towel, drying off quickly before slipping into my gown. Padding into the kitchen, I open the refrigerator and gaze longingly at the cheesecake Fallon brought over yesterday. Ten in the morning is too early to eat cheesecake, right?

I sigh and shut the door, but a knock at my front door holds me in place. Roman would have likely just broken in, Creek, Fallon, and anyone else in my family would have just used their key. I cross the apartment, opening the door and coming face to face with Kain.

"Hello, *mon amour*," he says as he sweeps into the room, capturing my face in his hands and kissing me sweetly. It's a kiss filled with so much love it warms me to my core. "I have been so worried about you. I heard what happened and have been trying to find out what is going on, but even my sources are slow in returning. How are you feeling?"

He pulls me into his arms, and I melt against him. Letting his warmth seep into me. "I'm okay—angry, sad, and confused—but mostly okay," I tell him as I step back and pour myself a mug of coffee, offering him one at the same time. "You truly know nothing?"

"I do not. You did not think me a part of it?" he asks, his eyes wide with hurt. His posture slips, and any reservations I might have had disappear completely.

"Never. I know you would never put me in harm's way

or want to hurt me."

"Good, *ma chérie*. I would never. All I want is to protect you. If I thought you'd let me, I'd have you on a plane before sundown, far away from this place and all that is coming."

"What do you mean?" I ask, confused.

"I told you of rumors I heard. They speak of creatures I have not faced in my many centuries. Creatures of nightmare brought to life." A shudder runs through me at his words.

"Let's hope they're just rumors to distract the rogues from banding together." I sigh, feeling the weight of it all on my shoulders. I roll my head on my neck, closing my eyes tiredly. There goes my relaxing day. I level a glance at Kain, twisting the obsidian ring on my finger, before asking, "Have you heard anything about a material that Hunters are unable to heal from? My dad was attacked, and I meant to ask, but I've been so wrapped up inside my own head, everything has just run away from me."

"Do not berate yourself, Remy. Others will try to pull you down with every opportunity as it is. You have been dealing with a lot, and once your awakening is complete, you'll be surprised to realize this happens to you a lot. You love working out puzzles, you always have, so not having all the pieces of your own mind is enough to drive you mad. You get lost, so far down that rabbit hole, sometimes you do not emerge until the process is already complete.

"You are doing well to be as present as you are. Many Hunters do not do so well. Why do you think your brothers and your father are so lenient with you right now? They all struggled much worse than you. That you were able to hunt alone already is a testament to how much stronger than most you are." He wraps me back up in his arms, and holds me close, letting the words sink in.

"As for this new weapon, I will speak to Luc to see what he can find."

"Thank you," I breathe, taking comfort in his arms.

"For you, I would break the world in two to discover all its secrets, so that you would know them."

"You say the strangest things," I giggle. "But that's part of why I love you."

I lift up and kiss him, showing him just how much I love him with the gesture.

"Well, isn't this just a pretty picture," Roman's voice fills my ears, and Kain holds me still in his arms.

"Roman," Kain says calmly, smiling at him.

"It has been a while, old friend," Roman replies, and my jaw nearly hits the floor.

"Wait, you two are friends?" I ask, taking a step backward out of Kain's embrace.

"The years are long, and when you are gone, friendship is sometimes what gets us through waiting for you," Kain responds easily.

"Well, slap my ass and call me Sally."

"Don't tempt me, princess," Roman says, his eyes heating at the thought.

"Oh hush," I tell him, still struggling to wrap my brain around this particular revelation. "What are you doing here?"

"The same thing he is, I imagine. Making sure you're okay. I tried to reach you before, but since this is your first time at home, it's the first time I've been successful."

"Sorry to inconvenience you," I sass, rolling my eyes at him.

"I am glad to see that some things never change," Kain chuckles, his smiling face makes me laugh.

"Well, maybe if he could just tone himself down a little," I say, dropping onto the sofa. This is... *a lot* to take in. "But as you can both see, I'm fine. Today is a me day, a day for relaxation before the memorials tomorrow."

"I understand *mon coeur*, we shall leave," Kain says, catching my hand and placing a kiss on it.

"I'm not going anywhere, not until I have more information," Roman grunts, and I swear if I roll my eyes any harder, I'll be able to see my brain.

"What information?" I ask, trying to be patient.

"The news of Lycans and Dracul working together has the packs up in arms. I've heard from ten of the twelve alphas across the world these last few days, each asking questions, none with any idea that this is why their rogue problem seemed to be dying down."

"I know no more than you at the moment, old friend. It would seem even the Hunters struggle to find information. Why don't we leave our heart in peace and see what we can find out?"

The key turns in my door and I panic, not knowing who could be walking in.

"Calm yourself, Princess. It's just the boy wonder," Roman says as Creek enters my apartment, his face thunderous when he takes in the room.

"Well, isn't this just fucking cozy," are the first words from his mouth, and I sigh. I really need to change the locks.

"Don't you start, boy," Roman growls as Creek slams the door closed behind him.

"Roman, your anger will not help this situation," Kain says, putting a hand on Roman's shoulder, as if planting him in his spot.

"You're seriously here with them, after everything that's happened?" Creek says to me, the anger rolling off him in waves.

"They had nothing to do with what happened. You know how I feel about them, why would they not be here?" I hold firm, refusing to back down. Despite his words before, knowing something and seeing it are two very different things.

"How do you know they had nothing to do with it?" he bites, and Roman growls again.

"You mind your words, boy."

"Call me boy one more fucking time," Creek snaps at him.

"Oh, for fuck's sake, take it down a level. I didn't invite *any* of you here. Today was meant to be a day for me to not stress the fuck out. But look at you. Each of you tells me that you love me, that you understand that I cannot choose, and yet you can't be in the same room without wanting to tear each other apart."

"Calm, my love," Kain says soothingly, making his way to my side. "Creek, I assure you, neither Roman, nor I, had anything to do with the attack on your people. My word has been my creed for a long time, so take it as binding."

"And I'm just meant to take you at your word?"

"You are. If anything, we are here to help. We each have our own resources. Imagine the possibilities if we were to pool them."

Kain's calm seems to reach out of him and settle around the room, tamping down the tempers of the other two.

"Fine, fine." Creek sighs, running a hand down his face, deflating before my eyes. "I came to make sure you were okay since you seemed so withdrawn the last few days. I guess I wasn't the only one."

"You're all more alike than you realize," I say with a small smile.

"I don't doubt that at all." Kain returns my smile and moves to my side. "However, now that we know you are safe, Roman and I will take our leave. We have much to look into."

Roman looks at Kain, questioning him, but says nothing. "I guess I'm going," he huffs to me. I stand, and Kain kisses me gently, but with so much passion it makes my toes curl. Roman must be able to smell it, because his chest rumbles, and Kain steps back.

Roman approaches me and takes me in his arms. "One day, very soon, I'm going to remove the scent of these two from you and make you mine." His mouth devours mine, and I whimper underneath him.

He pulls away, and heads to the door, Kain in tow.

"Until later, my love."

"Later, Princess."

The door closes behind them, leaving me with Creek, who looks like he's as turned on by their kisses as I am. He shakes his head, as if clearing his mind and clears his throat.

"They're... something else," he says, and I laugh lightly.

"You could say that."

"I really came here to see if you would consider not joining the hunt that I know is going to happen. I'm more than aware that you can protect yourself, but now that I know for sure that they're not behind it, I worry even more. I can't lose you, Remy."

"Why? Why would you ask that of me when you know better than most who I am? Would you sit it out? Stand by when the ones who mean the most to you in the world risk their lives? If I asked, would you stand down?" He has the decency to look embarrassed, but I can see he doesn't actually regret asking.

"I had to ask Remy. Your dad and brothers will feel the same. You have not completed your awakening, and that makes this so much more dangerous for you than it is for the rest of us."

"No, I will not stay behind, Creek. I know you mean well, I do. I love you for it, but no. Dangerous or not, the people who died were my friends too. It is my right to join the hunt, and I'm taking it. Everyone speaks of the legend that is Remington Bennett, but no one wants to let me become that person."

"That's because, sometimes, when you did the things that made that legend, you lost yourself. Doing those things broke you because even though your actions were justified, your heart has always been too big. The guilt would eat away at you for the lives you did not save or for those who died at your hand, who were only following the orders of their leaders. Becoming that person isn't something you ever wanted." I sigh, feeling the truth of his words, deep within the pit of instinct at the very core of me.

"You might be right. Regardless, if a hunt happens, I will be there alongside you and the others," I tell him firmly, not willing to let this argument continue any further.

"I don't like it, but I'm not going to try to stop you. I asked, so at least I know that I tried." He concedes, and I try my best to not to look too victorious.

"Don't sound so glum. We have the rest of the day to enjoy before the sadness of tomorrow takes over." I wink at him, wrapping my arms around his neck.

"Now that is something I can get on board with."

TWENTY EIGHT

Today is the day we hunt the ones who attacked us. I barely slept a wink last night thinking about it. Torn between worlds. My argument with Creek from a few days ago doesn't help matters, and things are still a little tense between us. He truly doesn't want me to join the hunt, and while he didn't press too hard about it, my brothers and my dad are on his side. They had no qualms with letting me know just how much they were on his side over mine. Only Maddie sided with me, telling them to let me make my own choices as they had the freedom to make their own. I take a deep breath and try to let go of the anger I've felt for the last few days over their nonsense.

The floorboards outside of my room creak. I hold my breath and reach for the dagger under my pillow. Climbing from the bed as quietly as I can, I find myself wishing I had worn something to bed last night. I slip on the shirt I discarded on the floor last night and make my way into the hall.

"It's just me," Roman calls out, and I straighten.

"You have got to stop breaking in," I say as I walk into the kitchen to find him leaning against the counter, holding out a mug of coffee for me.

"You need to get better security." He grins, and I take the mug from him, rolling my eyes.

"Look at you, being all domesticated." I smile, and his eyes slit in response. Some things never change.

"There's no taming a wild animal, princess." He grins, smug and provoking. I lean back against the doorframe, making my shirt part slightly and giving his wolf a peek of what could be his before I take a sip of the coffee. When his hands clench around the lip of the counter, nearly shattering it into dust, I'm more pleased than I'd happily admit.

I revel in these moments of control. They're few and far between, but they're guaranteed to get me wet in an instant, and he knows it. His nostrils flare, his silver eyes focused on me as the pupils restrict into two slits. I know he can smell my arousal, and I know it's making him lose the control he's so desperately trying to cling to.

"Why are you here? In my apartment, uninvited?"

I ask, taking another sip of the sweet nectar, acting like him devouring me with his eyes isn't doing something absolutely wicked to my insides.

"I came to ask you to not go tonight." My arousal suddenly dies at his demand, and from the look on his face, he knows it too.

"You don't get to ask that of me. If you're here, then you already know. You know that Ben was killed and who he was to me. *Family.* Lycans and Dracul banded together to attack us at my family home, Roman. It cannot go unanswered."

"I know that, I've spent the last three days looking into what the hell is going on. They are the pack deserters, banding together with the rogue Dracul. They're planning something, but the secret is well guarded, thus I haven't unraveled it yet. My instincts are screaming that something is going to go wrong, Remy. You need to stay home or come with me. But you cannot join the hunt tonight."

"No, Roman. That isn't who I am. I'm not going to let my family walk into the lion's den without me. Especially if this is an organized thing like you're suggesting."

"I said no, Remy," he roars. I slam the mug down on the counter, and it falls to the floor, shattering as I turn to him, my rage rising.

"You knew who I was, *what* I was, when you took me as your mate. Bond or not, I'm not going to change my mind or myself. This is who I am, Roman. You either love me as I am, or you reject me. We have not renewed the blood bond in this life. You do not have to stay if you cannot accept the life I choose."

"And what of the others? Have they accepted you as you are? Do they not object to you throwing yourself into this mess?"

"Kain respects my decisions. He never asked me to go because he knows who I am and would never ask me to change. And Creek might not be happy with my choice, but he wouldn't dare tell me what to do as you are trying to."

"And they accept sharing you?"

"You know they do. Kain was always aware, and Creek is as well. You saw it for yourself. I love them both, just as I love you despite our bond not having been sealed this time. The choice is yours, if you can accept me as I am—and that I'm in a relationship with them both. I will not force it. Just as you cannot force my decision here."

"And if I want you to myself? My wolf doesn't share well. He also doesn't like the thought of you in danger."

"Then you and your wolf need to have a talk and sort your shit out. This is my life, Roman. I will not have it dictated to me. Not anymore. I've made my decision."

"Those decisions could get you killed!" he roars, but I refuse to back down.

"They could, but if that happens, I know that I died being true to myself, not bending to the will of others. I want you in my life, Roman. You just have to decide if you want to be a part of it."

He growls and paces in front of me. "Fucking, woman. I should bend you over my goddamn knee."

I throw my hands in the air. I swear to the Fates this domineering, alpha asshole is pushing me to my limit. Though I won't lie, the thought of him spanking me doesn't exactly turn me off.

"I'd like to see you try it," I taunt him, playing with his control, knowing damn well I'm going to lose and end up with an ass as red as my blood.

Roman stops dead in his tracks, his body going eerily still if not for his chest heaving with the exertion of retaining his dominion over me and over himself.

"What did you just say to me, princess?" he asks rhetorically, I think. He turns his devastatingly handsome face toward me slowly, eyes boring into mine as though my taunting him is inconceivable.

"You heard me, Roman," I tell him, pushing the pieces of the shattered mug to the side with my foot and stepping over the spilled coffee, I take two more steps closer to his humming body. His fists are clenched at his sides, and a snarl inches up the side of his lip, and I smirk as I continue "I said I'd like to see you tr—"

I don't get a chance to finish my phrase. In an instant, I'm shoved up against the wall, his body flush with my now naked chest. Looking down at where my shirt has completely flown open, he grins like the killer I know he is, like a predator about to devour his prey. Like an alpha about to exert his control.

And I might just let him.

"Do you remember what happens when you play with my wolf, princess?" he asks. I know for a fact that question is rhetorical but screw it. I want his beast to come out and play.

"I get bitten?" I ask, leaning in and licking the seam of his mouth.

That's all it takes for him to pick me up and walk us the few steps to the sofa where he sits with me across his lap, my ass high in the air. My head practically hangs by his thigh. I'm laid bare to him with no underwear, no bra, and just a billowy shirt that offers zero protection from his large, calloused hands.

"What are you doing?" I squeal as I try, though not very hard, to get out of his grasp.

Gathering a handful of my hair in one hand, he pulls it to the side and tells me, "Watch me punish you."

Memories of Kain punishing me with his tongue flash across my mind. My men love to think that making me come is a punishment. Silly boys.

With his other hand, he pulls down my shirt until my arms are held prisoner by the cuffs. Making quick work of the material, he knots my wrists together and warns me, "That's because you defy me."

Wetness crawls down my thighs. His voice, the low baritone thick with his desire for me, caresses my skin with each syllable he speaks.

Taking a deep breath in, he chuckles. "You're wet, princess. My little warrior likes to be tied up, helpless," he taunts, firing me up with words that paint me as weak. I'll show him weak.

Arching my back in preparation to jump off his lap, I feel the first sting of his large, calloused hand. It hurts so good. My ass cheek flames with the sudden, harsh contact.

"That's because you dare talk back to me when all I want is to protect you."

I'm panting, fighting my natural urge to demolish the threat and my sudden desire to beg for more.

Roman slides his palm across my burning cheek, down between my globes and dips a finger inside my pussy, growling when all he finds is my warm juices. I'm so turned on right now, I couldn't hide it if I wanted to. But I don't ever want to hide my need from Roman.

I'm practically purring as his finger thrusts deep inside me, and I don't register the second slap.

Mother of all that is carnal, I want to rub myself on

his thigh, to brand him with my scent. A little friction on my clit wouldn't be so bad either. I want to come so badly already—I can almost feel the pain of it. Roman chuckles, widening his stance, so my pussy is no longer touching him.

I growl, turning my head to look at him, my eyes warning him that I can only take so much before I fight back. "That's because you taunt my inner wolf when I'm trying to be reasonable," he says, two fingers sliding inside my pussy, curling until he finds that sweet spot that makes me jump, making me want to cry out.

And I do cry out. I scream from the lack of friction. From the need to come. From the loss of sanity every time he touches me oh so briefly.

When his fingers slip out, he makes eye contact with me and brings his dripping wet fingers to his mouth, sucking on them and lapping up every drop of my juices.

"That's because I love the way you taste."

Next thing I know, he alternates cheeks as he spanks me like an errant child, fueling my cries and rubbing his palm on the sore spots from his punishing pleasure.

When he stops, I'm a blubbering, fidgety mess with only one need. To come. Now. I need the release or my sanity will forever escape me.

"I believe you owe me an apology, princess," he whispers, his hands deadly still.

"For what?" I breathe out, but he doesn't answer me. He slides one finger up the slit of my pussy, but he doesn't stop until he reaches the crease of my ass and circles my puckered hole.

Did I say I was losing my mind back there?

No, this is what will shove me over the edge of sanity. "Apologize and I'll let you come," he murmurs, almost crooning like I'm a wayward child who needs to be chastised.

My first instinct is to resist, but I *really* want to come, so I give in to his demands. "I'm sorry. I'm so, so…oh my Fates!" Pushing his thumb into my ass and hooking two fingers inside my pussy, he brings his thigh back underneath my clit and allows me to rub myself to orgasm as he fucks me with his fingers.

"That's my princess, come for me. Give me your pleasure," he croaks, his voice telling me he's just as affected by this little scene as I am.

Within seconds, my back arches, and I throw my head back on a scream that can probably be heard miles around us. Roman doesn't relent. He fucks me harder, plunges deeper until he can no longer take the sight before him. He picks me up, throws me on the sofa, my wrists still tied behind me. In one smooth move, he discards his clothes until he's standing over me, completely naked and hard as a fucking hammer.

I lick my lips at the sight of him. Big and thick. Tall and wide. He's the epitome of maleness, the reason women desire alphas. And he's all mine.

With my lip trapped between my teeth, I clench my thighs together. Fuck me, he shouldn't be allowed to be this hot. Roman kneels on the sofa and then picks me up, facing me away from him before impaling me on his steel-hard cock from behind. His arm wraps around me, and he wraps his hand around my throat, pulling me up until my back is flush with his chest while he fucks me.

With every thrust inside me, he tells me a story. Of a man who loves a woman.

Thrust.

Of a man who will die protecting the woman he loves.

Thrust in, pull out.

Of a man who slay all others if his love is in danger.

Thrust in and…

"Fuck!" we both cry out as he fucks me to within an inch of my life. I shudder, vision going blurry as he stiffens behind me.

When we both come down from what feels like a life-altering orgasm, he releases my wrists from their bonds. He turns me, wrapping my arms around his neck.

"I have lived without you for long enough, Remy. I do not know what I would do if something were to happen to you tonight, and I hadn't at least tried to stop you." The sincerity in his voice, a rare show of vulnerability from him, is like a knife to my heart. As much as being a Hunter is in my blood, being a protector is in his. I hurt him. I see that now.

"I'll do my best to make sure nothing does, so long as you promise to do that again," I tell him, resting my head on his shoulder as he lays us both down on the couch, a blanket suddenly covering us both.

"Deal," he whispers, tightening his hold and placing a tender kiss on my forehead.

TWENTY NINE

After spending the day wrapped up in Roman, I'm sore in the best of ways. I can still feel him on me. Even now as I'm geared up, ready to go avenge my friends.

The faction has been able to pull so little information about what's going on. How it's staying so under wraps is beyond me, and that alone has everyone more than a little on edge. What we did discover, thanks to Colt, is where the rogues disappeared to when they ran after the attack. They disappeared into a warehouse close to where we were that first night I went with him and Creek hunting. That feels like a lifetime ago now.

I pace the hall of my dad's house while I wait for the others. Creek watches me silently. Stillness is not something I want to feel right now. We're meant to be meeting the others in less than ten minutes, and they're all fucking around, making last minute changes, probably making sure to keep me on the sidelines as much as they can.

"Let's go," my dad's voice booms as he storms from the kitchen. It's so strange seeing him geared up. It's not something I think I'll ever get used to. Bauer and Colt follow him, so Creek and I bring up the rear, all piling into Bauer's newly modified truck. He spent most of the day replacing the glass and paneling to essentially make this thing a tank. A bulletproof tank.

He starts it as we buckle up, and silence descends as we head out in. We meet the others at the rendezvous point with seconds to go and then head up the envoy out of town. A few other Hunter families who were close made it in time for the hunt, but it's less than Dad was hoping for.

Regardless, no one was willing to wait any longer.

The trip is silent, the tension so thick you could cut it with a knife. Creek takes my hand and squeezes it. I squeeze his back and offer him a tight smile before I slip into that place inside me, the one where I'm not totally myself. I haven't dared reach into the pit of darkness before now, but not knowing what we're facing, I brace myself for the fall into whoever that Remy is. The cold, calm brutality of the pit washes over me. My body stiffens, and emotion drains from me. Darkness passes as the truck eats up the miles. The blackness of the night is only broken up by the light of the trucks.

We take a sharp turn, and we park. I climb from the truck, joining the others to debrief before we march toward our destination. We're still about a mile from the warehouse because approaching on foot is more discreet.

"We had a chance to scope this place out a few weeks ago," Colt says, his tone commanding, and it startles me that my carefree, cheeky brother is the same cold, calculating person standing in front of me. I guess I'm not the only one with darkness inside of them. He rolls out a blueprint of the warehouse on the hood of the car so we can all see what we're walking into.

"Exits are here, here, and here. There are only a few windows, and I'm thinking they're too high to assist anyone. However, there are three levels to the place with stairwells here, here, and here. We'll move in threes. With three people remaining outside should anyone try to bolt or if anyone calls in the cavalry. Understood?"

He barks out commands, and people break off into groups, double-checking their gear before we start the hunt. I hear my name and snap to attention.

"Remy, Creek, Bauer. You guys will take the back entrance that leads straight to a stairwell. Kody will cover the door." I nod and take a deep breath. Creek and Bauer can look out for themselves; I have faith that everyone here can, but I still worry that not everyone is making it out of here by the end of this.

"Let's go!" We move as one, merging with the shadows, steps silent as we cross the distance to our objective. There's no moon tonight, so the darkness is thick, and I'm grateful for my Hunter's sight. I can see just as clearly in the darkness as I can in the day.

Bauer taps my shoulder, and we branch off toward the back exit, following his lead. I only met Kody today. He's not much older than me, and he seems like he's a bit of a liability. I clear the thought from my mind and focus as the warehouse comes into view. I crouch beside Creek, hidden by the bushes that surround the warehouse, making sure the coast is clear.

I close my eyes and will my hearing to extend, but the warehouse seems silent. It's as if empty... or warded so that it seems that way. With no one in sight, Bauer motions for us to move closer. We reach the door, and he points to the rune symbol on the frame.

I was right, it's been warded, which means there could be Witches here too. Just fucking great. What the hell is this?

Bauer looks to his watch, and as the hands move into place, we breach the door. No one waits on the other side, so we move in like a well-oiled machine. Bauer takes the lead, gun at the ready, with Creek behind me. We move in the darkness as if we belong to it. Gunfire sounds in the distance, and I try not to let it in, to not think about whether they're our shots or theirs. We reach the first floor, slowly entering a room that spans almost half of the entire warehouse size. Once Bauer confirms it's clear, we move in farther. I go on high alert at the thud of footsteps racing above us, rushing toward where we stand.

We separate, moving for cover, and making sure to have eyes on the only other door in the space. It's situated near the stairwell to the next floor.

Dracul and Lycans flood the space, and we move forward, separating as we dive into the onslaught. I lose track of the others as I work my way through the Lycans and Dracul. I hate to think how many Kody has had to deal with, but the bottleneck should help him at least.

I pant as I shoot and slice, trying to clear the path, but it feels as if they're never-ending. How did so many of them congregate here without anyone knowing? I cut through the obstacles in front of me—not paying attention to the amount of blood covering me—until I reach the stairway to the second floor. I look behind me, and my eyes go wide.

Kain.

I rush to him, my heart racing. "Why are you here?" I ask, looking around to make sure Bauer doesn't see him.

"I came to help, to keep you safe. I did not intend to come in here, but I smelled your blood, and getting to you overrode all sense," he says, eyes taking me in.

"None of it is mine, well not much," I say, and he loosens a little. "But you can't be here."

"Remy, be careful!" Bauer roars and runs toward us. The last of the rogues in the room put down. I spin to face him and move to cover Kain. Creek stares in horror as Bauer raises his gun.

"Bauer, no!" I shout, but the gunshot rings out as I leap in front of Kain.

I hit the floor with a thud, Bauer still as a statue and looking at me like he doesn't know who I am. "Run!" I tell Kain, who looks at me, pain and devastation covering his features. He does as I ask and flashes away. I only hope he gets far from here, far from the Hunters who would end him without hesitation, as the burning in my chest grows.

"What the fuck was that?" Bauer roars as Creek appears at my side, applying pressure to the wound.

"We need to get the bullet out," Creek says, panic lacing his words. I nod at him and bite down as he pulls out a knife, opening the wound before reaching in for the bullet. The pain overwhelms me, so much so that I nearly pass out, but I hold on because... fuck! Bauer.

"Bauer, you don't understand," I groan. "He's not who you think he is."

"He is the head of the *fucking Dracul*, Remy. He is our enemy, and you just stopped me from killing him. Do you know how fucking long we've been hunting him? And then he shows his face here randomly. He must be a part of this; why else would he be here?"

"He was here for me. To try and keep me safe. To help us."

"You're out of your goddamn mind." He paces the space. Gunfire still sounds in the distance, but I can tell he's not focused on that anymore.

"Please, Bauer," I rasp, as Creek lifts my top to put a tourniquet bandage on the wound until I can get back to a Witch.

"You fucking betrayed us, Remy! How could you!" He storms off, up the stairs to the second floor, and a tear runs down my cheek.

"It's going to be okay, Remy." Creek tries to soothe me and scoops me up into his arms. I don't say a word, letting the tears fall because I know he doesn't believe his words any more than I do.

Creek carries me from the warehouse and back to the trucks where we left Marie and Fallon. Fallon rushes toward me, and Creek explains what happened. I stay silent, unable to speak, because I know everything is about to change.

"Oh, Remy," she gushes, as Creek places me gently on the ground. He removes the bandage, and she starts working to heal the hole in my chest. They talk above me, but I don't hear their words, lost inside my own mind. Memories flash in my head, this life merging with past ones. My mom's face front and center, soft, as if she stands before me, knowing and understanding. Knowing everything that I know.

My brother, the others, they will never forgive me. Even Colt, with his obvious love for Fallon, will not forgive this because they don't know. They wouldn't believe me if I had the truth to give to them. I know it, and that's why I haven't tried before. Because even when faced with the truth, my family wouldn't believe it. They'd cast me out before they believed their way of life to be wrong.

Fallon's hands lift from my chest and having barely felt the searing heat of the healing, I sit up, resting my back against the truck.

Waiting.

Waiting for them to come back and for my world to implode.

The smallest thread of hope remains, a bead of hope that maybe Bauer won't say anything. Maybe he'll cool down and talk to me first.

But when I see my dad walking toward me, covered in blood with Bauer on one side and Colt on the other helping Nate walk, I know that it's too late. There's fury on my dad's face, real rage, and I swallow around a thick lump in my throat.

I stand to face them, biting my lip until I taste blood as Creek rushes to his dad. I watch as he pleads with his dad, but Nate's face falls before hardening. He shakes his head at his son.

My dad reaches me and slaps me around the face so hard I fall to the ground.

"You are no daughter of mine. You betrayed your family and your faction with your actions. You are a disgrace to the Hunter name." He spits at my feet, and I wince.

"Denny," Marie starts, but he silences her with a look. "Place the traitor under arrest. She will face the Elders for her actions." He turns and walks away from me without so much as a backward glance. I look to Bauer who looks as sad as he is angry, but he turns and follows my dad.

"Colt," I start, but he shakes his head.

"How could you, Remy?" he asks, his voice thick.

"If I could just explain," I cry, but he too, turns away from me and joins the others. Marie reaches down to me and wipes the tears from my face.

"Don't let them see your pain. You own your choices, whatever they are." She looks at me, straight in the eyes, and I realize that she knows. Fallon looks guilty behind her, but I don't care. Not anymore.

"They will kill me," I tell her, defeated, though I take her hand and stand.

"There is more at play here than you know," she says, and Fallon's eyes go wide.

"What did you see?" she asks quietly, but Marie shakes her head. Creek approaches me, shackles in hand, and it breaks me.

"I am sorry, Remy. I tried to reason with them," he says, devastated.

"Don't. Keep it to yourself. All of it. There is no reason for you to be locked away alongside me," I beg him, and he shakes his head.

"No, Remy. I can't let them do this to you. Not when I knew and supported you. I can't let you carry this alone."

"You can, and you will," Marie says in a hushed whisper. "This is her journey; you must support her in other ways. You cannot help her if you are locked away as well." Creek looks to her, and she nods toward me, more meaning in the gesture than I can comprehend in the moment. I put my hands out in front of me and let him shackle my wrists and then my ankles.

"I love you," he whispers, with shining eyes.

"I love you too. Always."

THIRTY

I walk into the room I've only been in once before. The chamber of the Elders. The same place my ritual took place. Except this time, I am not received with honor and respect. This time, I'm received with distrust and fury. I've been here for two weeks, locked in a small room with no light, fed just enough once a day to keep me going until today. I'm covered in dirt and grime from the room I was kept in, which contained no more than a bucket in the corner to demean me further. I have not pleaded with them, though; I refused to speak until today. But I fear that they still will not listen.

I can feel the disgust in my father's stare more heavily than any of the other gazes focused on me. He doesn't understand, and I don't expect him to. He doesn't know.

How could he?

But the other factions are more than these people think of them. They are more than beasts that don't understand anything but the joy of the hunt, the kill, and the taste of blood. They are more like us than these people could ever know, more than these people have ever cared to know.

I feel it inside of me each time Kain looks at me, with each gentle kiss. I feel how much more there is to him. He is more than the head of the Dracul, more than the power that radiates from him. I know it with the way that Roman loves me, the way his need to protect me overrides all of his other instincts. They are not the beasts my faction makes them out to be.

Creek steps next to me, brushing his hand with mine. I don't know how I got to be so lucky, to be loved by these men so faithfully that they gave me the space to love them all, even if it has only been for a short time. I do not regret the decisions I made, in this life or the ones before, to love them. To be blessed with such love is a feeling like no other.

The candles illuminating the room flicker as the door opposite us opens, and the Elders enter the room, their faces hidden by the hoods of their cloaks as they step up on the raised platform before us. A Hunter I do not recognize comes forward and drags me to the middle of the room. My family stands to my left, with only Creek behind me in a show of support. The anger and confusion rolls off each of them, and it threatens to suffocate me.

"Remington Bennett. You stand before us here, with the witnesses of your kin, standing accused of betrayal of the faction of Hunters. With aiding the escape of one of our deadliest enemies, Kain Michaels, the head of the Dracul. The most dangerous and bloodthirsty of them all. How do you plead?" The Elder's voice echoes around the stone room, and I shudder.

"Not guilty. He is not who you think he is. If you would just listen…" I try to reason, but I know there is no use when I see that their shadowed faces remain beneath their hoods. They do not even lower them, not deeming me worthy of seeing them fully.

The people here have been fixed in their ways for centuries. I just wish I knew why. The stories from Kain of how life once was haunt me, but he did not know of the reason for the change. Without all of my memories, I'm clueless as to how to make a difference. If Ben had survived, things might be different.

"Your words betray you, as you betrayed your faction. Your pleading will do you no good here, girl. To sympathize with our enemies is to be our enemy, so you will be handed with the same fate we place upon them. The True Death."

"No," Creek shouts, but it feels a thousand miles away, and I sink to my knees. I knew the consequences of my actions when I took them, but I would do the same thing, time and again. My family, as much as I love each of them, is wrong. They are blinded by a hate that I have never felt. That I could never feel.

"Your mother would be ashamed of you," my father spits at me as Maddie and Nate hold him back. Bauer stares at me like he doesn't know me. My big brother, who I had hoped against all odds would have my back when the time came. Bauer, who turned his back on me and told my father what I had done. My heart breaks when I look at my family, all looking at me as if they don't know who I am. Colt is the only one who looks conflicted. Like he wants to speak out, to help me, but he's struggling with the betrayal of my actions. He stands with those who are against me.

"You can't do this!" Creek shouts, and I turn to find him struggling against the three Hunters who have him pinned to the back wall. A Hunter steps up beside me, Easton, my grandfather's right-hand man, and draws his bastard sword from the scabbard at his waist. I kneel on the ground and send up a prayer to any gods who might exist for the ones I love. To keep them safe when I no longer can.

"You choose not to fight?" The Elder asks, and I look up at him from where I kneel on the sandy ground.

"I am shackled and weaponless. It would be no real fight. I will accept the fate I have been dealt, but know that in every life, my feelings have remained true. I know your secrets; they will not stay secret for long. The world will know the truth, and when that happens, you'll wish you had made a different decision." I hold my head high as I say the words.

"Very well," the Elder says, waving his hand at the Hunter beside me who raises his sword, not looking even remotely fazed by my words. Thinking himself, all of them, to be untouchable. I look to my family, and a tear rolls down my face.

"I love you," I whisper to Creek and take a deep breath before bowing my head. The sound of metal slices through the air as I close my eyes. The ceiling explodes before the sword finds my neck, and chunks of rubble and dust rain down around me.

The Hunter beside me turns his sword to the man who is down on one knee in front of me. His black wings stretch out so far that they almost touch either side of the room. His head rises and shakes, the dust flying from his dark hair. Whispers ring around the room between the Elders and the Hunters. A real-life fucking angel just exploded into the room, and I can't think of a single thing to say.

"You will not harm her!" His voice echoes across the space. "She is bound to me, and I to her. Any harm against her is harm against me."

I gasp at his words because I have no fucking idea who this is or what the hell his words mean. But I know that voice.

He stands and turns to me, his gray eyes capturing mine, and my breath catches. I recognize him from a dream. I blush as I remember him and his touch. He steps closer, lifting my chin with a soft finger.

"Remy." He sighs. "Always causing so much chaos. Stand, please."

I stand up, and it feels as if the room itself is holding its breath. "Will someone fucking unchain her?" he growls.

"What is the meaning of this?" the Elder who sentenced me to death asks when he finds his voice. The Hunter who was going to kill me sheaths his sword and unlocks my shackles. My wrists are raw from the rub of the metal.

"You dare question me?" the angel's voice booms, and the room shakes, more dust falling around us. I look to my family who are all kneeling, as are the other Hunters around the room. Only Creek remains standing, looking unsure as to whether or not he can approach me.

"I am Leviathan, General of the Death Dealers, Archangel of War, and the creator of your faction. My word is your law, and you will do my bidding unless you wish to meet the fate you so casually dealt to her." The Elder shrinks back at the angel's words.

"This girl is the balance, the *Nisi Vita*, and should be treated with the utmost respect, not chained like some animal."

"She betrayed us!" another Elder speaks up.

"She did nothing more than she was meant to do," Leviathan answers and confusion clouds me.

He turns to me and tucks a fallen piece of my hair behind my ear.

"Hello again, sweetheart." He hugs me tightly. "Don't worry, you will remember." He winks and lifts me into his arms, before shooting into the sky, leaving the shouts below us.

To be continued...

TRANSLATIONS

Mon Amour - *My Love*
Ma Cherié - *My Darling*
Mon Coeur - *My Heart*

Fata vocant, ad hanc adducere nos ut in venator nobis.
Fate, we bring to you your hunter.

Rogamus autem vos, Angelus scientiam, ut restituat in aedis dedicandae se unum ex memoria vobis
We ask of you to return the memories of the one upon this alter who is angel born.

Angelus autem ducibus nobis dona puer hic noster de quo in suis bonis quasi unus accipit vera semita.
May this child be guided by the Angel, down the path of the past.
Ut rogatus est, et illud fieri.
As it is asked, so shall it be.

ABOUT THE AUTHOR

Sloane Murphy is the author of the international bestselling series, The Immortal Chronicles, as well as a range of other paranormal and contemporary romance. Sloane lives in Peterborough, England, with her husband & fur baby and over the years, she has developed an unhealthy appreciation for cheesy YA Films, cupcakes and bad pop music. She adores fairy tales, ballet and all things supernatural, drinks far too much coffee, and watches an ungodly amount of Netflix. When she's not busy writing, she can be found exploring the world with her husband and chocolate Labrador.

If you would like to send Sloane an email, you can reach her at sloane@authorsloanemurphy.com

Want to sign up for her mailing list? You can sign up HERE

Or come join her reader group on Facebook, Sloanes Little Monsters

facebook.com/sloanemurphybooks

twitter.com/SloaneMurphyBks

instagram.com/sloanemurphybooks

bookbub.com/authors/sloane-murphy

ACKNOWLEDGEMENTS

I have a lot of people to thank for this one, so strap in. First, to my husband, for leaving me to my brain babies for hours and days on end. For making me coffee and bringing me chocolate when those days when the words were streaming from me hard and I forgot to look after myself. Thank you for well, everything.

Jenna, without you this book would still just be a WIP in a word file from Nov 2018. You helped me believe that these guys were ready for the world, and it turns out, they really were! So thank you for the sprinting sessions, the pep talks and introducing me to the people who would become my tribe.

Eva, the peen whisperer. Thank you for all your help juggling these men and their wild, brutish behaviour. For the many hours in VOA and sprint rooms keeping me going! And to all the amazing authors in VOA for keeping me accountable during office hours! Danielle, Liane, all of you thank you!

To Sarah, my beautiful and creative assistant, for all your helps with edits, late night randomness, and really just everything you do to help me, when you really, really don't have to!

My beta team - you guys are awesome as ever. Thank

you for loving my book baby as much as I did, and giving me the swift kick up the ass that I need. Like always.

To Steph, Blake & Claire. For believing in me. For letting me be your guinea pig. For all of the things!

To Christine & Sam, for doing the final polish of Remy and making her sparkle shine bright.

Finally, to you, my readers, for sticking with me, because god knows it's been a bumpy ride, but without you guys, I wouldn't be here. So thank you for reading, for (I hope) loving these guys as much as I do. Here's to the future, and way more words to come!

ALSO BY SLOANE MURPHY

THE SEVEN REALMS SAGA
The Shadow Walkers Saga
(Reverse Harem Paranormal Romance)
A Crown of Blood and Bone
A Crown of Smoke and Ash
A Crown of Shadows and Secrets
A Crown of Thorns and Lies
A Crown of Fire and Wrath
A Crown of Pride and Ruin

The Shadow Weaver Series
(Menage Paranormal Romance)
Witch's Curse
Hunter's Heart
Demon's Blessing

The Shadow Queen Series
(Reverse Harem Paranormal Romance)
The Shadow Queen
Conquest
War
Famine
Death

THE IMMORTAL CHRONICLES SERIES
(YA Paranormal Romance. Complete Series)

Descent

Crash

Soar

Rapture

BLACK WATER ACADEMY SERIES
(Upper YA/NA Paranormal Romance. Reverse Harem)

Marked

Chosen

Hunted

DARK FAE DUET
(Paranormal Romance. Dark Fantasy)

Summer Princess

Winter King

OTHER AUTHORS AT HUDSON INDIE INK

Paranormal Romance/Urban Fantasy

Stephanie Hudson

Xen Randell

C. L. Monaghan

Sorcha Dawn

Sci-fi/Fantasy

Devin Hanson

Crime/Action

Blake Hudson

Mike Gomes

Contemporary Romance

Gemma Weir

Elodie Colt

Ann B. Harrison

CPSIA information can be obtained
at www.ICGtesting.com
Printed in the USA
BVHW071233210621
610124BV00001B/16